HAINT
& OTHER HUES OF BLUE

H M PALMER

This book is dedicated to three women. The three killed by their partners in the United States today and every day.

HAINT

& OTHER

HUES OF

BLUE

PLEASE NOTE: this book contains scenarios that abuse survivors may find distressing.

If you or someone you know has experienced or is currently experiencing any of the behaviors in this book, you are not alone, and there is a vast network of resources to help you get out safely and keep yourself safe.

Go to thehotline.org to find out more or call 1-800-799-7233(SAFE) for immediate assistance.

PROLOGUE

Jess

Sometimes Jess wished her fiancé would just hit her.

If that was his violence of choice, at least she would know what was coming. More tolerable, perhaps. She might have an idea of what to expect, when it was coming, and how long it would last. But mind games? Those were worse. She didn't know when they would start, what they would be, or how long she would have to endure them. They were effective, and in the end they could be lethal.

But the thing about games is two can play. The rules change. Tables turn. Power shifts. And the predetermined outcome shatters, like how the siren of the police cruiser flying past her house was obliterating the silence of the southern spring night.

As the blue and white strobes faded into the black, Jess moved away from the living room window to retrieve her phone from the kitchen table. Reaching for it, she could hear another siren brewing from the direction the cruiser had just come.

This one was a lower, longer wail. An ambulance. Hurrying back to the window, she watched as it passed, heading the same direction as the police cruiser. A fire truck followed. Thinking that was it, she returned her attention to the phone, her hands shaking because she knew where they were headed. She was about to make a call, but the sound of yet more sirens approaching stopped her. Unlocking the front door, she stepped out on the porch into the dark of the night as four more cruisers flew by. She didn't have time to return to her phone again before she heard the lonesome wail of another ambulance, cutting through the crisp evening air.

That's too many, Jess thought to herself.

She knew it wasn't uncommon for all available units to respond to a call in a small, north Georgia county like Hall. Everyone wanted in on the excitement when anything happened because it rarely did. But this was more than usual. And she knew enough to know tonight wasn't a case of the nosey Deputy Barney Fifes.

Looking back down at her phone, she tapped her fiancé's name on her recent call list. Then, she put the phone to her ear, knowing he wouldn't answer.

CHAPTER ONE

APRIL

Jess

Jess pulled her black Mercedes sedan into the driveway, exhaled, and moved the shifter to park.

Finally here, she thought to herself.

After two days, more than eight hundred miles, too many fast food drive-thrus, seven phone calls with her best friend from law school, Stacey, to pass the time, and one speeding ticket later—presumably Valley Alabama Police's only source of income—she arrived at her aunt's house.

Nina Wilton lived in Flowery Branch, a small town located in Hall County, Georgia. Hall was one of the southernmost counties of Appalachia and hadn't yet been swallowed up by the sprawling metropolis of Atlanta that had been creeping outward for decades, like the messy tendrils of a Kudzu vine. The town was situated on the southeastern side of Lake Lanier, and while it was much different than Highland Park in Dallas, Jess didn't feel too out of place. Probably because she grew up in a small town in northwest Texas not all that different from Flowery Branch. Trade the longhorn grill ornaments—yes, some people really have those like they do in the movies—for college football license plates and squat mesquite trees with tall, skinny pines, and Flowery Branch was essentially the same as the small towns of the Lone Star State. Small town gossip made its way around town via the few mom-and-pop stores still trying to hang on by their decades'-old—and in some cases, centuries'-old—roots in the big box store world of the twenty-first century.

She'd turned a few heads in her flashy German whip once she'd gotten off I-985, the interstate that connected small town north Georgia with Atlanta and its maze of intertwining interstates—complete with traffic that could turn the Dalai Lama homicidal. She chuckled to herself about her own Melanie Smooter *Sweet Home Alabama* moment. Although, there was a hint of *Legally Blonde* in her entrance, too—after all, she was an attorney.

Former attorney?

Minus the Bekins moving truck and Chihuahua.

"Alright, Piggs. We're here. Our new life...for now, anyway," she said with an exhale to Piggy, her Frenchie-mutt, who was nestled in his bed on the backseat, as she shifted into park. He snorted in response.

She wasn't sure how she'd feel when she pulled up to the Victorian home that graced Atlanta Highway, situated on the other side of the railroad tracks from the short downtown strip. But she quickly realized she'd made a good choice. She still had some healing and reflection to work through thanks to the events of the last few months; the ones that prompted her sudden career pause and subsequent move to help her mother's aging older sister. Flowery Branch offered her the distance she needed from Dallas to process how her life had spun off its axis and the comfort of her beloved aunt she'd grown close to in her summers spent here as a child.

Nina opened the front door, as if on cue. She had a bad hip and a knee that needed replacing, so she walked with a walker, but her mind was still sharper than a tack. The elderly woman smiled widely underneath her bifocals and waved at Jess with one hand and her house phone in the other. Jess guessed her aunt was talking to Jess's mother. If she was a betting woman, Jess would gamble her life savings that her mother had called every half-hour since she crossed the Georgia line on I-20 to see if she'd made it safely.

Jess returned the wave with a smile of her own and slipped off her seatbelt to step out into the balmy, spring sunshine. As she made her way to the porch, she gave the house a onceover. It had been years since she'd seen it. The home itself was equally interesting as its lone occupant. The bright colors typical of Victorian homes had been long ago painted over, and it now sported a drab dichromatic black and white ensemble. Thankfully, the home had not been stripped of all its character as it retained the quintessential deep south blue porch ceiling, crystal doorknobs, and a gorgeous foyer pendant lantern. Jess used to lay under it and stare after playing outside all day when she would come with her mom to visit Nina and her late uncle. The distinct smell of wood polish spilling out the door onto the porch transported her immediately back to her childhood.

"Listen, she's here now, Marcie, so I'm going to let you go. I'll call you tomorrow." Nina hung up the phone with Jess's mother and beckoned Jess to come give her a hug in the doorway, to which she obliged.

"Hey, Aunt Nina," Jess said over her aunt's shoulder as they embraced.

Nina held her at arm's length. "It's so good to see you, sweetie. I've been sitting here trying to count the years it's been since you last visited. I think it's been more than a dozen."

Piggy was still waiting in the backseat of the car with his nose smashed against the window, barking to be included.

"I was a teenager last time, so it's been at least fifteen," Jess said. Piggy's barking kicked up a notch as Jess broke their hug.

"Oh, well, don't keep the little fella waiting. You go and get him, and I'll getcha a bowl of water for 'em."

Her "'em" sounded like "eeyum" with her Georgia accent, not to be confused with a Texas drawl, which tends to lengthen vowels instead of simply dropping them like a southeastern accent.

Jess retrieved her excited pup and the first of her bags from the backseat. She didn't know how much cargo space the engineers at Mercedes had designed her sedan with, but she was pretty sure she'd defied the laws of physics with the amount of stuff she'd Tetris'd into the car.

After dropping her hodgepodge of bags and boxes in the foyer, she found Nina at the kitchen table and sat down to have a glass of sweet tea with her, Piggy at their feet.

"I wish I could help you, dear, but I'm afraid you'd be helping *me* up off the floor if I did," Nina said, tipping her glass toward Jess's bags in the foyer.

"Oh, don't worry about it." Jess waved her hand. "I haven't worked out in a couple of days. I need the exercise."

"I don't know why you even bother. You're skinny as a snap bean, darling." Nina observed.

Jess laughed and looked around, noting how little had changed since her last visit. The home phone was still mounted on the wall that sported the same magnolia bloom wallpaper, now faded from years of abuse by the sun. Her gaze caught on a few jars lining the backsplash beside the sink. Each jar had what looked like a banana peel soaking in water.

Nina must've noted her puzzled expression and explained, "Natural fertilizer for my plants. Why buy anything from the store when you have it at home?"

Waving her hand dismissively she went on, "Something your generation could learn a thing or two about. Hang around with me long enough and I'll *learnt* ya a thing or two," she finished with a wink.

Jess smiled, relieved to see time hadn't dulled her aunt's spunk. Standing up, she stretched in an effort to summon any energy the drive hadn't drained from her. "I think I might need a nap before the lessons start."

Nina smiled. "You can pick whichever bedroom you'd like, dear."

Jess had already decided on her room before she left Dallas. Nina's room was downstairs along with a guest bedroom. There were three more rooms upstairs off the large sitting area that spilled out from the top of the black walnut staircase. She would stay in the one on the right that overlooked the front yard. It was the room she always slept in as a kid with her cousins who grew up in Georgia.

As the years passed, her Georgia relatives moved off to college, one by one, or were transferred away for jobs like Jess's parents had done shortly before Jess was born. That's part of the reason Jess came east. Nina didn't have anyone left nearby to take care of her. She was a widow, and she'd never been able to have children of her own. And while Nina swore up and down she didn't need any help, the family knew she was one fall away from an extended hospital stay—or worse. That became clear a couple weeks back when Nina took the wrong dose of one of her medications and ended up in the hospital for a night.

Jess wasn't sure who would benefit the most from her time in Georgia, or how long she was going to stay. It was early April. She thought she would stay until fall and then consider heading back to Dallas, depending on what kind of arrangement they could work out for Nina. Jess had been raking in money as a single trial attorney and her savings would last for a while, so there was no pressure for her to decide soon. She might even take a part-time job while she was there; something to help pass the time through the heat of the summer.

That's a later Jess problem. I won't think about that right now. One thing at a time.

She tried not to let her mind wander too far past unpacking her bags. Lately, Jess had also been working on managing her expectations, those tricky things. Expectations—hers and society's—said she shouldn't have taken a break from her career, should've found a decent man by age thirty-three, should've bought a house already. But life hadn't panned out that way, and she didn't want to carry that toxicity into the new chapter of her life. Maybe the only thing she would gain from her time in Georgia was more time with her elderly aunt before she passed. Maybe it would yield a new career or the discovery of the elusive fountain of youth. Whatever happened, she decided before she left Dallas that she would be better off for it.

And with that settled, she carried her bags upstairs and started the unpacking process under the close supervision of Piggy.

CHAPTER TWO

Bryan

There wasn't a brick-and-mortar Georgia Bureau of Investigation office in Flowery Branch, yet. But north Georgia had experienced a population boom in the last few years, attracting folks from all walks of life with its mild climate and lower cost of living than the western states and New England. As a result, the bureau was struggling to keep up with the mounting caseload. Funding for a new office space was stuck in the proverbial maze of red tape that plagued publicly funded institutions. In the meantime, the GBI secured two small offices in the Flowery Branch Police Department's new building, smack in the middle of downtown, for a team of three agents that would set up a new regional office.

Bryan Whitley was reassigned from the Region Eight office in Cleveland, along with his colleague, Jason Thompson. Topher English, a bureau veteran, was moved from the Atlanta office in Decatur and given the supervisor position. Bryan was a Flowery Branch resident already, so he didn't mind his commute being cut from forty-five minutes to two. Jason lived a few miles up the road in Gainesville near Bryan's parents, while Topher had a house a few minutes south in Buford on a cove of the same lake that skirted the edge of Flowery Branch. The move suited all of them fine. They weren't exactly a dream team, but that didn't matter to the resource-starved office. Their superiors weren't looking for earth-shattering detective work; no one was reopening the O.J. case. They just needed bodies in the office to deal with the bodies in the manila folders.

Bryan was looking forward to working on more sophisticated cases than what they referred to as "chicken bone killings" in Region Eight. He'd grown tired of the simple murders that were the result of what many would consider minor offenses, except to those who were the recipients of them: mountain dwelling, Irish and Scottish descendants. Honor culture was still alive and well in their blood—staring at another man's woman a second too long kind of thing, or siblings fighting over family land. In those circles, they would throw hands and pull triggers without batting an eye, yet held to the honor code so tightly they would rarely speak with the cops even when they'd been wronged. This kind of behavior made Bryan's job difficult to solve crimes that should've been simple open-and-shut cases. He'd had his fill of those and was ready to work cases that would bring more recognition.

Of course, he already had name recognition going for him with his father being the Hall County Sheriff, but a little extra hometown heroism as detective extraordinaire certainly wouldn't hurt when it was time for him to run for his father's position whenever the old man finally retires.

And now that the bullshit investigation that almost ended his career was over, he could focus on his next move. He had some leads that would allow him to make a name for himself if he handled them carefully and under his boss's radar.

Topher, who was his superior, operated under a different philosophy than Bryan. Topher played the long game. Who had time for that? In the law enforcement world, leads go cold, witnesses disappear, and the criminals slide into new aliases if you give them too much time. And sometimes, they needed a little help from Bryan to get them into position so GBI could take action. They would've gotten there anyway in Bryan's estimation. Why not help things along so they could reallocate their resources to catch the bigger fish who could do more damage to the community? This giving-them-time-to-hang-themselves bullshit that Topher bought into wasn't doing anyone any favors, including Bryan.

"Hey, man," Bryan acknowledged one of the city cops, Eli, as they passed each other on Bryan's way into his makeshift office at the police department.

Eli saluted in response and jumped into his squad car, not lingering for any small talk. That was fine with Bryan. He preferred to keep their conversations brief and out of the ear shot of others.

A few minutes later, he was at his desk eating a greasy breakfast sandwich he'd grabbed at a drive-thru on his way in when his work phone buzzed on the desk beside his personal cell. Throwing a glance at it—he was planning to ignore it if it was the boss man, as it was too early to deal with Mr. Oldschool—he saw it was one of his confidential informants. He answered quickly. It was unusual for a CI to call that early. They usually stayed in bed sleeping off the previous night's bad choices until at least noon.

"I've got some information you might want to know about," a young man's voice on the other line started, his enticing tone pushing Bryan out of his seat.

"Talk to me." Bryan was already putting on his sunglasses and heading out the door to his truck.

CHAPTER THREE

Jess

Jess's first few days in Georgia were mostly uneventful. She and Nina spent hours catching up, though Jess noticed Nina was being careful not to mention her work. They reminisced on the summers Jess spent in Flowery Branch as a child, and even dug out some photo albums from those days. Jess was more at ease than she'd been in weeks. She couldn't remember the last time she'd laughed so hard. They even shared a few tears remembering Nina's late husband, a sweet man who died from a heart attack when Jess was a teenager.

One evening, the ladies sat on the porch enjoying some lemonade from Mason jars Nina spent most of the day and her energy making. Their glasses sweated, and the ice tinkered like miniature wind chimes as they sipped the tart, nectary drink.

"You always were my little history sponge. You remember when we used to watch the Discovery channel before bed whenever you came to stay?" Nina asked.

"Yeah, didn't I beg you to record late ones on VHS so we could watch them the next day?"

Nina chuckled and replied, "That sounds about right. I had to practically peel you off the living room floor to get you to go to bed.

One night, I had to threaten to call your mother if my memory serves me correctly."

A timer started going off on Jess's phone that was sitting beside her on the swing.

"Medicine time," Nina chimed.

"I'll go get it. Lipitor, right?" Jess pushed off the swing to head inside.

Nina shook her head. "Should be time for Metoprolol."

Jess sighed. "Lord help us. I'll check the chart."

It didn't take long for Jess to become overwhelmed as Nina's caretaker. Her aunt needed nearly a dozen medications every day in the form of pills, liquids, and shots, each with its own specific dose and time it was supposed to be administered. Jess was used to a hectic schedule and things coming at her fast—she was a trial attorney for crying out loud—but this kind of work was outside of her wheelhouse, and she was always worried about Nina falling.

Later that evening, she called her mother from Nina's porch.

"I don't know, Mom. She's worse than I expected." Even though Nina was inside, Jess kept her voice low so she wouldn't hear her. "I mean, she's in good spirits, but there's *a lot* of medications, and I'm struggling to help her get out of bed in the morning or out of a chair when she's been sitting for a long time."

"I was afraid that might be the case," Jess's mother, Marcie, said with a troubled sigh.

Jess wrapped an arm across her midsection. "I mean I can do it, but I am afraid of administering the wrong dose, or the wrong medication at the wrong time. The shots are the hardest. I feel like I bruise her every time."

"Shots? I didn't know she was taking any shots."

Jess sighed and focused on the fern in the hanging basket swaying with the breeze at the far end of the porch. "I didn't know, either, until I got here. She takes them weekly for her blood sugar. I honestly don't know how she didn't end up in the hospital sooner."

"Oh, goodness. Well, that's not something you should be doing, hon. I'll talk to your father tonight about a caretaker. If I know my sister, she'll whine about the cost, but we'll pay for whatever Medicare doesn't cover. And Jess..."

"Yeah?"

"Thank you for all you're doing. I hate that I can't be out there with her myself. I'm going to try and come whenever I can get some time off," Marcie said.

She ran the office at a logistics company that transported organs being donated. It was a small operation, and they were often short-staffed. Simply put, until they could hire another office manager, Marcie was single-handedly in charge of making sure people on death's doorstep got the lungs, hearts, and kidneys they needed to see the next sunrise. Everyone understood her situation, including Nina, but Jess knew her mother was beating herself up about not being able to come out.

"That would be nice. I'm sure Nina would love to see you. But don't worry about it so much. You know how she doesn't like anyone fussing over her."

"How're you doing?" Her mother's tone signaled she was fishing for anything Jess wanted to share about her healing journey, not so much her role as Nina's caretaker.

"I'm good," Jess answered, keeping her tone light. "I think I'm going to check out a farmers' market across the tracks in the morning. I'm tired of eating frozen dinners."

Her mother laughed. "Nina never did pay much attention to the cooking portion of home ec. She was too much of a free spirit for that. Kind of like you."

"Well, this free spirit is about to crawl in bed. Let me know what you and dad decide."

"I'll call you soon," Marcie assured her. "Love you."

"Love you, too." Jess hung up and relaxed back into the porch swing, drinking in the warm evening under the robin's-egg blue of the porch ceiling.

Her heart longed for home, but she knew she wasn't ready to go back, yet. She needed to make peace with the past before she made any big moves. Jess wasn't the type to wallow in self-pity, but the scandal had knocked her for a loop. She wasn't fired, but there was no way she could stay in a work environment where her colleagues acted like she was radioactive material after she'd stood up for herself.

Jess never doubted she would rebound, but she didn't feel any closer to a comeback now than when she'd left Dallas, not even an inch. She thought she'd start feeling better within a few days of being in Georgia, but she was coming to realize it was going to take her longer to regroup than she'd expected. For the moment, she would take things as they came and squeeze every bit of enjoyment she could from her temporary home, starting with the farmers' market in the morning.

CHAPTER FOUR

Bryan

Jess wasn't the kind of woman you slept on. Bryan could tell that within the first few minutes of seeing her at the farmers' market. He thought she was beautiful with her long hair and toned legs. But what piqued Bryan's interest most was the way she carried herself. She walked with her shoulders back like she wasn't afraid to take up space. It was a stance that demanded respect but not necessarily attention.

Flowery Branch shut down Main Street in front of the shops that lined both sides of the narrow downtown road by the railroad tracks every Saturday morning during the spring and summer months. The locals sold vegetables from their gardens, baked goods from their kitchens, and there was a fit blonde that usually stopped in after her morning run and bought asparagus from the westernmost booth on the south side of the street.

Bryan couldn't care less about waking up before the sun or shopping for organic vegetables, but he made an exception on farmers' market Saturdays. He was waiting for blondie to make her arrival, scanning his way through the booths when he saw a new face.

Having grown up in Flowery Branch, Bryan knew everyone that wasn't a newcomer. That wasn't an exaggeration. He really knew everyone. And what was in everyone's underwear drawers, how many nudes they had on their phones, and how many other people's phones those same nudes were on. What he didn't know from his work as a GBI agent, he learned from his sheriff father. But he didn't know the pretty brunette making her way up the street. He was already wondering what was in her underwear drawer.

Her light brown hair was pulled back in a loose ponytail under a distressed ball cap, not in a grungy way but in a purposefully tattered, stylish way that screamed, "suburban white girl who's never had a ball cap long enough to naturally look like this." Bryan noticed she sported high-end running shoes with aggressive outsoles that suggested she wasn't all show, no action based on the wear. She also wore clean, well-fitted yoga pants and a lightweight, long-sleeve athletic top that showcased her tapered waist. He guessed she was in her early thirties.

She was polished but not too primped. Based on the neutral colors of her attire and her straightforward posture, he would place her as someone who worked in a male dominated profession. Not law enforcement, though. She was a touch too reserved—Bryan's female colleagues tended to land on the emphatic side of the demeanor spectrum—and not quite observant enough of her surroundings for his field. Maybe finance. Probably law. Bryan couldn't help but profile her. That's what he did. Law enforcement was a part of his DNA. Most importantly, no ring. In fact, not much jewelry at all, save for a pair of small, unassuming pearl earrings.

He stopped at a booth selling homemade soaps and shave bars, pretending to smell through their selection as he watched her from across the market. The brunette was chatting with a booth owner named Clive who claimed to have the best radishes in Georgia, a title Bryan was sure no one would ever fight him for. As she moved through the market, he continued to trail behind her by three or four booths, occasionally studying an item and smiling at the vendors along the way. She purchased a couple more items, paying in cash and dropping her change in any tip jars the booth owners had set up.

Once she'd shopped the length of the market, she turned and made her way toward the east end of downtown in the direction of the railroad tracks, bags secured on her wrist. Not wanting to draw any more attention to himself than necessary, Bryan didn't follow her directly. Instead, he made his way one street over to where he'd parked his Dodge Ram while throwing glances her way under the cover of his ball cap.

By the time he cranked the engine, she had picked her way over the railroad tracks and was waiting for a clearing in the traffic to cross Atlanta Highway. The landscape dropped off on the far side of the tracks. He could only see her hat through the driver's side window until he pulled his truck out of the parking lot and headed toward the railroad track crossing about thirty yards south of where the brunette was darting across the street. The stoplight turned green as Bryan was pulling up to it, and he punched the gas while flipping on his blinker. He took a left onto Atlanta Highway toward her direction and caught sight of her slipping through the front door of one of the historic homes that lined the main drag through town. He was pretty sure it was Nina Wilton's home, if she still lived there. Her late husband had a lumber business Bryan had worked at during the summers in high school.

The door closed behind her as Bryan passed. He was already on the phone with one of his buddies from high school before he hit the next stoplight. If anyone in the county knew who she was, Bryan would also know by lunch.

CHAPTER FIVE

Jess

All her life Jess had felt as though she were a hybrid. A mix of old and new. Like the conterminous where two oceans meet but don't mix because of their differing densities. She could regale the anguish of missing a call from a crush on a landline yet keep up with her younger cousins on their smart devices. She felt like she'd won the generational lottery. This had set her up for a killer career in the legal field that was dominated by a generation largely removed from technology but was also becoming more intertwined with said technology. She quickly figured out how to mint herself into a puzzle piece that connected the two worlds, and it had paid well.

Outside of her profession, this disposition felt more isolating. At this stage in her life, she was too old to identify with college students or young professionals in their twenties, but she didn't fit in with most women in their early-to-mid-thirties, many of whom were leaving their careers or scaling them back as they entered motherhood. Her constant outside of her hobby of DIY furniture restoration projects was her career, and even that was disrupted. In some ways, Jess was thankful for it. The distance from work over the past few weeks enabled her to see she attached too much of herself to her job. For as long as she could remember, Jess knew she wanted to go from high school straight to college and follow up her undergrad with law school. Everything else in life was going to have to fit around that plan. That's exactly what she'd done, and it had taken up the whole of her identity without her realizing it. This break was the first time in her life she'd taken a step back to evaluate her path.

All these thoughts were swirling through her head one evening, as she drove to the marina across the railroad tracks that was tucked back in a quiet cove of the lake away from the main channel. She'd decided to take herself on a date. After grabbing a Cuban salad to go from the seafood restaurant at the marina, The Coral Social, she grabbed her current read, a historical drama, out of her car and walked down to the docks that lined the cove with boats of all kinds. She opted for the dock that held the houseboats, not wanting to be bothered and thinking the size of the houseboats would conceal her from any chatty retirees taking their pontoon boats for evening joy rides. At the end, she spotted a bench that was begging for her company where she plopped down and opened her to-go box.

Spring was pushing through the last of the winter brown that had been clinging onto the landscape. The azalea bushes were bursting with blooms, and the tulips had awoken from their slumber to bring new life to the yards she'd passed on her drive to the lake. She took a few minutes to eat and soak in the golden sunlight before cracking open her novel.

She didn't get two chapters into her book when she was interrupted by a whirring sound. Looking up, she noticed a man on a bass boat was using the trolling motor on the bow to maneuver slowly through the docks as he threw a cast into each empty boat slip he passed. Soon, he directly in front of Jess as he rounded the end of the dock.

Jess recognized him. She was pretty sure she'd seen him at the farmers' market two weeks ago. She'd caught him checking her out in the reflection of a shop window—he had been wearing basketball shorts and a t-shirt which made him look younger. Today, he looked closer to Jess's age, maybe a couple of years older. He was in shape with a trim waist and the bottom of his tight biceps were rounded, like there were coiled snakes peeking from beneath the sleeves of his shirt, flexing with each cast. His angular face was offset by a strong jawline and framed with a short beard that matched the burnt umber of his hair. He was good-looking but not her type. Well, not anymore. She'd dated the jock stereotype enough to know her future partner wasn't one. Their physiques often couldn't make up for the lack of intellectual stimulation Jess craved in a partner.

"Howdy," he acknowledged her, tipping his ball cap in her direction like the main character in a spaghetti western.

Jess gave a small smile in return, unsure how much she wanted to engage. Thinking about her situation had put her in a mood she wasn't ready to claw her way out of to be social—yet. She refocused her attention on her book. He took the hint and didn't linger. She heard the whir of the motor kick back up and saw the boat head for the fueling dock below The Coral Social out of the corner of her eye.

Jess read until it was too dark to see the pages of her book and the night picked up a chill. When she left, there was no sight of the man on the boat.

A couple days later, Jess got Nina situated with her Judge Judy reruns after dinner and made her way back over to the marina. When she arrived, she grabbed the book she'd tossed in the passenger seat, but she didn't start reading immediately. Instead, she spent some time meandering the docks, taking in the sights and sounds of the lake and reveling the feeling of the evening sun kissing her skin.

Eventually she came to the same bench she had dinner on earlier that week and sat down to read.

As she found the place she'd left off in her novel, the same man on the fishing boat from earlier in the week slowly idled past her and headed toward the fueling dock again. He offered a smile with a wave as he passed. There was something about the man she couldn't place her finger on. She couldn't identify the feeling as good or bad. It was just...something.

She tried to concentrate on her book, but it wasn't long before the man reappeared in front of her.

"Mind if I bother you for a minute? You happen to be right over the honey hole," he said with a coy smile that told Jess there was no honey hole full of fish; he just wanted to talk with her, and she wasn't sure how she felt about it.

Because of what had happened in Dallas, her guard automatically went up when a man approached her. This man didn't seem unsafe, but he wasn't exactly giving her Hallmark-movie-hometown-good-ol'-boy vibes, either.

"Bass or catfish?" Jess asked over her book without closing it.

"Pardon?"

"Are you fishing for bass or catfish?"

The man seemed a little taken aback that she knew her fish facts based on the way his eyebrows pulled upward and his head cocked to the side. It took him a moment to respond. "Bass, of course."

"Then, you should know you'd probably have better luck past that dock where it's shallower and the fish are on bed." She pointed to the neighboring dock that sported a corrugated tin roof over the boats bobbing in their slips over lighter green water.

She had no idea her weekends being dragged out on the lake with her dad when she was a kid—for long days of fishing—would pay off. Not that she had any interest in showcasing her aquatic expertise; she just wanted the man to quit hitting on her so she could get back to reading.

"Spoken like a true fisherwoman," he observed. Then, apparently thinking this was his opportunity to introduce himself, he followed up with, "I'm Bryan, by the way."

"Jess," she responded in a clipped tone, refocusing her book.

"Any other advice you'd like to share, Jess?"

"Talking scares the fish," she deadpanned, searching the page for where she'd left off. Her southern decorum reserves were drained at this point.

Bryan threw his head back and laughed. Jess looked up to see him shift his foot on the trolling motor pedal, turning the boat so he was facing her directly. "You never figured out that it was just our parents trying to get us to shut up when we didn't know better than to ask hundreds of questions about everything?"

"No one ever let me in on that joke," she replied, still not looking up from her book.

"Alright, I'll make you a deal," he said like a game show host. "If I miss this pitch from here into that boat slip without getting tangled in the lift, I'll leave you to your evening," he said, indicating the last slip of the covered dock, directly to Jess's right about fifteen yards. "*But*...if I make it, you have to go on a date with me."

Jess eyed the slip with its tangle of metal between the dock and the boat lift. Seemed like a feat if he could pull it off—and like a juvenile dare—but Jess felt confident failure was imminent, and she'd soon return to her solitary date in peace.

"Alright. Deal." She snapped her book closed and dropped it in her lap.

"Do I get a practice cast first?" Bryan asked.

"Nope, you should have included that in your initial complaint if you wanted it."

"Ah, an attorney?" He studied Jess, as if her reaction would confirm his suspicions. She said nothing, not wanting to keep the lines of communication open any longer than necessary. "Well?" he pressed.

"Guilty," she admitted, looking at him from under a lowered brow.

"Pun intended?" he asked with a grin.

Not sure if she was more irritated at him for not taking a hint or herself for entertaining him as long as she did, she rose to her feet, secured her book under one arm, and turned to leave.

Bryan stopped her with, "Alright, alright. I'll cast."

He shifted his foot on the trolling motor pedal a couple times, turning the boat, so that he was facing the slip. With finesse, he opened the bail on the reel, swung the rod out to the side, and then whipped the rod toward the slip.

Ding! The lure ricocheted off one of the steel support poles surrounding the slip, which conveniently dropped it into the water in the middle of the boat lift. Bryan reeled quickly to extract the lure before it sank too far and became tangled in the boat lift system.

He looked over at Jess with his eyebrows raised and a grin climbing up the right side of his face as if to say "well?"

"That was luck," she contended.

"And I'll take all the luck I can get. So, about that date…"

Jess thought for a moment. It could be nice to know someone her age in town. A way to meet friends.

"Okay," she heard herself say flatly.

"Tomorrow night. At the restaurant," he said, swinging his rod in the direction of The Coral Social.

"I'll meet you there at seven," Jess answered over her shoulder, as she headed up the dock to her car.

She didn't want this man showing up at Nina's to pick her up. One, she didn't know who he was, and two, she didn't want Nina reporting back to her mother that Jess was dating. It was a sensitive subject, since her mother couldn't understand why landing a husband wasn't Jess's top priority at her age. Not that she was averse to the idea, she just wasn't going to chase a man down. Her career had kept her busy enough, and she found great meaning in helping the innocent retain their freedom and try to retain a modicum of their dignity along the way. Now that her work was on hold, maybe it was time to meet someone.

CHAPTER SIX

Jess

Jess stood in front of the mirror the next evening assessing her outfit choice for her date with Bryan. It's funny how much one's taste changes in a decade. Twenty-something-year-old Jess would have been appalled to wear the medium-wash, high-rise jeans and cream top with pleated sleeves she'd pulled out of her armoire. She would've preferred something with a lower neckline and no doubt spent at least ten more minutes on her hair. In older Jess's defense, the top was cropped and hit right at the top of her jeans. She felt like she deserved some cool points for that.

Satisfied with her outfit, she swiped mascara on her lashes, dabbed concealer under her eyes and blush on the apples of her cheeks, grabbed her purse, and went downstairs to make sure Nina was situated before she left.

"You look nice, dear. Where are you headed?"

"I got invited to dinner," Jess said, leaving out any details that would indicate it was a date, which was futile as Nina's smile indicated she already knew.

She hoped her aunt wouldn't say anything to her mother, but she wouldn't be surprised if Nina phoned Marcie as soon as the front door closed behind Jess.

Jess let Piggy out, and then drove to the marina. She pulled in a couple of minutes before seven and reminded herself to enjoy the night.

At the least, you might end up with a new friend.

A Dodge Ram rolled in at seven on the dot and circled the parking lot before parking next to her. Bryan hopped out and smiled at her. She wondered how he spotted her so quickly in the lot full of cars, but maybe he'd watched what car she'd gotten into the night before as the marina and restaurant shared a parking lot that was visible from the lake where he'd been fishing.

He was put together in a rough-around-the-edges way. Under a fresh ball cap, his hair was closely cropped with neat sideburns as if he'd just gotten it cut. His beard was also short and well-groomed, and he was wearing a navy polo and khaki tactical pants.

He smiled at her with the corners of his eyes creasing. "You came."

Jess shouldered her purse and closed her car door. "A woman of my word."

Bryan motioned for her to walk ahead of him toward the restaurant, only stepping ahead of her to grab the door.

She caught the slight scent of a musky aftershave as he held the door for her to enter first. Once the hostess seated them in a cozy booth by a large window that overlooked the cove, Bryan slid his sunglasses around to the back of his neck, smiled at Jess over his menu, and told her she looked nice.

"Thank you." Jess smiled softly, enjoying the compliment, and brushed away a strand of hair that had fallen across her forehead.

"You look like an app girl. You want an appetizer?" Bryan asked.

"An app girl? What does that mean?" Jess had never heard such a thing.

"I don't know. I just made it up because I wanted to order an appetizer," he said with a wink and a grin.

The comment broke the ice and amused Jess. She suggested the fried calamari or the crab dip.

"It's settled. We'll get both," he said and set his menu on the edge of the table.

A young, bubbly waitress appeared to get their drink orders—a pilsner for Bryan and margarita for Jess—and Bryan ordered the appetizers for them.

As the waitress walked off, Jess shifted the conversation. "So, my jargon gave my profession away yesterday, and your pants are giving yours away today."

"Oh, yeah?"

"Yeah, it's clear you're in IT," she responded.

Bryan threw his head back and laughed. "You know I almost was. But I just couldn't figure out that whole email thing, so I had to move on."

Jess grinned and asked, "Are you local law enforcement or state?"

"What makes you think I'm in law enforcement?" He gently challenged.

"Besides the pants? You made sure you sat where you could see the door, you've profiled everyone that's walked through it, and you already noticed I'm a leftie."

"How do you figure I know you're a leftie?" He leaned back against the booth and turned his head.

"You slid the menu toward my left hand," Jess answered.

"Guilty," he responded, seemingly impressed with her observation skills based on his surprised expression. He went on, "I'm a GBI agent, so state level. You might've heard us referred to as 'God's Best Investigators,' which is true, but of course, we come second to GSP, otherwise known as 'God's Special People,'" he said in a facetious tone.

Jess tilted her head and looked at him quizzically. "Not following you."

"Georgia State Patrol," he answered. "They think they're deities."

"Ah, I see. Well, that makes sense. I think I passed a dozen of them waiting on the side of the highway between the state line and Atlanta when I got here a few weeks ago."

Jess asked more about his job, and he explained that he got into law enforcement following in his dad's footsteps, the kinds of cases he worked on—general investigations which included homicide—and that he was part of a small team opening a new regional office for the bureau in Flowery Branch.

"Sounds like you've got quite the resume," Jess noted.

"Ah, it's good enough for government work," Bryan joked with a shrug.

Jess laughed, reveling in his carefree attitude. She slowly felt the listless feeling she'd been bogged down with fade into the background. For the first time in a couple of months, she wasn't ruminating on the crossroads her life had come to and was glad she agreed to the date. She felt the tension that had been pulling at her neck ease.

The waitress appeared with a loaded tray and slid their drinks, appetizers, and two small plates in front of them with a smile and asked if they were ready to order.

Bryan indicated for Jess to go first. She ordered the Creole shrimp pasta with a side salad, and he followed up with a grouper sandwich.

After the waitress scooped their menus from them and headed for the kitchen, Bryan grabbed the smaller plates and set one in front of Jess first, and then himself. He dished out some of each appetizer on her plate before adding some to his own.

Jess was impressed at the gesture. She couldn't remember a date where a man had gone the extra mile like this.

"So, I guessed attorney correctly, but what area of practice?" He asked.

Jess had been wondering when he would get to that, and she smiled up at him amusingly. "Probably not your favorite kind," she said before taking a bite of fried calamari.

Her reply made him pause halfway to his mouth with his fork. He cocked his head to the side and said, "You've gotta be kidding me."

Jess laughed and shrugged as she continued to munch on the calamari.

"A defense attorney?" Bryan asked.

"You guessed it...again," she said with a smile and jab of her fork in his direction.

"No shit?" he asked rhetorically. "Now, I have to reassess my opinion of you." His words were tinged with playfulness.

Defense attorneys and law enforcement had a tepid relationship at best. Local and state investigators like Bryan bore the burden of being the eyes and ears for the prosecution. And it was the job of defense attorneys, like Jess, to systematically dismantle the prosecution's argument, often by exploiting any errors in the cornerstone of the prosecution's stance: the investigation. But learning this fact about her didn't seem to deter Bryan. If anything, he seemed even more intrigued by her, asking her questions and dropping jovial jabs at her when an opportunity presented itself. Perhaps he had a taste for forbidden fruit.

A battle of wits was Jess's love language, and any lingering reservations were melting away the further their conversation went.

After dinner, Bryan suggested they stroll the docks below the restaurant where Jess had been sitting when he asked her on a date. There was a cool breeze coming off the lake, so he detoured them to his truck first and grabbed a light jacket for Jess that she pulled around her shoulders.

Bonus points for Bryan.

"So, what brought you out here?" Bryan asked, as they meandered down the dock past boats of all kinds seesawing on the waves created by the vessels cruising through the cove to the open water.

"Uh, well..." Jess chastised herself for not preparing an answer for that question. It wasn't like her to not have one. "My aunt needed some help, and I was burned out with my job. It wasn't a great work environment, so I decided to head out here and help my aunt while I figure out my next step."

"I see," he said, nodding.

Jess was sure he knew there was more to the story since he was an investigator, but he didn't press. Instead, he asked, "How're you liking Georgia?"

"It's been lovely so far. I can't get over how much the area has grown since the last time I was here," she answered.

"Yeah, Hollywood likes the tax breaks the state offers, so they've started filming shows and movies here. It's moved a lot of people to Atlanta, pushing the locals farther and farther out." Bryan explained that one of the most popular shows on TV depicting a family entangled in criminal activities was partially filmed in Flowery Branch.

"Does any of that go on here in real life?" Jess asked. She hadn't thought of Flowery Branch as a dangerous place, but his story made her wonder.

"You'd be surprised," is all Bryan offered in response before pulling up short beside one of the slips toward the end of the dock.

"You want to take a ride?" He motioned toward a slip that housed the boat she'd seen him on the previous day.

"Uhm," Jess wasn't sure how to respond.

She didn't expect a sunset cruise would be on the agenda. He seemed harmless enough, but she listened to enough true crime podcasts and streamed enough documentaries to know those were the ones to watch out for.

"I won't bite. I promise. Work told me I had to quit doing that, or I'd get fired," Bryan joked, as he stepped onto the bow of the boat, stretched his hand out toward her, and winked. "I'll have you back before curfew."

"Tempting." Half of Jess wanted to go since tonight was the most she'd enjoyed herself in Georgia so far, but the other half of her was hesitant. She reminded herself to go slow and said, "But I regretfully have to decline. I need to get back home to check on my aunt."

She could've called Nina to make sure all was well, but she wanted to end the night on a high note. And there wasn't any harm in leaving Bryan wanting more.

"Fair enough," Bryan answered, sounding a little dejected but also understanding. "I'll walk you back to your car."

When they reached her Mercedes, he opened her door.

Jess slid into her seat and Bryan leaned against the top of the open door, smiling at her. "I had a great time tonight."

"Me, too. Thank you for dinner. Sorry I have to go, but she's been mixing up her medications lately, and I'm a little worried about her."

"Well, you can make it up to me with a second date." A smile relaxed Bryan's features as he awaited her response.

"Okay." Jess smiled and pulled her phone out.

They exchanged phone numbers, and he promised he'd be in touch.

"Be safe," he softly instructed, pushing himself up off her door.

She gave him a slight smile. "I will."

He grinned with soft eyes and pushed her door closed before shoving his hands in his pockets.

Jess reversed out of her space and gave a small wave before driving off. Bryan returned the wave and watched her pull away, and she caught herself smiling as she drove home.

CHAPTER SEVEN

MAY

Bryan

TRAIN BEER!" the waitress yelled above the call of the train whistle wailing outside, swinging a towel above her head in a circular motion.

After learning they both preferred whiskey on their first date, Bryan decided to take Jess to a distillery for their second. There was one a few minutes north in Gainesville in an old industrial district by the railroad tracks. It had a good barbecue restaurant beside it that sold cheap draft beer for two dollars whenever a train rumbled past. He decided they would start their evening there before walking across the parking lot to the distillery for drinks.

Tonight, the joint was filled with a mix of families, dates, and work colleagues. Bryan and Jess stepped around the towel-wielding waitress to order at the front counter. After they selected their choices—they both ordered the brisket and beer—Bryan paid, and the cashier handed him a metal holder with a number card stuck on the top. Bryan motioned for Jess to lead the way into the dining room to the right of the cashier counter. She selected a high-top table by the front window. Bryan pulled Jess's chair out and waited for her to get situated before taking the seat directly across from her.

They sipped their local IPA beers out of chilled glasses and engaged in the normal second date small talk about what each of them had been up to since their first date earlier in the week. When the food came, Bryan made sure Jess liked her brisket before he started eating his. His mother raised him to make sure the lady was taken care of first and foremost.

He paid close attention to Jess's mannerisms, watching for any signs she was a flirt. When she excused herself to the restroom, he watched to see if she sent any signals to any of the other men in the restaurant, like single women sometimes do. His ex-girlfriend would do that sort of thing, and he couldn't stand it. He hadn't seen anything on his first date with Jess to indicate she might be femme fatale, but, of course, everyone was on their best behavior in the beginning.

She was beautiful, intelligent, and independent. The triple crown for Bryan. But he learned over the years that you had to be careful with the independent type. He loved the challenge of the strong-headed assertiveness that came with professional women, but that same trait led them to stray outside the lines of appropriate relationship behavior from time to time. They would play off the infractions by saying things like "it was just a lunch work date," as if sharing a meal with the opposite sex was acceptable behavior for someone in a relationship. That wasn't something he would address right now, but if the opportunity presented itself, he would act.

Perhaps the most intriguing thing about Jess was that he couldn't find out much about her. After he'd seen her at the farmers' market, he'd asked around, but no one had any information. He could always pull her up by searching Nina Wilton's name in his GBI software or running Jess's tag. Because they were a smaller satellite office, Bryan and his colleagues did their own research instead of sending it to the back office. But he had to keep a low profile, not knowing if there were any lingering eyes on him from the investigation. And right now, flying under the radar was imperative to his current investigation; the one that wasn't exactly authorized but was more important than all the previous cases he'd investigated over the course of his career. This one had the potential to make or break him—maybe even get him a federal position with a cushier pension and secure the approval of his father—if he didn't get himself killed in the process. Considering that, he had no choice but to let the information come to him organically— something he hadn't done in a long time.

Lucky for Bryan, the Flowery Branch Police Department building that housed his new office was situated directly across the railroad tracks and Atlanta Highway from Nina Wilton's home, where he'd seen Jess go after the farmers' market. His office window gave him a direct line of sight to the house. He wasn't in the office as much as usual with his side project becoming increasingly demanding of his time. But when he was there, he watched the house to see if he could catch a glimpse of Jess and intercept her. He'd seen her leave one weeknight, head across the tracks in her Mercedes, and head in the direction of the marina on the edge of town where he kept his bass boat. He'd jumped in his truck, headed for the marina, and the rest was history.

He finished his beer and dropped their food trays at the designated counter by the time she returned to the table from the restroom.

"Are you ready?" She asked as she approached, smiling.

He noticed she'd applied fresh lipstick and took it as a sign she was enjoying the evening.

"Yup, let's go," he said, as he led her to the door.

Leaning, he opened it with one arm so she could pass through in front of him, gently placing his hand on the small of her back as she did. They walked across the parking lot to the distillery next door where they ordered drinks before picking a spot outside to enjoy the warm evening. There were a few other couples around, lounging in the Adirondack chairs and playing the yard games the establishment had set up.

After their first drink, Bryan asked if she wanted to play cornhole.

"Sure, let's do it," she replied.

"Alright, we only have time for one game, though," Bryan informed her.

"Oh?"

"I want to take you somewhere for dessert that closes kind of early. It's one of my favorite spots. I think you'll like it."

CHAPTER EIGHT

Jess

O kay," Jess agreed, wondering what Bryan had in mind.

Bryan won the yard game by a landslide. She could tell he was going easy on her the first few throws and called him out on it. He accepted the challenge and turned up the heat. Jess enjoyed the competition—she was an attorney after all—and didn't mind the loss. He won fair and square. After the last throw, she downed the remainder of her drink, and they headed for the truck.

He opened the door for her, and she felt his hand brush at the small of her back again as she climbed in. Jess took note of how clean the truck was while he circled the hood, something she'd missed when she'd hopped in at Nina's. The dash was dust-free and lustrous, the rubber floor mats were almost spotless, and the leather seats gleamed with a slight sheen.

They cruised through the downtown streets to a different part of town that quickly shifted in its architecture and culture. The unassuming brown brick and stately white stucco buildings near the industrial area gave way to a much more vibrant, bustling scene.

"Welcome to Little Mexico," Bryan announced as he steered them onto a street lined with brightly colored buildings that sported signs in Spanish.

As they waited at a stoplight, he switched on the radio and flipped through stations until he found a Latin one and turned it up, bobbing his head to the beat.

He sent her a wink across the seat. "I want to make sure you get the full experience."

This garnered a laugh from Jess, who couldn't say she wasn't surprised. A culturally immersive date wasn't what she was expecting from a cop. "I didn't know there was such a large Hispanic community here."

"Well, here's your fun fact for the day: Gainesville here," he waved his hand out his open window like Vanna White on Wheel of Fortune, "was built on chicken money. It's the poultry capital of the world. The poultry processing plants attract migrant workers. Legend has it, there's a sign in Mexico that says something like 'Go to Gainesville, Georgia to find work,' or something like that. Oh, and it's illegal to eat fried chicken with a fork here," he finished.

"You're kidding." Jess was convinced he made the last fact up.

"Nope. City ordinance from the 1960s. You can Google it." He steered them into the parking lot of a small strip mall.

Their destination was a small *cocina* sandwiched between a check cashing joint and a no-contract cell phone store. Bryan backed into a space—such a cop—and cut the engine.

"Miss Lola has the best *sopaipillas* this side of the border," he explained as they crossed the small parking lot.

"Oh? And how do you know this?"

Bryan grinned and pointed to a red and orange hand-painted sign hanging in the window that said exactly that in response.

"Ah, I see."

Bryan stepped ahead to open the door for Jess and then filed in behind her. The place was small, maybe a little wider than a car length, and only had two tables. It looked like most people took their food to go based on the large stack of white Styrofoam containers that almost touched the ceiling in one of the back corners of the kitchen, the entirety of which was visible from the ordering counter.

"Mr. Bryan!" a woman Jess presumed to be Miss Lola exclaimed with a Latin accent, complete with a rolling "r," as soon as she saw them walk through the door.

"*Hola,* Lola. *¿Cómo estás?*"

Spanish? Jess was momentarily taken aback.

"*Muy bien, amigo. Veo que hoy has traído a una amiga,*" Lola responded, eyeing Jess with a friendly smile.

"*Si, lo hice. ¿Puedes ayudarla mientras uso el baño, por favor?*" Bryan asked.

"*¡Claro que sí!*" Lola exclaimed with a nod.

Jess wasn't fluent in Spanish, but she'd retained enough of her elementary knowledge of it to know that Bryan was going to the restroom, and he asked Lola to help Jess while he did.

"I'll be right back," Bryan said as he slipped behind the counter and walked past the kitchen staff into a hallway in the back.

"What can I get you, dear?" Lola asked Jess warmly, switching to English.

She was a stout, short woman with her black hair pulled neatly away from her face. Her floral apron was streaked with flour, and she wore a gold crucifix necklace that hung just above her large bosom.

"Uhm, well, what do you recommend? It all looks so good," Jess asked, scanning the rows of mouth-watering options behind the glass display in front of her.

"The sopaipillas are good if you're looking for something filling and not too sweet. I make those myself. If you want something a little sweeter, maybe you'd like the *fresas con crema* or the *churros,*" she explained, pointing to each option as she spoke. "But those two are made by Pedro, so they're not as good as my *sopaipillas.*"

"*Aye!*" a man called from the kitchen area. He continued, spouting off a few things in Spanish that sounded like insults, which were met with Miss Lola's presumed insults in return.

The whole kitchen staff burst into laughter, and Pedro turned a little red.

"He's my nephew," Lola explained, leaning over the glass display case toward Jess with a gleam in her eye. "It's my job to keep him in check."

Bryan emerged from the bathroom, and they decided on the sopaipillas. The square pastries reminded Jess of the world-famous beignets at Café du Monde in New Orleans. Bryan ordered four of them. Lola bagged six with a wink, threw in some honey packets, and rang them out.

"*¡No te mantengas alejado tanto tiempo!*" Lola called after them as they headed for the exit.

"You know I can't stay away from you too long, Miss Lola. Just trying to watch my figure is all." Bryan pushed the door open for Jess with the hand holding the desserts and patted his belly with his other.

Lola's laughter faded away as the door swung closed behind them.

"I didn't know you spoke Spanish," Jess said as they shimmied their way between the cars parked in front of the *cocina*.

"I don't," Bryan responded, prompting Jess to look at him sideways. "I speak Mexican," he explained. "And I couldn't write a word of it to save my life. But it's easier than waiting for a translator when you're trying to find someone quickly."

"Ah, I see. So you picked it up along the way?"

"More or less. I know how to ask for the bathroom, order food and beer, count to twenty, tell someone to fuck off, and ask 'how does life without parole sound,'" he explained, garnering a chuckle from Jess.

Bryan dropped the tailgate for them to eat on. He used a napkin to pull one of the pastries from the bag, drizzled some honey on the top, and fed the first bite to Jess.

He eyed her for a reaction. "Do you like it?"

"It's delicious." She licked the honey from her lips and took the rest from him.

Neither of them said a word as they ate. The warmth of the bread and sugary sweetness of the honey was intoxicating, making Jess want to go back and order as many *sopaipillas* as Lola could make. Jess noticed Bryan staring across the street at a rundown motel that looked like it was built in the 1950s and never updated. The red and cream block-letter sign read "Juliana Motel." He seemed to be studying the same area each time he looked at it, toward one of the rooms on the right side of the motel.

"Everything okay?" Jess asked following his gaze.

He broke his stare and looked over at her. "Yeah, sorry. Sometimes I get lost in my head. Are you ready to head back?"

"Sure."

Bryan opened the passenger door for Jess on his way to throw their trash in a bin on the sidewalk.

As they took a left on Atlanta Highway to head back down to Flowery Branch, Jess noticed him looking in the rearview mirror for longer than normal. Jess thought the behavior was somewhat odd but passed it off as him just being a cop, just like backing into the parking space.

He dropped her off at Nina's—she let him pick her up this time since Nina already guessed she went on a date when they first went out, and the cat wasn't going back in the bag—and asked her on a third date.

Jess agreed and moved to open her door, but Bryan stopped her by taking her hand. Pushing the bill of his ball cap up with his thumb, he leaned over the console, hooked the thumb of his other hand behind her ear, and kissed her. Jess's stomach somersaulted as she tasted the honey from the *sopaipillas* on his lips that seemed to fit perfectly with hers and her skin tingled beneath his touch. She wanted to crawl across the console and find other areas of him that fit well with her. But a full-on make out session in front of her aunt's house at thirty-three felt silly, so she pulled away and slipped out of the truck with a smile.

"Thank you for a nice evening," she said and closed the door.

Bryan rolled down the passenger window and asked, "Would you like me to walk you to the door?"

"Thank you, but I'll manage," she assured him over her shoulder with a wink, not breaking stride. "Goodnight, Bryan," she cooed.

"Goodnight, Jess," he echoed her with a smile before dropping the truck in reverse and slowly backing down the driveway as she made her way up the front steps.

She slipped inside, watched Bryan's headlights slowly fade away, quietly retrieved Piggy from Nina's dark bedroom, and then padded upstairs to wash her face. The kiss replayed over and over in her head as she got ready for bed, giving her a headrush and making her feel like a teenager again.

Oh, get a grip, Jess. Stop it with the middle school swooning shit. You're a grown-ass woman with a law degree.

But that didn't stop her from texting her friend, Stacey, a recap of the evening and slipping into sleep with a grin.

CHAPTER NINE

Jess

Jess hadn't even thought of dating in Georgia. In fact, the last time she had a serious boyfriend was almost five years ago. He was a nice guy, but it was clear he wanted to move onto the white picket fence and minivan phase of life, while Jess was just getting started in her career, so they drifted apart. After that, she'd dated a few men casually, but nothing stuck longer than a few months.

Now that she'd met Bryan, she was starting to wonder what her next step should be. She had enough money saved up to coast for a while, especially now that her lease in Dallas was ending in a couple of weeks. Not knowing what to expect when she moved to Georgia, she'd taken a chunk of her savings to pay off her car, so she didn't have any debt. Her student loans from law school were also paid off, which she made contingent upon her employment with the firm she'd started working for in Dallas straight out of school. She negotiated her salary to such that it would allow her to pay her loans back in five years if she lived a minimalist lifestyle during that time. Her friends weren't sure what to make of it when they learned she was denying jobs that said no to her request.

"Are you crazy?! This isn't the medical field where they do that sort of thing. Do you want a job? You can bet that's going to get around. You know how rumors fly in this town. Dallas isn't *that* big, and you're going to hurt your chances at other firms if they find out," Stacey told her when Jess explained how her job search was going.

"Maybe. Or maybe it will weed out the wrong places for me," Jess argued, ever the attorney.

As it turned out, Jess was right. One day while she was grocery shopping, she got a call. To her surprise, it was one of the founding partners of a large, prestigious criminal defense firm located in downtown Dallas.

"When I heard of your request, I knew I wanted to bring you in for an interview. Anyone with that kind of chutzpah so early in her career has the potential to make a solid attorney, especially with a résumé like yours. I believe you could be a great addition to our team. Can you come in next week?" He asked.

She heard herself say, "Yes, I can make that work."

He told her his office would be in touch to set up a time.

Jess hung up the phone in shock. She'd been working toward her goal of being an attorney since she was on the debate team in high school. It was hard to believe the final puzzle piece had fallen into place.

Jess called Stacey to tell her the news, and they went shopping for an interview outfit that afternoon. The plain navy and black suits she had from law school moot court would've been fine, but Jess wanted something new. She steered away from the stuffier styles like pantsuits that hadn't changed since women had entered the legal field and were expected to look like men to be taken seriously. It was winter at the time, so she picked out a navy velvet pencil skirt that accentuated her curves in a way that preserved professionalism. She paired it with a cream silk top under a tartan print blazer that complimented the navy skirt. Stacey stood behind Jess as she assessed her outfit choice in the dressing room mirror and told her she'd make her Highland ancestors proud.

Jess furrowed her brows. "I don't think I have any Scottish ancestry."

"You're bull-headed enough to be," Stacey replied with a soft prod to Jess's ribs.

Jess lifted her chin as she straightened the lapels of her new blazer. "I'll take that as a compliment."

The call that she'd been offered the job came on a Wednesday a couple of weeks later, and she started the following Monday. A year-and-a-half into her career, she hit her stride as a trial attorney. One of the senior members of the firm took her under his wing as her mentor and showed her the ins and outs of which approaches won cases and the tactics that tended to lose them in the courtroom. She soaked up everything and studied each end of a trial from jury selection to appellate strategies, often not leaving time for anything else in life. But Jess loved every minute of it.

Her efforts didn't go unnoticed by the firm partners. Five years into practicing, she was selected to be lead counsel on a case that garnered more media attention than expected. As a result, the Innocence Project, an organization dedicated to overturning the convictions of the wrongfully accused, reached out and asked her to become a project ambassador and work with them on some cases with similar fact patterns.

She was thrilled to partner with them and happily accepted some cases to review. Her nights and weekends were spent pouring over the case files. Some of the cases were heart-wrenching. Young men and women in jail, some had already been there for decades, for murders, rapes, robberies they didn't commit. DNA evidence had even proved their innocence, and they were still incarcerated as they couldn't afford legal counsel to advocate for their release, or their cases were being worked on but stuck in the quagmire of the legal system. All the while, these wronged individuals were losing more and more of their lives.

Jess was moved to tears on more than one occasion reading over the court transcripts. She considered quitting her job with the defense firm and joining the Innocence Project full time, but part of her also wanted to make partner in her firm. Torn between the two, she continued to work with her firm and volunteer for the project when she could.

Three years after she started working with them, she received an email from a staff member at the Office of the Attorney General. The email didn't say much, only that Attorney General of Texas, Justin Bennett, was requesting a meeting to discuss her work with the Innocence Project. The staffer didn't specify any further, and Jess was afraid she was in trouble.

That's silly. I'm an ethical practitioner. I haven't done anything wrong.

Still the request struck her as odd, and frankly, she didn't have time for it. She was neck-deep in cases for her firm and a case for the project. Jess tried to have them speak with her paralegals, but Justin refused to work with anyone else. She notified the project, but there wasn't much they could say. The man was the top legal official in the state of Texas. She didn't have much of a choice. Frustrated, Jess replied a curt affirmative to the staff member who'd reached out.

Like Jess, Justin achieved success early in his career. He was in his late forties and attractive with a salt-and-pepper beard. Jess had seen him around town at events like the Governor's Inaugural Ball and the State Bar of Texas Christmas parties in the past but was only briefly introduced to him for the first time at the State Bar of Texas's Christmas party a few months prior to his request to meet. They exchanged pleasantries, but they each had their own dates to keep them occupied so the interaction was minimal. Still, she picked up an odd energy from him. Something in the way he looked at each woman that passed by during their brief interaction made Jess uncomfortable, and she wasn't looking forward to having dinner with him.

Scavenging through her closet, she managed to find a dress that was fitted but conservative. She capped it with a blazer to retain an image of professionalism. Heels felt too sensual, and that was the last image she wanted to convey to this man, so she opted for a smart pair of flats. She wore her hair and makeup the same as she did to work—minimal neutrals—and grabbed her briefcase instead of a purse.

Jess arrived at the dinner early, and Justin arrived shortly after, dropped off by a car service.

Great, he probably intends on over-consuming if he didn't drive himself.

Jess forced a smile as she shook his hand and wished time to move faster so she could go home and shower off his touch. She felt the same slimy sense she'd gotten from him at the Christmas party. Her gut told her to keep her guard up and be ready to set some boundaries if he started talking about anything other than work.

It didn't help that the restaurant he'd chosen was a swanky, white tablecloth spot downtown with private booths, impressive chandeliers, and Art Deco style that felt like more of a place you'd go on a date than a business dinner. As they took their seats, assisted by the maître d', Justin explained he'd chosen that spot precisely for the privacy it offered, so they could discuss the sensitive subject matter that was the trial. Jess felt that was probably just a bonus, and they wouldn't end up speaking much about the trial.

She was right. He asked her a few questions about her defense work, the trial he claimed he wanted to talk to her about, and her career plans until he found a wormhole to dive into a more personal discussion, asking her where she was from and what she did outside of work.

She kept her answers as bland and boring as she could, only reciprocating his questions to the extent necessary to not be rude. Justin seemed undeterred by her tight-lipped nature. The booth was a semicircle, and each time he shifted to reach for his drink—a top-shelf vodka with two lemons, carcass out—he inched closer to Jess. She wasn't amused and excused herself to the bathroom, making sure to take her bag with her.

When she returned, she sat as close to the edge of the booth as she could without falling off, not caring about the image the move portrayed at this point. It was past time for Justin to take a hint. And if he didn't soon, Jess was going to make sure he took one.

Dinner finally came, and Jess busied herself with tossing her salad. Justin took a few bites of his steak while continuing to sing his own praises, with Jess crooning short responses that affirmed he was, indeed, the greatest man on earth in hopes he wouldn't return the conversation to her. Eventually, the moment Jess had been dreading came.

He slid his hand on her knee underneath the tablecloth.

Jess locked eyes with him, hoping that was enough to back him down. It wasn't. His fingers slowly moved, caressing her knee.

"I'm sorry, Justin. I was under the impression this was a business dinner. I'm happy to discuss the law with you, but I will not be engaging in anything further. I apologize if at any point during this dinner something else was conveyed to you. I assure you that was a mistake that I will not be making again," she said with an iciness that indicated she was not at all sorry or confused if she accidentally gave him anything close to a mixed signal.

"Jess," Justin began with feigned innocence. "Of course this is a business dinner. I came to congratulate you on your tremendous success as a project ambassador and thank you for what you've done for the people of our great state," he went on without withdrawing his hand.

Oh, fuck off with your fake praise.

While removing his hand from her knee with her own, she responded, "Thank me for which part? Highlighting the incompetence of your prosecutors or showcasing the flaws of your investigators?"

Justin remained calm, but a shadow crossed his face, and his tone turned menacing. "That's no way to speak to someone who can determine the trajectory of your career with one phone call to the Texas State Bar."

Jess knew he had no legitimate power over anyone at the state bar, but she also knew someone of his political stature could call in a favor and make life a misery for Jess. If he was so brazen to make a complaint against her, or convince someone else to do the dirty work, she would have to go through an investigation process with the bar and defend her license. She doubted he would follow through with his threat, nonetheless, it unnerved her.

"And with that inappropriate statement, I'll take my leave," Jess said, as she scooped up her bag and headed for the door, almost knocking into a waiter carrying a tray of glasses as she hurried out.

She sat in her car for a moment with a white-knuckle grip on the steering wheel trying to process how royally she screwed up by snapping back at him instead of politely holding a boundary. After a few minutes, she cranked the engine and drove home to a sleepless night.

She spent the next couple days debating if she should let the incident go. Ultimately, she felt like she needed to take action. It wasn't her goal to cause unnecessary trouble, but she was sure this man had taken advantage of others based on how boldly he stepped across the line from business to personal and his behavior at the Christmas party. She sought advice from her mentors in the field on how to handle the situation as she saw no reason to destroy the man's career. But she did want to hold him accountable and hopefully make others safer. Unfortunately, someone in her mentor circle—or someone related to it—had loose lips. Before Jess had time to formulate a plan, she was presented with a cease and desist letter by Justin's office. The letter was also sent to her work email address.

Infuriated, Jess decided to tell everyone what happened that night. She called a meeting with the firm partners and detailed how the evening went down. She could tell by their faces that some believed her, and others weren't so sure. They all wore pained expressions, and Jess felt like it had to do more with the trouble this could cause the firm than feeling sorry for her. She left the meeting feeling worse than when she went into it.

She understood her firm was between a rock and a hard place. They didn't want to fire Jess, but they also didn't want to be blacklisted by the state attorney general who could make their lives a living hell and put the future of the firm in jeopardy, affecting the lives of dozens. Ultimately, after some tough conversations, Jess decided to step away from the firm. She was angry with the partners for being such cowards, for not standing up for justice, what they'd taken an oath to do as attorney. But she soon realized the bitterness was only going to hurt her, not them, so she decided to take a week-long trip to a resort in Arizona in hopes of figuring out her next step.

It was during that trip her mom called to tell her Nina had been hospitalized for a night. Worried for her sister, Marcie called the police department to conduct a welfare check after Nina didn't return her call for a day, since Nina always called back within a few hours, and they found her unconscious. Nina played the incident off as a simple medication dosage mix-up, but Jess's mom and dad felt she might have not been telling the whole story. Nina was independent to a fault, and it wouldn't surprise anyone in the family if she was in worse health than she let on.

Jess cut her trip short and returned to Dallas. On the flight home, she decided she would head to Georgia to stay with Nina while the dust from the pieces of her life settled. With her condo lease winding down, she spent a day moving whatever she wasn't taking to Georgia into her parents' basement an hour north of the city.

Now that she had been in Georgia for more than a month, Jess's initial worries about Nina's needs that she'd voiced to her mother the first week after her arrival were confirmed. Nina needed more help than what Jess could offer. WebMD had Jess convinced she'd just killed Nina every time she distributed a dose of medication. Overwhelmed, she called her mother again.

"I think she needs a professional. I don't know what I'm doing, and she's dealing with a lot more issues than she led us to believe when I came out here," Jess explained.

"Well, your father and I have been discussing options since you and I spoke about it last, and we both agree with you. We've decided we're going to hire a caretaker. I started calling some places today. Once we find someone, can you still stay for another week or two to help Nina adjust? We all know she's going to push back, so you'll probably have to help convince her. And if anyone can win an argument, it's my little attorney. Anyway, after that, you can come home. And I'm going to try to come out to see Nina for a few days and then ride back with you. I think we'll have more staff soon. Management has been holding a lot of interviews, finally," Marcie explained.

Jess felt a mix of emotions. On one hand, she was relieved there was a plan to get Nina the care she needed. On the other hand, she was apprehensive about how that would impact her situation. Once the caretaker was in place, Jess might not have to stay in Georgia anymore. But she didn't feel like she had a reason to head back to Dallas, either. Everything she had there, besides Stacey and a couple other friends, was gone. And now that she'd met a man who intrigued her, the situation was becoming even more complicated. Her heart ached under the weight of uncertainty.

"Are you sure y'all can afford that?" Jess asked.

"We'll figure it out," her mother assured her.

"What do you mean?" Her parents weren't poor and had grown a nice nest egg for themselves, but they didn't have Texas oil money, either. And Jess knew in-home medical care could be very expensive.

"That's not for you to worry about. Everything's going to be fine."

"Okay, well...I'm not sure I'm ready to come back to Dallas just yet."

"Oh? Is it getting serious with that guy?" Her mother asked.

Nina must have spilled the beans on Bryan even though they hadn't talked about it directly.

Not wanting to get into particulars, Jess changed the subject, "It's more about me trying to figure out what to do with my career. I still haven't decided, and I've felt more peace here than I have in a long time."

"Well, alright then," Marcie conceded in a hesitant tone. "I suppose you know what's best for you."

"And, I can cover any nights Nina needs help, so you won't have to hire around-the-clock care."

"Listen, you know I'd love to have you closer to home, but I believe you if you say you're better off there. I want you to be happy..." her mother trailed off, and Jess knew she was trying not to cry.

"Thank you, Momma. At least for now. And maybe y'all can come out here for the holidays this year if I'm still here."

It was only May, so Jess might've been getting a little ahead of herself, but she hated the thought of her mother being upset.

"That sounds like it might be fun," her mother's tone instantly lifted. "I'll talk to your father about it when he gets home from work."

"Alright, well I think Nina is due for another round of medicine. I love you, and I'll talk to you soon."

They said their goodbyes and hung up with Marcie promising to call with the caretaker details as soon as she had more information.

So, it's settled. I guess I'm staying for a while.

She thought of Bryan and smiled. He represented hope and a fresh start for Jess. Like the single wildflower that had somehow made it through the fire, standing defiant and tall, and providing life and color in a devastated landscape. She wasn't sure how far the relationship would go—they'd only been on two dates—but she hoped they had a future. She liked that he seemed to be cognizant of taking care of her in a way that wasn't overbearing. His open mind for other cultures was intriguing. And she'd be lying if she said she didn't want to get her hands on him and see what was beneath the tactical khakis.

Her daydream of Bryan was interrupted by intrusive thoughts about what she was going to do for work. If she was going to pursue a relationship with Bryan, it was important to her that she signal to him she wasn't planning to be a freeloading slob.

She sighed and thought, *I can't imagine being anywhere outside of the legal field...*

She immensely enjoyed being a trial attorney. Even now, Jess could feel her heart start racing when she recalled standing at the defendant's table with her client and hearing the jury foreman say "not guilty" after months, or sometimes years, of pouring her soul into a case. She loved the heart-pumping thrill of returning someone's life to them and crushing the prosecution.

The pay was also great, but the hours were brutal. Working sixty to eighty hours most weeks was burning the candle at both ends, and it showed in the number of litigators that burned out after fifteen years and went into other areas of practice.

As she stood at the crossroads her life had come to, Jess would be lying if she said she wasn't giving some thought to moving into a new area of practice herself. But she didn't know where else to go. Many of the attorneys she went to school with that went into family law had decided to switch gears and focus on criminal law. If so many of her colleagues preferred counseling murderers to dealing with custody battles, Jess couldn't find anything that drew her to the domestic sector of the legal world, either. Working on a contingency basis in personal injury cases could be lucrative, but she found no passion there when she took a fellowship at a personal injury firm when she was a 3L—third-year law student—like she thought she would. Real estate, trademark, and contract law were also solid career choices, but she found the idea of eating cardboard more appealing than playing semantic judo all day, arguing the meaning of "is" in front of a judge.

Ultimately, she knew her heart was in the criminal justice system, and her run-in with Justin and the subsequent letdown of her firm's reaction hadn't dimmed that flame. The satisfaction that came from a not guilty verdict was a high Jess knew she wasn't done chasing. She knew that was where she needed to be. And maybe, she hoped, something would come up and show her a new path down the road.

Before getting into bed that night, she signed up for the next bar exam—Georgia was not a Uniform Bar Exam state and required attorneys to take its own test before practicing law—which was scheduled a few weeks away in July.

CHAPTER TEN

Jess

On their third date, Bryan asked Jess why she left Dallas. They were dining on the veranda of Magnolias, one of the nicer restaurants in Flowery Branch that sat on the northside of downtown in an old house with a large, wrap-around porch. His question was fair, and Jess would be wondering the same thing if roles were reversed. She sighed and told him the story, hoping he would believe her.

"Wow, I'm sorry you had to go through all that," he said when she finished. After a pause, he added, "I know how it feels."

"Oh?"

"Yeah, I was investigated a few months ago. An unfortunate situation went down when I was undercover." He was staring at his beer, speaking slowly, as if he was trying to choose his words carefully. "Basically, I got accused of killing someone. When I was working undercover, a rival gang member was pissed we were close to his turf and opened fire on us like a coward from his car, hitting the guy I was trying to extract information from. Anyway, I tried to keep him alive by doing chest compressions until EMS got there, but he was already gone when they arrived on scene."

Bryan paused before continuing, "It was...the worst night of my life." He didn't look up at her immediately; he just kept rotating his beer glass on the coaster it was sitting on with his brow pulled down in concentration, as if the beer might suddenly fly away if he let go. "So, anyway, yeah, I uh, unfortunately know how it feels to not be believed is what I'm getting at, I guess. It really sucks, and I hate you had to go through it, too," he finished and finally looked up at her with pain projecting from his eyes as he reached for her hand across the table.

"Wow. That's terrible. I can't even begin to imagine." Jess asked, enjoying the warmth of his hand on hers. "When did that happen?"

"Last summer. It's been almost a year now," he answered. "The investigation on me is closed, but the case is still open." After another brief pause, he continued, "His name was Thomas Ravello. If you want to look into it, I'd understand. Anyway, I uh, yeah," he stumbled over his words. "I just wanted you to hear it from me first."

"Sounds like we should both be in therapy," Jess observed, half-joking.

He smiled and shrugged. "Yeah, maybe."

There was an immediate shift in their energy. Jess felt a stronger connection forming between them as they shared their awful experiences that were disturbing, shameful, and few others understood. She smiled and squeezed his hand, feeling her heart settle into him a little more.

Bryan placed his napkin on the plate in front of him, then made a handwriting motion to the waiter, who nodded and disappeared inside the kitchen, returning shortly with their check.

"You want to take a ride?" Bryan asked Jess with a grin, swinging his head in the direction of the marina they'd met at a couple of streets over.

"On the boat?"

"Yeah, why not? The weather's great, and I've got some fuel to burn so it doesn't eat my carburetor," he explained.

She nodded. "Let's do it."

Bryan dropped a few bills in the check holder, while Jess finished off her old fashioned, and they made their way to his truck.

He reached out his hand and held hers on the console as he drove the short distance to the marina, his thumb softly stroking the back of her hand just below her knuckles.

The birds welcomed them with their chirping from the trees that lined the cove. They made their way down the dock at a leisurely pace, enjoying the evening. Bryan boarded the boat first, then helped Jess on. He tucked their phones away in one of the watertight compartments, cranked the engine, untied the ropes that held the boat in the slip, and slowly motored them through the cove toward the open water.

Jess saddled up beside Bryan on the leather bench seat. The mid-May night was balmy, but the air was cooler on the water in the shadows of the channel where the trees blocked the sun, serving her a chill whenever the wind cut at the right angle. She melted a little farther into Bryan, who shifted so she could tuck in closer and put his arm around her shoulders.

The lowering sun emerged from the trees once they hit the open water. Jess swooped her hair back into a ponytail with an elastic band.

Bryan leaned in close to her ear and said, "I'll go slow so you're not cold."

Jess smiled at him and tilted her head back, so he could plant a kiss on her lips. She could taste a hint of beer and smelled the musk of aftershave, his stubble tickling her chin.

They spent some time cruising around and bobbing in the wake of the larger boats, enjoying the evening sun. Jess kicked off her shoes and turned her face to catch as much sunlight as she could.

"You want to see something cool?" Bryan asked as he cut the throttle back and looked over his right shoulder down into the water.

"What is it?" Jess asked, trying to peer over the side at whatever he was looking at.

He started pressing buttons on a small screen that was mounted on the boat just to the right of the steering wheel.

"Is that sonar?" Jess asked.

"Yeah, it'll take a second to load, but it's pretty neat once it does."

Jess watched as the device slowly came to life with arched lines materializing here and there. Bryan slightly increased the throttle while adjusting the wheel.

"What is that?" Jess squinted and turned her head.

"A bridge," Bryan answered, his attention still focused on the screen to make sure they were driving straight over the structure.

"How'd it get down there?"

"This lake was built on top of a town by the U.S. Army Corps of Engineers in the 1950s. There's all kinds of stuff below us."

"Why would they do that?"

"Why does the government do anything?" He asked rhetorically. "Money to burn or a back to scratch, probably. And that there," he pointed to the dam that loomed ominously a few hundred yards away, "supposedly has a deep underground bunker called 'the witch's broom.' It's a local legend."

"You're kidding." Jess had noticed the dam at the end of the lake as they emerged from the marina cove earlier.

It was a massive, concrete structure that towered above the jetty of boulders surrounding it with a semi-circle of orange buoys in the water to keep watercraft from getting too close. A large, red sign was affixed to the front of the structure that read: "Restricted. Stay Back 500 Feet."

As the sun descended lower in the sky, it illuminated the back side of the structure, casting dark shadows on the front that made it look even more ominous.

"Nope, there's a few more, too." Bryan fished a small flashlight out of his pocket, turned it on, and held it just below his chin, like a kid telling ghost stories around the campfire. He went on with a low tone and animated eyes, "Legend has it there are catfish the size of Volkswagens that lurk at the bottom of the lake down near the dam in the deep water."

"Do you believe that?" Jess asked, amused at this looser version of Bryan that was emerging.

"Yeah, why not?" he shrugged.

"Really?" she pressed, trying to gauge if he was being serious or pulling her leg.

"Sure," he answered with a smile as he clicked the flashlight off and threw it on the dash between the steering wheel and the small windshield.

"There's no way."

"Oh, come on. You got to believe in some crazy stuff. Life's too short not to. In fact, I might just find me one tonight," he replied with a mischievous grin spreading across his features.

"I'm not sure I like where this is going." A mix of excitement and apprehension started brewing in her gut.

"See, that's the thing about you attorneys. You're too literal. Everything has to be black and white and inside the lines," he said, standing up. *"Boring."*

"What're you doing?" Jess scooted sideways across the seat as he stepped past her toward the center of the boat.

"Going to find me a mega-catfish," he answered, grabbing the back of his shirt and pulling it over his head to reveal his chiseled physique in one quick motion.

Jess had to peel her eyes away from his midsection to catch the rogue expression on his face before he dove off the side of the boat toward the dam in his jeans and boots.

Jess anxiously clambered over to the side where he'd exited, the scratchy carpet pricked at her knees as she leaned over and looked for him. He didn't immediately emerge, so she shifted to the other side of the boat to look just as he was breaking the surface, the cool water splashing on her.

He shook the water out of his eyes and smiled up at her. Jess couldn't help but laugh at his playfulness.

"What'd you find down there? Any mega-catfish?" she asked animatedly.

He played it off as he treaded water. "Nah, not today. They must've known I was going to come looking for them." His large chest muscles pumping momentarily distracted Jess.

"How's the water? Looks cold."

"Feels great. Probably about sixty-eight degrees or so. Basically a hot tub," Bryan answered while shaking his head to the side in what looked like an attempt to drain water out of his ear.

He stopped and looked at her, another flirtatious grin brewing on his tanned features as he brought his arms forward to tread water back toward the boat.

"Don't you dare," Jess warned, pointing a finger at him.

"What?" he asked innocently, a full smile breaking onto his face.

"You know *what*." Jess shifted farther back in the boat to sit on the far side.

Bryan laughed as he launched a wall of water toward her in one quick, powerful stroke of his arms. Jess shrieked and shifted to avoid it. Most of the water landed beside her thanks to her quick reflexes, but some large droplets landed on her legs and chest, soaking through her sundress.

"Might as well go ahead and get in at this point," Bryan observed, his eyes daring her.

"What happened to keeping me from getting cold?" Jess lightly scolded him.

"Well, I wouldn't make you cold if I wasn't planning on warming you up after," he said, his expression turning more sensual as his chin dropped and his eyebrows raised. "But I'll need your help to get me out to do that."

"You think I'm going to fall for that?" Jess cocked her head to the side.

"It's either that or watch me tread water until I drown."

"What would happen if you fell in while fishing by yourself?" Jess pressed, enjoying the banter.

"I'd die," he said without missing a beat.

"Okay, I'll help you up," Jess chirped as she scooted over to the driver's seat and removed Bryan's phone from the watertight compartment he'd stashed it in.

Then she moved to the side of the boat, holding his phone in her left hand and extending her right one to him. She was confident he wouldn't pull her in with his cell phone held hostage.

Bryan looked at the phone in her hand and smiled, his eyes dancing with mischief. He stuck one boot against the side of the boat and grabbed her hand. In one quick motion, he pulled himself out of the water just enough to knock the phone from her other hand onto the carpeted floor of the boat and yank her, sending her flying over his head into the water.

Jess emerged to find Bryan holding onto the side of the boat, hooting with laughter.

"You should've seen your face," he said between laughs.

The water was freezing but invigorating. Jess was surprised at the move but decided to embrace the moment and swam up to Bryan. She wrapped her arms around his neck, lowering a seductive gaze at him with her lips parted, eyes teasing. Bryan held onto the boat with one arm and wrapped his other around her. Their lips met, and she ran a hand down the ridges of his chest and stomach muscles to the top of his jeans. She slipped two fingers inside the waistband just behind the button and felt his breath catch and his core tighten. She tightened her hold around his neck to melt her body into his as far as she could and gently bit his bottom lip. She didn't care about the scruff of his beard scratching her face; she couldn't get enough of him. They stayed locked in their embrace until a shrill wail coming from the direction of the dam interrupted their moment, sounding something like a Midwest tornado siren.

"That doesn't sound good," Jess said looking over the boat toward the dark structure looming in the distance.

"They're about to open it up," Bryan explained.

"What?" Jess snapped her head back around to face Bryan, eyes wide.

"Scheduled water release," he went on. "The sirens give anyone in the river on the other side of the dam a heads up to get out before the water rises."

Jess suddenly became aware of the sunken town and the probably-nonexistent-but-maybe-real giant fish lurking below them and wanted back on the boat.

"We should probably get out," she said, her body starting to shiver.

"Yeah, let's get you warm," Bryan agreed in a husky tone that was such a turn on it made Jess want to pour it all over herself.

He planted one more kiss on her lips before pulling himself in the boat. Next, he leaned back over the side and scooped Jess out with one arm like she weighed nothing. She wrapped her arms around herself to ward off the chill and sat down on the taut leather of the seat. Bryan rummaged around in a couple of locker compartments near the bow until he found two beach towels. He wrapped one around her shoulders and draped the other over her lap before pulling his shirt back on and securing his phone that she'd tried to hold hostage.

He sat down beside her at the wheel and wrapped his arm around her shoulders. Before cranking the engine, he turned and nuzzled his face in her hair by her ear and said, "Now, let's get you home."

CHAPTER ELEVEN

Jess

Jess walked from Nina's to the police department across the railroad tracks. Bryan had called her earlier in the day and invited her to a cookout his office was sponsoring along with the city police department they shared the building with. The event was to kick off the local chamber of commerce's "First Fridays"—a campaign to encourage the town to shop local instead of patronizing the big box stores.

She spotted Bryan manning the grill surrounded by a small crowd of city officers in uniforms, two other men that were dressed similarly to Bryan in khaki pants and three-button polos, and a few women that looked to be their wives sitting nearby in lawn chairs. A few kids that looked to be three or four ran around the lawn playing tag while the younger ones ate popsicles.

One of the men tipped his Coke can in Jess's direction and said something, prompting Bryan to look her way. He smiled and passed off the tongs he'd been holding to one of the officers.

"Hello, gorgeous," he called to her as she neared.

"Hey." She smiled and stepped into his hug.

Bryan turned and started introducing her to the group one by one, starting with the officers and their significant others.

He turned to the men in polos last. "And here we have Jason, the finest janitor in town." He grabbed a smaller man by the shoulder with one hand and gave him a playful shake.

Jason gave a fake laugh and extended his hand to Jess. "Special Agent Jason Thompson, ma'am. Nice to meet you."

"Nice to meet you, Jason," Jess said, shaking his hand.

Bryan turned to the other man in a polo and started, "And this is—"

"Topher English," the man finished, offering his hand. "Pleasure to meet you, Jess." He had a lean, athletic frame with broad shoulders and was an inch or two taller than Bryan. His dark blond hair was longer on top than on the sides, and the faint beginnings of smoker lines were showing up around his mouth.

Jess smiled and took his hand. "You, too."

As their hands parted, Bryan stepped in between them to reassume his position as grill master, asking everyone how they wanted their burgers cooked.

One of the women stepped over and introduced herself as Courtney, Jason's wife. She asked where Jess was from and how long she'd been in town. Then, she introduced her to the other women and the kids. Jess smiled and returned their waves.

"We like to support each other in the blue line community, so you let us know if you ever need anything, okay?" Courtney drew out the last few words.

Jess thanked her, then returned to Bryan's side to help transfer food from the grill to the picnic tables set up on the lawn.

There wasn't assigned seating, but the groups stuck to their own, with the officers taking up two tables, and Bryan, Jess, Jason, Courtney, and Topher claiming their own. Topher and Jess ended up across from one another. Bryan and Courtney were the chattiest of the group and carried most of the conversation.

Jess reached for a ketchup bottle in the middle of the table at the same time Topher did. His fingers brushed against hers as she took hold of the condiment.

"Sorry," they both said at the same time as Topher retracted his hand.

Jess squeezed a glob onto her burger, then handed the bottle over to Topher. He accepted it with a grin, and Jess noticed he had green eyes like hers.

Her thoughts were interrupted by Bryan asking her if she wanted another burger. "Or a hot dog? I think we have a pack of those in one of these coolers somewhere around here."

"I'm full. But thank you."

"Alright." He checked his watch. "Let's get the rest of these cows cooked. School is letting out, so the crowds will be here soon."

Everyone got up, cleaned their messes, and pitched in to cook the rest of the food. The women assembled the burgers after the men got them off the grills and passed them out to the throngs of shoppers passing by as they made their way to the shops.

Jess noticed Topher made sure every kid that came by left with a sticker badge and even showed his real badge to the few that seemed particularly intrigued. She wondered what his story was. With a lack of a wedding band and no significant other there like everyone else, she felt bad for him. Especially since he seemed to enjoy interacting with the kids.

He stood up from kneeling to take a picture with a little boy who wanted to hold his badge and caught her staring. He smiled at her with kind eyes, and she awkwardly grinned back before looking away.

Courtney came over to help Jess refill a drink cooler and then coaxed her over to the lawn chairs to socialize with the other women.

Jess didn't spot Topher the rest of the evening. He must've slipped away into the crowd without her noticing.

One afternoon the following week, Jess was nearly home from running some errands when she got stopped by a train at the railroad tracks across Atlanta Highway from Nina's. Between taking care of Nina and dates with Bryan, she hadn't had much time for herself since she'd moved to Georgia. Needing to replenish some of her beauty essentials and a new pair of running shoes, she'd spent the first half of the day running errands. She was able to enjoy them at a leisurely pace since Nina now had a caretaker in place.

It had taken Jess and Marcie some time to find the right person to help with Nina's needs. With her mother joining virtually, they'd interviewed several people that didn't seem like a good fit or didn't have the right qualifications. Finally, they found Ruth, who had all the necessary experience and hit it off with Nina. Jess had expected Nina to object to an outside caretaker and insist she didn't need the extra help, but when she met Ruth, her tune changed. The women had so much in common from the same generation—although Ruth was ten years younger and in better health—and growing up in the area to being widowers. Ruth fell right into place, starting the day after she interviewed. The agreement was for her to work three to four days a week, depending on Nina's doctor appointment schedule, and a few hours on the weekend as needed.

It was lunchtime, and Jess's stomach was rumbling right along with the behemoth slowly passing in front of her. She used her thumb to flip through the radio channels with the buttons on her steering wheel, settling on a 90s hit from Jewel to pass the time. By the second chorus, Jess was singing along about who will save your soul if you won't.

At the conclusion of the third verse, Jess noticed the train was slowing down, and it hadn't been moving quickly to begin with. She watched with frustration as it continued to slow all the way to a dead stop.

She tapped an icon on the car's screen that took up most of the dash's real estate, and a voice came through the speakers reading off her texts. Stacey had texted her twice: once to ask the name of someone they went to law school with, and then again to say never mind, she figured it out. Jess chuckled and made a mental note to call her later. The next message was one from Bryan saying he hoped she was having a good day, making her smile. Every guy she'd dated in the past had done sweet things like that at first, but it had always tapered off. So far, Bryan hadn't shown any signs of slowing.

She pressed the voice command button on her steering wheel and instructed her car to call Nina's house phone.

Her aunt picked up on the first ring. "Hey, dear."

"Hey, I'm almost home, but can you let Piggy out for me? The train just stopped, and I'm not sure how long it will take me to get across the tracks."

"Yeah, he probably needs to go potty. I cleaned out my fridge earlier, and he was closer than the trash can," Nina informed her with a chuckle.

Jess groaned, envisioning a night of cleaning up diarrhea. "Wonderful."

They hung up, and Jess noticed cars making U-turns behind her in the rearview mirror. She followed suit and picked her way northward through the short, narrow downtown streets in search of a crossing that wasn't blocked. As she passed by one of the downtown shops, something caught her eye. She slowed down to get a better look of the vintage accent cabinet that was beckoning her attention in the window of an antique shop. The structure of the piece was beautiful. It looked like it might have been hand-carved, but someone had painted it a yellow that was so abrasive on the eyes they should've caught a felony charge for selecting such a color. The piece was topped with a small marble slab that was stunning, and Jess's DIY spidey senses were tingling. She had flipped a few pieces of furniture from the thrift store for her college apartment and still liked to take on projects when she could make the time for it.

With a car coming up behind her, Jess had to get back on the gas. She decided she would go to Nina's and offload her morning purchases to make space in her car so she could come back and get the piece. A couple streets north of downtown, she found a crossing that wasn't blocked by the train, turned on Atlanta Highway, and then waited for a break in the traffic to hang a left into Nina's driveway.

She cut the engine, quickly bounded up the porch stairs, and through the front door. Piggy came running out of the kitchen to greet her, wiggling and wagging. He followed her upstairs where she changed out of her jeans into workout clothes and grabbed some old towels out of a linen closet. Piggy passed her on the way back down the stairs and ran back into the kitchen, no doubt hoping Nina needed a garbage disposal again.

Jess yelled she was stepping out again from the front door and then drove back across the railroad tracks to purchase the accent cabinet. She wasn't sure how she was going to fit the piece in her car and knew she should probably wait until Bryan got off work to use his truck, but she wanted to go ahead and buy it in case someone else had their eye on it. After some tricky maneuvering and help from the store employee, she was able to shove the cabinet in her trunk with the back seats down, stuffing the towels around the piece so it would pad it for the bumpy drive across the railroad tracks. She drove back gingerly, worried if she ran over them too hard, the trunk would fly open.

Back at Nina's, she popped the trunk and gave the console a good tug. The resistance of the seats and towels had wedged the cabinet snuggly. Rather than risk damaging the piece or her car, she decided to wait until Bryan got off work to come over and help. It was time he met Nina, anyway.

She texted him to ask if he would come by that evening. He replied quickly, saying he would come straight there once he wrapped up for the day.

Ruth was leaving early that evening to babysit her grandkids, so she stopped in the kitchen on her way out the door to let Jess know which medications Nina still needed that evening.

"Allopurinol, prednisone, and a baby aspirin," Jess read down the list Ruth handed her.

"You got it," Ruth confirmed.

"Shaken, not stirred, right?" Jess joked.

"And two olives." Ruth went along with it, making them both laugh. "I'll see you tomorrow," she threw over her shoulder on the way out the door.

Jess got to work making spaghetti. She dashed a small amount of red pepper on the top of the bubbling sauce to finish it off as Bryan texted saying he would be on his way soon.

The evening wasn't too hot as spring was doing its best to fend off summer, and the nights were still somewhat cool. She decided to set up the front porch for them to eat, helping Nina outside first, and then bringing out three glasses of water. Nina instructed her to leave the front door open with the screen closed to let some fresh air in the house.

CHAPTER TWELVE

Jess

Jess saw Bryan's truck pull in the driveway from the kitchen window as she was dishing the spaghetti onto three plates. She pulled some garlic toast out of the oven and added a piece to each. Then she balanced a plate on her forearm just like she'd done as a waitress in undergrad, scooped up the other two plates, and headed for the porch. Bryan was already on the porch, leaning back on the railing and chatting with Nina who was sitting in her favorite wicker rocker. Seeing Jess approaching through the screen door, Bryan quickly crossed the porch and opened it for her. They both stepped back as Piggy came running out from behind Jess and plopped down in the middle of the porch to keep an eye out for any food that might drop.

"How can I help?" Bryan asked.

"If you'll grab your plate..." she nodded toward the overfilled plate in her right hand, "I can handle the rest."

Bryan did as instructed, and Jess handed Nina one of the remaining plates before taking a spot on the porch swing, inviting Bryan to join her.

"I see you two have met," she said, looking at Bryan, then Nina, and back to Bryan.

Nina nodded and Bryan answered, "Indeed we have."

They picked their conversation back up, with Nina asking Bryan questions about his job. He answered them respectfully in between bites of his pasta.

"You said your last name was Whitley?" Nina asked.

"Yes, ma'am," Bryan answered.

"You must be Todd's boy, then."

"Yes, ma'am, that's correct," Bryan affirmed, nodding his head.

Jess interjected, "You know Bryan's dad?"

Nina explained, "Back in the day, pretty much everyone in the area went to church at the same place in Gainesville. Probably, oh I'd say around thirty or thirty-five years ago, the church split up into two or three smaller churches. But I knew your family when we all went together in Gainesville. Your dad was probably in his twenties last time I saw him in person. Now I just see his face on the campaign signs all over town every election year," she finished with a chuckle.

Bryan nodded, setting his empty plate beside him on top of the porch railing. He leaned his elbows on his knees, clasped his hands together, as though to get comfortable and said, "Yeah, he always wanted to be the sheriff, and he finally won a few years ago."

Jess sipped her water and listened as Bryan and Nina caught up on the small-town talk. At one point, Nina commented on the state of her lawn, lamenting that the yard service she paid was a week late and the grass was getting out of control.

"I can help," Bryan said, then turned to Jess. "I'll go grab my equipment if that's okay with you?"

"I don't mind." Jess was charmed by the gesture. It warmed her heart to know his chivalry extended past her to encompass her loved ones, too.

"You know, that would be mighty nice of you, if you don't mind," Nina said.

"Oh, it'll be easy," he said lightly with a wave of his hand. "I can knock out the whole yard in less than half an hour. I'd be happy to."

A warm feeling across Jess's chest. She felt another piece of her heart soften as the guard she'd put up after what happened in Dallas slipped down without effort. Bryan was a riddle she'd yet to figure out—rough yet soft, witty yet kind, bold yet gentle—and she was intrigued to solve it.

She beamed as he gave her a peck on the cheek before jumping in his truck to get his lawn equipment from his house. Jess took the plates inside to wash. Nina followed her in to catch her favorite evening shows, taking Piggy with her—they'd started a nightly habit of Piggy keeping Nina company in her room until Jess was ready to go to bed. Jess followed them inside, and before she disappeared into her room, Nina instructed Jess to cut off some chocolate cake on the kitchen counter and give it to Bryan. Jess located the cake and cut a large piece off for her and Bryan to split, grabbed a mystery novel, and a pitcher of cold lemonade she found in the fridge before returning to the porch swing.

Bryan returned a few minutes later with a small trailer behind his truck and pulled in sideways to get the trailer out of the road. He unloaded the push mower and got to work. Jess found it increasingly difficult to focus on her book when Bryan's forearm muscles were begging for her attention. He caught her staring as he mowed down a strip of grass beside the walkway that connected the porch and the driveway, and his face broke into a smile. Her stomach did a somersault when he followed that up with a wink. She smiled back and bit her lip. Her thoughts were probably too impure for her aunt's front porch, but she couldn't help herself.

Once he finished with the yard and loaded his equipment back on the trailer, Bryan joined her on the porch. He took the glass of lemonade Jess handed to him with a, "thank you."

He downed half of it in one long chug and sat beside her on the porch swing. With his heels planted on the ground, he flexed his feet back and forth to sway them gently. They took turns feeding each other forkfuls of cake, trying to smear icing on the other's nose. Dusk was starting to fall, and the crickets were warming up for their nightly concert as they swung in silence in the fading light.

"Thank you for doing that," Jess said, tilting her drink glass with her free hand toward the yard.

"You're welcome. I like doing yard work, and I needed to get a good sweat in," he said, wiping his hand down his face and stifling a yawn.

They'd been together almost every day since their third date, often going out on the boat and not allowing much time for anything else.

"That reminds me. Tomorrow is the first basketball game of the season. Want to come cheer me on?" he asked, letting go of her hand and slipping his arm around her shoulders to pull her closer.

"You're on a team?" She pulled away slightly to look at him.

This was the first Jess was hearing anything about a team or game, but it made sense since he was in such good shape.

"Yeah, we play a short season every year around this time. Cops versus firemen," Bryan explained before landing a peck on the tip of her nose.

"I thought that was a softball thing?" Jess asked, dropping her head back onto his shoulder beside her.

He rubbed his thumb back and forth on her arm with the hand he'd wrapped around her, igniting a small fire on the surface of her skin. "Most places, yeah. We like basketball better, though. It usually draws a crowd. You can get to know some of the guys' wives and girlfriends you met at the cookout better."

"Oh, that sounds fun. Count me in," she answered in a light tone.

"Great, I'll swing by and pick you up tomorrow night around five-thirty. Game starts at six." He stood up and stretched.

Darkness had fallen, but the glow from the streetlights that lined Atlanta Highway illuminated the porch enough that she could still see the mischievous look on his face when he looked down at her, took her drink, set it on the porch railing, and grabbed her hand, pulling her up off the swing. He towed her behind him down the porch stairs and over to his truck. The driver's side faced the house, blocking the streetlight. Once they were in the shadows, he pushed her back up against the truck and pressed his body against hers.

Jess let her body melt into the hardened lines of his as their mouths found each other. She ran her hands up his back and clenched at his shirt, trying to remove every remaining atom of space between their bodies. He buried his face in her neck, and her entire body felt as though it was pulsing with energy.

Eventually, they reached the threshold where they had to decide whether they were going to take themselves to Bryan's house or take a cool down lap. As much as Jess had been wanting to rip his clothes off and find out how his skin felt on hers, she didn't want to move things too fast and let a romp in the sheets complicate what felt like the start of something that could last. She pulled her hands around to his chest and slowed their kiss. He caught on and left gentle pecks along her jawline and back to her lips. With their breathing still heavy, he framed her face with his large hands and rested his forehead on hers.

"I'll see you tomorrow," he said with a smile.

She leaned up and pecked him on the lips. "See you then."

He climbed into his truck, waved goodbye before backing the trailer out, and headed north.

Jess went inside and headed for Nina's room to see if she needed help getting ready for bed and to say goodnight. She found her already in bed, reading her Bible by the light of the lamp on her nightstand with Piggy curled up at the foot of the bed.

Nina looked up as Jess padded into the room and smiled.

"Did you take all your medications Ruth laid out? Do you need anything before I go upstairs?" Jess asked.

"No, I think I'm okay for the night. Thanks, dear. And yes, I took everything. You can check under the bed if you don't believe me," Nina responded.

Jess ignored her last comment and folded one leg underneath her as she sat at the end of the bed beside Piggy. "What do you think about Bryan?" Nina was the only person she'd introduced Bryan to, and she was interested in her impression.

Nina placed a bookmark in her Bible and set it down on the bed beside her. She thought for a moment before responding, "He seems like a nice man, but I think a more appropriate question is what do *you* think about Bryan?"

Caught off-guard, it was Jess's turn to pause before answering, "Well, it's still early, but I like that he makes me feel taken care of."

She detailed how he served her first at dinner and took initiative in planning dates, and how it surprised her that she was delighted by such behaviors. Jess had been so independent she never realized how nice it felt to take the back seat sometimes and not have to be the one figuring everything out. "He's also good at communicating, and he's intelligent..." Jess continued listing her favorite qualities about Bryan.

"All that sounds wonderful, dear. I hope you continue finding wonderful things about him that you like. But..." Nina paused, and her gaze shifted toward the ceiling as if she were searching for the right words before continuing, "don't forget that it takes time to get to know someone."

Jess felt like there was more Nina wasn't saying. She was a straight shooter and didn't often stop to choose words carefully. "What exactly are you implying?" Jess asked curiously, reaching out to give Nina's blanketed foot a squeeze.

"I don't think you know this, but I was married before your uncle," Nina answered. This was news to Jess. She didn't know how to respond, so she waited for her aunt to say more. "I was young— younger than you—and the marriage didn't last long. Let's just say, the man wasn't who he said he was or who I thought he was prior to our vows. And he hid it well." As she finished, she looked down at her hands she'd folded together over her midsection. Jess wasn't sure what her aunt was feeling—maybe shame—but it wasn't like Nina to be so reserved.

"It's hard to think anyone could fool you," Jess responded.

Nina looked back up at her and smiled. "Well, dear, it's hard to see red flags when you're wearing rose-colored glasses. It could happen to any of us. You're a smart woman. You'll figure it out," she finished lightly.

Then, she reached for her Bible and opened it back up to where her bookmark rested.

Jess told her goodnight and scooped Piggy up. She let him out to do his business through the back door off the kitchen, making sure he didn't wander too far into the overgrown lot that bordered Nina's backyard, and then called him in to head upstairs.

Her mind was too wound up to let her sleep, so she opened the armoire to rifle through her clothes and pick up an outfit for the game as she sorted through her thoughts.

She grabbed a boyfriend-style t-shirt and studied it while her mind mulled over Nina's comment about rose-colored glasses. Was there anything about Bryan that she could be brushing over? She popped the hanger that held the t-shirt back on the bar in the armoire and grabbed a flowy blouse, fluffing the bell sleeve as she contemplated the item. He looked good on paper, and he'd always been a gentleman to her. Deciding against the blouse, she replaced it and thought about Nina's first marriage as she flipped through her other shirt options. She wondered who the man was and what he'd done for Nina to divorce him. Toward the end of her options, she landed on a vintage Guns N' Roses single-stitch concert t-shirt from the 90s from the "Use Your Illusion" tour. She and her dad shared a love for rock bands, and she'd scored the shirt at a thrift store in Dallas a couple of years ago.

Deciding she would pair the shirt with some stonewash jeans and top it off with a light flannel button up, she set the outfit on the upholstered bench at the end of her bed. She scooped Piggy up, snuggled him into a cocoon in the blankets on the bed, and crawled in.

CHAPTER THIRTEEN

Jess

Bryan picked Jess up at five-thirty as promised, giving a honk as he pulled into Nina's driveway. Jess made sure Ruth was staying with Nina until she got back and then left out the front door.

"Hello, handsome," she said as she opened the truck door.

She hopped in and leaned across the console, landing a kiss on his cheek. He took her hand and kissed the back of it in response before steering them out of the driveway.

As they drove, Jess explained her plans to start interviewing and take the next bar exam. She hadn't said anything to him yet because she wanted to think about it for a few days to make sure that was her move, and she now felt it was.

She expected Bryan to respond supportively, or at least ask some questions. Instead, he kept his eyes on the road and seemed to grip the steering wheel a little harder than before as he let out an "Mhmmm…"

"What?" Jess asked, confused at his response.

"Are you sure you're ready?" He looked over at her, his features pinching together.

"Yeah, it's been long enough. I'm getting restless now," she explained. "Besides, it's not like anything will happen overnight. The interview process will take time, and I'm going to tell anyone I interview with that I'm not going to start before I take the bar, since I would be limited on what duties I could perform before getting licensed to practice in Georgia, anyway."

He nodded, pursed his lips, and kept his eyes on the road. Jess could tell he wasn't sold on the idea, and it was starting to bother her.

"What's the problem?" Jess pressed. "I thought you liked independent, working women. Or were you just trying to blow smoke up my ass?"

Bryan's serious mask broke, and he began to chuckle. "It's one of my favorite things about you. But…I'm not sure you're ready. I thought you wanted to talk to a therapist first. Make sure you've worked through all that…shit." He waved his hand as he said "shit." "I just don't want to see you hurt." His tone turned to pleading. "I think it's great you want to get back out there. Just don't let it be too soon where it triggers you. I'm sure you know how the long hours and stress of the work eat at you. God forbid you have to deal with another harassment situation. You'd be a mess, and I'd be in jail for shooting the motherfucker."

Jess sat silent for a moment while his words sank in. While she felt he was underestimating her, she did wonder if he was making a good point. The only direct thing she'd done to address the hurt and defeat that had precipitated her work hiatus was head east to Georgia and hope the memory faded more and more with each mile marker sign she passed.

He went on, "Maybe you should just give it a little more time and wait until after you get your results back from the bar in the fall is all I'm saying. I'll cover any bills that come up for you between now and then. It'll be here before you know it, and you might be wishing you'd taken more time to heal. I just want to make sure you'll be okay."

His offer surprised Jess, and she thought it was odd. But it felt like a distraction, and she tried not to let her frustration show. She was tired from studying for the bar all day and didn't want to argue anymore.

"I'll think about it. Like I said, I probably won't hear back from anywhere I interview right away."

They left it at that as they were pulling into their destination.

The court, which was a tennis court, was on the grounds of the University of North Georgia's Gainesville campus, a few miles north of Flowery Branch. It was one of the lesser-used courts, so the college let the guys drag a basketball goal onto it and play any time they wanted.

Bryan headed for the court, and Jess took a seat on the top row of the short metal bleachers that sat just outside the court fence.

Topher pulled up in a navy Toyota Tacoma in a spot directly behind where Jess was sitting. She turned around at the noise of the truck shifting into park, and he gave her a smile and a wave as he killed the truck's engine.

She grinned, giving a small wave in return.

"How're you?" Topher asked as he rounded the front end of the truck en route to the passenger door.

"Good," Jess responded. "Yourself?"

"Can't complain," he answered in a laid-back tone, grabbing a duffle bag from the floorboard of the passenger side. "Are you the cheer team for us this year?" He stepped over toward her and placed his duffle bag down on the bleachers a few feet to her right to dig through it.

"I think water girl is more my speed," Jess replied facetiously.

"Did they already hold the tryouts for that?" Topher asked.

Jess looked at him inquisitively, trying to gauge his seriousness.

"They didn't tell you about the half-court shot contest? Winner gets to be the water girl," he deadpanned while fishing a water bottle out of his bag.

Jess's wit kicked in, and she kept the joke going, "Oh, yeah, they decided to cancel it this year out of fairness for the other competitors." She made like she was shooting a basket.

Topher laughed and said, "Fair enough."

He then excused himself and headed to the gate that led inside the court.

Jess searched the crowd of players that had converged on the turned court and spotted Bryan chatting with one of the Flowery Branch officers on his team. Jess was pretty sure the man's name was Eli. His brother, Emery, was a firefighter and played for the other side. She met them both at the cookout, too, and while she hadn't interacted with them much, she saw enough to know she didn't like them. They seemed shallow and acted as if they never found the exit of the high school football locker room. Based on the parts of their conversations she overheard at the cookout, everything was seen through the lens of "getting some ass" and "fucking shit up." It was no secret to Jess that this kind of mentality came with the territory for many cops and firemen, but these guys didn't have an off switch for the jock-talk like some in those fields do. Their maturity never moved past the age of sixteen.

Topher was the different one of the group. She and Bryan grabbed drinks with him one night after the cookout. Bryan mentioned that it wasn't a common occurrence for him and Topher to socialize outside of work, but it was a casual, enjoyable evening. Over beers, Jess learned Topher was a widower after his wife passed away from breast cancer five years ago. They never had kids, so he threw himself into his work. She also knew he was ex-military—commission: Army. Jess didn't know what his rank was, but she suspected he wasn't a bullet catcher—probably some kind of special operations based on his calm demeanor and quick wit.

He and Emery busted each others' balls in trash talk on the court. Emery was in the Marine Corps; the "sticker warriors" as Topher called them. Jess didn't understand what that meant until she saw a car with four Marine Corps insignia stickers on the back, and then she noticed every time she saw a car with some kind of Marine accoutrement, they always came in pairs.

The trash talk decibel reached a crescendo as Jason—who was acting as referee for the game—walked to the middle of the court with the ball. One of the city officers stepped up for the police, and Emery took position for the firefighters. After a few more jovial jabs from each side, they tipped off and got the game started.

A few other wives and girlfriends that had been at the First Friday event, including Courtney, were there in a group on the front two rows of the bleachers that sat just outside the court fence. While they were nice and welcoming, the bulk of their conversations were about their kids. Jess smiled and said, "hello," opting to sit at the end of the group so she didn't look antisocial but didn't have to engage in a conversation she couldn't relate to.

During the first half, it looked like Team LEO (cops) were winning, but Team Basement Savers (firemen) started giving them a run for their money. Team LEO called a timeout to regroup, and Bryan jogged over to the fence to chug some water.

"You bringing home that W?" Jess called out.

"Just for you, babe," he said breathily with a wink.

He took another swig from his bottle, and then poured the remaining contents over his head, matting his hair to his forehead.

Jess slid her sunglasses from the top of her head down her face to the bridge of her nose and kicked back to watch the rest of the game.

Bryan, Eli, and the officers on Team LEO were all good athletes, but their main strategy seemed to be aggression; Topher, the final member of Team LEO, had finesse. She watched as he played the thinking man's game. The others had worn themselves out and were quickly losing steam. Topher had to pick up the slack and ultimately led the police to victory through strategy. Jess watched as he wore the Basement Savers down by charging to get fouls, which seemed to drop the firemen's morale, and wear out their defense by making them play aggressively with quick passes before Topher shot three pointers.

After the game, the guys hung around for a while on the court, talking and trying to shoot from half-court. The women started packing up their cushioned stadium seats and wrangling kids into minivans.

Bryan trotted over to her on the bleachers with a cold bottle of water for her from the cooler on the court and asked, "Did Topher make you uncomfortable earlier?"

The question came out of the blue. Jess paused a beat before responding, "No, he was just saying hello."

"Okay, good. Just making sure he wasn't creeping you out," Bryan explained. "You okay staying for a few more minutes?"

Jess nodded. "I don't mind."

Bryan handed her the water bottle and headed back to the court.

Jess noticed Topher grab his things to leave without much fanfare. He smiled at her as he passed and left as quietly as he'd come. His low-key nature intrigued Jess and made her wonder what his secrets were. She had no idea it was only a matter of time until she knew.

CHAPTER FOURTEEN

JUNE

Jess

Jess took a break from studying for the bar at Nina's and walked down the driveway to get the mail. She pulled a flat cardboard envelope addressed to "Jessica Graylon" from the mailbox and tore the string at the top to open it as she made her way back to the porch. It contained a formal separation letter her mother had forwarded from her Dallas firm, which explained in dry, sterile language the termination of her benefits and information regarding who she needed to contact to roll over her retirement account.

Even though Marcie had texted to let her know she'd dropped it in the mail, it unexpectedly brought back a flood of emotions, and she sat down on the front porch steps to process her thoughts. Anger burned deep in her chest, cut with sadness.

Her phone dinged in her back pocket, and she pulled it out to see a text from Bryan offering to cook her dinner at his house. Part of her wanted to spend the rest of the day curled up in her room, avoiding the world, but her stronger side won out. She texted him to name the time. Then she went upstairs, changed into her running clothes, and jogged down Atlanta Highway. She ran until she reached the marina where she'd met Bryan and meandered the docks until she felt better. Not fixed, but better. Checking her watch, she decided it was time to head back and jump in the shower.

She blow-dried her hair straight and kept her look minimal with some joggers, slouchy t-shirt, and some mascara. Downstairs, she found Nina in the kitchen with Piggy and tried to round him up to go with her, but he decided to stick with Nina who was feeding him table scraps.

"Traitor," she scolded him. He snorted in response before turning back to Nina to beg some more.

"You want me to bring you some dinner on my way back?" Jess asked.

"No, Ruth will be back from the store shortly, and we're going to Reid's to get something. Thank you for asking," Nina responded, referring to her favorite diner across the railroad tracks on the downtown strip.

Jess smiled at how Nina and Ruth had become close as she walked to her car. She didn't realize how lonely Nina had been until she saw how she and Ruth would sit on the porch for hours and laugh. It also made Jess feel less guilty about spending so much time with Bryan.

Her tires crunched on the broken concrete of Bryan's driveway as she rolled in at seven on the dot and pushed the ignition button to kill the engine. As she stepped out, she felt a flutter in her chest at the mental image of living here with him if they made things official.

The house was a quaint, two-bedroom craftsman home that looked as though it was built a century ago based on the architecture—Jess had learned a thing or two about design styles from the DIY home makeover social media pages she followed. Like Nina's, it sat directly off Atlanta Highway, just a third of a mile to the north. It had a garage that looked as though it had been a later addition. The place was clearly a bachelor pad that could use a woman's touch. Jess felt like it could shine to the level of its former glory with a couple cans of paint and a DIY project or two. Her favorite feature of the home's exterior was the Frank Lloyd Wright-style leaded glass windows that flanked the front door. Their geometric shapes and stained glass gave the space some character of a bygone era that Jess would love to step into if time machines ever existed one day.

The garage door was open, so she made her way inside and found herself in the kitchen where Bryan was collecting seasoning shakers from a cabinet by the fridge.

"Hey, beautiful," Bryan greeted her.

He dropped the seasoning shakers on the counter beside steaks that were soaking in a dark liquid and made his way around the island to kiss her.

Jess smiled and leaned in for a peck on the lips. "How was your day?"

He pulled out one of the stools that sat below the bar side of the island for her, opposite where he was preparing the steaks.

"It was a blast. I started out by doing some paperwork, then I helped Jason with some paperwork before completing some more paperwork over lunch. Then, we had a team meeting to discuss—"

"Paperwork?" Jess guessed, dropping onto the stool.

"How'd you know?" Bryan asked rhetorically with a gleam in his eye as he headed back around the island to tend to the steaks. "The citizens of Georgia can sleep well tonight knowing the red tape dragon has been slain," he added in a dramatic documentary narrator voice.

"Sounds like a productive day," Jess observed.

"Fuck no." Bryan snorted as he worked the cap off a spice shaker. "I work for the government."

Jess laughed and watched as he prepped the meat with dashes and pinches of seasonings and herbs. Once he finished, she opened the back door since Bryan had his hands full with the food, then dropped into one of the patio chairs while he turned his focus on the grill. On the drive over, she decided she wasn't going to mention the separation paperwork she'd gotten in the mail earlier and instead focus on having a relaxing night with Bryan, but he picked up on her energy and asked her what was wrong as he was placing the steaks on the grill.

Jess sat back in her chair with her arms crossed, exhaled, and said, "I got the formal separation paperwork in the mail today, and it just brought back all that shit from the past. I'm not sure why it bothered me so much."

In response, he closed the lid to the grill and stepped toward her, pulling her out of her chair into an embrace.

"I'm so sorry, babe. It must have been awful having to face those people every day. That place never deserved you. I'm glad you're out of there," he said into her hair.

The tears Jess had been fighting all afternoon let loose. He listened intently while stroking her hair as she released her frustrations into his chest and asked questions when her tears subsided. They didn't feel probing, but like he was trying to fully understand the situation.

Finally, he pulled back and planted a kiss on her forehead. "You're better off now."

Jess nodded. "Yeah, I think so," she answered softly, wiping her face. "And now I'm starving. I'll go get us some plates," she offered and turned to head inside.

She stepped into the half-bathroom off the living room and splashed some cold water on her face before grabbing plates, a couple beers, and heading back outside.

"Thank you," Jess said as she handed Bryan his beer.

"For what?"

"For believing in me when no one else has."

"Of course, babe. That's what I'm here for. I'm your biggest cheerleader. I'll always support you. And I'll always believe you. You know I know how that feels. To be called a liar and feel like everyone's against you for something that wasn't your fault."

Jess smiled, and they sat down to eat.

That night, she stayed over, and it was the first time they slept together. After dinner, Bryan had led them upstairs and traced her body with his fingertips, letting her set their pace.

As she lay in his arms after, his chest moving rhythmically against her back, she finally felt like she was home.

Bryan felt like home.

CHAPTER FIFTEEN

Bryan

Bryan pulled the SIM card out of his burner phone and broke it in half. His current undercover work wasn't exactly aboveboard, so he was rotating his number more frequently than usual. He pocketed the pieces to further destroy later and dropped the phone in a nearby trash can. He didn't worry about smashing it since it wouldn't be in there long. The parks department emptied the trash cans at the Buford Dam parks every Wednesday and Sunday afternoons, and it was just after lunch on Wednesday. Bryan continued down the sidewalk and followed it down the hill as it looped around to the lake.

Just as he'd anticipated, there was a man with a straw cowboy hat sitting in a folding lawn chair with a line in the water fishing for catfish. The man looked up as he heard Bryan approaching from his left and gave a simple nod before turning his attention back to the water. Bryan passed behind him and took a seat in the empty chair to the man's right. Reaching into the cooler that sat between them, Bryan felt around to make sure what he came for was in there. At the bottom of the ice, he felt a plastic bag, confirming the man had delivered what Bryan was expecting. He swiped a beer can before closing the cooler and cracked it open.

"Any luck?" he nodded toward the man's fishing line.

"Nah, *ese*. Slow today," the man said with a Latin accent.

Bryan nodded and continued sipping his beer. Once he finished, he grabbed another can out and set it beside the man's chair before scooping up the cooler and heading back to his truck.

85

CHAPTER SIXTEEN

JULY

Jess

Jess didn't remember much of June. Once the calendar hit one month out from the date she was to take the bar exam, she hunkered down and studied every day until her eyes hurt from taking practice tests to sear the black letter law she would be tested on into her memory like a hot iron. Bryan had backed off voicing his concerns and had been supportive by making her meals, texted her inspirational quotes each morning, and even scheduled her a massage and drove her to it.

A hot day in July, two weeks out from the exam, Jess needed a change of scenery from studying at Nina's. She walked across the tracks with her laptop to a quaint coffee shop on the older side of the downtown strip.

A bell dinged as she made her way inside to find the joint buzzing. Small dining tables dotted the inside to the right and left occupied with breakfast goers, and there was a staircase that led to a second story just beyond the tables on the left. She joined the back of the ordering line to the right of the stairs. While waiting, she admired the place's original charm with its exposed century-old brick and wood beams. Once she made it to the front of the line, she ordered a plain coffee and a buttery pastry from the young worker who smiled and told Jess she would bring her order once it was ready, pushing a metal stand with a number on the top across the counter toward Jess.

Jess decided to head to the second level to find a quieter corner to do her research. She picked a spot in the corner, sat down, and opened her laptop.

The smiling employee from downstairs delivered her order just as her computer booted up. She sipped her coffee while navigating through job listings online. There were a few postings for defense attorney positions but none nearby. As she kept scrolling, she came across several assistant district attorney positions in the surrounding counties: Banks, Dawson, Gwinnett, and Cobb. She stopped on one and read through the description and salary estimate. She'd be making less than half of what she'd pull in on a good year as a defense attorney. The income discrepancy wasn't news to Jess, but she didn't realize exactly how much less they were making on average. Her math skills weren't great—she was an attorney after all—but a quick calculation told her that was less than fifteen dollars an hour.

With an exhale, she clicked out of the browser window and maneuvered to her email. Her inbox was flooded daily with emails from her legal journal subscriptions. Something caught her eye mid scroll: another mention of Gwinnett in the same sentence as the Innocence Project. An idea popped into her head.

She reached for her phone on the table behind the laptop and called Nina's house phone.

"Hey, dear. Is everything okay?" Nina's voice popped on the line.

"Yeah, I, uh, just need to know where Gwinnett is?" Jess managed to ask while she continued scouring the article for information, her brow pinched tight over her nose. "Isn't that close to here?"

"It's the next county down," Nina replied.

"Okay, thanks. I'll be home in a little while," Jess said and hung up.

She Googled the Gwinnett County District Attorney, finding out his name was Jack Hardeman. She then went back to the job listing page and started applying to the assistant district attorney position in his office.

Jess knew she needed to bring something to the table to prove her worth and solidify her place in the district attorney's office as something other than an assistant district attorney, groveling around at the bottom. One of the administrative staffers in the Gwinnett DA's office reached out two days after she submitted her application to set up an interview for the end of the following week.

During this time, she devised a plan to pitch the idea of forming a conviction review unit; something larger cities were creating in the wake of the criminal justice reform movement that had been gaining steam over the last decade. High profile exonerations spearheaded by organizations like the Innocence Project were fueling the movement along with each podcast clip and documentary sound bite that went viral.

Jess wasn't political on the issue and felt that the legal system should be a part of the movement to better itself with real change coming from the inside. The responsibility to right the wrongs fell on the system's shoulders, which should redress the convictions before the pressure from the outside gained steam. In addition to the moral obligation, Jess felt they could mitigate the bad press and preserve funding, which was always in jeopardy to begin with.

She was confident she could find at least one case that could be overturned as DNA evidence had been used around the country to prove the innocence of several decades-old cases where the alleged criminals were convicted on questionable forensic practices, what defense attorneys loved to call "junk science," and trials riddled with Brady Violations. These infractions were unfortunately not all that uncommon in Jess's experience and happened when the prosecution omitted evidence that could have been beneficial to the defendant during the accused's trial. Sometimes it was a flagrant act where the evidence was purposefully omitted from the discovery process, and other times it was because the police and other subordinate offices that provide the DA with their evidence for a case left out information when they fed the results from their investigation to the DA's office.

She had two rounds of interviews with assistant district attorneys, which Jess felt had gone smoothly, and the final interview was with the district attorney himself at the end of August, almost two months after she'd submitted her application. It was the first time she'd met him, but it was far from the first time she saw his face. In preparation for the interview, Jess dove into every article she could find about Jack Hardeman. By all accounts, the man had a stellar career. So far, no scandals. In fact, Jess couldn't dig up anything derogatory on the man.

Jess arrived at the Gwinnett Justice and Administration Center— a modern courthouse that included its own food court—early for her interview with the DA and didn't have to wait long in the pulsating fluorescent lighting situation of the waiting area before being ushered into Hardeman's office by a young staff member. Jack turned away from his computer screen and took his glasses off with one hand and extended the other toward Jess.

"Jack Hardeman. Pleasure to meet you," he said, giving her hand a firm shake.

Jess pulled her face back into a smile. "Jessica Graylon. Please call me Jess."

As she settled into the armchair opposite the desk from Jack, Jess noticed an article pulled up on his desktop that sat on a separate desk over his right shoulder. It was an article with the Innocence Project's logo at the top of the page, and her heart rate kicked up a notch. She decided to wait until she felt like she had built rapport with him to pitch her plan, so she smiled and waited for him to speak.

"Okay, Jess," he started with his hands folded on the desk in front of him. Jess picked up a slight northern accent clinging to some of his words. She would guess New York or New Jersey, but it could've been Boston. "Whose résumé did you copy?"

Jess wasn't following. "Pardon me?"

"I'm joking," he said softly, ducking his head and leaning forward with a twinkle in his eye.

Jess chuckled nervously. "Oh."

She hadn't been expecting such a jovial character. Most DAs were stuffier in their demeanor. The legal field attracted a lot of austere, Type A folks who made sure their appearances were serious and straightlaced. Jack reminded her of a warm grandpa who liked to prank his grandkids. He was a breath of fresh air.

"Your résumé is extremely impressive, and I have to ask, what makes you want to work here? Looks like you could have any job you want making a substantial amount more money. Why the DA's office?"

Jess decided to match his energy. "I really enjoy long hours for almost no pay."

Jack laughed and asked her a few more questions regarding her expectations for a position in his office. He sat back in his chair and listened intently with folded hands, nodding periodically. When she answered the last of his questions, he paused and exhaled with his head tilted back before leveling his gaze with hers. "Unfortunately, I'm going to have to say no," he said gently.

Jess was taken aback. The interview seemed to be going well. A pit opened in her stomach as she realized he might've found out about what happened in Dallas if he'd called her old firm.

"Beg your pardon?"

"You're clearly sharp as a whip, and I feel like your talent wouldn't be put to use here," Jack explained. He snapped his fingers and continued energetically. "I've got a friend at a firm downtown. It's a great office. Good culture there. They're hiring, too, which they don't do often. I can put you in touch with them if you're interested."

Jess was relieved his hesitation didn't appear to have anything to do with her past, and she wasn't easily dissuaded. "I'm sorry, Jack, but I'm having a hard time understanding why you feel like this job wouldn't be a good fit for me. I understand the sacrifices I'd be making, and I..."

"Well, what this office needs is stability. You know better than anyone that the rate of turnover in DA's offices is high. I need someone who's going to plan to stick around for a while, and I think someone with your career experience would get bored here. An inordinate amount of the staff's time is devoted to hiring, and I'm really trying to crack down on that. The turnover impacts our relationship with the police and the investigators...eh, it's a snowball effect, you know?"

It was time to shoot her shot. Jess swung her head toward his computer and asked, "Are you on the Innocence Project's radar? I might be able to help you with that."

He paused, tilted his head, and steepled his hands in front of him. "Alright. Let's hear it."

Jess launched into her elevator pitch. She briefly explained her work with the Innocence Project and then laid out her proposal for assembling a team that would focus on reviewing convictions. The team would be tasked with analyzing which cases were most likely to get overturned based on new evidence or new tests that could be run on old evidence, then focus on getting those convictions reversed in a way that preserved the dignity of the office. She stressed how doing it in-house instead of the Innocence Project coming in and attracting a firestorm of national press would mitigate any undermining of public trust in the office.

At the conclusion of her pitch, he sat silent for a moment and pursed his lips. Jess knew it was likely his first question would be cost-concerned. She was right, and like a seasoned trial attorney, she already had an answer for him.

"I just don't see how we'd be able to pay you anything near what you're probably looking for. I'd be embarrassed to even start throwing numbers out."

"I can get you off their radar," she pointed to the Innocence's Project article, "with one phone call." Reading Jack's furrowed brow,

Jess knew she had to sweeten the pot. "And I'll work on an hourly basis until we get a conviction overturned. Then, we can discuss a salary."

He pursed his lips as though considering her offer.

"Oh, and one more thing," she added before he could respond.

"What's that?"

"I want to work remotely three days a week. That will save office space for the team. And I'll only need two investigators to start."

He exhaled sharply before replying, "I can't make any guarantees."

"Of course not. But just think of what a wonderful opportunity it would be to be the model for the state of Georgia, or even the national model, for conviction review units. The press that would bring would no doubt be reflected in your budget in years to come. And with that, I rest my case. I'm sure I've taken more than enough of your time, Jack. My cell is on my résumé. I have a printed copy for you here." She pulled it from her briefcase and placed it on the desk in front of him.

"And I look forward to hearing from you soon." She finished with her courtroom smile and saw herself out the door.

CHAPTER SEVENTEEN

AUGUST

Jess

"Wait, let me get this straight. You want to work *for a DA*?" Bryan asked.

"Yeah, I think that's the plan," Jess affirmed.

He knew she'd gone to an interview, but she'd left out the part that it was for an assistant district attorney position. She didn't want to say too much or get her hopes up about any of them, so she'd kept most of the details to herself, not sharing much information with anyone.

She and Bryan were having dinner that night at The Coral Social, the same place they'd met for their first date. Jess couldn't even wait for their fried calamari to arrive before she told Bryan her plan.

"Jess, you spent your career slaughtering DAs at the base of the bench...why would you go to work for one? Conviction review unit or not. I mean I get what you're saying about the potential there, but going from top dog to bottom of barrel, on the other side no less, would be a huge change."

Jess sensed he wasn't a fan of the idea that she would be reviewing and criticizing the investigative work of his colleagues. Investigators take pride in preparing their cases. They live and breathe justice, and Jess wanted to make sure the right kind of people were reviewing the cases that might be overturned. She didn't want a team who made the prosecution and the investigating agencies that answered to it look like monsters. These units needed people who were going to face the facts and handle them appropriately without pushing an agenda or using them to dismantle the legal system.

She explained all of this to Bryan over dinner. Occasionally, he would ask a question or make a curt statement about the time commitment and little-to-no pay.

"They don't pull outsiders in for this kind of shit. You're going to have to go in at the ground level and grovel around for a few years, and then *maybe* you'd get a shot at joining that team. There's going to be a pecking order when it comes to who works that unit. They're going to hand-select people they know won't make them look bad. How do they know a defense attorney from Dallas who they don't know from Adam isn't going to come in and start making them look like idiots to boost her career?" He paused to take a swig of beer. "I hear what you're saying, but it feels like a long shot, and I don't want you getting your hopes up and then hurt when they slam the door in your face. I mean, don't you think you've been through enough in the past year?"

His words stung, but she could understand his hesitation. When Jess decided she was going to do something, she didn't always see the problems in the situation; she saw the opportunities and the challenges she was confident she could take on. It might not be the most practical approach, but she didn't think that was a reason to scrap the whole plan. The sting turned to a burn, and it irritated her.

"To be honest with you, Bryan, I'm a little surprised. I thought you were more open-minded, and I thought you'd be excited for me."

Bryan softened his face and his approach. "It's not that I'm not excited for you. I love seeing your passion come back. There's a sexy fire in your eyes I haven't seen before. I just don't want you hurt.

That's all, and I apologize if it comes across as being insensitive. It comes from a good place, I promise."

"I know you're trying to protect me, and I appreciate that, but I know what I'm doing. This is my next move," she finished confidently as the waiter dropped calamari in front of them.

A couple of expressions passed over Bryan's face. The empathy slipped away, and it appeared his frustration returned as his lips pulled in a thin line, but Jess could tell he was trying to hide it by looking down at his beer or toward the lake with his hands clasped in front of his face.

After a moment, he looked at her with a crooked smile that didn't quite make it to his eyes and responded, "Okay, it sounds like you've thought this through. Welcome to the dark side." He raised his glass and clinked it against hers.

Jess smiled back, but something told her neither one of them was sold. She felt he wasn't buying that she was making the right decision, and Jess wasn't convinced by his smile that his hesitation was solely out of concern for her mental well-being. It seemed there might be more he wasn't saying.

It's probably nothing. Maybe he had a bad day, and this is how it's coming out. And he's right. I probably should go to therapy. Maybe that's the tension I'm feeling. Knowing I should go but not wanting to. Or maybe he's worried if I jump back in too soon, I'll get overwhelmed and decide to go back to Dallas.

Jess reached across the table and took his hand with a squeeze. "What's new with you?"

He looked down at her hand and flipped his over to take her hand into his. The tension in his shoulders relaxed, and she sensed his mood lighten.

"Oh, you know, interviewing suspects who don't know their asses from a hole in the ground," he replied, as he looked out across the lake beyond the deck they were seated on. "I did get a break in the robbery case I'm helping Jason with, though. We caught the driver and convinced him to be a CI in exchange for probation and no time."

"Which case is that?" Jess asked, she was starting to lose track of everything Bryan was working on.

"The one where someone stole all that heavy equipment off the construction lot up in Lula. Over a million dollars' worth. Banks County Sheriff's Office brought us in after all their leads went cold," Bryan explained. "Oh, and that reminds me, I'll probably be out late the next few nights doing surveillance work for that case and a couple others, too," he added, giving her hand a squeeze.

"Please be careful," Jess said apprehensively.

"It's not dangerous. We won't be busting down any doors. Not this week, anyway." His tone picked up a hint of irritation as he finished.

"You sound disappointed," Jess noted.

His eyes lit up. "I'd be lying if I said it wasn't one of the better parts of the job. Anyway," he changed the subject, "I'd like to make up my absence over the next few days by taking you to meet my family next weekend if you're up for it? My folks are having a cookout for the college football season kick-off, and I'd love to introduce you."

His offer caught Jess by surprise. They hadn't had the official "what are we" discussion yet, but Jess hadn't felt pressure to bring it up since they'd been acting as though they were in a relationship for the last couple of months with her spending the night at his house more frequently. They had met in April, and it was now the end of August. It seemed like the logical next step in their relationship since he'd already met Nina. She hadn't thought about it since her focus was now on finding work whenever she wasn't with Bryan or helping Nina when Ruth wasn't around.

"Just don't make me wear a University of Georgia jersey," Jess responded. She was afraid she'd be kicked out of the University of Texas Alumni Association.

Bryan winked. "I think we can make an exception for you."

CHAPTER EIGHTEEN

LABOR DAY WEEKEND

Jess

Jess met the remainder of the Whitleys on a warm, end-of-summer evening. Even though it was Labor Day weekend, you wouldn't know it wasn't a holiday for the start of SEC football if you were from another country. The sport was celebrated almost as religiously as Sunday church in the South.

Jess opted for a simple, white cotton V-neck, jeans, and leather slides. Casual and comfortable but also polished enough to meet his family. She pulled her hair up in a ponytail to keep it off her neck. Georgia summers were just as unforgiving as Texas's, and she didn't want to spend the evening peeling moist strands of hair off her nape.

Bryan picked her up from Nina's and drove them a half-hour to his parents' house on the north side of Gainesville. Their home was situated in a quiet cove on Lake Lanier, or, as Jess had sometimes heard the locals call it, "Murder Lake." She inquired about the story behind the moniker as they pulled onto his parents' street.

"That's a bit of an exaggeration," he said dismissively. "There are a lot of deaths associated with it, but they're usually boating accidents or people driving off the bridges in bad weather. Things like that."

"So, no real murders?"

"Well, I wouldn't say that. It does happen from time to time."

His answer did little to comfort her. She made a mental note to not get in the water again when they went out on the boat.

They pulled into the driveway of a brick ranch with a sprawling manicured lawn that spilled into the lake on the back side of the house. Jess was slapped with a round of nerves at the sight of a couple cars already there. Bryan pulled them into the side yard and dropped the truck in park under an old oak tree.

"Alright." He clapped his hands together. "Let's go meet Ma and Pa."

Jess unbuckled as Bryan opened his door and slid out of the truck with ease as he never wore his seatbelt. When Jess mentioned it to him, he cited his dangerous job was more likely to get him killed. Jess felt his answer to be a bit childish, but she didn't press the matter. He was a grown man. If he wanted to die eating the steering wheel of his truck, that was his prerogative.

Bryan held the front door open for her to enter first. As soon as she stepped inside, she smelled a mingle of scents from savory to sweet that made her mouth water. She wasn't sure if it was the smells or the nervousness of meeting Bryan's family making her stomach churn.

He closed the door behind them. "Everyone should be in the kitchen."

He placed a hand gently on Jess's lower back and guided her toward the sound of voices through the foyer, the formal dining room, and into the kitchen.

"There she is! I've heard *so much about you*," a woman who Jess presumed to be Bryan's mother exclaimed as soon as Jess and Bryan entered the kitchen.

"Well, it's good to see you too, Momma," Bryan said over Jess's shoulder. "Jess, this is my momma, Pattie."

Pattie was a little shorter than Jess's five-foot-eight inches, but her bubbly personality made up for what she lacked in height. She wore her dark hair in a closely cropped bob that swooped away from her face with caramel highlights accenting the style.

She had been cutting peaches when Jess and Bryan walked in, so she stopped to wipe her hands off with a paper towel. "Oh, hush. You know I've been wanting to meet the woman you won't quit talking about," she directed at Bryan before turning back to Jess.

She removed her apron, throwing it on the counter beside her. "It's so nice to meet you, dear. Let me have a hug."

Jess leaned in and embraced her. "It's nice to meet you, too, Mrs. Whitley."

"Oh please, call me Pattie. Mrs. Whitley is Todd's mother. You'll meet him in a minute. He's outside manning the grill."

"Just don't call her a bad cook. Last time I did, she held out on me for a month, if you know what I mean," a bald man said, coming into the kitchen through the sliding glass door that led to the back deck overlooking the lake.

Jess presumed the man to be Bryan's father, Todd, based on the fact they had the same angular face structure with straight noses under dark brown eyes.

"Dad, can we at least eat dinner before you try to update us on your and mom's sex life?" Bryan's nose scrunched, and he looked like he wanted to crawl in a hole.

"Thank you for having me today, Pattie," Jess smiled, enjoying Pattie's southern momisms.

"You just make yourself at home. We've got enough food to feed an army and...*excuse me*," she turned her attention to Todd, who'd just made a grave mistake by going for the closest towel he could find to wipe his hands with, which was a pretty one with lemons on it hanging on the oven door.

"The decorative towels are *off limits*," Pattie said, as she snatched it from him and then proceeded to swat him with it before returning it to its home on the oven handle. When she turned around, she gave Jess a look that said *men,* accompanied with an eye roll.

Jess had a feeling Todd was well aware of this rule and decided to regularly ignore it based on how unfazed he seemed by Pattie's rebuke. "Yes, ma'am," he said while locating a new roll of paper towels under the sink.

"Jess, this is my dad," Bryan tipped his hand toward Todd, introducing him to her.

"Pleasure to meet you, Jess. If you'll excuse me, I've got to get some stuff off the grill before it burns. Like Pattie said, please make yourself at home. Our house is your house," he said, slipping out the sliding back door.

"And if you'll excuse *me* for a minute, I'm going to go call Bryan's sister and find out where they are. The food's going to be cold when they get here if they don't hurry up," Pattie said, heading toward a side hall Jess assumed led to his parents' bedroom.

Bryan reached behind Jess to retrieve a couple of paper plates off the counter. He started to hand one to her, then pulled it back toward himself as if he thought better of it.

"Why don't you sit on the other side of the bar here?" He suggested and guided her around the counter to a row of barstools.

Jess gently rebuked him. "I can make a plate for myself."

"You'll do nothing of the sort. You're our guest, and you'll be treated as such," Bryan answered.

He stepped back around the counter and retrieved the apron Pattie had been wearing earlier, making a show of donning it and tying it around his waist. Then, he went into bartender mode. He charismatically asked for her order—a Jack and Ginger—pretending to take it down with a fake pen and pad while nodding enthusiastically.

"One Jack and Ginger for the lady. Coming right up!" Bryan exclaimed.

He secured a can of ginger ale from the pantry on the far side of the kitchen, tossed it up, and caught it behind his back. He set it down on the counter in front of Jess and briefly disappeared into the dining room on the other side of the pantry. He returned with two stemless crystal glasses in one hand and a fifth of Jack Daniels in the other. After filling the glasses with ice, he poured the Jack from a dramatic height while making typical bartender chatter.

"First time here?" he asked with a glint in his eye, as he switched to pouring Jack in the second glass.

"Indeed, it is." Jess went along playfully.

"Well, then this one's on the house," he said with a smile, slapping his hand down on the granite countertop, pouring the bubbly ginger ale over the amber whiskey.

He stirred their drinks, set them on the bar in front of Jess, and then moved to add some buffalo chicken dip, pigs-in-a-blanket to a plate, and a few items from the veggie tray. Then, he removed the apron, scooped the plate up, and came around the bar to sit on the stool next to her.

It was just the two of them for a few moments until Pattie returned and announced Bryan's sister, Mallory, was almost there. She disappeared as quickly as she appeared, muttering about finding some lipstick and consciously running her hand through her hair to fluff it.

"Mal's got two little kids. You'll love them," Bryan informed Jess, popping a pig-in-a-blanket into his mouth.

They turned around at the sound of the sliding glass door opening behind them.

"Ah, golden boy's here," a man in a red University of Georgia football jersey said as he stepped inside.

He slowly made his way over to them, beer in hand.

"Jess, this is my cousin, Nathan. Our tolerance for him is directly related to his level of intoxication," Bryan said jokingly, but Jess knew Bryan well enough at this point to sense he might not be entirely joking.

"You know we put those out for profiling purposes, right?" Nathan couldn't resist returning his cousin's insult, indicating the carrots on the plate Bryan fixed for him and Jess.

Bryan mock laughed at Nathan's retort.

As Nathan drew closer to them—a little too close—Jess could smell the alcohol on him.

"You know I'm just busting your balls," Nathan said.

Jess could see Bryan's body stiffen out of the corner of her eye when he replied, "We have a lady here, Nathan. Manners, man."

Nathan swung toward Jess and said, "Oh, I'm sorry, hon. You see, since Bryan here never had a big brother, I've always felt an obligation to make sure he doesn't get himself a big head, being Mr. GBI and all."

"Well, it seems like you've got some work to do," Jess said with a wink directed at Bryan, trying to put him at ease.

They were saved from the discussion, and Nathan's breath, by the creak of the front door opening followed by the clomping of children running. Two young kids came barreling into the kitchen. The boy looked to be around six years old, and the girl had to be his younger sister by a year or two.

"Uncle Bryan!" they said in sync.

The siblings raced to their uncle, pushing and shoving each other the whole way.

"Hey, guys." Bryan chuckled as he stepped off his stool and squatted down to greet the kids.

Nathan slinked back outside silently, and Jess relaxed a little in his absence.

Having won his uncle's attention over his sister, the boy dropped the backpack he was wearing and wrestled out a transformer toy. He beamed as he showed it off to Bryan, eyes bright as Christmas morning.

Bryan spent a moment admiring it and asking questions to the boy's delight. The girl had run back toward the front door, shying away after seeing Jess, and returned with a woman around Jess's age. Upon her arrival, the kids didn't stick around for any further grown-up action and took off giggling through the living room toward the other side of the house.

"Hey, Mal," Bryan said, rising to his feet and leaning in to give his sister a hug.

"I'm not here to see *you*," she said as she reciprocated the embrace. "Heard you were bringing someone."

Bryan laughed, broke the hug, and pivoted so Mallory could see Jess sitting at the bar behind him. "You heard right. This is Jess." He then turned to Jess and introduced Mallory as his older sister.

"It's so nice to meet you," Mallory said, stepping toward Jess and spreading her arms open for a hug. "We've heard so many wonderful things about you."

"It's nice to meet you as well, Mallory," Jess said over the woman's shoulder as they hugged.

Mallory pulled away and said, "You can call me 'Mal.' Everyone does. Now, please excuse me while I go round up my offspring before they break something."

A couple more cousins and some neighbors joined the party over the next half-hour, and Bryan made sure he introduced Jess to each new guest as they arrived. When it was time to eat, everyone gathered on the large porch that overlooked the water underneath a canopy of fans that helped keep the heat and flies at bay.

The pregame show was playing on the TV mounted at the end of the porch as they made their plates. Todd said grace, and then everyone dug in, only coming up for air to "call the Dawgs"—a loud cheer complete with dog-barking—as the game kicked off.

After eating, and Pattie insisting everyone have at least seconds, the group spread out with some playing horseshoes in the yard, others heading down to the dock to jump on the jet skis, and the rest—including Bryan and Jess—huddling around the TV to watch the game. Jess noticed Bryan sat close to his dad and tried to talk shop with him during the commercial breaks.

Just before halftime, Jess went inside and used the restroom Bryan had pointed out to her earlier down the hall that sprouted off the living room. She decided to detour to the kitchen on her way out for some peach cobbler. As she was making a plate, she heard footsteps coming from the living room and looked up to see Nathan coming into the kitchen by the bar where she and Bryan ate the appetizers. She wondered how she'd missed him when she went to the bathroom.

"You know, you'd be a lot prettier if you smiled more," Nathan said, acknowledging her with a wobble to his step as he came around the bar into the kitchen and opened the fridge.

"Come again?" Jess stopped scooping the cobbler and asked, although she heard him as clear as day. Her question was an opportunity for him to rethink what he'd just said, not for her confirmation that she'd heard him correctly.

Nathan didn't get that memo. He cracked open the can of beer he'd just pulled from the fridge door, turned to her, and responded with slurred words, "You should smile more. People don't like serious women."

Jess opened her mouth to speak, but Bryan beat her to the punch.

"The fuck you just say?"

Oh, shit.

The color drained from Nathan's face as he whipped his head to see Bryan coming into the kitchen from the formal dining room. He must have followed Jess in and used the bathroom attached to his parents' bedroom, where Pattie had disappeared to earlier. Bryan closed the gap, standing a couple of feet from Nathan and asked again, "What the fuck did you just say?"

"It's fine, Bryan. It was just a poor attempt at a joke," Jess nervously stepped toward them.

"It was a *joke*. Like she said," Nathan defended himself. "Nothing to get all Mr. Cop about," he said, waving his hands around, spilling beer.

Jess could tell Bryan was fighting an internal battle to keep his cool as he stared his cousin down. For a second, she thought he might swing.

"After you apologize to my girlfriend, you're getting the hell out of here. I don't care if you Uber or walk, but you can't stay here," he bit out from behind clenched teeth.

This was the first time she'd heard Bryan refer to her as his girlfriend, which added a new layer of complexity to the situation for her as her mind oscillated between elation, fear, and getting turned on at Bryan being protective of her.

"This ain't your house," Nathan tried to argue back, taking a step toward Bryan, which prompted Bryan to take a step toward Nathan, putting them nose to nose.

Jess's stress level climbed another notch, trying to decide how to intervene when Bryan's dad came in through the sliding glass door. He must've seen what was going on from the back deck where he'd been watching the game.

Jess guessed this must not have been an isolated incident, because Todd jumped into action. "Nathan, why don't I give you a ride home, son?" He asked while crossing the kitchen and grabbing his keys off the counter. Todd's tone indicated there was no question, and Nathan got the hint.

Stepping around Bryan, Nathan sat his beer on the kitchen counter and said "sorry" to Jess before heading toward the front door behind Todd.

"Come on. Let's go back outside." Jess grabbed Bryan's hand and took a step toward the back door.

Bryan didn't budge, staring a hole into his cousin's back until he was out of sight. He looked down at Jess and said, "I'm sorry. He's a fucking idiot. Did he say anything else to you?"

"No, that was it. He was drunk. It's fine," she assured him.

"No, it's not fine," Bryan countered. "I'll call him tomorrow once he's sobered up."

He grabbed a hand towel—not the lemon one from the oven handle as his father had—and wiped up the beer his cousin had spilled.

The incident had soured the mood. "Do you want to stay here and finish the game or head out?" Jess asked.

"Let's head out," he answered, taking her hand and walking them to the sliding glass door.

They found his mother and Mallory swinging Mallory's kids on the swing set in the backyard. They made their way down the deck stairs to hug their goodbyes.

Jess was hugging Mallory goodbye when she heard Pattie ask Bryan why they were leaving so early. "Nathan," was all Bryan said, and Pattie shook her head as if she wasn't surprised.

Before his mother turned them loose, she made Bryan promise to bring Jess back soon. It was safe to say she'd passed the family test.

Bryan was quiet most of the drive home. Jess could tell he was embarrassed and pissed at his cousin's behavior. She wanted to take his mind off the unfortunate event and get clarity on where they stood now that she'd met his family.

"Did you mean to say 'girlfriend' earlier?" She asked from the passenger seat.

"Yes, I did," he replied, reaching over to take her hand and planted a few kisses on the back of it, interlocking their fingers together and holding them over his chest. "If it were 2010, I would say we're 'Facebook official.'"

Jess laughed and asked, "If it were 2005, would I be your top friend on Myspace?"

"Mmmmm," he tilted his head and pursed his lips before answering, "That might be pushing it, but top three for sure." He gave her hand a squeeze and threw a wink in her direction.

Jess scoffed and pulled her hand away in fake offense.

"You know I'm kidding." He reclaimed her hand and gave it another squeeze.

They were both so distracted by each other that neither noticed Bryan had driven them straight to his house without dropping Jess off at Nina's first.

Jess looked over at him as he shifted the truck into park in his driveway. He grabbed the handle to open his door, then paused. He let out a chuckle and looked over at Jess.

"Sorry, I forgot...well, why don't you stay here tonight?" He asked. "I can take you back in the morning."

"Okay," Jess agreed, smiling.

Bryan went inside to shower, and Jess called Ruth, who reported that all was well with Nina's medication schedule and that Nina was happy to look after Piggy for the night.

Since Jess had been staying over a few times with increasing frequency, she already had a toothbrush in the medicine cabinet in his bathroom and had a couple of outfits there, too.

Before they fell asleep that night, Bryan proposed an idea. "You should just move in."

"I'll think about it," Jess answered in a playful tone.

"Oh, don't you think we're a little past playing hard to get at this point?"

"I've got to keep you on your toes somehow."

"Fair enough," he conceded with a sigh. "But we both know you can't resist. I give it two days before your hair products are covering every surface in that bathroom," he said, pointing to the doorway.

Jess softly laughed in response and snuggled into Bryan, letting sleep take over.

The following weekend, Jess and Bryan finished moving her things into his house. She'd already had her car packed by the time he got off work.

Bryan had pulled into Nina's driveway as Jess was loading the last box into the front seat of her Mercedes. Piggy was nestled in the backseat between two boxes of shoes, launching an attack on a squeaky toy like he had some personal business to settle.

"You ready?" she asked Bryan over the roof of her car.

"You're already packed?" He asked, coming toward her to plant a kiss on her lips.

"Well, I only brought to Georgia what I could fit in my car, so it really wasn't all that much to pack back up," she replied, patting the roof.

"Well, alright then. You want to say goodbye to Nina?" He asked, taking a step toward the front porch stairs.

"Ruth took her to an appointment. I told her I'd probably be gone when she left. I'll stop by tomorrow to check on her," Jess explained.

"I'll follow you," Bryan said with a smile.

Jess led them on the short drive to Bryan's, and they spent the next half-hour unloading Jess's car. She dropped a box containing Piggy's toys—Jess promised Nina she would bring him by at least once a week to spend the night—on the kitchen floor and made a beeline for the freezer to cool off. A swirl of frost greeted her as she swung open the door and threw a couple of ice cubes on the floor for Piggy. She peeled her sweat-soaked shirt away from her body as she leaned her head into the freezer, savoring the stinging of the cold on her flushed skin.

She planned to spend the rest of the day setting up her office in the spare bedroom upstairs, but Bryan had other ideas.

He scooped her up from behind and carried her up the stairs, and based on where his hands were roaming, Jess was pretty sure it wasn't to unpack anything.

CHAPTER NINETEEN

OCTOBER

Jess

Jess received a call from Jack Hardeman's office six weeks after her interview with him asking how soon she could get the conviction review unit up and running. She'd been in touch with them every couple of weeks, and her hope was starting to wane until they finally came through with the go-ahead to start putting a team together. The call came shortly before she got the email that she passed the bar.

With renewed purpose, Jess threw herself into setting up the unit. As promised, she used her contacts at the Innocence Project to back them off the Gwinnett case they had considered taking on by assuring them it would be her top priority as head of the conviction review unit. The case was that of David Jessup, a man convicted of murder who was serving a life sentence. The project was more than happy to reserve their resources for districts that didn't have review units and promised to halt their work on the case so long as Jess's team was tackling it.

The first few weeks were long hours trying to secure office supplies and get the staff set up. Her first hire was a young investigator from a local city police department named Shauna, who was sharp and hungry to effect change. Jess hired her at the end of her interview. Jess tasked Shauna with hiring an additional investigator, while Jess spent her time diving into case files to decide which cases the team should try to tackle first in addition to the David Jessup case.

She worked late and kept working when she got home. Eventually, she could feel her schedule begin to wear on her relationship with Bryan. He'd backed off his initial concerns and tried to be supportive during the first few weeks, but it was quickly becoming clear they weren't spending enough time together. They were ships passing in the night some days, and Bryan had been complaining about it with increasing frequency. Each time he did, Jess could feel the tension between them thicken, but she promised him that her schedule would even out once the office found its rhythm.

At the end of her third week, Jess walked into the house to find him stirring something on the stove. Jess dropped her purse and briefcase in one of the kitchen chairs and kicked off her heels. Piggy broke away from Bryan's immediate vicinity, where he usually took up post as fallen food patrol, to snort and wiggle his hello before returning to his post.

"Need some help?" Jess asked, shedding her blazer and throwing it over the back of one of the kitchen chairs.

"Yeah, can you do me a favor?" Bryan asked.

"Yeah," Jess responded, crossing the kitchen toward him.

"I need you to make sure you get yourself a beer and make yourself comfortable," he said over his shoulder.

Jess stepped over, leaned into his back, wrapped her arms around his waist, and said, "I really don't mind helping."

"I've got two more minutes on this." He nodded down toward the vegetable stir fry he was working over the blue gas flame. "And the steaks are already done."

"Well, if you insist," Jess conceded.

She opted for a glass of wine over a beer and opened a bottle of her favorite kind, Amarone. She only kept one or two bottles around at a time, because they were pricey. Tonight felt like a good time to bust the cork on one to celebrate having her team completed for the conviction review unit. She had two investigators, an attorney, and a legal assistant. Everyone would be working for the unit part time until they got a conviction overturned. Jack agreed to a reevaluation of everyone's roles and pay at that time.

Locating the aerator she'd purchased on a recent Walmart run—how silly of her not to pack the one she had in Dallas when she moved—Jess popped it over the mouth of the bottle and helped herself to a generous pour.

Wine glass in hand, she took a seat at the table and grabbed her phone to check her email before she even realized what she was doing. She caught Bryan's face pull into a frustrated expression when he saw what she was doing as he was coming over with the pan of vegetables he'd been stirring. He didn't say anything, but instead dished out a couple scoops onto the plates he'd set out for them on the table. Jess quickly finished scanning the subject lines to make sure there weren't any emergencies, then dropped her phone back into her briefcase, and tried to shut off work mode.

Over dinner, although she was already working from home a few days a week, she told Bryan she would only spend one day in the office the following week so they could spend more time together even if she had to work late, and maybe squeeze in a breakfast date or two.

"Oh, I forgot about Nina's appointment. I have to take her to the doctor Monday afternoon. Ruth had something come up," Jess explained.

"What time?" he asked, not doing much to hide the irritation in his voice.

"It's a little later. Around four I think," Jess answered.

"Don't you think that was unfair to you?" Bryan asked.

Jess didn't like where this might be going. "What?"

"How your family expected you to come take care of someone who clearly needs a medical professional's assistance. And right after you went through one of the hardest times in your life," he elaborated.

Jess was taken aback. "I offered to help."

"Did you, though?" Bryan's voice lifted into a mock-questioning tone.

"Yes," she asserted. "It was my idea. And we didn't know the shape she was in until I got out here. Nina didn't tell us how bad it was over the phone," Jess explained in the most even tone she could manage, growing annoyed that he was trying to foment...exactly what she wasn't sure.

He must have sensed her resistance building because his energy shifted and he changed the subject. "Well, anyway, I think we need to take a trip. A few days where you don't have to worry about the unit or Nina or anything else, and I won't have to think about work, either."

"What did you have in mind?"

"I already booked us a trip to Asheville for the first weekend in December," he answered before taking a bite of steak.

"Oh?" was all she managed to say as his response was unexpected.

This was the first she'd heard of a trip, and it caught Jess off-guard since they were both so busy with work. But a vacation sounded amazing. The grind she'd been running since starting the unit was starting to take a toll on her, too, not just their relationship. It was currently the first week of October, so it would give Jess something to look forward to the next few weeks. "What's in Asheville?"

"More breweries than you can imagine, great hiking, and the Biltmore Estate, which will be decorated for Christmas. I booked us tickets for a tour. My mom goes with her friends every couple of years and says the tickets sell out fast."

"Wow, I had no idea you were into that kind of thing," Jess observed, pleasantly surprised.

He winked. "There's a lot of layers to this onion." Sitting back in his chair, he rubbed his hands down his chest to Jess's laughter.

Once they finished dinner, Bryan scooped up their plates and insisted he would take care of the clean-up.

Jess left him to it and went upstairs to change. Keeping with her *treat yourself* theme for the night, she pulled out her silky pajama bottoms and matching camisole. She clipped her hair up, washed her face, and then made her way back downstairs where Bryan had taken to the couch, flipping through streaming services. He had already refreshed her wine glass and had it waiting for her on the coffee table. Jess hoped he never stopped doing small gestures like this for her.

"Thanks, babe," Jess said, picking up her wine glass. "Before we get into a show, I've got another case to run by you." She caught him lifting an eyebrow with a less-than-thrilled expression.

Based on his reaction, he already knew she was referring to an exercise Jess had dubbed "courtroom." She would pitch him a scenario pulled from one of the cases she was deciding whether to have her team review, get his input from a prosecutorial investigator's side, and then Jess would try to refute it to find ways to strengthen her case.

"It's not one of mine, I promise. No work talk," Jess explained, grabbing her glass and sinking down into the opposite side of the couch. She stretched her feet out toward him and wiggled her toes against his leg until he set his beer down and massaged them.

"Alright. Shoot," Bryan said, grabbing the remote and turning down the volume on the TV.

She broke down a case the Innocence Project was working on in Kansas. Upon reading about it via a news article in her inbox that morning, Jess had spent most of the time she should've been reviewing her own cases that day researching it. She laid out the details of the trial—adding that the investigators were suspected of planting the murder weapon at the son's house—and then waved her hand toward Bryan, signaling for him to give his opinion on the case.

He sat with the information for a moment with his lips pursed before starting, "Who else had motive but the son? You said everyone that testified said the father was abusive to the son. And two weeks before he was killed, the employees of the family business overheard the conversation where the father told the son he wasn't going to be taking over the business and was cut out of the will. If that's not motive, I don't know what is. So, even if there's speculation the gun was planted by the investigating officers, a five-year-old could tell you who pulled the trigger," Bryan explained.

"So, you're saying the ends justify the means?" Jess asked.

"If you want to interpret it that way..."

"*Weak,*" Jess scoffed, getting up to refill her wine glass.

"Okay," Bryan said in a lighter tone with an inquisitive expression as she passed by him. "Then, who do you think did it?"

Jess continued from the kitchen, "I don't know who did it. I wasn't there, and neither were you," Jess said as she replaced the aerator with a stopper in the bottle. "And if it was so obvious there was no one else with motive, why did they need to plant the weapon? They should've left the gun where they found it in the father's truck instead of hiding it at the son's house. That makes me think there was someone else involved. Someone they were trying to protect, perhaps. Just admit the investigators blew it."

"Just admit that the son all but fully incriminated himself with his actions, and no one else had motive," Bryan countered, raising his voice from the living room.

"That you know of," Jess argued. She returned to the living room and sat closer to him on the couch, folding her feet underneath her. Raising an eyebrow, she pressed him. "You're one of those, 'show me the man and I'll show you the crime' guys, aren't you?"

"There's a lot of truth to that," Bryan said, looking toward the TV and tipping his beer outward at nothing in particular.

"You know who said that?" Jess asked.

"No, but I'll bet my life savings you do." He looked at her with a smile and a tap on her leg.

"One of Stalin's closest confidants," Jess informed him. "His chief of police to be exact," she added with a tip of her glass in his direction before taking a swig.

"So, that automatically negates any truth in the statement?"

"I would, at the very least, hesitate to make it a motto to live by, considering the source."

"Ah, we all have some bad in us," Bryan said flippantly, looking her directly in the eye.

"Oh yeah? What's your bad?" She asked with playful intrigue.

"I have many," he replied, tucking his chin and looking up at her from a lowered brow. Jess didn't get the feeling he was intentionally trying to make himself look like sinister, but there was something about it that felt ominous. "And so do you," he added.

Jess waited him out for a longer response, knowing he was several beers in and loser-lipped than usual.

Bryan delivered with, "See, here's the thing." Downing the rest of his bottle, he leaned over to place it on the coffee table. He went on, leaning back into the couch. "If there's anything I've learned as an investigator, it's that good people do bad things with the right cocktail of conditions."

Jess listened and sipped on her wine.

He continued, "People don't like to believe that, but it's true. I've seen it play out time and time again." He looked down and licked his bottom lip with narrowed eyes as if recalling a memory. "The look of remorse and shock on their faces sitting in the interview room after being interrogated as the weight of realization about what they've done sinks in. And it could be any of us in that chair at any time."

"Your little distraction is cute, but I won't be dissuaded. Prosecution blew it. You know it. Admit it," Jess said as she pushed herself off the couch and headed for the kitchen.

She had been planning to save the rest of her bottle of her expensive Amarone for the following evening but decided to polish it off now instead.

"Bring me a beer, please," Bryan deflected, lifting his voice so she could hear him in the kitchen.

"Concede, and I'll give you more than that," she answered from the fridge.

Bryan's tone changed from mildly annoyed to enthusiastic and got louder as he got up and made his way to join her in the kitchen. "Royal fuck up. Absolutely no excuses. Drop the charges with prejudice. Fuck twelve," he finished, using a slang term for cops.

He strolled in the kitchen with a pep in his step and a mischievous smirk on his face.

They were standing on opposite sides of the kitchen island as Jess finished pouring the Amarone in her glass and took a sip, staring Bryan down playfully over the rim. She put the stopper back in the bottle on the kitchen island and made it halfway to the fridge before getting swept up from behind. Bryan wrapped her in a tight embrace and nuzzled into her neck. His kisses wandered up to her ear as his hands roved their way over her curves and lingered in the soft places.

It was safe to say "courtroom" had concluded for the night.

CHAPTER TWENTY

Topher

Topher sat on his living room couch pouring over the final report from Bryan's investigation last year. He'd been hit with some questions while he was in the shower, so he sat in nothing but his towel as he flipped through the file. He picked up the sandwich he'd grabbed on his way home, unwrapped it from the butcher paper, and took a bite, a glob of mayonnaise plopping onto the butcher paper placemat below.

The investigation into Bryan's involvement in the shooting of Thomas Ravello—a young man caught up in the cartel gang street wars—was closed months ago, but the details about it were starting to eat him up. When the incident happened, Topher didn't pay much attention to it. He didn't have a reason to since he and Bryan weren't working together at the time. Once they were both assigned to open the Flowery Branch office, Topher began to have some questions. Bryan hadn't done anything explicitly wrong in their first few months together, but Topher didn't like the way he operated. When they conducted their first interrogation together, Bryan went into bad cop mode right out of the gate. He later told Topher that he was expecting Topher to step in as the "good cop."

"I don't do that movie shit," Topher responded sharply, irritated at Bryan's rogue behavior, and ordered him to never behave that way in an interrogation with him again. That was a small-town-investigator-who-didn't-know-any-better tactic. Not something that was going to fly in his office.

Most recently, Topher caught sight of some red flags when he asked Bryan how his investigation into a cartel link by the street name "Tweety Bird" was going. Bryan usually had a lot of details about his cases. Despite his awful interrogation tactics, he was good at surveillance and thorough in his reports. But whenever Tweety Bird came up, Bryan didn't have much information and would look for an opportunity to change the subject and talk about a different case.

Topher mulled removing Bryan from the case and taking it on himself, but the Atlanta office had fed the case to Bryan because of the links he already had with some known criminals that were believed to be connected to Tweety Bird. Ruffling feathers wasn't foreign to Topher, but he didn't do it unnecessarily. Right now didn't seem like the best time to rock the boat when he'd just recently gotten his own office. Not that he cared all that much about having power—he only had two subordinates, so he barely had any. It was more about not having a boss breathing down his neck from the next office over like he'd had the last fifteen years since he started with GBI.

Not to mention Topher had recently learned that the head of the GBI had been Sheriff Whitley's partner when they were Hall County Sheriff's Deputies working the road at the beginning of their careers. It made Bryan almost untouchable. Topher would bet that, had there been more distance from the investigation for Bryan, he would've been head of the new office instead of Topher. Still, even with the head of the bureau in Bryan's corner, Topher wasn't going to let him get someone killed or their office shut down. He kept a close eye on Bryan and decided to dig into his past to find out who his subordinate was.

Topher's initial reason for pulling the report was to see how Bryan operated undercover. He wanted to know if he was working with a loose cannon, or if Bryan had simply gotten unlucky in a wrong-place-wrong-time scenario. At the conclusion of the report that summarized the events the night Thomas Ravello was killed, Topher was leaning toward the former option. The facts weren't sitting well with him, and he was starting to wonder if Bryan had more of a role in the young man's death than just a witness. And if there was one thing Topher hated, it was a dirty cop.

The kid—he wasn't even a decade younger than Topher, but the way he carried himself put them generations apart in Topher's mind—had ridden in on his daddy's coattails and had some infatuation with impressing his old man it seemed. Name recognition still gets you a long way in a small southern town. Topher understood why and didn't care that much about it.

Politics always had been and always would be a game of back scratching, sometimes to the point of corruption, but Bryan didn't even try to add anything to the community beyond a carrier of the Whitley name. And there were doubts that he was the sheriff's son. Rumors had swirled around the community in the past that Bryan's mother was fond of what could be described as "extracurricular activities" once upon a time with one of her activity partners rumored to be Todd's brother. The accusations weren't exclusive to his mother, either, if you asked enough people in town, Sheriff Whitely had a taste for extracurriculars himself. Those rumors could've also simply been a smear campaign from his opponents running for sheriff.

Topher wasn't the kind to live and breathe law enforcement, but as a bachelor, he didn't have much else to do but work. His wife had been diagnosed shortly after they'd started trying to have a baby, and the cancer took her quickly. So now it was just the work, fitness, and beer for Topher.

He dropped the report on the coffee table in front of him and pushed himself off the couch to retrieve a Corona from the fridge.

Some days he wished he had a dog he could train to fetch it for him. A companion would probably do him good. But Topher had an aversion to bonds, of the human sort or other. From his usually absent parents during childhood, to the loss and carnage he experienced at war in Afghanistan, to his wife passing, life had been one letdown after another. People don't stay, and if they did, they did damage. So it was easier to keep everyone and everything at arm's length. Topher knew it probably wasn't the healthiest strategy, but it mitigated the pain enough to get out of bed every day. He used fitness first thing in the morning to keep most of the demons at bay, and work took over the remainder of his mental bandwidth. His caseload had been heavy since being put in charge of the new field office, but he knew his concerns would keep eating at him until he checked into Bryan.

Topher normally didn't bother with the small-town he said she said bullshit of Flowery Branch—he kept to himself. Not that he hid in the shadows like a slinking cat—more like an old dog that found a sunbeam streaming through a window in the winter. He couldn't be bothered. He might tilt an ear to some interesting information and even open an eye to some particularly salacious chatter—he was human after all—but it was rare for him to involve himself.

He was making an exception to that for Bryan's case, because if he was going to be responsible for Bryan as his superior, Topher wanted to know exactly who he was. And so far, he wasn't believing the good cop façade Agent Whitley paraded around. The one that had gotten him on the local news and a national morning show for his acts of service in the community when he was a beat cop before getting on with GBI. Topher wasn't going to hold Bryan's family against him, but he was going to take a microscope to every other area of the agent's life. He was convinced the Thomas Ravello shooting held the key to uncovering exactly who Whitely was, and he wasn't going to stop until he found what he wasn't even sure he was looking for.

CHAPTER TWENTY-ONE

Jess

The calendar said that summer should've concluded weeks ago in September, but Georgia, like much of the South, wouldn't get the memo that it was time to pack away the warm weather for good until sometime in November. There were still a couple of lake days to be had before winter moved in and stole the sun.

Over dinner recently, Topher invited Bryan and Jess to hang out on his boat one Saturday in mid-October. Jess thought it was interesting as Bryan didn't make it seem as though he and Topher had ever been anything more than coworkers, but she was looking forward to spending some time in the sunshine before the cooler weather moved in. Bryan had already winterized his boat and put it in dry storage for the season.

They met Topher at his house. He lived in a cove on the lake a few minutes south in Buford. His house was small, sandwiched in between two larger homes, and had a dock where he kept his boat. It looked like a house on the Gulf Coast, with its light blue and white paint scheme, and large front porch with palm leaf ceiling fans.

They parked in front of the house beside Topher's bureau car—Jess wasn't sure why he had one, as she'd never seen him drive it—and his Tacoma, walked around to the back, and spotted Topher in his wake boat down at the dock digging through some of the locker boxes on the front deck.

"Hey, man. Nice boat," Bryan greeted Topher as they approached, throwing him the bag of subs he and Jess had picked up on the way.

Topher had a couple of the lockers on the front of the boat open and had been digging through the contents. "Thanks. It's not really my style, but it came with the house. I'm not sure if I have a third life jacket somewhere or not," he said as he caught the sandwich bag and set it down on the bench seat behind the console before digging through the compartments again.

Bryan stepped off the dock and onto the deck of the boat. Once steadied, he turned to Jess and grabbed the bag she'd packed full of towels, sunscreen, and snacks. He held out his other hand to pull her onboard, making sure she was steady before he let go.

Having located the third life jacket, they were ready to set out for the day. Topher cranked the engine and idled them out of the slip. Bryan sat in the back by Topher, so they could talk while Jess sprawled out on one of the front couches, stretching her toes toward the bow. She kept her athletic shorts and t-shirt on until the sun had warmed her skin enough to shed them to reveal the bikini she had on underneath. Most of the guys' conversation was lost to the hum of the engine and the whooshing of the wind, so Jess didn't spend much time trying to decipher what they were discussing. Probably something to do with work based on their serious expressions. She did catch Bryan saying something about Emery and Eli and rolled her eyes, wishing Bryan wasn't friends with the immature brothers.

They spent an hour or so riding around enjoying the sunshine and some beers. Topher maneuvered them around families on sailboats, couples zipping around on jet skis, and a few wakeboarders in wetsuits flipping tricks. The hair that escaped Jess's ponytail whipped around like jellyfish tentacles, stinging her skin wherever they landed. She soaked in the sun's caress and savored the cool feeling of the spray from the lake as it misted her.

Two beers in, Topher steered them to a small island with a beach and guided the boat to a gentle stop on the sand. He cut the engine and jumped on the couch opposite Jess to hop overboard and finish beaching them.

"You want another beer, babe?" Bryan asked Jess from the back.

"Sure."

He tossed her a can, and then one to Topher. They grabbed the sandwiches and towels and joined Topher on the beach. The guys continued their work discussion down the beach near the bow of the boat, as if they expected it to suddenly take off. Jess sat a few yards away in the sun on a towel, cracked open a novel, and enjoyed the feeling of her toes in the sand. She tuned them out for the most part, but a name caught her ear.

She turned toward them and asked, "Did you say Enrique Suarez?"

"Yeah," Topher acknowledged without elaborating.

Jess closed her novel and pushed herself up off her towel to look over at the men. "You got eyes on him?"

"He's a person of interest right now for a murder I'm working on. I can't find him, though. But I'm pretty sure he's back in Central America. Are you looking for him, too?" Topher asked.

"Yeah, I need a DNA sample from him. I'm pretty sure it'll get one of my guys free if I can. Locating him has been consuming a large part of our resources lately," Jess explained.

"I might be able to help you on that," Topher offered. "I've got a couple leads I'm working on, and I'm feeling good that one is going to stick."

"That would be great. Can you update me if you hear anything?" Jess asked.

"Sure, no problem," Topher replied.

Jess thought she might've seen a troubled look pass across Bryan's face for a moment. But it could've just been the shadow from the pine trees on the island playing tricks with the light.

They decided to head back as the sun started dropping and the air grew chilly.

Back at the dock, Bryan hopped off first to tie up the boat, so Topher extended his hand to help Jess out.

She accepted it and stepped over the side onto the dock. She couldn't decide if her mind was messing with her, or if the feel of his skin on hers was making her want more of them to be intertwined than just their hands. Forcing her fingers open, she made her hand release his.

CHAPTER TWENTY-TWO

Topher

Topher thought back over the day. Everything was falling into place nicely. He would wait a while to give Bryan more time to screw up and then meet with Jess to discuss the case Enrique Suarez situation. But that wasn't the main objective of meeting with her. Topher needed to build her trust for what might be coming with Bryan, even though it might not be for a while. He learned long ago that one had to have patience and play the long game when it came to investigations. He didn't have the full picture of how far-reaching the situation that Bryan seemed to be entangled in was, but he knew he had to start planting seeds now.

His focus wandered away from the investigation to Jess. Whitley had snagged a good one. It didn't make sense to Topher. Jess seemed too...something for Bryan. He couldn't place his finger on it, but he knew she was too good for the sheriff's son. Maybe it was her intelligence. He didn't think his thoughts stemmed from jealousy. Even though his wife's passing was several years ago, Topher still wasn't interested in dating, holding fast to his "people always leave whether they want to or not" philosophy. However, there were offers ranging from casual sex to full-blown relationships. Every now and then, he indulged in the casual offers only to be met with unfulfilled angst later. He always told himself he'd date again when the right one came along, but he couldn't bullshit himself and knew he was kicking the can down the road.

His thoughts drifted away from his past forays back to Jess. His mind's eye played clips from the day like an old movie reel. He recalled the spray of the waves misting her sun-kissed skin, and the bow of her upper lip with its near perfect curvature. The way the sun highlighted the lighter strands of her hair as the wind flung it about. The swell of her breasts in her bikini top. And the feel of her hand in his as he helped her off the boat.

A stirring in his chest let him know it was time to turn off that stream of thought. He forced his mind back to the investigation. Picking up the file on his coffee table, he flipped through the photos of the Thomas Ravello crime scene and the witness statements, searching for what he knew must be there but couldn't find. Yet.

Snapping the folder shut, he got up and threw some leftovers in the microwave and grabbed a beer. Over dinner, he surfed around his fake social media profiles to see if anything was new in the criminal world that would help solve his cases without much luck.

Night fell, and he checked his watch. It was nine o'clock. The perfect time to head out for a couple of drive-bys and find out why Bryan spent so much time on the phone with Emery and Eli when he talked so much shit about them.

CHAPTER TWENTY-THREE

Jess

Jess stared at the case files on her desk at work, not actually seeing any of them. She'd sent everyone away to find empty jury rooms to work in and shut the door so she wouldn't be bothered by anyone while she narrowed down the cases the unit was going to take on in addition to David Jessup's. For the past ten minutes, she'd been staring at the pile, chewing on the end of her pen.

How does one decide who gets a chance at freedom first?

As if that wasn't enough of a mental load, her mind was drifting back to the weekend when they went on the lake with Topher. She wondered if he was going to call, and more importantly, why she was wanting him to. That was a dangerous train of thought. She was in a relationship with a thoughtful man. So why was she thinking about Topher and the way it felt when their hands touched?

Forcing her mind back to work, Jess finished drafting some post-conviction relief motions for Jessup before getting ready to meet with Shauna over lunch to discuss updates in his case. She pulled her blazer on and headed for the justice building's food court where Shauna was waiting for her.

Shauna wasted no time as they took their seats after snagging some sandwiches at a deli. "As you know, he's currently serving time at the state prison a few hours south in Reidsville. The paperwork has already been completed to transfer him to a closer facility, or here to Gwinnett County Jail down the road. I don't know if we'll get that lucky, but I'm hoping we can at least get him to the state prison about half an hour from here. It's a minimum-security facility, so I'm not sure if they'll do it, but he hasn't had any behavior issues while incarcerated. I'll keep you updated on that. You know it has to go through a committee, then get approved by the warden and all that. In the meantime, I'm working on some potential suspects we can start looking into based on my research."

Jess was surprised. She'd hired Shauna for her work ethic, but this was even more than she'd expected. "Hit me with it."

"I've narrowed it down to three people based on possible motives. Two I was able to locate easily through social media. The third is actually David's cousin. He was harder to find, but I think I figured out where he is now via skip tracing."

Jess nodded. "Nice work. Obviously obtaining DNA is top priority, but let's go ahead and pull their records while we wait on getting warrants signed for that. Check every county they've lived in and the surrounding counties as well. I want to be as thorough as possible. If any of them stole a candy bar when they were five, I want to know about it."

"Sounds good. I'll pull everything I can find and update you by the end of the week," Shauna said with a nod.

Having settled the business part of the conversation, their discussion diverted into more general chatter. Shauna started explaining her frustrations with her mother-in-law.

"She's not a bad person I don't think," she elaborated. "But she's so hard to deal with sometimes. I'm dreading the holidays this year. It's our turn to host, and last time I spoke with her, she mentioned staying for the whole week at Thanksgiving. She invites herself. It doesn't matter that I have kids and other commitments to deal with. She assumes I'll swing my front door wide open and roll out the red carpet for her any time she calls. I just don't know how I'm going to do it this time," she finished, staring at her sandwich with her brow pulled low over her eyes.

Jess tried her best to empathize. "I'm sorry. I can tell you're a little overwhelmed. How long have you been married?"

"Seven years. And you'd think we would've been able to get on the same page at some point along the way. Every time I bring it up to my husband, he dismisses it and changes the subject," Shauna went on. "Anyway, I just can't imagine treating any of my kids' spouses that way. I mean, my oldest is four, so that's a ways down the road. But I would *never* do that."

Something about that statement was unsettling for Jess. It was an innocuous comment, but it gnawed at her.

"Careful with that," she warned her colleague.

"With what?"

"You never know what you might do that you never thought you would."

Shauna stopped chewing her sandwich momentarily as she digested what Jess had said.

"What do you mean?" She asked, lowering her sandwich and looked at Jess quizzically.

"I just wouldn't be so sure about things like that." Jess paused before continuing, "I know I'm not much older than you, so please don't think I'm trying to be patronizing or bestow some kind of sage wisdom on you, but I've already done a lot of shit I said I never would. And I'm sure I'll do some more, too."

Shauna cocked her head to the side and thought for a moment. "You know, I've never really thought about it like that."

Jess balled up her sandwich paper and got up to throw it away. "I hope I'm wrong."

She got home to find Bryan walking down the side of the house with a window screen headed toward the backyard as she pulled in the driveway. She drank in the sight of his muscles working under his shirt. Stepping out of her car, she shed her blazer and threw it across the console into her passenger seat before approaching Bryan.

He looked back over his shoulder toward her at the sound of her car door closing and said, "Hey, babe," without breaking his stride.

"What's going on?" She asked.

"I think someone tried to break in," he explained, as he finagled the screen back into position. "Looks like they popped the screen out of the frame, and they bent it a little bit when they did. I had to straighten it back out with a hammer."

"What?" Jess didn't hear anything past "someone tried to break in." "In the middle of the day? Is Piggy okay?" Her stress level immediately spiked, and she instinctively turned back toward the open garage to go inside.

"He's fine. I checked on him first thing," he reassured her.

"Oh, good." Turning around to face Bryan again, exhaling a sigh of relief.

He finished replacing the screen and stepped over to kiss her. Pulling away, he asked if she wanted to go grab dinner.

"Are you not worried about this? Did you look around to make sure nothing is missing, or if any other screens were damaged?" Jess walked toward the back patio, scouring the area.

"Of course, babe. I checked everything out. It's fine. I'm pretty sure it was some juveniles that have been stealing people's stuff off porches. The city police investigators are working on catching them. Don't worry about it."

"You're sure?" She asked, still looking around.

He replied patiently, "Yes, babe. I'm sure."

His confidence assuaged her fears enough to drop it. "Okay."

"Do you want to go eat?"

"Uh, sure. Let me change and let Piggy out for a few."

"Okay. I'll grab a shower real quick," he said, trailing behind her into the house.

Bryan headed for the stairs, and Jess beelined for Piggy's crate. He danced, wiggled, snorted, and spun around at the sight of her.

"Hey, buddy. Let's go potty."

She followed him out the back door and waited while he sniffed and snorted his way around the yard. Looking to her right, she saw the window Bryan had just replaced the screen on. She studied it from where she stood, not wanting to disturb the space as she surveyed the scene. Something didn't sit right with her. The screen wasn't slashed. Bryan said it had been popped off, which could easily be the case but cutting it would be faster. A daytime break-in attempt would mean time was of the essence. Taking the screen off took more time, and that would make sense if you didn't want anyone to know you'd broken in. Most criminals—kids or not—who were only looking for valuables didn't care about that.

Her gaze dropped to the ground. The mulch bed below the window was receding toward the yard, leaving bare dirt directly below the window. From what Jess could tell, the shoe prints all matched. She couldn't find two different sole patterns, and the prints looked to be from a boot like what Bryan wore to work. Nothing else in the area seemed disturbed.

Odd.

Calling Piggy, she stepped back inside so she could change.

They left for dinner, grabbing some barbecue and chatting about their days while they ate.

After dinner, Bryan steered them east toward the commercial shopping center that sat on the opposite side of the highway.

"Where're we headed?" Jess asked.

"Home Depot. I want to see what kind of security systems they have. Seems like we ought to put something in place. I should've done it a long time ago."

"Can you drop me off at Walmart on your way across the parking lot? I need some paper for the printer. I've got a lot of documents to print, so I can make notes as I review them. I'll meet you at Home Depot."

"Sure," he replied.

Bryan did as she asked, dropping her off at the Walmart storefront. She spent some time wandering the office supplies aisles, grabbing some file folders and highlighters in addition to the copy paper, and headed for the self-checkout. Scanning her items, she tried to avoid looking at her image being displayed back to her by the security screen on the checkout station, because it could make Naomi Campbell look like a frump. Jess understood it helped keep shoplifting down, but damn, couldn't they let you select your own filter? She felt like a sunless tanner or cosmetic company was missing out on some good advertising.

Scooping up her loot, she made for the exit. As she was walking through the first set of sliding doors, she saw a hand swipe at the bag in her right hand, and she instinctively snatched it toward her body, taking a step to her left as she whipped her body around to face not the masked thief she'd expected but her boyfriend.

Bryan laughed and said with pride, "Nice situational awareness, babe. Good job."

"Oh my God, Bryan. I thought you were in Home Depot," Jess exclaimed, trying to come down from the fright he gave her.

"I had to go to the bathroom," is all he offered for an explanation as he reached for the bag again. "Let me carry your stuff."

She handed over the bags. "Thanks."

He could've used the bathroom in Home Depot...was he trying to keep tabs on me?

She was too drained from work to bring it up and potentially start a fight with him, so she acted like everything was fine. They drove across the parking lot to the Home Depot on the other side of the shopping center and perused the security system section. Bryan opted for a package that contained four outdoor cameras and two panic buttons for inside. They hit the self-checkout sans selfie cam, then headed back home. He installed the system, while Jess reviewed some court transcripts and tried to keep the questions plaguing her at bay.

She told herself she was overreacting, and that Bryan had seen too many things as a cop to not secure his own home.

"There we go," Bryan said as he shut the plastic door to the panel on the alarm keypad he'd just mounted to the wall by the door that went to the garage.

Jess looked up from reading transcripts at the table. "All done? That was fast."

"I'm in IT remember? The pants tipped you off." He winked at her, and she couldn't help but laugh. "So, the code is zero four two eight."

The numbers sounded like a date. "Is that the day we met?"

"Indeed, it is," Bryan affirmed. "And the panic button is right here."

He stepped to the right of the keypad into the living room and pointed to the other side of the wall, indicating the button was directly behind the keypad. "You can reach around, press the button, and it's connected to 911." He made his way over to her and planted a kiss on her head. "Now you won't have to worry while I'm away."

"When will you be away?"

He stepped around the table and sat opposite her. "We'll have to do some training a few hours away in Macon early next year. And something could always come up before then if there's a big case where the bureau needs to reallocate resources. It doesn't happen often, but it's always a possibility."

"Oh."

Bryan slowly slid a finger under the flap of the file folder that held the transcripts she'd been reviewing and looked at her with a flirtatious grin as he flicked his finger to close the file.

"Alright, I'll put work away for the night," she said, returning the grin and sliding the folder back into her briefcase.

CHAPTER TWENTY-FOUR

END OF OCTOBER-DECEMBER

Jess

Life chugged along in its new rhythms through the fall. Jess and Bryan spent their weekends completing DIY home improvement projects, restoring the accent cabinet Jess had purchased before she moved in with him, and enjoying all that the new season had to offer. Texas couldn't compete with fall in Appalachia in terms of the foliage. The reds, yellow, and oranges made the mountains look like they'd been set aflame, burning with the final warmth of the year before winter invaded the landscape and stripped all the color.

After selecting the perfect pumpkin for carving one Sunday at a small-town pumpkin patch nestled at the foothill of the mountains, they spent the remainder of the afternoon cruising the two-lane mountain roads, enjoying the colorful foliage. They pulled off at a scenic viewing area to take some pictures of the two of them with the rolling mountains making a most romantic backdrop. Bryan proudly showed her Tallulah Gorge, which he boasted was the deepest canyon east of the Mississippi River. Jess felt like she could've taken his word for it instead of hiking the nearly eleven hundred steps down into the earth and back up the other side, but the breathtaking waterfalls surrounded by the fall foliage were worth a week of sore calves. Their relationship blossomed like a spring flower with each autumn adventure.

In December, they took the trip to Asheville that Bryan had booked in October. It was a relaxing few days filled with winery tours, horseback riding, massages, and large, late dinners filled with all the best carbs. They even drove part of the winding Blue Ridge Parkway that curled its way through the highlands like a snake, with views that demanded adoration.

"We should come back here next fall. I hear the leaves are incredible in mid-October," Bryan said.

"Let's do it." She smiled back and squeezed his hand.

On their last day of the trip, they went on the tour of the Biltmore Estate Bryan had booked them. As they emerged from the forest path that separated the parking lot from the grounds of the home, the Châteauesque monstrosity rose before them, majestic and romantic. Jess felt like she'd been transported through time to nineteenth century Europe. It was a scene straight out of a Jane Austen novel. America's largest home wowed them with its soaring ceilings, indoor garden, and maze of bedrooms fit for a royal family. Every room was decked out in the most elegant Christmas decor, complete with trees showcasing ornaments the size of Jess's head. Her favorite feature was the immense flowerpots in front of the house, so large she could climb inside them and take a nap. And the immense staircases that were so ornate and colossal they could've been in a European castle. It was the closest thing to a fairytale Jess had ever experienced.

After touring the home, they decided to have lunch in the cozy café that was housed in the home's former stables. They wined and dined and talked of their upcoming projects for the house. Jess thought a sage green would be an appealing accent color for the wall that led up the stairs. Bryan agreed and told her to buy whichever shade her heart desired, promising to help her paint it.

She noticed he became quieter at the end of the meal. She passed it off as tiredness. They'd been going nonstop since they arrived in Asheville.

After taking care of the check, Bryan suggested they explore the expansive terrace on the other side of the mansion. Jess agreed, wanting to feel the sun on her face while it was out. They wound their way through the crowds congregating at the front of the home and were relieved to find some quiet on the terrace.

They strolled around hand in hand, taking in the incredible sight of the Blue Ridge Mountains pressing against the skyline in the distance.

"I wonder if the other gardens are within walking distance," Bryan said. "Let me ask these people." He dropped her hand and walked over to a small group on the far side of the terrace.

Jess wondered why he wanted to walk the gardens in December. They had already seen the winter garden inside the house. He was taking his time chatting with them, so Jess pulled her phone from her jacket pocket and took some photos of the mountains. She texted a couple to her mom and one to Stacey.

She sensed stirring behind her and turned to find Bryan kneeling. It took a moment for it to register that he was down on one knee with a small, teal blue box in his hand.

"Will you marry me?" The world stopped spinning, and Jess's brain stalled. Her jaw fell open and she cupped a hand over her gaping mouth.

For a moment, it felt as though she was outside of her body watching the scene from above. As she regained her senses, what felt like a kaleidoscope of butterflies behind her navel rippled its way up through her chest. Every girl imagines the moment she'll get proposed to dozens of times growing up, but Jess had stopped that when she decided she was going to focus on her career. Now, with Bryan kneeling before her, she was immensely elated and flooded with happiness.

"Jess?" Bryan beckoned her attention.

"Yeah?"

"Will you marry me?" Bryan repeated himself, his smile starting to fade.

"Oh, yes," Jess answered excitedly with a wide smile. Tears pushed against her lower lids and her throat felt heavy as she whispered, "Yes, I'll marry you."

A smile burst across Bryan's face, and he quickly rose, bringing her in for a kiss by cupping a hand behind her neck.

Clapping and cheers ensued from the small crowds that had stopped wandering the grounds to watch as he slipped the ring over her knuckle. It was an impressive piece with a solitaire diamond pronged in what looked to be a platinum setting that floated above a hidden halo and yellow gold band—he must've noticed that was her preferred metal based on the few pieces of fine jewelry she wore on occasion.

The woman Bryan had gone up to returned his phone and congratulated them. They thanked her and swiped through the photos.

"There should be a chilled bottle of champagne and some chocolate covered strawberries waiting for us right over here," Bryan said as he led her to a small side garden with a fountain a few yards away.

"Congratulations Mr. and soon to be Mrs. Whitley," a man dressed as a butler said, removing the cover from a silver tray that sat in front of the fountain.

"Thank you so much," Jess gushed, and Bryan echoed her sentiment.

"I'll leave you two to enjoy each other's company, but I'll be right over here should you need anything." He turned and pointed toward the mansion. "And I already have a car warmed for you when you're ready to retire to your suite," the man explained before stepping away.

"Suite?" Jess looked at Bryan.

"Yeah, we got an upgrade for the night. I felt the occasion called for it," he said before pulling her in for another kiss.

They took a seat at the table and held hands as they sipped champagne. Bryan commented on how cold Jess's hands were and moved his chair closer so she could put her hands under his shirt to warm them. The strawberries were delectable, and Jess wondered out loud if they could order more to the room.

"I'll have that taken care of for you, future Mrs. Whitley," Bryan said with a smile.

Jess beamed and suggested they head to the suite. Bryan stepped away to locate the butler, and Jess stretched out her left hand in front of her to admire the new addition to her ring finger.

As she stared at the dazzling Tiffany piece—*how the hell did he afford a Tiffany ring? I've never even mentioned Tiffany around him before*—a small whisper in a remote corner of her mind voiced concern. Something inside her already knew the thunderheads were rolling in, even though she wasn't admitting it to herself yet. And then for some reason she couldn't explain, she thought of Topher.

CHAPTER TWENTY-FIVE

Topher

Topher pulled two cigarettes out of the pack and threw it back on the patio table. He lit one and shoved the second one behind his right ear. A habit from his days with his late wife. Even though it had been years since she passed, he couldn't bring himself to pull out just one.

It was a warm day for December, so he opted to unwind on the deck until the chill returned with nightfall. He took a long drag and settled back into the metal chair on his back deck that overlooked his small backyard and the dock. Scratching his chin with the thumb of the hand holding the cigarette, he thought back over the day. He'd spent most of it haggling with a used car salesman at one of the Hispanic-owned buy-here-pay-here car lots in Gainesville. He had no use for another vehicle; his Tacoma suited him just fine, but the activity gave him a good cover for keeping an eye on the Juliana Motel situated across Atlanta Highway from the car lot. The suspected drug supplier that the Atlanta office had tasked Topher with following frequented the seedy 1950s establishment.

Between Topher's broken Spanish and the car salesman's basic English, it was not a successful negotiation. However, Topher got more than he bargained for when it came to figuring out what Bryan's undercover activities were.

A CI informed him that Tweety Bird had been hanging around the motel and even had a room number: 310.

He'd been sitting on a bench outside the small trailer that housed the car lot's office, pretending to review some finance forms the salesman gave him to consider, when a familiar truck pulled into the parking lot of the motel. The red Dodge Ram with a USMC logo down the side of the bed by the taillight quickly backed into a space beside the exterior stairwell, so that it wasn't visible from the street. From his vantage point, Topher could see the breezeway between the stairwell and the first-floor rooms. After a moment, a man emerged into the breezeway behind where the truck parked and climbed the stairs to the third floor and entered room 310.

Son of a bitch.

There was no mistaking it. It was Emery. The sticker warrior firefighter. He emerged from the room after about ten minutes and quickly drove away south on Atlanta Highway toward Flowery Branch.

Topher threw the clipboard of papers on the bench behind him as he made a break for his truck. He caught a left out of the lot as soon as he could and fought to catch up with Emery. He took Atlanta Highway all the way back down to Flowery Branch but never caught sight of the truck again.

Frustrated, he continued southward home. The clock on the dash read three on the dot. Anticipating a long night, he stopped by a gas station and grabbed a fresh pack of Marlboros and a large black coffee.

Topher didn't like the way this was looking. Emery had met with Tweety Bird—or someone close to him—and wasn't a stranger to Bryan's recent call list. There was no reason for a firefighter to meet with a supplier unless he was buying or selling drugs. Topher was leaning toward the second option, although he hadn't seen him leave the room with anything. But it was possible he'd tapped it to his body under his loose-fitting shirt or filled his pockets.

Sitting on his deck smoking the Marlboros, he ran through his options. He could bring Jason in to help. Jason was sharp and could help put eyes in other places and on people that needed to be investigated, but the chances of a slip-up jumped astronomically with each additional person that got involved. He also had a suspicion a federal agency might already have the situation on its radar, given the potential scope of this drug ring. There wasn't any concrete evidence to indicate the feds were stepping in, but his gut told him it was only a matter of time if they hadn't already.

Ultimately, he decided he needed more information before he could make any moves. Blowing out a swirl of smoke, he grabbed his burner phone and started making calls.

CHAPTER TWENTY-SIX

Jess

*T*iffany?" Stacey scoffed on the other end of the line. "Did he get an advance on his inheritance?"

Jess broke into a laugh. This is why Stacey was her closest friend. She had absolutely no filter, and Jess loved the authenticity. What you saw was what you got. A true breath of fresh air in a world saturated with shiny veneers of aesthetic social media accounts trying to conceal messy lives.

"You know I was wondering the same thing," Jess responded, keeping her voice low as she was shopping at J&J, the local grocery store.

"You don't even like Tiffany. Simple solitaires aren't your style," Stacey pointed out.

Jess looked down at the ring and wiggled her finger to watch it sparkle. "Yeah, but I like this one."

"How many carats is it?"

"I think it might be close to two."

"He's selling drugs," Stacey said with finality.

Jess laughed at the absurdity.

"Jess, he's a *cop*. Two carats...from *Tiffany*? That's got to be worth half his pension."

"He probably went to his parents. And he's been a bachelor, so he's been able to put away money, like I did after I paid off my school loans."

"Y'all haven't had the money talk yet?" Stacey sounded surprised.

"No, not yet. We've both been swamped with work, and I didn't want to bring it up while we were enjoying Asheville. But we will soon, I'm sure." Jess added it to her mile-long to-do list.

"Well, whatever." Her friend relented. "When am I going to see these two carats in person?"

"Soon, I hope. I was thinking about planning a long weekend in the spring."

"Will you be bringing cop boy?"

"Yes, *Bryan* will come with me as long as his work allows, and you have to be nice to him if he does."

Stacey sighed. "Fine. I'll give him a shot. I just hate that he's taking my best friend away from me is all."

Jess laughed. "He's not taking me away. Honestly, I think I was going to stay here for a while, even if he hadn't proposed this soon."

"Not if I had anything to say about it you weren't," Stacey argued.

"You're welcome here anytime. You and the fam. Speaking of, how're the kiddos?"

Stacey and her husband had toddler twin boys that Jess adored. Her heart felt a little heavy thinking about how much bigger they must be now since the last time she saw them. It was hard to believe her once free-spirited best friend that had influenced half of their law school class to go skinny dipping after their second-year exams was now a strict routine-oriented mom who planned her entire life around her kids and their nap schedule. Jess would bet she even knew how to fold a fitted sheet now.

"Oh, you know, when it's not poop smeared on the walls, it's something shoved up a nose. And I know I'll miss these days when they're grown, but sometimes it takes everything in me not to look at the little crotch fruits and go, 'What the *fuck*, man?'"

Jess laughed until tears were brimming up against her lash line, and she made a snort sound akin to Piggy's stubbed-nose noises.

"And if I have to go to urgent care for one more X-ray to see what one of them has swallowed, I'm sure they're going to call Child Protective Services on me. And you know what, when they show up, I might just hand them the other one, too. See what you get to look forward to?"

"Whoa, whoa. I just got the ring. Let's not get ahead of ourselves."

Stacey started to reply but was interrupted by a loud crashing noise followed by a small wail that gradually turned into two screams. "Oh my– they jus– I gotta go. I'll call you this week."

"Oof, hope that wasn't too expensive. Bye," Jess said as she hung up, still trying to catch her breath from laughing.

She dropped her phone in her purse and wheeled her cart to the produce section.

Speaking of growing up, there are certain things no one prepares you for in adult life.

Jess stared in disbelief at the different kinds of small potatoes, the number of varieties.

What the hell is the difference?

They were hosting Bryan's parents for dinner that night, and he was in an anxious state—Jess noticed he tended to stress out when he was around his dad, wanting to make sure everything was perfect—trying to get everything ready, so he'd sent her to J&J for baby red potatoes, but they only had baby Yukon Gold and Purple Majesty potatoes. Jess didn't even know there were purple potatoes.

She called him and asked which to get.

"Yukon Gold is fine," he answered.

"Okay, I'm almost done, about to check out. See in a few. Bye." She hung up right as he said, "Bye, I—"

Oops. Unintentional.

She dropped her phone back in her purse as she scooped up a bag of the Yukon Golds. As soon as she set them in the cart, her phone started ringing. Bryan again.

"Hey," she answered.

His tone was serious. "You didn't say 'I love you.'"

"Uh...I'm sorry, just had a handful, and I'm trying to get to check out," Jess said, trying to keep the frustration out of her voice.

"Why didn't you say it?"

"Like I said, I'm in a hurry to get back so you can start cooking. I know your parents will be there soon."

"While you're there can you grab another six-pack?" Like a switch had flipped, his tone was a complete one-eighty from the one he'd used when she answered.

She started slowly pushing her cart again. "Sure."

"Okay, bye, love you."

"I love you, too," she answered and waited for him to hang up so she didn't get the third degree again.

Odd.

CHAPTER TWENTY-SEVEN

Jess

On Christmas morning, Jess woke to the smell of pancakes cooking. She stretched, shoved her feet into her slippers, and went downstairs to find Bryan still in his boxers and tousled hair laying out a feast for breakfast. He'd cooked them eggs, pancakes, bacon, grits, and already had her coffee ready the way she liked it—one tablespoon of honey and a light pour of cream.

"Merry Christmas, babe," he said with a smile as she walked over to where he was flipping a pancake on the stove to kiss him good morning.

She took in the spread of food laid out on the island. "Merry Christmas. This looks amazing."

Bryan nodded toward the stove. "I'm almost done if you want to go ahead and make a plate. I made sure to put your collagen in your coffee, too."

Jess shot him a look. "Are you trying to say I'm looking old?"

"Just making sure you're taken care of," he said, smacking her ass.

They shared Christmas memories from their childhoods over breakfast. Jess told him how her dad would rub flour on the bottom of his boots and walk around the living room to leave "snow footprints" from Santa when she was little. Bryan told her about how he and Mallory made a plan to stay up all night to catch Santa on the roof and see if reindeer could really fly, but they got caught trying to sneak out the back door by his mother. They laughed and enjoyed a second cup of coffee before opening their presents from one another in the living room.

Bryan gifted Jess with a pair of new pearl earrings, since she'd lost one from the set she often wore, a brad nailer she wanted for her DIY projects, and a new leather briefcase for work.

Jess gave him some new running shoes, a custom engraved wooden storage box for his watches, a new stainless steel watch band for the one he wore every day, and a seat belt cutter.

"What's this?" Bryan asked, examining the tool.

"It's a seat belt cutter," Jess explained.

He looked at Jess over the tool and smirked. "Are you trying to tell me I should start wearing my seat belt?"

"What do you think?" She asked with a raised brow and head tilt over the rim of her coffee cup.

"Why would I need a seat belt cutter?" He pressed, still smirking.

"In case you get in an accident and are pinned by it," Jess explained.

"Then, it would make sense not to wear one in the first place," Bryan countered.

Jess rolled her eyes. "You know, you're starting to sound like an attorney."

Bryan threw his head back and laughed heartily. "I guess you're rubbing off on me," he said, reaching across the couch to squeeze her foot.

"Speaking of rubbing things on me..." he yanked her foot to slide her down on the couch to where her back ended up on the seat. She squealed and pulled him on top of her as he moved closer.

She locked her legs around him and tangled her hands in his hair as he buried his face in her neck and his hands under her clothes.

Of the weirdest things to do after sex, video chatting with her parents had to be up there for Jess. As they were pulling their clothes out of couch cushions and Bryan was fishing Jess's panties off the curtain rod, her phone started ringing. She swiped Bryan's t-shirt off the coffee table to find her phone underneath. It was her mother trying to FaceTime her.

"Shit. Put your shirt on!" She flung it at Bryan who was hopping off the back off the couch, panties in hand.

Jess grabbed a throw to cover her naked bottom half, sat on the couch, and tried to smooth her hair down before answering on the last ring.

Her mom's face filled the screen from a low angle, her readers blocking much of her eyes. Bryan finished pulling his shirt on and sat down beside Jess on the couch.

"Merry Christmas, y'all!" Marcie exclaimed. "Oh, boy do y'all look flushed. What've you been up to?"

"Uh, we uh, just got back from a run," Jess blurted out.

"Yeah, we were...running," Bryan chimed in, not sounding any more convincing than Jess.

"Oh, okay. Well, your father and I wanted to say Merry Christmas, and we can't wait to see you in a few weeks to give you your presents and finally meet our soon to be son-in-law in person," Marcie said.

Jess's dad was in the background waving and saying something Jess couldn't quite make out.

"We can't wait, either," Jess responded. "Are y'all doing anything fun today?"

"We're going to go to church, and then to see the lights at the botanical garden. That was one of your dad's presents to me," her mother explained with a gleeful smile full of holiday cheer lighting up her face.

"And then we might go for a run ourselves," her father said in the background with a chuckle.

They said their goodbyes, and Jess hit the end button.

"They knew we—" Bryan started.

"Had sex? Yeah," Jess finished with a nod, dropping her phone on the coffee table along with her dignity.

"Awesome," he said sarcastically.

"Yup."

"Well," Bryan said, squeezing her knee, "I guess we better get going. We've got some ground to cover today."

"Yeah," Jess said, still staring at her phone, embarrassed.

They showered and were getting ready to head out the door to Nina's when Todd called and needed help cooking. Apparently, he got a late start with the turkey and Pattie was threatening divorce if Christmas dinner wasn't served on time.

"You go ahead. I'll hang with Nina for a while and then come up when Ruth gets there for the evening," Jess said.

"Are you sure?" Bryan looked at her with concern.

"Yeah, it's fine. I'll take Piggy, too, and leave him over there tonight to keep them company," Jess assured him.

"Alright. Let me know when you're headed up," he said, leaning in for a kiss.

He turned to head out the door when Jess stopped him by saying, "Wait." She stepped into the living room and grabbed the seat belt cutter and handed it to him. "Put it in the truck so you don't forget it," she said with a wink.

He threw it up in the air, caught it, and said, "I'll put it in the glove box for you."

"Fair enough," Jess conceded. She wasn't going to try and parent a grown man any longer.

"I love you," he said, starting to close the door.

"I love you, too," she answered before turning her attention to rounding Piggy up to take to Nina's.

CHAPTER TWENTY-EIGHT

JANUARY

Jess

On a bleak January day, Jess and Bryan did a walk-through at an event venue in the neighboring town of Buford after work. It was a romantic, white home built in the early 1900s. It looked similar to Nina's house with the black trim around the windows and the porch ceiling was a similar shade of pale blue. Bryan had asked her if she wanted to get married in Dallas in accordance with the tradition of marrying in the bride's hometown. Jess was touched by the offer, but the idea of starting her marriage in a town that still put a bad taste in her mouth when she thought about it was as appealing as eating glass. Jess also wasn't sure if Nina would be up to traveling that far, and she couldn't imagine a wedding day without her aunt there.

The venue coordinator, a polite, graying woman in what Jess would guess to be her sixties, met them out front shortly after they'd arrived and showed them the grounds. The manicured yard was framed with towering magnolia trees that made the perfect backdrop for a southern wedding. The woman headed for the porch to take them inside when Bryan's work phone rang. He told Jess to go in without him and took the call. Jess was a little irritated, but Bryan had already told her whatever venue she picked out he would be fine with, so she followed the woman inside, the smell of wood polish and Pine-Sol raking her nostrils. They went room by room as her tour guide explained a typical wedding day.

At the end, the woman smiled and handed her a brochure, pointed to her direct line on the back, and instructed Jess to call her with any questions. Jess thanked the woman before rejoining Bryan outside. He was pacing the driveway behind the truck, still on the phone. When he saw her, he quickly hung up and smiled, asking how the rest of the tour went. She filled him in as they climbed into the truck.

Bryan interrupted and said he'd heard of a good Thai restaurant just across the railroad tracks, the same ones that ran through the middle of Flowery Branch, suggesting they grab some and take it home. Jess called in their order, and Bryan dropped her at the front of the restaurant.

On the way home, Bryan asked which date she wanted to go with.

"At the venue?" she asked.

"Yeah."

"Babe, did you hear how much it is? It's more than ten thousand dollars. We agreed we wouldn't spend more than eight on a venue."

"Yeah, but I also saw the way your eyes lit up at the magnolia trees. I know those are your favorite. That's the venue you want."

"I mean it's beautiful, but it seems like it wouldn't be a smart move financially. We should probably save that money and invest it or something. I don't want to need a rainy-day fund and not have it."

"You worry too much. If you want that venue, then we're going to get that venue. My bride is going to get the wedding of her dreams. After all, we're only going to do it once."

Jess smiled in return, reveling in the feeling of his confidence and thoughtfulness. "Let me talk to my parents and see what dates would work best for them, since they'll have to travel."

Bryan agreed, and they left it at that.

Once they got home, Jess started sorting the boxes on their back patio table, while Bryan went inside to change out of his work clothes. Jess was ravenous since she'd skipped lunch, so she went ahead and started eating straight from the container, her mind flipping through wedding details while she enjoyed the glowing pink sunset illuminating their backyard.

"What are you doing?" Bryan asked when he came back outside in basketball shorts and a t-shirt.

Jess looked up from the container of rice she'd been shoveling food into her mouth out of and asked, "What do you mean?"

"Why didn't you wait for me?" He asked as he gestured toward the white box in her hand.

"I'm starving. I didn't have lunch today."

"Why not?"

Jess paused before answering, not liking the direction the conversation felt like it was heading in. "I was trying to catch up on some work."

"Well, we're about to be a family now, Jess. And families eat together."

What the hell is he talking about?

"Right...which is what we're about to do now that you're here," she answered hesitantly.

"No, this isn't how we do it. We say grace over the food, and then we start together. I know that wasn't a thing for your family growing up, but it's really important to me." His voice wasn't elevated, but she could sense the angst in him; he was escalating. But Jess was over it.

"So, you want me to stare at my food and wait until you sit down, even if it's ten minutes before I take a bite of my food? I'm pretty sure God will forgive me if I take a bite before grace is said." She had just enough attitude in her tone to flip his switch.

"You know what? You're being a disrespectful bitch right now." His tone was venomous as he threw down the fork he'd been holding and launched into an assault. "I buy you a nice dinner and all I ask you to do is wait a couple of minutes so we can enjoy it together. What's the rush? What's more important than spending time with your almost husband?"

Her mind couldn't work fast enough to formulate a response, so she just sat there staring at him. His face grew red, he grabbed his container of food and his drink, then stomped inside to eat alone.

CHAPTER TWENTY-NINE

Bryan

Bryan knew he'd been a little harsh the other night. Not that he regretted the message that she should be starting to think more like a family—Jess needed to know that she'd upset him and think twice before doing it again. However, he could've been better with his delivery. Things had been tense between them since, making their conversations short. At first, he felt like she needed a day or two to calm down, but when her attitude hadn't changed after the third day, he knew it was time to make it up to her.

While she was working from Nina's, he left work and passed by the house to make sure nothing was going on that he should be aware of, like a strange car. He drove down Atlanta Highway to a jeweler in Buford called Teena's Fine Jewelry. The locals simply referred to it as "Teena's." It was the go-to place in the area for all things custom and designer jewelry. Bryan stepped through the front door and gave a salute to the officer on the other side of the plexiglass to his right.

After a robbery some years back, the owners had remodeled and added an entrance that resembled an airlock on a spaceship. If anything looked suspicious, the officer could lock both the door to the outside and the second door that led into the store until backup arrived to sort things out.

The officer nodded back and buzzed Bryan in. Once inside, he swung left and browsed the watch cases. They were a Rolex dealer, and while he had never been someone overly flashy, he had been making enough green the past few months to consider one. But a conversation piece like a Rolex would turn too many heads, and that's the last thing he needed right now. He'd already pushed the envelope getting Jess a Tiffany engagement ring.

He headed back toward the middle of the store that held the women's jewelry. Valentine's Day was a few weeks out, and the store had red and pink reminders positioned around in various places. A friendly young blonde woman greeted him with a smile and asked how she could help. He told her he was looking for a necklace. On the drive there, he'd decided what he was looking for. A diamond seemed too cliché, and he thought an emerald stone would be nice. He envisioned it highlighting Jess's forest green eyes, but he quickly realized why he didn't see many emeralds worn when he glimpsed the price tags.

"Maybe something blue," Bryan said to the sales associate.

Moving to another case, she pulled out a navy sapphire pendant the color of the deep ocean and a light blue topaz option out of one of the cases and set them on a black velvet mat for Bryan to consider. The blue topaz was nice, but it reminded him of Windex and felt more suited for a little girl, not an intelligent trial attorney. A sapphire was the obvious option for Jess. The navy would match with her neutral work clothes and seemed to be more distinguished and timeless than brighter-colored topaz, but she already had a couple of sapphire pieces.

The woman seemed to pick up that Bryan wasn't sold on either stone and mentioned she might have another hue he might like around the corner in another case. He followed her as her heels clinked on the marble floor, like a pick stabbing ice, her blonde locks bobbing up and down with each step. She stepped behind a case, unlocked the back of it, and pulled out a few more options. They were all the same color. Not quite the navy of the sapphires but a darker blue than the topaz. Bryan would describe them as greenish blue, much like the color of the Chattahoochee River that fed into Lake Lanier.

"These are tourmalines. Perhaps they're more along the lines of what you're looking for?" The associate looked up at him quizzically, awaiting his response.

He studied the options and decided on a long, rectangular piece—the woman called it an emerald, which was confusing for Bryan, because she had just said tourmaline, and the price tag was also much different than the emeralds in the other case. The main stone was haloed by petite diamonds and hung on its long edge from a delicate rose gold chain.

Bryan waited as the woman disappeared to package it in thick, gold paper. When she returned, she congratulated him on his wonderful choice—he suspected it was to make him feel good right before asking for his payment method. After checking out, he headed back through the airlock and up the road to Flowery Branch.

He texted Jess on his way, letting her know he'd made reservations for dinner.

CHAPTER THIRTY

Jess

Jess left Nina's a little earlier than planned to get ready for her date with Bryan. His text had caught her by surprise. She was still upset about his dinner outburst two nights ago and had been giving him the cold shoulder. She had a lot of work to do on the David Jessup case and had been fighting with the Georgia Department of Corrections all day in an effort to have David transported to the Gwinnett County Jail so she could interview him in person. If she couldn't get him to Gwinnett, she would have to travel to him with Shauna and likely pay the expenses out of her own pocket to preserve the review team's minimal budget. Long story short, she didn't have the energy to fight Bryan anymore and agreed to dinner.

She wrapped up her emails, then headed home. He wasn't there, but she went ahead and jumped in the shower and then curled her hair.

I wonder if he has some news. Maybe he got promoted. Or it's an apology dinner.

It turned out to be the latter. He got home as Jess finished getting dressed. She found him in the kitchen unloading several grocery bags of goodies.

"What's all this?" She asked as she approached the island where he was dumping his loot by turning the bags upside down.

"For you," he said with a smile.

Jess sorted through the contents and found her favorite snacks, candy, a pair of fuzzy socks, some fancy lip balm, and a cylindrical box. Jess grabbed the box and picked it up for a closer look.

"You got me a menstrual cup? Am I PMSing so bad I need a whole care kit?"

"A what?" Bryan set the grocery bag he was still holding down and leaned over the counter to look at the box.

Jess turned the box around for him to see and said, "This is a menstrual cup. It's basically a reusable tampon."

"Uhhhh," Bryan said, turning his head like a puppy that heard a squeaky toy and squinting at the box.

Jess burst out laughing. "What...did you...think it was?" She asked in between waves of belly-aching laughs.

"A stress ball," Bryan answered sheepishly, making Jess laugh harder.

"How?" she managed, close to tears and out of breath.

"Well, it was on an endcap at the store with all the women's self-care, treat yourself stuff. And it says 'stress less' on the label," Bryan tried his best to explain pointing at the box, flustered and embarrassed.

Jess pulled herself together, set the box down on the counter, and met him on his side of the island to bring him in for a hug.

"Thank you for my self-care, treat yourself goodies," she said, wrapping her arms around his waist.

"You're welcome. Sorry it was a major fail," he said dejectedly and planted a kiss on her lips.

Jess pulled away, tilted her head to the side, looked up at him and said softly, "It was very thoughtful of you."

He went in for another kiss but pulled up short and said, "But wait, there's more. The best part, actually."

"Oh?" Jess wasn't sure what to expect next. Maybe a bottle of lube he thought was hair gel.

"I'll be right back," he said as he pulled away from her and headed for the door to the garage.

Jess leaned on the island counter and opened a package of Reese's while she waited for him to come back.

He returned to the kitchen with his right hand behind his back and a smile on his face. He sauntered over to her with a playful expression, like a kid trying to hold in a secret.

Jess raised her eyebrows and waited.

He pulled his arm around to reveal a small gold-wrapped box and handed it to her.

Jess wiped her Reese's fingers off with a paper towel and took the box from him. It opened to reveal a beautiful rose-gold pendant necklace with a center stone the color of the deeper parts of the Caribbean Sea, somewhere between navy and turquoise.

"Bryan," Jess gasped. "What on Earth?"

"I'm not taking it back so don't ask me to," he said, gently taking the box from her. "Turn around," he softly ordered.

She did as told, lifting her hair out of the way, so he could clip it around her neck.

"It's a tourmaline. The lady that sold it to me said that it's guaranteed to increase your sex drive." His tone was salacious.

Jess snorted and rolled her eyes. "I hope you kept the receipt."

Bryan kissed her softly on the back of the neck and said, "Now let's go find an outfit upstairs that matches it for dinner."

CHAPTER THIRTY-ONE

At the end of January, Jess's parents came to stay for a long weekend to meet Bryan and visit with Nina. Bryan had called and asked for her hand over the phone, and they'd video chatted with her parents a couple times, but they'd never met in person.

Her parents opted to stay with Nina, since Bryan and Jess's guest bedroom also doubled as her remote office. They spent the weekend exploring local shops and enjoying the finest food they could drive to. Jess and her mother got a massage, while her dad and Bryan went to the gun range. It was a wonderful couple of days that went by entirely too fast. Jess wasn't ready for them to leave when she and Bryan dropped them off at the airport. Marcie only got out of the car because Jess promised to visit soon.

Jess was wholly unprepared for what happened the following evening with Bryan on their way to his parents' house for dinner. They had just gotten in his truck when he asked her why she hadn't posted anything about their relationship on social media.

"It makes me feel like you're not that invested in the relationship. Like you're embarrassed of me or something," Bryan griped pitifully, which irritated Jess, because she hated people playing the victim when she dealt with real victims at work but also gave her pause and made her wonder if she was being selfish.

"Babe, I haven't updated anything on my accounts in a year and a half. Look," she said as she pulled her phone out of the pocket on the side of her leggings and navigated her way to the social media folder. She pulled up each app and read off the date of her last post on each one.

"So, I'm not worth a new post? Is that what you're saying? I'm not newsworthy enough for a new profile picture that takes a whole ten seconds to post?" Bryan countered, doubling down.

Jess pushed back. "You haven't posted anything about us, either. So, why are you jumping all over me?"

He looked over at her with a concerned expression and said, "For your safety. You notice how I don't list a hometown, or where I live?" He asked rhetorically before going on, "I don't ever post where I am, either. Or tag anyone else. One of the undercover guys over at Gwinnett Special Investigations blew his cover that way. Almost ruined a three-year investigation and put his family in jeopardy. Jess, we are dealing with the *cartel*, not Waffle House workers selling meth out the back door. I would be putting you in harm's way if I posted anything with you or about you."

"Then why even have social media? What's the point?" Jess threw up her hands, exasperated. "Seems like more trouble than it's worth," she said, her voice rising with her frustration level.

"Because it's one of the ways I keep track of what's going on," he said, grabbing his phone out of the side pocket of the door and waving it in his left hand as he drove with his right. "It's part of how we keep our finger on the pulse and identify key players in our investigations."

"You can do that with a fake profile."

"We have those, too," he rebutted, unfazed.

"Then why do you need your own?" She pitched.

"Why do you need your own if you haven't posted anything in a year and a half?" He bunted.

"Why do you keep your phone in the door when we're together?" Jess asked. That one caught him like a left hook to the jaw. He looked over at her, and his mouth opened to answer, but nothing came out.

"Hiding something?" she pressed with a head swing in his direction and a raised brow.

He remembered how to speak and answered, "Habit. That's where I always put it in my truck."

"Right..." Jess said in a mockingly convinced tone, nodding.

She might as well have reached over the console and slapped him across the face.

His face flushed, and he reacted with a vengeance. "You need to understand something," he started through gritted teeth accompanied with finger-pointing in her direction. "I'm looking out for you, and I don't appreciate your bitch attitude about it. You're so ungrateful." He paused for a moment.

When he spoke again, his tone had changed from angry to exasperated. "At this point, I don't know...Jess. I just don't know," he said cryptically.

"What do you mean you *don't know*?"

"I don't know if this is going to work. You don't seem like you really want this relationship to work," he answered. Jess sat silent, stunned. He went on, "I don't feel like you appreciate me. Like you give me any credit."

"Bryan," Jess began, "this has nothing to do with me not wanting to be with you or not appreciating you. I've had a lot on my plate with abruptly moving halfway across the country, taking the bar, starting a new job, moving in with you. Updating my social media is one of the furthest things from my mind right now."

"You check your stories every day, you get alerts on your phone, I just don't believe that," Bryan continued. "I think there's something more. I feel like you're ashamed of me. Am I not good looking enough? Were your ex-boyfriends better looking? Or is there someone else out there you don't want me to find out about? Huh? Is that it?" He cut his eyes at her.

Jess started to pull inside herself, stunned. "No, that's not it. I can't believe you'd even say that."

She turned her head to look out her window. They were traveling parallel to the railroad tracks. Bryan slowed them to a stop at a red light. Both sat in silence. Jess could feel the tension pulsating from Bryan. The rage in him was building again. She tried to keep her demeanor as calm as possible, hoping it would diffuse him.

She could feel the rumbling of a train coming up on the railroad tracks. As if on cue, the train blew its whistle as it blasted by them. The light turned green, and Bryan accelerated. Jess continued to watch the train cars as they went by as a distraction from Bryan's antics. Eventually, they caught up to the same speed as the train. Jess wondered how fast the train was going when it passed Nina's. She discreetly peeked at the speedometer out of the corner of her eye. Fifty-five miles per hour.

Her thoughts were broken by Bryan saying, "You never answered me."

"What?"

"Whether or not you want to be in this relationship."

"Is that a real question?" Jess came back out of her shell. "Are you serious?"

Bryan looked at her and waited.

She hated herself for falling for the waiting tactic as she said, "We're not in middle school. If I wanted to leave, I would just do it."

"Oh, so you *have* been thinking about it. Okay, I see," he said as he looked in the side mirror and flipped the blinker on to change lanes.

"Do you hear yourself right now?"

"You mean the way you make me?"

"Take me home," Jess demanded, done playing his rigged game.

She wasn't going to sit there and get blamed for everything and wondered if he realized he was cultivating a seed of doubt in her mind about the sturdiness of their relationship. If she was being honest with herself, this wasn't the first time she'd had such thoughts. But the closer she got to the final days of David Jessup's post-conviction relief ruling, the less mental stamina she had to examine the pitfalls in her and Bryan's relationship. She needed to get past this case before she did any deep soul searching on how to proceed with Bryan.

The existence of the conviction review unit likely depended on getting Jessup out of prison. Hardeman, as nice as he was, had been dropping subtle hints to her that he hadn't been able to secure any supplemental funding. That meant Jess was going to have to make a miracle happen or lose the office, which would put other people out of work and leave more innocent people in prison for crimes they didn't commit. She could only take on so many problems at one time, so as irritated and confused as she was at Bryan's behavior, she pushed out the larger questions about their situation, promising herself she'd come back to them after the Jessup case had wrapped up.

Bryan dug in. "No, my parents are expecting us for dinner."

"I don't care," she told the window.

He banged his hand down on the steering wheel. "*Exactly*. Case in point. You don't care. I'm glad you finally admitted it."

Jess whipped her head around to face him. "Are you *insane*? You know that's not what I meant."

"Listen, Jess," he brought his tone down. "All I need is to know that you care. That you want this as much as I do."

They were nearing his parents' house. Jess wondered if he would've backed down had they been going anywhere else. She suspected not. He didn't want his parents seeing trouble in paradise and asking too many questions.

"So...you need me to declare my love for you to the world by adding your picture to a photo sharing app that I haven't used in over a year? To your earlier point, wouldn't that put me in jeopardy? It would make sense that neither of us should post about one another if you're worried about safety. After all, it is the *cartel* we're dealing with here."

"You know what. Forget it. You're right. That was juvenile of me. Maybe we should just both delete our accounts. That would probably be the smartest thing."

He exhaled long and slow as he pulled into his parents' driveway and cut the engine. Before she could climb out, he stopped her by grabbing her hand.

"I love you," he said as he looked at her with sorrowful eyes. "I hate upsetting you."

Jess didn't say anything, staring straight ahead.

"You forgive me?" He asked, giving her hand a squeeze.

"Yeah, just stop picking fights about stupid shit," Jess gave in, wanting to get out of the truck.

He laughed and moved his hand to squeeze her thigh playfully. "Okay, deal. Let's go eat."

CHAPTER THIRTY-TWO

FEBRUARY

Jess

Jess and Bryan were streaming a documentary on serial killers to decompress from a day of investigating and interrogating criminals, when Bryan said something that turned Jess's blood cool in her veins. The forensic psychologist being interviewed on the TV was waxing eloquent about how murderers choose their murder weapons.

"The best way to kill someone is to make it look like suicide," Bryan commented before popping half a chocolate-chip cookie in his mouth. "You can always find a reason for someone to kill himself if you have enough information on him. That or salt."

"Salt?" Jess inquired.

"It's naturally occurring in the body. Allowing you to hide your murder weapon in plain sight." He let that sit for a moment before adding, "There's probably enough in the kitchen to kill both of us."

Jess wasn't a stranger to death and murder. Her firm had defended men and women who had committed all sorts of heinous acts. That kind of evil came with the territory, but her position as one of the trial attorneys had insulated her from some of the grislier details of the cases her office took on. The 3L interns and paralegals spent more time analyzing the crime scene photos and autopsy reports. They boiled it down to the particulars Jess needed to know, while she focused more on formulating the best strategy for how to present the evidence. Still, she had seen and heard evil. And something about Bryan's comment didn't sit right with her. A small twinge in her chest told her that he might not be simply spitting facts for shits and giggles. But she didn't know how to respond, so she turned her attention back to the documentary.

Bryan injected again a minute later, "The best way to dispose of a body is to chop it up and disperse it through the woods. Animals eat it. Learned that from a serial killer I interviewed." He paused to eat another cookie. "Especially in an area where there's hogs. They'll eat everything including hair and teeth."

"What if that's not an option?" As uncomfortable as Jess was with his comments, part of her was intrigued, and her legal mind was always eager for more information on how to bolster a case.

"Assuming you don't have a vat of hydrochloric acid lying around, water would probably be your next best option," Bryan answered. "The longer anything, a body, evidence, a weapon," he lists off, "sits in water, the less likely any biological evidence can be pulled from it."

"Good to know," Jess replied in a sarcastically light tone, hoping it would cover up the fact that she was creeped out.

The episode ended, and she got up and started making sure anything that had a lock in the house was secured.

Bryan's phone went off in the kitchen, and he popped up to retrieve it. She heard him answer, and the back door in the kitchen swung open, the blinds banging against the window. It wasn't news to Jess that investigators worked around the clock, but still, the number of after-hours calls seemed excessive.

"Who's that?" She raised her voice from the living room.

He paused just outside the door frame. Jess had never pressed him on who he talked with, so the question probably caught him by surprise. He tapped on his screen—muting himself—and explained, "Eli's getting divorced." He grabbed the door and shut it behind him before she could respond.

She wondered why he needed to go outside for that kind of conversation. Jess didn't know his wife outside of seeing her at a basketball game once and couldn't even remember her name.

Irritated and still feeling unnerved from his comments, Jess decided to head upstairs and run a bath. She stopped in the kitchen first to refill her wine glass.

"Come on, boy," she called to Piggy as she headed back through the living room for the stairs. He launched from his bed and beat her up the stairs.

She ran the hot water on full blast and stripped off her clothing. Piggy made himself comfortable on the mat in front of the vanity with a bone, while Jess debated which bath essentials to use. She normally opted for Epsom salts to soak out any muscle tension, but Bryan's salt comment made her reach for the liquid bubble bath instead. After pouring a healthy amount straight underneath the water stream, she grabbed her phone and scrolled mindlessly through apps and updates while she waited for the water to cool down enough for her to get in.

She couldn't shake the comments he'd made. Or maybe it was the delivery that bothered her more. Something in his tone felt sinister. With her phone still in hand, she debated texting Stacey.

But what would I say? Bryan made a comment about salt being used as a murder weapon, is that weird?

Jess's trial attorney mind kicked in again, and she reviewed the arguments on both sides. From the outside looking in, one might conclude it was a completely harmless comment, since he was a homicide investigator and has seen worse murders than salt overdose—officially called hypernatremia, according to the Google search she'd just conducted. And maybe that's all it was.

She was also nervous about alerting Stacey to anything. If questions started being asked and Bryan found out, he might overreact like he did with social media incident.

Is that normal? Why do I need to worry so much about what upsets him?

Jess combed through her memory, revisiting her past relationships to see if she could remember feeling this way with someone before.

Her thoughts were interrupted by the back door closing downstairs and Piggy's head popping up at the sound with a snort. He must have finished his call. Dipping a toe in the water, the temperature had cooled enough that she could step in and try to let the water wash away the worries.

CHAPTER THIRTY-THREE

Jess

Jess took Nina to an afternoon doctor's appointment Ruth couldn't make and decided to take the rest of the day off. She sat on the garage floor with her back against the wall, surrounded by her tools and a small heater since the door was open to let fumes out. Scrolling through her social media accounts, she followed a few more DIY furniture restoration pages. After a few minutes of virtual idea-gathering, she stared passed her phone at the antique hutch sitting on the other side of the garage from her. Mocking her. It didn't matter how much paint stripper she used, the hideous red someone had painted it lingered like blood stains. She saw it sitting in someone's yard at an estate sale as she and Bryan were driving down Atlanta Highway to dinner last week and convinced him to turn around and get it. The piece had a lot of potential, and Jess had started it with high hopes.

She dropped her phone into her lap and shifted her gaze from the hutch to the can of paint stripper sitting on the ground next to it. She could see the words "Highly Flammable" in bright red block letters written on the can. She considered looking for a matchbox instead of a paint scraper. The piece had been difficult since she'd started working on it a few days ago. First, the hardware had been difficult to remove. Then, as she worked to strip the paint from the counter on the lower half of the hutch, she figured out why someone had painted it. There were several rings that looked like water stains underneath the red. After that frustrating discovery, she'd left the project alone for a couple days.

Her common sense prevailed, and she refrained from reducing the piece to ashes. Grabbing her scrapper, she pushed herself off the floor and got back to work.

When Bryan pulled in half an hour later, she was still at it. The red was almost gone from three sides, but so was the paint stripper, and the water stains remained.

Jess shook the can as Bryan walked into the garage with a couple of black convenience store bags in hand.

"Looks like you're making some progress, babe," he said as he approached.

"I think I've inhaled more fumes than a meth lab today." She dropped her paint scraper on the ground, letting it clatter on the concrete. "Do you mind grabbing me some more of this?" She lifted the can to show him.

"Sure," he said, taking the can from her. "I should be able to get some tomorrow."

"They sell it at the hardware store off Highway 53. The other stores don't have that brand."

"Does it matter?"

"Yeah, it's the only thing eating through the paint. The first stuff I tried was less effective than tap water."

"Then I'll get you some muriatic acid instead," he said as he passed behind her and smacked her on the ass en route to the door.

"What's that?" Jess asked, following him inside.

"It's better at stripping stuff," he explained, kicking his shoes off just inside the door.

"Have you used it before?"

"No, but if it's more effective than bleach at wiping DNA from crime scenes, I'm confident that paint doesn't stand a chance. Just make sure you dilute it with water first."

Jess couldn't argue with that logic, so she dropped her plea.

After dinner, she grabbed a few twenties out of her purse off the kitchen counter and held them out to Bryan who'd already parked it on the couch.

"What's that for?" He asked over the sound of Netflix loading on the TV.

"The acid," she explained.

"Ah, don't worry about it," he waved his hand dismissively and turned his attention to the TV.

"Is it expensive?"

"It's not a big deal. We can work out an arrangement for reimbursement," he said with a wink over a deviant smile.

Jess let her arm drop back to her side and cocked her head to the side. "Bryan," she said, her tone saturated with exasperation.

He looked up at her. "If I take the cash, will you shut up so we can watch a movie?"

"Yes."

Without a word he extended his palm toward her, and she handed over the bills.

"Now sit down and let's pick something," he said, slapping the seat cushion next to him on the couch before dropping the cash on the coffee table in front of him.

Jess kicked off her shoes and dropped them in the tray by the door leading to the garage where Bryan had stashed his earlier. She used the hair elastic on her wrist to swoop her hair up on top of her head as she plopped down on the couch beside him. Thankfully, he picked a comedy. She was tired of murders.

After the movie, she was cleaning up the kitchen before bed and rolled her eyes at the grocery bags Bryan had left on the counter unpacked. He'd already gone upstairs.

Hope there isn't anything that needs refrigeration, she thought as she opened the first bag. The contents stopped her in her tracks. Four boxes of Norton's salt.

You gotta be fucking kidding me.

Jess wanted to scream. She wanted to pound her fists on the counter. Why would he come home with a shit ton of salt after his comments the night before unless he was trying to make a point or drive her crazy?

She left the bags on the counter without unloading them and climbed straight into bed, not wanting to interact with Bryan anymore that night, so she pretended to be asleep when he emerged from the bathroom after his shower.

She thought about ignoring it, not giving him the reaction he was looking for. Ultimately, her stubbornness won, and she decided to confront him the next morning.

Bryan was already in the kitchen making some oatmeal when Jess came downstairs. She made a beeline for the coffee maker without looking at him or answering his "good morning."

"Are you planning on canning something?" She asked as she measured out the beans and added them to the grinder on the top of the coffee maker.

"What?" he asked over his shoulder as he stirred the oats on the stove.

"All that salt you got. The only time I've seen someone buy that much was my grandmother when she had dozens of jars of beans from her garden to can for the winter," she said as she swung her hand toward the bags containing the salt on the island between them.

As he started to reply, Jess slammed her finger down on the button to start the grinder, drowning him out. She had no interest in his reply, which was probably something like "the store had a BOGO sale." It was too convenient that he'd made those comments about salt the other night and then showed up with boxes of it the next day. She couldn't help but feel he was trying to send some kind of a message to her.

But why would he do that?

"Did you hear me?" Bryan asked from the table where he'd sat down to eat.

"What?" she busied herself by refilling the decorative honey jar on the counter while the coffee brewed so she didn't have to turn around and face him.

"I got it so you can remove the water stains from the hutch. I read through some blogs, and they said salt might help," he explained in a calm tone.

Jess's mind went fifteen directions at once. She had been sure he was trying to mess with her. But he seemed so sincere in his answer.

Maybe I'm being too sensitive.

Still, her chest felt tight.

She tried to shake it off and changed the subject. "I'll be ready to start painting it soon. Do you think I should paint it cream or blue?" Jess already knew she was going to go with the cream.

"The blue would look nice," Bryan said through a mouth full of oatmeal.

"Yeah, I really like it, but I'm not sure that it will look good with the sage walls."

"Then go with cream," he offered.

"Want to help me paint it?"

"I'm not very good at that kind of thing," Bryan commented pitifully.

"You can paint the back then," Jess suggested.

"Why don't I cheer you on from the sidelines?"

"Fair enough."

"Speaking of sidelines, basketball is starting up again. We're going to practice next Monday before the season starts," Bryan informed her as he put on his shoes in one of the kitchen table chairs.

It was Tuesday. Jess mentally checked her calendar. "I'm going to have dinner with Nina and Ruth Monday for Ruth's birthday."

"What time?"

"I'm not sure yet," Jess said.

"We're not starting until seven-thirty, so you can come after," Bryan said with a tone that indicated the matter was settled.

Before she could respond, Bryan got a text on one of his phones, which kept him busy on the way out the door. She heard his truck door close and the engine crank, which reignited her anger. He could leave without saying goodbye, but Jess got treated like a Gitmo prisoner if she didn't say "I love you" when she hung up the phone.

It might be an Irish coffee kind of morning.

She didn't have time to stay mad. David Jessup had finally been brought to Gwinnett County Jail, and she anticipated it was going to be a long day.

CHAPTER THIRTY-FOUR

Bryan

Bryan was getting brain fog. He'd been working on a robbery case in the office all morning, and it was starting to feel like he was moving backward. His CIs on his other cases haven't had good news for him in weeks, and he felt like Jess had started pushing away from him; he was in a shitty mood to say the least.

Deciding to run it off, he went to his truck and grabbed his workout clothes. He changed in the bathroom, grabbed his sunglasses off his desk, and headed out the back door. The air was chilly, but the sun was out, making it a tolerable temperature. The narrow downtown grid had a couple streets with some decent inclines that he knew would get his blood pumping. His knees protested for the first quarter mile but settled down once he warmed up.

Once he found his stride, he thought about Jess and why she seemed so obstinate lately like she had been with the social media situation. They'd had good days since then, but it was still eating him up, and he didn't want it happening again. That was always the problem he ran into with the independent types. They forgot how to operate inside relationships. He didn't get why it was so hard for them to understand it was for their own good. The times Jess pushed back on him was just him trying to look out for her.

As a cop, he saw things most wouldn't notice and knew things most didn't want to. He had a unique perspective, which was an asset. Jess must have felt like it was putting a cramp in her style, and he was getting pretty fucking sick of it. But he knew he had to be patient with her, and she would come around. And, besides, he always liked a challenge. Like breaking a mule.

After a couple laps traversing the downtown streets, he took a short break and peeled his sweaty shirt away from his body. He checked his watch; it was almost four. Jess would probably be home soon. He decided he would pop into the small florist shop on the downtown strip, then head across the railroad tracks to surprise her when she got home.

CHAPTER THIRTY-FIVE

Jess

Jess pulled in the driveway and took a deep breath before cutting the engine. As anticipated, it had been a long and heavy day at the jail with David Jessup.

David was middle-aged now with graying hair. He'd been in jail for more than twenty-five years and had maintained that he was innocent every step of the way. At first glance, Jess tried to disprove his claim. She never believed anyone off the bat. But the man had a compelling story. He'd become a jailhouse lawyer, drafting his own post-conviction relief motions, and helping others do the same. After the initial pleasantries, Jess got straight to the point and asked David why he was in jail if he wasn't the one who did the crime.

He took a deep breath, stared down at his shackled hands, and then started telling a story that Jess could've finished for him; she'd heard it too many times in her career. It started with a young boy from a troubled home and ended with a life sentence.

David had a long history of run-ins with the law that started in middle school. None of the offenses were felonies or violent. But he was a pain in the police's ass until he wasn't. One day they figured out they could use him. As soon as there was a murder that could be blamed on him, the police jumped on the opportunity. He was quickly booked, arraigned, and tried for murder. He couldn't afford the six-figure bond, so he remained in jail during the pendency of his trial.

The prosecution built its case on circumstantial evidence, and they did a damn good job of pulling something out of almost nothing. They convinced the jury that this man must have been the murderer, because he was spotted in the area the night a woman was robbed and stabbed to death by a man about David's age, build, skin color, and someone dressed in dark-colored sweatpants like David had been wearing the day of the murder. David's appointed defense team did the best they could, but the jury believed the story the prosecution crafted and convicted him.

During his incarceration, he missed his children's birthdays, the deaths of his parents, and countless other significant life events. All while the true offender was out living the moments of life David was missing. This was the kind of case that inspired the making of documentaries. The ones that breed public resentment for law enforcement and the court system. A few bad actors tarnishing the reputation of the entire judicial system.

Jess was trying to change that with the review unit. She felt like she could put pressure on the field in a dignified way to bring positive change. She knew you caught more flies with honey than vinegar, so she wanted to make sure the pressure was applied in a way that allowed them to save face and not fight the conviction review movement. But it was going to be a process, and now that she was home, it was time to put that on the shelf for the day.

Grabbing her briefcase, she went inside. Her briefcase hit the nearest chair, and she flung her heels off in separate directions. Piggy came racing toward her, sliding into her shins in a flurry of snorts and whines.

"Looks like someone escaped their crate today, huh?" She looked over to his crate across the kitchen underneath the window to see his crate door wide open. "If you tore anything up, you're going to be in a world of trouble. I guess we'll have to get some clips to secure that door, you little evil genius," she cooed in a baby voice as she bent down to scratch him under his muzzle.

Her stomach rumbled, and she made her way over to the fridge. She immediately groaned after opening it. They were down to a wilted bag of lettuce, orange juice, a few water bottles, four eggs, and various condiments.

She grabbed her phone out of her briefcase to start a grocery list. Passing through the living room en route to the stairs, she got the fright of her life.

"Hey, babe," came from behind.

Her phone went flying out of her hand, and she stubbed her toe on the coffee table as she whirled around to find Bryan sitting in a chair in the corner. She slapped her hand over her chest and tried to catch her breath.

Bryan chuckled and stood up. He held a bouquet of white roses.

"Are you trying to kill me? You almost gave me a heart attack."

Bryan grinned. "I wanted to surprise you."

"Consider me surprised," Jess said as she looked back down at the flowers in his hand. "Those are pretty."

He held them out toward her. "Not as pretty as you."

"Thank you. Let me put them in some water," she said as she took them and headed for the kitchen.

She stopped short and turned around. "Where's your car?"

"At the office. I went for a jog."

"Oh..." she turned to find a vase in the kitchen.

Of course there wasn't one, because Jess didn't think to throw one in her car leaving Dallas, and Bryan's bachelor pad had probably never seen anything glass that wasn't a beer bottle.

"I might have to run to Nina's and borrow a vase."

He'd followed her in the kitchen and grabbed a water bottle out of the fridge.

"Nah, we'll go get one. You'll need one, anyway. Those definitely won't be the last flowers you'll get," he said with a smile. "We'll grab some dinner, find you a vase, then you can drop me back at my truck."

"Okay. Let me change. Will you let Piggy out, and then put him up in his crate?"

"Sure."

Jess quickly slipped into a pair of yoga pants and a V-neck leisure shirt. She thought Bryan's surprise move was kind of odd but tried to set the feeling aside and focus on the gesture. The flowers were also a nice touch. She located a light jacket and a pair of socks, and padded downstairs to find her tennis shoes. Once she was ready, they stepped outside, and Bryan made a beeline for the driver's side, wasting no time with the push start. Jess slid in and started scrolling through DIY blogs for furniture restoration tips as Bryan steered them out of the driveway.

Out of nowhere, Bryan asked, "Why is your passenger seat heat on?"

Jess looked down to the dial beside the gear shifter, and then up to Bryan. He didn't return the look but instead kept his eyes on the road with a steel grip on the steering wheel. He had the same emotionless expression he'd worn when he drilled into her about why she didn't post photos of the two of them on social media.

"It was already on when we got in," he went on.

Jess turned to face ahead and took a deep breath. The grateful feeling she'd been trying to focus on was instantly replaced with dread. She knew he wasn't going to believe her—that he was already running scenarios in his head, and none of them were innocent. Her palms grew moist, and she shifted uncomfortably in her seat. Jess forced herself to stop, knowing it made her look guilty, even though she wasn't.

"I used it to try and keep lunch warm the other day," she finally said.

Bryan paused for a moment and looked at her before speaking. "You serious right now?"

The question was rhetorical, but there was nothing Jess could do other than to steel herself for the imminent barrage of accusations and subsequent interrogation.

"Are you serious?" He enunciated each word, his eyes never leaving the road.

"Stop, Bry," Jess pleaded softly. She'd now learned the only way out of a Bryan investigation was through it.

"Why are you fidgeting right now?" He asked as he motioned to her hands in her lap. She looked down to see she was twisting her engagement ring with the neighboring fingers. "You're acting like a criminal. I don't know why you think you can lie to me."

Jess turned her face to the window so he wouldn't see the corners of her mouth turn down as she fought the tears bubbling up in her eyes. But that part of Jess that would fight back was tired. Tired of having these conversations. Tired of not being believed and having the truth twisted to make her seem like the bad guy for small or nonexistent issues like starting to eat her meal before Bryan sat down. She argued for a living, and he'd still managed to wear her down.

"Oh, so you're going to try the silent treatment on me today? Yeah, that'll work." He laughed a cold, humorless laugh.

Jess kept her gaze out the window and tried to keep herself as calm as possible. The silence was even worse because she knew it wasn't over. The air in the car felt energized, like it held a charge. He was winding up, and she couldn't gauge how much when he wasn't saying anything.

Without warning, a loud snap reverberated through the car. Jess's head whipped around instinctively to find Bryan had slammed his water bottle on the floorboard between his knees. The plastic top had broken, allowing water to spread across the floor mat in a maze.

"I don't know *WHY*...you always have to do this. Why you have to ruin a good day. Why you have to lie to me. Just tell me who you had in the car, Jess. I'm sick of your sneaky shit. Just tell me and get it over with."

She felt like a perp sitting in a dark room on a cold metal chair with a bright light shining directly in her eyes, and Bryan was the cop who was there to get one thing and one thing only: a confession.

Breaking her silence, she fought to keep her tone even. "Bryan, I haven't had anyone in the car. I turned it on when I went to pick up lunch for the unit the other day. We got soup, and I wanted to keep it warm."

Wrong answer.

Abruptly, Bryan stomped on the brakes and whipped them into the right-hand turning lane. The maneuver was violent, slamming Jess's chest against the seatbelt and her left knee into the center console. Bryan aggressively shifted them into park. He gripped the wheel with his left hand and twisted to face Jess.

"Tell me," he demanded.

"There's nothing else to tell you. Can we please get going? There was no one in the car with me," Jess insisted, her voice rising defensively. The anger growing inside of her was the only thing keeping her from crying.

"You know I'll find out if there was anyone in here with you."

Jess fixed her eyes on the road ahead. "I'm glad you don't have anything better to do with your time than chase ghosts."

"You might regret saying that."

Jess's head snapped around to face him, like her neck was on a swivel. "What do you mean?"

"Just hope I don't find anything," was all he offered in response.

For some reason, her mind turned to Topher. She hadn't seen him in a while and wondered if he could help. They weren't hanging out with him like they had been in the fall. It seemed like that stopped as soon as they got engaged. Jess figured it was the hustle and bustle of the holidays, but now she was starting to suspect there could be more to it. Maybe Bryan didn't want her around Topher for some reason.

She didn't know how quickly that was about to change.

CHAPTER THIRTY-SIX

Topher

Topher hadn't called Jess to set up a meeting in the fall to compare notes on Enrique Suarez as he'd intended. Other cases with bigger fires to put out had taken him away from looking into Bryan. Murder rates usually climbed around the holidays. For some reason, the magic of the most wonderful time of the year inspired more people to end a life than normal. Topher also knew that if he backed off and gave Bryan enough rope, he'd end up hanging his own ass. His hands would eventually get so dirty that Sheriff Daddy and his ex-partner at the helm of the GBI wouldn't have a shot in hell at getting his son off the hook this time. And then Bryan and Jess had gotten engaged, which made things infinitely more complicated.

After he learned of their engagement, he thought about nixing his investigation into Bryan's secrets all together but swiftly decided that could never be an option. For one, he wasn't going to willingly let a dirty cop stay on his team. Topher didn't give a damn if Bryan was related to the president. He wouldn't turn a blind eye like everyone else had been doing. But the second reason was the one that kept him up at night. He wouldn't be able to live with himself if anything happened to Jess.

Cartels were brutal. They had a never-ending stream of creative ways to torture and kill people. If someone was in their way when they wanted to expand their territory, they would shoot them execution-style, or worse—whatever got the job done was fine. When they wanted to send a message to a person or entity that was disrupting their agenda, they would torture victims mercilessly before finally offing them. Because Jess was tied to law enforcement, Topher feared she could suffer the second fate if Bryan pushed his luck too far, whatever he was doing.

Topher looked forward to seeing her when Bryan mentioned dinner, or when they came out on the boat with him. He couldn't care less about Bryan, but he needed him close to monitor any changes in his behavior and to see if he would slip up and say something after a couple of beers that Topher could use to further his investigation on him.

Uncovering new pieces of information was painfully slow. He might learn one new piece of information a week, and some of them didn't mean much. Bryan was covering his tracks well. In fact, Topher was finding more out by the absence of information available to him.

He was torn between telling Jess or keeping her in the dark. Ultimately, he decided he had to tell her. It was the better of the two horrible options. He didn't want to scare her too much by telling her everything or run the risk of coming on so strong she wouldn't believe him. She might even have her own suspicions and be able to help Topher fill in some blanks. But if she took what he told her and ran to Bryan with it, he would know he couldn't say anything else to her and would have to finish his investigation alone.

Regardless, he needed to get to Jess for his conscience's sake. And maybe there were other reasons he wasn't ready to admit to himself... yet. Either way, Suarez had recently been caught, and it gave him the perfect opportunity to call a meeting with her.

When Topher left the Atlanta office, the clock on the dash said it was nearing noon. He grabbed his phone out of the cup holder, called the Gwinnett County Justice Building, and asked for the DA's office.

CHAPTER THIRTY-SEVEN

Jess

Topher called Jess at her office, wanting to meet with her to discuss what she knew about Enrique Suarez, the man they'd discussed on the lake last fall. He'd been caught in California and extradited to Georgia. He was being held in Gwinnett while awaiting trial, facing a combined total of more than two hundred years in prison if convicted on all counts, which included murder and RICO charges. Jess didn't know much outside of his charges, but she'd heard some chatter around work about it, so she agreed to lunch. Topher suggested a place known for its burgers just off the square in Lawrenceville, not far from the justice building where her office was located.

They pulled into the parking lot at the same time. Topher waited for Jess to park and then pulled in next to her sedan. He waited at the back of his bureau car for her to grab her briefcase before they went inside.

He stepped ahead of her to get the door, and Jess noticed the slight scent of soap and the veins webbing his forearms that someone with a fiancé probably shouldn't be eyeing too hard.

Topher asked for a table outside on the heated patio, which was empty as the air still had a nip in it.

Once they'd sat down and ordered drinks, Jess asked him what he needed from her, referring to Suarez.

"Anything helps," he answered.

She told him everything she'd heard through the grapevine, only pausing when the waiter dropped their drinks and took their food orders. Topher listened intently and sipped his beer, keeping his eyes on her as she spoke. Jess noticed he didn't take notes, and he didn't ask as many follow-up questions as she'd anticipated.

Topher shifted forward in his seat, resting his arms on the table. "Thanks. I need to talk to you about something else."

Jess set her tea down. "Oh? And that is?"

"Did you mention this to Bryan?" He motioned between them with a wave of his hand.

Jess's brows pinched together in confusion. "No, I haven't talked to him since I left home this morning. What's going on?"

He leaned in and dropped his voice. "You know the kind of cases we're dealing with right now involve some cartel members, and we've been briefed by our Atlanta office and the FBI on the level of risk involved." He paused for a second, and his eyes narrowed slightly. "Bryan was more dismissive of that information than I'd like to see. I wanted to let you know that it's wise, and I recommend, you watch your back, especially when you're out. Don't have the same routine every day for things like your route to work. Habits make you predictable. At least until we get some of our current cases closed and behind us. And please don't mention any of this to him. Like I said, he wasn't hearing it, and the last thing I need is fighting within the office. I'm sure he's told you how swamped we are right now. Anyway, I thought you should know so you can keep yourself safe."

Not knowing how to respond, she managed, "I'll keep that in mind."

They left it at that, Topher paid the check, thanked Jess, and they left. She drove back to work with her thoughts swirling like a hurricane. At one point she grabbed her phone to call Bryan, but she stopped herself, deciding it would be better to talk to him that night when he wasn't distracted at work or around Topher. At her desk, she tried to look like she was doing something, but she couldn't focus. She had no idea how much time she'd spent looking like she was trying to organize her files when Shauna interrupted her.

"You okay?"

"What?" Jess looked up to find her standing in the doorway.

"I asked if you were okay," Shauna explained with a concerned look on her face, leaning against Jess's office door.

"Uh, yeah. Just a little...overwhelmed," Jess answered, still shuffling papers around on her desk with no objective.

Shauna pushed herself off the doorframe and took a step into the office. "You're looking pale. Maybe you should call it a day. I can handle anything you have on your calendar this afternoon."

Jess had stopped fake organizing and was holding her face with her hands, thumbs cupped under her jaw and index fingers pressing into her temples. She looked up at Shauna, tempted to take her offer.

"Seriously," Shauna went on. "You need to head out. Things are only going to heat up from here on in these cases." She waved at the files in front of Jess. "You know how it goes once the motions we're preparing get filed. All hands on deck."

"You're right," Jess said at the top of a long exhale.

Shauna had a point; the workload had the potential to get hectic in the coming weeks. Things were going to start moving quickly in the David Jessup case, and they'd also taken on three more cases. Tomorrow Jess's schedule was full of interviews to find a paralegal to help her with drafting and filing motions, and another part-time investigator to help Shauna sort through existing and collect new evidence. With the unit gaining ground on the Jessup case and pulling in good press coverage as a result, Jack had been finally able to secure a little more funding. It wasn't much, but she would make sure it lasted through Jessup's case—even if that meant forgoing her own pay.

Handing the ropes off to Shauna, Jess headed home. She started a load of laundry, cleaned the kitchen, fed and walked Piggy. Still, her mind wouldn't let her think about anything else besides her lunch with Topher. Deciding a run might do her some good, she laced up her tennis shoes and left out the garage door.

She tried to pound out the intrusive thoughts that had been plaguing her all afternoon with each step, but no matter how hard she tried to keep her focus on the scenery, a new question would pop up every couple of minutes.

Why would Bryan be dismissive of danger that could impact me?

Is Topher making it up to drive a wedge between Bryan and me? Does he want to date me?

It didn't match his character. Not to mention the fact that Topher seemed largely uninterested in a relationship based on Jess's observations. She'd never seen him look twice at a girl when she and Bryan had gone to dinner or hung out on the boat with him.

Does he want to take Bryan down to reduce competition for his next career move?

Jess couldn't come up with any plausible explanation as to why Topher wouldn't be telling her the truth. After running three miles around town, purposefully avoiding the area surrounding the police station, she went home and showered before Bryan got home.

I have to ask him.

Jess had decided to confront her fiancé despite what Topher had said. But he came through the door clearly distracted and barely acknowledged her. Jess sensed the same heavy charge saturating the air that was in the car during seat heat gate, giving her pause. All the words she'd been planning to say slammed against the back of her teeth. She forced them back down with a swallow.

He ate his dinner quickly, not saying much, and then went upstairs to change into workout clothes. Jess heard him answer a phone call on his ear buds as he stepped into the garage. She couldn't make out what he was saying over the sound of him hitting the punching bag.

Not knowing what to do, she went into her office upstairs and tried to make sense of some court transcripts she'd brought home, but her images of drug deals and cartel headlines kept intrusively invading her mental space. After maybe fifteen minutes of fighting to stay focused, she realized work was futile and decided to go to Nina's.

She went downstairs to find Bryan and tell him where she was going. But the low sound of his voice made her pull up short just before she opened the door to the garage. He was still on the phone, and she could just barely make out what he was saying.

"Stop calling me about this shit. You know where to find me."

Jess waited a few seconds before she opened the door and found him slamming his fists into the punching bag again.

"I'm going to Nina's!" She yelled over the sound of the chains that suspended the bag snapping with each hit.

"What?" he asked, pulling out an earbud.

"Nina has dessert for us. I'll be back in a few."

Based on the thin line his lips were pulled into, he was clearly upset at whatever news he'd gotten on the phone call and didn't protest her departure.

She drove past her aunt's and went to the gas station to fill up her tank, gathering her thoughts before having to act like nothing was wrong when she got to Nina's.

Ruth was bringing Nina out onto the porch as Jess approached the front steps. Her aunt had a jar of steaming tea in one hand and pushed her walker clumsily with the other.

"Nina, it's *February*." Jess scolded her aunt.

"I've *got* to get out of that house," Nina said resolutely, pointing to the door behind her. "Ruth is going to get me some blankets, and I'm going to sit my ass out here for a few minutes and get me some fresh air. If I wanted to stay inside until spring, I would live up where the yankees do with all that awful snow on the ground." Her jowls jiggled as she finished with a curt nod.

Ruth looked at Jess with apologetic eyes and a shrug as if to say, "I tried."

Jess sighed and helped her aunt into her wicker chair. "Well, I would try to talk you out of it, but I know how that would end."

Ruth went inside and reappeared with two comforters that they cocooned around Nina before disappearing inside again to get her nightly medications ready.

Jess perched on the porch swing, trying to stretch the tension out of her neck and caught sight of the robin's egg blue ceiling.

"What's the story with the blue? Isn't it associated with an old wives' tale or legend or something?" Jess asked her aunt.

Nina finished her drink and set the glass on the wicker table beside her chair before explaining, "It's a tradition that started in the low country. It originated with the slaves if I'm not mistaken. The idea was that ghosts, or 'spirits' as they called them, couldn't enter a house with a blue ceiling." She pointed upward. "It's often called 'haint blue.' Something about spirits not being able to cross bodies of water, or the ghosts would think the ceiling was the sky and pass through it instead of entering the home. *So*...they would paint their porch ceilings with haint and other hues of blue for protection against evil. Between it and my Bible, ain't nothing getting in this house," Nina declared with a chuckle. Her tone then turned serious before she said, "Speaking of ghosts, you look like someone just walked over your grave."

"Hmmmm?" Jess had zoned out momentarily, squinting up at the pale blue ceiling and wondering if the legend had any credence.

"I said you look like someone just walked over your grave. Is everything alright?" Nina's brows furrowed behind her glasses.

"Yeah, sorry," Jess shook the thought off and snapped back into the present. "That's neat. I didn't realize that's where the blue came from."

The uneasiness that had started creeping on her since lunch with Topher was getting harder to keep at bay. But the more she pushed it away, the more it pushed back. The temperature wasn't the only thing making her shiver.

192

CHAPTER THIRTY-EIGHT

MARCH

Jess

Jess found she preferred interviewing murderers to other criminals. Of course, some maintained they were innocent even after conviction, but with others, the usual pretenses were dropped. They may not come right out and say they took a life, but often they didn't deny it. And sometimes, they did come right out and say it. Jess didn't always know whether it was the truth, or for "street cred," or because they were a bona fide psychopath. Jess wasn't sure which kind she was sitting across the table from in an interview room today—at his request—but she bet she would have him pinned by the end of their interaction.

His name was Scar. Legal name: Enrique Suarez. The man she'd discussed with Topher at lunch the week before. His moniker came from the ugly brown scar that ran down the left side of his face from the outside corner of his eye toward his ear. But that wasn't even the most interesting embellishment on his face, which was heavily inked. Jess's personal favorite was the black widow spider that looked like it was crawling out of his right eye.

"I understand you wanted to speak with me," Jess spoke first, scrolling through emails on her phone.

Despite his conviction, she wasn't worried about him hurting her. He was shackled at both his hands and feet, and a sheriff's deputy was posted up outside the door. The deputy had stayed in the room with them at first, but Jess politely sent him outside. Criminals didn't like to say much in front of cops for some reason, and Jess didn't want this to take any longer than necessary. She needed Scar to cut to the chase so she could get back to work.

"That's right," he spoke with a hint of a Latin accent.

Jess whipped out her phone and started checking her emails while she waited for him to talk. Even though she wasn't going to stay long, she also wasn't going to pander to a convicted felon to get him to speak.

Eventually, he filled the silence again. "Is this being recorded?"

"There're closed circuit cameras in every interview room thanks to your tax dollars. Well, I guess not yours as I take it you probably weren't disclosing your black-market funds to the state treasury or the IRS before you landed yourself in this fine establishment for the next few decades."

"A little presumptuous, don't you think?" He retorted.

Jess was impressed with his wit. This wasn't a garden variety criminal. He must've been higher up the cartel food chain. Definitely not a mule or a plug.

"Am I wrong?" She countered, dropping her phone down on the table between them. She clasped her hands on top of her crossed knee and met his gaze.

He let out a small chuckle that didn't reach his eyes. "I was asking about the cameras for your benefit. Not mine."

What the hell?

"I appreciate your consideration, but there's nothing I can do about the cameras." She kept her tone cool, disliking him toying with her.

"Fair enough. I've got some information you'll want to know. I heard you're the head of conviction review."

The ability of prisoners to obtain information never ceased to amaze Jess. Someone on the outside was clearly feeding this guy intel.

"I'm also late for my lunch break," Jess said as she picked her phone back up and returned to her emails, her patience beginning to wear thin.

"And I'm sure you're familiar with the Ravello murder case that's still open," Scar went on, unfazed by her bitchy tone.

She involuntarily looked up at him from her phone at the name of the man whose murder Bryan was investigated for, waiting for more.

"I've got your killer."

I doubt it. She learned early in her career convicts could be quick to pass along or fabricate information in exchange for early release.

"Even if you have information on his whereabouts for me, I have no power to commute your sentence," Jess informed him.

He wasn't fazed. "I know. I made peace with my fate long before I was even in custody."

"So, what's in it for you to rat someone out?"

"Justice for my brother," he answered.

She assumed he was referring to the gang member who Bryan suspected killed Thomas Ravello in the drive-by.

And take out some of the competition. Jess knew the gang wars weren't exclusive to the streets. The drama continued inside the cinder block walls.

When Jess didn't respond, he continued, "He didn't shoot Ravello, and he shouldn't go to jail for it or have to spend his life in hiding when the killer is in plain sight."

"Alright, give me the name." Jess conceded, expecting to hear the name of a rival gang member.

"Special Agent Whitely of the GBI."

The fuck?

Jess's heart rate spiked, and she was sure her face must've made some kind of twitch that betrayed her, but she held as steady as she could.

"I think you're familiar with that name?" he asked rhetorically with a glint in his eye and a smile, making the black widow look like it was creeping farther out of his eye.

Ten minutes later, Jess burst through the doors of the jail as fast as she could professionally maneuver in her designer pumps, pulling on her coat as she beelined for her car. The clacking of her heels was drowned out by catcalls and greasy pickup lines yelled by the inmates playing basketball in a highly secured court that was situated near the public entrance. Jess paid them no mind. She didn't even notice them. All her mental space was trying to process what Scar had just told her. She only caught bits and pieces of what he said after he dropped the bomb of Bryan's name on her. Even in her brain fog, she did clock him saying something about there being video evidence of Bryan murdering someone—or so he claimed.

She was already calling Topher before she made it to her car. Bryan had called him from her phone one time when he'd forgotten his at home, and she'd stored it in her contact list.

"Yeah?" he answered on the first ring.

"Where are you?" Jess demanded.

"Jess? I'm at headquarters in Decatur. Are you okay?"

Her breathing was labored. "We need to talk. Can you make your way to Lawrenceville?"

"Sure. I'll be there in half an hour."

"There's a pub on the square—"

"Yeah, McKenzie's."

"Meet me there," she said and hung up the phone as she swung open her car door, threw her briefcase across the console, and dropped into her seat.

She sat for a moment staring at nothing through the windshield with her hands gripping the wheel, replaying the encounter with Spider Face Scar. She combed her memory for what Bryan had told her last year when he mentioned the investigation on their third date. He hadn't said much about it.

Did Bryan kill someone?

Her mind couldn't compute this information. She needed Topher to weigh in and confirm this guy was bullshitting her, but an ominous feeling brewing low in her chest told her he might not be.

Jess got to the pub before Topher and ordered two beers at the bar. She gulped down one of them as soon as the bartender put it in front of her. The bartender didn't bat an eye. He'd probably seen much worse being in such close proximity to the justice building. Not every case was lost with grace.

Topher came through the door a few minutes later, pushing his sunglasses on top of his head, and eyed the empty glass with a quizzical expression as he approached and took the seat on the far side of her, so he was facing the door.

Jess opened her mouth to speak, but Topher stopped her with a raised hand.

He mouthed "phone" to her. She fished her cell out of her bag and handed it over. Topher whistled to catch the bartender's attention and slid both of their phones toward him as he approached. Without question, the man scooped them up and put them in a cabinet behind the bar underneath the colorful bottles of liquor glowing bright from the lighting behind them.

"Those are basically just listening devices that happen to make phone calls. Better safe than sorry," Topher explained.

Jess knew this meant he knew more than what they initially spoke about, and now she did, too.

She cut to the chase. "Tell me what's going on with Bryan."

He looked at her sideways. "What do you mean?"

"He's taking a lot of calls at night. He seems distracted and on edge. You know more than what you told me before. What is it?"

Topher paused for a moment, as if debating how to answer. He finally spoke, "I think he's working undercover on something I haven't signed off on."

"Does it relate to the Thomas Ravello incident?"

His brow lowered, shifting his neutral expression into one of concern. "It could. Pretty much everything in that world connects if you go down the rabbit hole far enough. Why are you asking? Is anyone following you?"

She caught him up on her meeting with Scar, including the part where he claimed to have access to video evidence of the Ravello shooting. "Who is he talking about getting justice for?"

Topher explained, "Jesus Silva, the suspected Hellcat driver. He's probably back in Central America. Ravello's murder isn't likely to be solved unless he's apprehended in the States for something else and pops up in CODIS or NDIS like what happened with Suarez."

"You think Suarez is telling the truth?" Jess asked.

Topher cocked his jaw to the side and thought for a moment without saying anything. "You said he's not trying to bargain?"

"No, didn't ask for shit. Said he wanted justice for his 'brother,' " Jess answered using air quotes. "How do we get our hands on that video if it's real?"

"I'll see what I can do—"

Dropping her voice and leaning toward him, Jess cut him off, "No, I'm not sitting around waiting to see if my fiancé is a *fucking murderer*, Topher."

"I've got a few folks in my contact list that might know something. And no, I'm not taking you with me." Topher looked her in the eyes as he finished.

"So, I'm supposed to go home to Bryan and act like nothing's happening while you chase this video down?"

Topher matched her posture and moved in so they sat knee-to-knee, their faces maybe a foot apart. His nearness made her nervous in a different kind of way than the nerves she was feeling about Bryan right now.

He started, "Okay, then amuse me. Tell me your plan. You going to drive around the lower side of Buford Highway in your high-end Benz and walk up to everyone that looks cartel related and start asking them questions?" He was referring to the impoverished neighborhoods where Ravello was killed. Not a place known for low crime rates. "Sounds like a great way to end up sex trafficked while your Benz finds its way to a chop shop."

Jess's eyes narrowed. He had a point. "So what do you suggest I do?"

Topher sat back in his seat. "Don't say anything to him. As far as we know, this guy is trying to play you. Trying to gain leverage to negotiate the pending charges that haven't gone to trial, yet. It might not even be real."

Jess ran a hand through her hair, as if trying to push everything away. "I don't know how I'm going to do that, Topher."

He leaned over and grabbed a cork coaster down the bar. "Okay, let's play this out." He tapped the bar with the coaster as he made each point. "If you confront him, you run the risk of him beating us to the video, if it's real, to cover his tracks and tie up any other loose ends out there. And he'll either deny it, *or*, if he admits to it, he'll claim self-defense."

Jess stared at him. Not knowing what to say as a numb feeling started to take hold of her chest.

Topher dropped the coaster and leaned in again. "Go home. Go to Dallas for a few days. You work remotely a lot anyway, don't you?"

Jess exhaled through her nose and stared at the bottles behind the bar for a moment. It wasn't a terrible idea.

"I have a cousin that's getting married this fall, and she's been asking me to get fitted for a bridesmaid's dress. I've just got to figure out a way to keep Bryan from trying to come."

"Let me handle that. I've got something that will keep him busy for a couple of days," Topher offered. "I have to schedule who goes to the quarterly training down at the state patrol this week. We can't all go at once. I'll send Bryan first."

"When?"

Topher waved down the bartender. "I can send him as soon as tomorrow."

The bartender picked up on Topher's cue and slid their phones back down the bar to Topher who handed Jess's to her and said, "Unlock it."

She input the password and handed it over without question.

"What's your aunt's caregiver's name" He asked.

"Ruth?" Jess's response came out as more of a question.

He typed and swiped for a minute before returning it to her.

"What did you do?"

"Put my current throwdown number in. It's saved under Ruth's contact as her home number," he said, pulling a flip phone straight out of 2003 from one of the side pockets of his tactical pants.

"And we're probably going to have to move this underground," Topher explained. "Text me only if you find out anything else, but don't say much. And if you're feeling unsafe, I'm only a call away. Otherwise, I'll come to you."

"Are you going to drink that?" Jess asked Topher, pointing to the remaining beer.

He pushed it toward her in response, and she downed fast enough to make a frat boy proud.

CHAPTER THIRTY-NINE

Topher

Topher pulled his personal cell out of his pocket and swiped to an app. Once it loaded, he could see Jess's location, a blue dot moving back toward the justice building. He had a small amount of guilt for not being upfront with her about everything he'd done with her phone. But the less she knew the better. She wouldn't have to act like she didn't know about something she had no knowledge of.

His mind shifted to Bryan and this alleged video.

There was only one way to find out if it was real. He pulled out his burner cell and started setting up meetings with each of his CIs that might have connections to Gwinnett or Suarez's gang.

Waiting for a call back from one of them, he phoned his old Army buddy, Josh, who now ran the crisis intervention division at the Georgia Public Safety Training Center in central Georgia, or "Gipstick," as the law enforcement community referred to it. Josh owed him a few favors since Topher had saved his ass more than a couple times, so he agreed for Bryan to be a late addition to his class starting the following day.

With that settled, he drove home and pulled his truck in the garage. He switched out his license plate on the back, added an NFL plate to the front, and slapped large "AT&T Contractor" magnets on his driver and passenger doors, taking care to cover up any identifying dents and scratches with the magnets. Then, he replaced the case folders in his passenger seat—those would have to wait—with a fluorescent vest and a hard hat off his workbench. Hopping back in the truck, he smashed the clicker to open the garage door, pulled out of his driveway, and headed south.

There was a Latin kitchen down Buford Highway that Topher used to visit from time to time when he worked in the Atlanta office. It had top-notch empanadas, and one of the cooks, Mateo, fed him information. He wasn't a CI, just a good dude that volunteered at his church on the weekends and wanted to help keep crime down in his community.

Topher entered through the back door, finding his target helping one of the busboys washing dishes.

Mateo turned around at Topher's footsteps. "Friend!" His face spread wide, revealing a smile that didn't have all its teeth. He'd been brought to the States when he was a child, so his accent was slight.

Topher had never given his name, and Mateo had never asked. Mateo turned to the young worker and gave him some instructions in Spanish. The boy nodded and disappeared through the door to the dining room.

Mateo grabbed a towel to dry his hands. "Long time no see, my friend."

"I've been busy." Topher shook his hand. "Listen, Thomas Ravello, what do you know?"

"Ah yes, very sad. I knew his dad when we were niños. Thomas was a good kid."

"Do you know who killed him?"

"No, but his *tío* put out a cash reward for information. I remember it was a lot of money, like over a hundred thousand or something like that. And then, it was weird, it just went away." Mateo finished with a shrug.

"Who was his uncle that was offering the reward?"

"I don't know his real name. They call him something like an animal." Mateo flapped his arms and whistled a "tweet" noise. "Something like a bird."

"Tweety Bird," Topher offered, feeling his trap muscles draw up with tension.

"That's the one!" Mateo exclaimed.

The hair on the back of Topher's neck stood up, but that's all he needed to know, so he changed the subject.

"One last question. You know anyone by the last name Silva?"

Mateo looked away and pulled his brow low, as though he was wracking his brain. "No, but I know where you can go where they might."

Mateo gave him the address to a convenience store. Topher thanked him and spent the rest of the evening and late into the night connecting the dots on Bryan's secrets, only pulling into his driveway when the sun was coming up.

CHAPTER FORTY

Jess

One of the first tenets law school had instilled in Jess was that a good attorney never asks a question to the opposing side that he or she didn't already know the answer to. She was back in her office after meeting Topher at McKenzie's, pacing the floor with the door closed.

Six times she'd grabbed her phone to call Bryan and six times she'd set it back down. She didn't know the answers to the questions she needed to ask him, and she wasn't sure she was prepared to hear them from the man she loved. There was something else at play, too. It was as if there was a black hole with Bryan at the center, and the gravitational pull was tugging harder at Jess with each passing second. But its draw didn't give her the warm fuzzies; it was a sinister feeling. As though she wouldn't be able to break away from Bryan if she tried. It wasn't all that different from the feeling when he brought home the salt.

All she was certain about at the moment was that she needed space, and she needed her mom.

Picking up her phone a seventh time, she texted Bryan that she had a meeting with Hardeman and expected it would run late. Then, she ordered food delivery and spent the rest of the afternoon booking a plane ticket and calling her mom and dad to let them know she was coming home for the weekend.

"You're going to fly to Texas to try on a dress?"

She'd just told Bryan she'd be leaving in the morning as she sorted through their bedroom closet to locate the one suitcase she'd brought from Dallas.

"Yeah, I've got to have time to get it altered if it doesn't fit. And besides, I haven't been back home since I moved out here."

"Can you go next week? I'd like to see your family again before the wedding," he asked behind her from the closet doorway.

"No, I think all the bridesmaids have to be at this appointment. They got us in at the last minute, and I don't want to start any drama for my cousin. It's only three days. Today's Wednesday—I leave in the morning, and I'll be back on Sunday. Not a long trip." Jess pulled an explanation out of thin air, disturbed at her ability to do so.

Bryan genuinely sounded sad. "Alright. Well, I'll miss you."

I'm sorry, what?

Jess was expecting a fight about her "hiding him," like he claimed during the social media argument. Every fiber of her being was braced, ready for action.

Bryan went downstairs as Jess packed her suitcase. She took a deep breath and tried to roll the tension out of her shoulders as she indiscriminately threw clothes in her bag. Once she was finished, she checked the time on her phone. It was only eight-thirty. She debated laying down for the night, but then Bryan called up the stairs saying he was waiting for her to start the show they had been streaming the past few evenings.

She changed into a t-shirt and sweats and joined him on the couch. He pulled her over into him and threw a blanket on top of her.

She couldn't help but study his hands as they worked the remote. Had they ended someone's life? Did he shoot Thomas? Was he capable of that kind of evil?

Bryan's comment from the fall when they were playing "courtroom" came back to her. *Good people do bad things with the right cocktail of conditions.*

Jess couldn't turn off her defense attorney brain no matter how hard she tried. It was constantly scanning for wherever there may be doubt. Maybe he did do it, but it was an accident, and he didn't want to lose his job. She had a hard time believing the man who'd accidentally bought her a menstrual cup trying to be sweet had killed someone in cold blood.

Sure, he had his moments. Jess didn't like when he went on a tangent about something minor and made them fight. But all couples fought. Right? And why would she trust a convicted killer over her fiancé?

The more she tried to make sense of the facts, the more she realized she didn't know what she didn't know.

CHAPTER FORTY-ONE

Jess dropped Piggy off at Nina's the next morning before heading to the airport. Ruth promised he wouldn't be a burden, and Jess knew Nina had missed him. On the drive to the airport, she kept checking her rearview for a cartel hitman, but it didn't seem like anyone was following her. She made it to the parking lot where Bryan had helped her book a parking spot the night before. While she was waiting at the gate, she called Stacey to set up dinner plans for that weekend and did her best to soak in the feeling of normalness that talking to her best friend brought her.

She stared at her engagement ring for what felt like half of the flight, trying to forget about the way Bryan held her on the couch last night. With her thumb, she twirled it around her finger mindlessly. A visual representation of how her insides felt. Her stomach coiled tighter at the thought of breaking off the relationship with Bryan. She didn't want to leave the man she loved. The man who made sure she liked her food before he started eating his in case she wanted to switch plates. Subconsciously, she knew it wouldn't end well if she left. But did that mean she needed to bury all her fears and intuitions and move along as if Topher and Scar had never put doubt in her mind?

Part of her wanted to take the ring off. See if it felt like a weight was lifted from her when she did. But she knew someone at home—her parents or Stacey—would notice it was missing and ask about it, so she left it on. Or, God forbid, she lost it. She didn't even want to think about how Bryan would handle that.

Her flight to Dallas arrived on time, and she picked up her rental car. Marcie had insisted on trying to take off work early to pick her up, but Jess wanted her own car so she wouldn't have to bum rides off her parents all weekend or rely on the handful of retiree Uber drivers that all knew her from her childhood. She would never be able to get them to stop chatting and "catchin' up" once she got in the car with them, and she didn't want anyone asking why she'd left Dallas.

She drove out of the city to her parents' house, feeling incredibly weird navigating the same streets she used to drive when she worked in one of the tall glass buildings downtown in another life. The narrow city streets with their flashy foreign cars slowly gave way to suburbia with its chain restaurants and minivans. Jess arrived home: a quiet neighborhood where the suburbs met the large, sprawling cattle ranches a couple hours after she'd touched down.

It was late afternoon by the time she was rolling her suitcase through the front door. Her dad greeted her with a hug and carried her bag upstairs to her old room while her mother wrapped up a phone call in the kitchen on her cell phone.

Jess didn't know who she was talking to, but she quickly hung up and came over to smother Jess in a tight hug.

"There she iiiiiiis." Her mother hugged Jess tightly, like she hadn't seen her in years.

Her and Jess's features favored one another, but Marcie was several inches shorter, so her arms wrapped low around Jess's waist.

Jess wanted so badly to tell her mother everything. How she was worried about what was going on with Bryan but didn't know what to do or even believe at this point. She wanted to tell her she was scared and how her insides twisted when she contemplated breaking off the relationship. But the words were held back by the same fear that wouldn't let her take her ring off. Fear of not knowing what Bryan would do but knowing what he was capable of as a highly trained homicide investigator at his physical peak. Not to mention his potential entanglement with the cartel.

"Are you hungry, dear?" Marcie asked, pulling away. "I just made some chicken salad, and we've got some leftover barbeque and a few other things in the fridge."

Her mother usually only made chicken salad when they were expecting company. Jess guessed she was considered company now.

"That sounds good, but I want to change first. Actually, I'll probably go ahead and shower, and then maybe we can go to dinner after instead."

"Okay, we can do that. I'll make sure your dad doesn't start any projects, so we'll be ready when you come back down."

Jess climbed the stairs and breathed in the scent of her old room as she entered. Her parents still used the same detergent with a floral fragrance, and the smell brought memories flooding back, making her a little emotional. This room was always her safe space growing up. It had been painted so many colors, including the rite of passage mint blue that all teenage girls in the early 2000s painted their rooms. Once she'd moved to college, her parents had painted the whole house, and the room now sported a smart beige color. She closed the door and flopped on the bed. Her mind told her she needed to text Bryan, or he would be checking up on her. But she held off a little longer. She wanted to soak in the feeling of normalcy and safety that had been slipping away ever since Topher approached her last week. Eventually she peeled herself off the bed, texted Bryan she'd made it to her parents, and headed for the shower.

She let the warm water penetrate her tense muscles and washed her hair. She wished she could stay there the rest of the day so she didn't have to face the questions she knew her parents would be asking over dinner about wedding planning. When they talked on the phone, Jess had been able to wiggle out of wedding talk, but she felt like she wouldn't be able to keep their curiosity at bay any longer. After all, she was an only child and knew her parents were looking forward to having grandchildren sooner rather than later. Jess stayed in the shower, stalling until the hot water ran out. After towel drying her hair, she got dressed and grabbed her blow dryer from her suitcase. She was about to start styling her hair when she heard a familiar voice downstairs.

No.

That can't *be him.*

Before she knew it, she was running down the staircase to investigate.

Her suspicions were confirmed when she made it to the kitchen and almost ran smack into Bryan's back.

"Bryan?" she asked in disbelief.

"Surprise," he said as he turned around to face her, flashing a wide smile.

It reminded Jess of a politician's smile. He could fool almost anyone with it. Maybe even a jury.

CHAPTER FORTY-TWO

Now Jess knew why her mother made the chicken salad.

"Oh, my goodness. I'm so glad I don't have to keep it a secret anymore," Marcie said. "I almost slipped up three times this morning and said something."

Act. Happy.

"Hey, babe," Jess said, trying to sound excited. "I can't believe you came all the way out here."

"Well, I figure it's a trip I need to get used to making. I expect we'll be spending half of our holidays out here now. And, lucky me, they had seats on the flight right after yours." He closed the distance between them to plant a kiss on her cheek.

"Oh, did you hear that?" Jess's mother excitedly asked her father, who had emerged from the garage. "Y'all will have to come for Christmas dinner this year. Maybe you can drive Nina out here for a week or two."

"Speaking of dinner and Aunt Nina, why don't y'all decide on where to eat, and I'll give Ruth a call to make sure all is well with Nina," Jess said, grabbing her phone off the kitchen counter to head outside.

She called Topher under Ruth's contact as soon as she got out of earshot of the house in the far part of the yard. She knew her mother would keep Bryan busy for a few minutes, chatting his ear off.

"I thought Bryan was at training?" She rage-whispered into the phone as soon as he picked up.

"Yeah, he left today," Topher said, breathily.

"He left today and came *here*."

The sound of something like a weight dropping onto concrete reverberated through the phone. "He's where?"

"HE'S FUCKING HERE, TOPHER." She had to work to pull her tone back down. "At my parents' house. *In Dallas.*"

She could hear Topher exhale sharply through his nose.

Jess went on, "I thought you said you had an assignment for him?"

"I did. I sent him to Macon for that bullshit training. Used a favor to get him in the class last minute, too. I guess he got lost and ended up at the airport on the way." The last part sounded as if it came out through gritted teeth. Topher might've been more pissed than Jess was.

She didn't know if she could put a name to what she was feeling, even if she had a gun to her head. It was a lot of everything and absolutely nothing at the exact same time. Her mind and her body were warring. One was trying to keep her alert, and the other was trying to distance her from what was going on since she couldn't fight or flee.

"Alright. Just act normal, and I'll deal with this," he said reassuringly.

"What are you going to do?"

"Make some phone calls. Don't worry, I'll get him back here. But he'll be there through tonight. If you need to call me again, my phone will be on."

"Okay, but I doubt I'll be able to find more time to get away."

Jess could hear the masked anger in Topher's voice. "I'm sorry, Jess. I'll keep a tighter leash on him once he gets back. Try to enjoy your time with your family."

"Thank you," she said, not sure how to end the call.

"I'll, uh. I'll talk to you soon," Topher said, apparently not knowing how to end the call, either.

"Okay."

"Bye."

"Bye." Jess hung up, painted on a smile that only ran skin deep, and went back inside.

"They're not trying to talk you out of the wedding, are they?" Bryan asked as they laid in bed that night.

As Topher promised, he found a way to get Bryan back to Georgia. Bryan got a call at dinner he stepped outside the restaurant to take. When he came back inside, Jess could tell Topher had cracked the whip. Bryan wore a frustrated expression, but he tried to set it aside and be jovial the remainder of the dinner. After they got back to her parents' house and said goodnight to them, Bryan told her he had to head home early the next morning for a regional meeting. Topher had come through as promised.

Jess searched the shadows of his features in the dark room, trying to come up with an answer to his question. "No, they would never do that."

"Just making sure you're not getting cold feet," he joked as he tugged on a lock of her hair.

They were snuggled under the comforter, lying on their sides face to face.

Instead of lying, Jess responded by snuggling into his chest. It seemed like the less dishonest option. He stroked her hair softly.

"I really like your folks. Hopefully, they can come visit us when we can't make it out here."

"Mmmhmmm," Jess murmured into his chest as his word from a few months ago replayed in her head about it being unfair they expected her to take care of Nina.

"When I talked to your mom on the phone this morning, she said they were good with a May date."

Jess wasn't following. "What do you mean?"

"For the wedding. That's when the magnolia trees will be blooming. I called the venue, thinking they wouldn't have anything this year with May a little over two months away, but they had a cancellation in the middle of the month. I went ahead and put a deposit down."

"You what?" Jess snapped her head up to look at him, even though she couldn't see much in the darkness.

"I wanted to surprise you," he explained with a hint of hurt in his voice.

"I am very much surprised. Do you know how long it takes to plan a wedding? There's no guarantee I can get a dress in that timeframe. Sometimes they can take weeks to come in if I have to order one."

"When's that dress thing?"

"Tomorrow," Jess lied, unable to get out of that one.

"Sounds like the perfect time to look for your own dress. And your mom can go with you. She probably wouldn't be able to go with you if you shopped in Georgia. Besides, we can move the deposit to another date. I just wanted you to have the option of getting married with the magnolias blooming, since you like them so much."

"Well, thank you for thinking of me." Jess tried to insert as much gratitude to her tone as she could to hide the fact that she was alarmed.

"I already miss you," he mumbled sleepily into her hair.

"Me, too." That one wasn't a lie. Jess missed herself more with each passing day.

CHAPTER FORTY-THREE

Topher

Bryan wouldn't get in for a couple more hours, and when he landed, he would get an email that the meeting Topher had set up to get his sorry ass to Georgia was canceled. But, according to Topher's CIs, Bryan still had plans in Georgia for the day. Agent Whitley apparently set up a meeting late last night, and Topher decided to add himself to the guest list. A gut feeling told him that the feds were close, and he needed to know how close.

He caught Jason coming into the office just after lunch. "Hey, man, I need to borrow your kid's seat."

Without a word, Jason turned and exited the building through the door he'd just come in, Topher in tow.

"Don't fuck it up. Those things are expensive," Jason instructed as he handed the car seat over.

"You'll have it back tomorrow none the worse for wear."

"Tomorrow? What's going on?" Jason asked.

"You know my favorite thing about you, Jason?"

"What's that?"

"You usually don't ask too many fucking questions," Topher replied as he placed the car seat in the second row of his truck.

Jason nodded. "Noted," he said and turned back toward the office.

Topher climbed in and headed toward the nearest car rental lot. Slapping contractor magnets on the side of his truck and changing his plates wouldn't work this time. Today, he had to be a master of disguise. He was going for the influencer mom look, hoping for a swanky SUV. The rental car employee had a sense of humor, and he ended up with a minivan that was more "2000s soccer mom," than "click the link in my bio for a discount on gluten-free beach towels." The minivan would provide more cover, though, so he decided to roll with it. He paid in cash and swiped the keys off the counter.

Back at his truck, he dug out the ball cap, visor sunglasses, and camera he'd stashed in his truck console, and transferred them to the van before grabbing the car seat out of the back. It had a mystery amber substance that made his fingers stick to the side of the seat. He set it down in the second-row seat and gave it a soft push on the side. It toppled over easily. That wouldn't do. He worked with the seatbelt to secure the car seat but had no idea what he was doing. Ultimately, he ended up buckling the belt over the front of the seat, stretching the belt to its limit, and hoping the tint on the second-row windows was dark enough to conceal his ignorance.

He had to get on the road, and he had to be on his game. This wasn't a typical surveillance sojourn. He was going to have to be creative and think on his toes. Casing an agent wasn't easy to do. It was like trying to commit arson at a fire station. But Topher had a couple things working for him: more years in the field than Bryan and less ego, too.

The senior agent had a lot of ground to cover before he got into position for the evening. First stop: thrift store. He needed to complete the look, and his spartan closet options ranged from "probably ex-military" to "definitely a cop," along with one suit that doubled for weddings and funerals. He popped into a thrift shop in Gainesville and scoured the men's racks, settling on a baseball popover that made him look like a traveling baseball dad. It even color-coordinated with his hat and visor glasses. He shrugged off the three-button polo he was wearing and slipped the popover on top of his undershirt.

Taking a gander in the mirror, he saw a Topher of another life. One where his wife hadn't died and he was a father. He still wondered about having kids every now and then. Outside of his wife dying, he'd never made plans to have them, because he didn't think he'd live long enough. Between the military and law enforcement, he never expected to see thirty-five. Now, in his mid-forties, he didn't know what to do with the rest of his life. Too old to change careers, too young to retire. But, what about a family? There might still be time. Something stirred in his chest. The same sensation he sometimes had when he thought about Jess. A feeling. But feelings don't get shit done, so he left the thought in the mirror and headed to the checkout counter.

Next up: The Juliana Motel. See if he could catch anyone slipping around the supplier. He pulled over in an industrial park a half mile from the motel. A white, middle-class baseball dad hanging around the area of the motel could raise some eyebrows. He didn't have the time to haggle with the used car salesman again, so he needed a new cover.

With a few quick twists, he removed the valve stem cap on the back passenger tire and let out a few pounds of air, praying the air hose he was headed for worked. He merged back into traffic with his flashers on and pulled over into the car wash beside the motel. The establishment was almost as squalid as the motel it neighbored. He spent a few minutes finagling with the air hose, buying him time to assess the situation at the motel. Nothing noteworthy happened and any more lingering might draw too much attention, so he jumped back in the van.

Final stop: snacks. The most important stop of the day. Topher learned in his early days as an agent there were a few necessities for a successful stakeout: a few unneeded calories, a bottle to pee in, and a lot of patience. He popped into a convenience store and loaded up on beef jerky and Gatorade. What a dinner.

Now it was time for business. He unlocked a smart phone he'd picked up the evening before at a low-cost, no contract service provider and opened an app. A map popped up with a few colored dots. One was Jess at work, the second was Bryan—who looked like he finally made it to work. Jess's was blue because it was downloaded to her phone. Bryan's was green, because his tracking device was a physical bug on his vehicle instead of an app like on Jess's phone. In fact, Bryan had two dots. Topher planted one on Bryan's personal truck and his bureau car. He knew Bryan kept magnetic key boxes on the vehicle frames in case he locked himself out. As long as Bryan didn't lock himself out tonight, Topher's trackers would be safely tucked away in the boxes. He'd switch them out with the keys tomorrow. Hopefully, he wouldn't even need the tracker. Topher already knew where Bryan was supposed to be thanks to one of his CIs, but then again, a smart criminal often changed the meeting location at the last minute to throw the other side off their game. Any plans they had for an ambush or a setup would be out the window.

The informant said tonight's meeting spot was Lavender Park in Gainesville. A sprawling development home to a marina, playground, dog park, walking trails, and baseball fields. minivan heaven, so he wouldn't have a problem blending in. He just needed to figure out which part of the park Bryan would pick to meet Tweety Bird.

Topher decided the boat ramp would the most logical options as it gave the most cover, and any areas that had kids like a playground would have the most eyes looking for danger. This park had one of the biggest ramps on the lake. Lots of large boats, trailers, and trucks would provide the best concealment the park could offer to hide in plain sight.

He drove through the park to the boat ramp at the end and surveyed the scene. It was early evening, and there was a decent amount of activity with fisherman and sunset cruisers launching. Topher circled around and chose a spot at the end of the lot between two SUVs and behind a truck that didn't have a boat trailer behind it. The location gave him a view of both entrances to the lot, the boat ramp, and the dock where boat drivers pick up whoever parked the trailer. He waited a moment until he made sure everyone in the lot was preoccupied before climbing into the third-row seat and settling in low where he could just barely see out the windows.

219

CHAPTER FORTY-FOUR

Topher

Topher wished he'd bought another Gatorade. It was a warm day in the mid-seventies—one of Georgia's cruel habits was making its inhabitants believe that springtime was a handful of summer days intermingled with the final days of winter—and he was going to lose a lot of fluid by sweating if Bryan didn't show up in the next hour or two.

Topher pulled up his tracking app to see how far out Bryan was, but a car circling in the lot gave him pause. He watched as it pulled a similar maneuver as Topher had done when he'd first pulled in. It was a black, luxury SUV with blacked out wheels and an illegal tint. The kind often driven by either rappers and drug lords, or a fed that had confiscated it from one of the earlier two. It parked on the other side of the lot from Topher, disappearing behind the trucks and boat trailers.

After a moment, a man and a woman emerged from the area the car had just parked in and headed for the walking trail that paralleled the wooded side of the lot. The woman wore a neat ponytail that was slicked back with so much gel it looked like a mirror—definitely ex-military—and the man had a clean haircut, no beard. Dead giveaways for undercovers. They both wore workout clothes that were a little too high-end for most people in Gainesville unless they were going to go work out at the country club on the north side of town. Dumbasses might as well have shown up in a white conversion van with seventy-five antennas on the roof and "FEDERAL SURVEILLANCE VEHICLE" painted down the side in bright red paint with flashing neon arrows pointing to it.

His suspicions were confirmed: the feds were joining the party. Could be Homeland Security or FBI but probably Homeland Security. Feebs—the state level agents' pet name for their FBI counterparts—would have better intel and dressed more appropriately for the locale. Either way, the guest list was getting crowded, and Topher's frustration about the situation hit a new level. Not only was Bryan disrespecting Topher and the office, he was putting lives in danger.

Speaking of, the guest of honor arrived as the sun was sinking below the horizon, casting a pink glow on the landscape. Bryan's Dodge Ram slipped into one of the open spaces between a couple of large boat trailers. Nothing happened for around five minutes. Then, Bryan emerged and headed down to the floating dock. He was dressed frat boy-esque in khaki shorts and a solid, pale blue polo.

As Bryan reached the end of the dock, a man Topher didn't recognize was idling up in a center console boat that Bryan stepped onto. He grabbed onto one of the poles holding up the Bimini top, and the boat driver turned and headed back through the no wake zone until they disappeared across the water.

Topher sat as still as possible. A skill he had to master in his military career to stay alive. The Army preferred to work under the cover of night, and he knew that the human eye looks for movement more than anything in the dark.

With minimal movement, Topher slipped on a night vision device when the light had dimmed enough. He didn't want to miss a single potential piece of evidence. If Bryan came back with one less button done than how he'd left, Topher wanted to know about it.

The boat returned around half an hour later, dropped Bryan at the dock, idled backward a moment, and then turned for the open water again. Everything looked the same as when Bryan had boarded the boat. No extra occupants, and Bryan didn't seem to have added anything to his person. No large, bulging pockets or anything immediately obvious.

Topher figured the intent of the meeting wasn't to exchange drugs or cash. He was likely having Emery and Eli do most of the dirty work. So the only thing he could've gotten was information. Which was sometimes more dangerous than the other two options. It was starting to feel more and more to Topher like he was juggling bottles of gasoline beside an open flame.

The fed couple had returned and looked like they were going to be Bryan's tail for the night, following him out of the parking lot. Topher destroyed the cell phone, returned the rental by putting the key in the drop box, transferred the car seat back to his truck, and went home to stare a hole into the ceiling above his bed, wrestling with thoughts of Jess that were always waiting for him when he couldn't fill his time with anything else.

CHAPTER FORTY-FIVE

Jess

The day after Jess returned from Dallas, she worked remotely from Nina's. Ruth had taken the day off since she worked through the weekend while Jess was away. Shauna called her first thing about some motions that had been rejected by the court in the Jessup case, and Jess spent most of her day putting out that fire. In a sense, it was a welcome distraction as a large part of her didn't want to face the mystery in her own life.

Nina had a cold and was spending the day in bed sleeping it off. Jess had set up shop at the kitchen table and was so engrossed in drafting a new motion to send to her paralegal for e-filing, she jumped when there was a knock at the back door on the other side of the kitchen. Expecting to see Ruth, she walked over and pushed the curtain aside to find Topher.

She quickly unlocked it. "Topher? Hey, what's going on?" Her brow furrowed.

He pushed his way past her so he could slip into the house and spoke in a low tone, looking past her. "We need to talk. Where's your aunt? Is anyone else here?"

Jess's stomach jumped into her throat. "She's in bed. It's just me and her. What's going on? Is everything okay?"

"Is this the basement door?" He pointed to the door in the short hallway between the kitchen and the foyer.

Jess nodded. "Yeah."

In response, he held a finger over his lips and motioned for her to follow him. He went to open the door but stopped before he twisted the old, crystal knob. He turned, pulled his phone out of his jeans pocket, and mouthed to Jess, "Where's your phone?"

She pointed to her bag on the table between where they were standing and the back door he just came through.

Topher flicked his fingers toward his wrist in a "give it here" motion. Jess grabbed it from the side pocket and handed it to him. He fumbled through a few kitchen drawers until he found some aluminum foil, wrapped their phones individually in a layer of foil, and then together in another layer of foil. Jess knew he was making a makeshift faraday cage. Bryan mentioned to her that he would wrap confiscated phones in foil until he could get them in the bureau's safe rooms to prevent someone from remotely wiping the phone. He claimed most of that technology couldn't be effective if the phone had no signal.

Topher then placed them in the microwave, quietly closed the door, and headed for the basement. Jess filed in behind him and pulled the chain hanging from the single lightbulb on the wall just inside the door as she stepped down onto the first stair.

Once at the bottom, Topher turned to face Jess and then looked above her head at the door. Jess had pulled the door behind her, but it didn't shut all the way. Without a word, he quickly bounded back up the staircase, pulled it until it latched, and then rejoined her at the bottom.

He took a deep breath, leaned against a support beam, ran his hand through his hair and down the back of his neck, and exhaled while looking at his feet.

Jess's mind was going a hundred miles an hour in seventeen different directions. "How'd you get here? Did anyone see you?"

"I keep a ghillie suit in the truck," he deadpanned.

"Huh?"

"Never mind. No one saw me. Anyway, listen..." he started, and then paused, pushing off the beam and placing his hands on his hips.

"I don't like the sound of that." Her stress level shot even higher, and the muscles in her lower back tightened.

His lips pulled into a thin line, and he ran a hand through his hair. "I think this is a lot deeper than we realized," was all he offered.

He then dropped his gaze and zeroed in on her wrist. Her smart watch.

Reaching out, he grabbed her arm, flipped her wrist over, popped the silicone band open, and ran it back up the stairs. Jess heard the crinkling of foil, and then he reappeared at the top of the steps, shutting the door behind him again.

Jess's eyebrows knitted together, and her stomach clenched as she watched him descend the stairs again. "Isn't this overkill? Please tell me what the hell is going on."

"Devices can be accessed even with the battery removed. Phones, watches, tablets, laptops, you name it. We used to do it in the Army. It has to do with the chips and some microtechnology I can't talk about. Also, the government keeps extra tabs on people that it spent a lot of time and money telling its darkest secrets to, like yours truly." He sticks a thumb to his chest.

Once he hit the bottom, he moved past without looking at her and walked up to the dryer against the far wall that might be as old as Jess. He twisted and pushed at the knobs until it cranked to life with a frightening clatter. Then he turned and plopped down in an old iron patio chair with white paint flaking off and falling like snow underneath him.

He looked up at her—she opted for standing—then wiped his hand down his face and raised his voice just enough to be heard over the drone of the dryer. "Remember how I mentioned the feds might be getting involved?"

"Yeah…" Jess said, unsure she wanted to know what he was about to say next.

Topher leveled his gaze at her, speaking calmly, "I think they could be crashing whatever parade Bryan is leading within the next couple of weeks."

The news hit Jess like a punch to the stomach. "Why?"

"I followed him Friday night, and he picked up a tail that I would bet my career was undercover feds."

Jess processed the news, taking a seat at the bottom of the stairs. Her mind went back to Scar. "Did you find a video?"

He shook his head slightly. "Still working on it."

Sitting made her feel even more nervous. She pushed off the stairs and started pacing the floor in an unconscious effort to regulate her nervous system. "Alright so you said you think he might be working undercover. For what? To find out who shot Ravello? Why? Why would he be undercover without your approval? None of this is making sense to me." She stopped pacing and turned to look at Topher. "What's the motivation here?"

"One of two things," Topher started, leaning his elbows on his thighs. "Either he's trying to work the case by himself so he can prove his worth to his daddy, or he's doing it for the money. My thoughts are he's trying to impress his dad and set himself up for an FBI position. He's already approached me about writing a recommendation whenever a spot opens at the Atlanta field office."

She took in what he said and turned to face him, one arm crossed in front of her waist while her other hand rested on her chin. "There's more. I can see it on your face."

"That's all I know," he said, opening his hands in front of him.

"Bullshit, Topher. What else?"

"I don't *know* anything else," he pushed back.

Jess's small amount of remaining patience was teetering. "Leave the semantic arguments to us attorneys. I know you don't *know* anything else. But you have suspicions. What are they?"

He stared back at her. Two professional interrogators squaring off, studying each other for the slightest twitch that would betray them and say what words wouldn't.

Topher finally cracked. "Might also be blackmail. Retribution for Ravello's death if Bryan did kill him. A compromised cop on the inside to do your bidding is worth ten cops in the ground for someone running a black-market empire."

"Why wouldn't he just tell you or the bureau if he felt like they were out to get him?"

"Would you risk having an investigation to determine whether or not you killed someone reopened? My guess is Bryan would rather die than go down disgraced and spend the rest of his life in jail. You know how they treat cops in the pen."

"And what exactly is he doing?"

Topher took a deep breath, blew it out, and answered, "I think he's running interference. It's two-fold. He's keeping these guys he's working with off our radar so we focus on the competition—other drug dealers—instead. And he's probably taking a cut of the money in exchange for giving them protection."

"Why would he be taking a cut if he's being blackmailed? Wouldn't he be doing...whatever it is they want him to do for free if that was the case?"

"I don't know exactly what's going down, it's probably one or the other."

If Bryan was working with the cartel for cash, her Tiffany ring made more sense now. And she did see him pay in cash often. But there were some puzzle pieces still not fitting together for her. "And you haven't intervened because?"

"Has Bryan mentioned who the big boss is at GBI?"

"No, it's never come up."

"He's Sheriff Whitley's ex-partner from when they were Hall County Deputies working the road thirty years ago."

Jess felt like all the air had been sucked out of the room. She squeezed her eyes shut and rubbed her forehead as if trying to wipe away the problem. "*Fucking* hell, Topher. We've got to find out if that video is real."

Neither of them said anything for a moment. Jess leaned against a support beam, wrapped her arms around herself, and looked at her feet. Topher shifted to sit back in the chair, more paint flakes floated to the concrete beneath him.

A thought hit her. "Why would this video—if it's real—be coming out now when the shooting happened months ago?"

"Could be a number of things. Information is traded like currency in the drug world. Someone could've saved it until they needed a favor from a rival. Or it could've been used as a peace offering,"

"Peace offering?"

"Let's say someone encroached on rival territory. A rookie gang member who made a mistake. Instead of waiting for retaliation, the erring side might have offered up the video as retribution," Topher elucidated.

Jess wished the floor would open up and swallow her whole. Just a year ago she was a trial attorney kicking ass in the courtroom with a beautiful condo in a high-end neighborhood and hopes of achieving partner status before her thirty-fifth birthday. She'd moved to Georgia to start over. This isn't what she had in mind when she was planning her reset. Now her life was in shambles with an engagement that felt like a million-pound burden, not to mention the fact that she had to constantly look over her shoulder to make sure a cartel hit man wasn't following her home.

Topher broke through her thoughts. "If it's out there, I should be able to get my hands on it soon. But, Jess, I think we need to get you out."

Jess stared at him trying to process what he'd just said. "Like leave Bryan?"

He opened his mouth, as if formulating a response, but Jess spoke before he could. "How do we even know this is all real? All we have is an accusation from a psychotic criminal, and the fact that Bryan has broken some protocol by failing to have you sign off on some undercover work and takes too many phone calls from Emery and Eli." She threw her hands up, exasperated.

Topher brought her back to the present. "What's your gut telling you, Jess? If you think this is all bullshit and Bryan is squeaky clean, then I'll never say another word about it. But if there's even a *hint* of doubt in your mind, then you need to listen to it."

Jess shook her head. She looked over Topher's shoulder and pursed her lips as she stared at the cinderblock wall behind him. "I don't know."

Topher cocked his head to the side. "Then ask yourself this question: Why'd you come to me about the video? Why didn't you go straight to your fiancé?"

There was no malice in his tone, but the question hit Jess hard. He had a point. Jess couldn't argue it, and she couldn't answer the question. Or maybe she didn't want to answer it. Something in her mind was trying to push those kinds of thoughts down.

After a moment, Topher stood up and took a step toward the stairs. "You've got that number. Call me if you need anything. Otherwise, I'll let you know once I've got the video—if there's one out there to get."

He turned and left, closing the door at the top of the staircase gently behind him.

Jess lowered herself into the chair he'd been sitting in. The truth, she was coming to realize, was more painful than simply Bryan's potential malevolence. If her relationship with him unraveled, she would have two major failures on the books in just a year's time.

Leaving Bryan, the man she'd fallen in love with, would feel like another escape. And she was tired of feeling like she was running away from life.

CHAPTER FORTY-SIX

Whose truck was that at Nina's today?" Bryan asked nonchalantly over dinner.

Jess's first thought was Topher, and dread washed over her, turning her blood cool in her veins. But then she remembered the handyman had stopped by. She tried not to let it show on her face, but it was too late. He'd already seen the fork pause ever so slightly on its way to her mouth. He didn't speak, but his eyes narrowed.

She kept her voice as light and calm as possible. "A handyman. Her upstairs toilet wouldn't quit running. She asked me to help her get it fixed."

"A handyman with no advertisements on his truck? Looked like a personal vehicle to me." Bryan wasn't going to let it go. He was a dog with his jaw locked on a bone in a junkyard fight, and Jess was the bone.

"Yeah, Ruth knows him. He mostly does stuff on the side. Extra cash kind of thing. Nice, older man." She hoped his jealousy wouldn't rage as hard if he knew the man wasn't boyfriend material.

"Why didn't you call me? I can fix that sort of thing. It's usually just resetting the chain with the rod. No big deal."

"I don't want to bother you at work with that sort of thing. Why were you driving by at that time of day anyway? That's in the middle of the workday." The question was benign enough, but the expression his face shifted into was anything but. She immediately realized her screw-up once it was out of her mouth.

"Why are you getting defensive?" He asked, his voice a little louder and firmer than his previous questions.

Jess's voice automatically ticked up a notch as her anxiety level rose. "I'm not. It's just weird…"

"You know what's weird? I'll tell you what's weird. It's weird that you're getting defensive over a simple request that you let me help. Makes me think maybe it was more than a handyman at Nina's today. Or maybe not even a handyman at all. She didn't bring that friend's nephew around again, did she? The one she mentioned she would set you up with if *you were ever single again*," he said, using air quotes after dropping his napkin.

"She said that right when I moved here. Before we were dating. Where is all this coming from, Bry?" She stared at him in disbelief.

His eyes were nearly void as he stared back at her, never breaking his gaze. After a moment, he looked down, grabbed the burger off the plate and took another bite, chewing his food in quick motions. His eyes met hers again as he chewed. The little life that was left in them had turned dark and morphed into utter contempt, disdain, and loathing.

"It seems like you don't want me around. You didn't like the idea of me helping. So it's either because she's trying to set you up with someone, or you're embarrassed of me. Huh? Is that it? Think I'm not man enough for that kind of task?"

"Of course not. Like I said, you were at work. I didn't want to bother you."

"Bother me?" he shook his head, dropped his burger onto his plate, pushed back from the table, and walked over to the fridge, licking mayo off his fingers as he did.

"You know, it's always an excuse with you," he said into the fridge as he grabbed a beer. "I don't get it. Most women want their man to do that kind of thing." He closed the fridge door with a dramatic swing. "They're proud of it. This is just another example of how you don't appreciate me. Of how you doubt me."

He walked back over to the table, pausing only to use the bottle opener mounted on the wall. The sound of the lid clanging into the small metal bucket hanging below the opener intensified Jess's anxiety, and she realized how hard she was gripping the fork.

He plopped back in his chair and threw back a large gulp of beer.

"Babe," Jess said, trying a softer approach, "that's not it at all. But I'm sorry. Next time I'll call you. Okay?"

He cocked his jaw as he stared another hole through her. "Yeah, whatever."

Not sure what else to do, Jess tried to finish her salad as normally as possible, even though her appetite had evaporated faster than water in the desert sun.

With a humorless chuckle, Bryan stood up and made his way through the living room and up the stairs. Jess let her shoulders fall a bit and sat back in her chair, dropping her fork in the salad bowl. She thought back over the handyman situation and wondered if she didn't do the right thing. Maybe she should have called Bryan about it. She didn't have much time to ruminate on the matter before her thoughts were abruptly penetrated by an ear-piercing crash of glass shattering that came from the bottom of the stairs, almost making her jump out of her chair.

Jess sat still for a moment, listening. No other noises followed, so she slipped out of her chair softly to peek in the living room. She saw the fragmented remnants of the beer bottle scattered over the hardwood at the base of the stairs with intermittent white splotches of foam. Drips of beer streaked down the wall toward the baseboards as tears spilled over and streamed down her cheeks. As unpleasant as his word salad barrages were—about things like social media and her seat heat use—those were all she'd thought she had to worry about. But since he'd slammed the water bottle down in the car and now this, she wondered if he might start getting physical with her. The thought scared her shitless.

She retreated further away into the deep caves in her mind that seemed to be her dwelling place more and more these days, slipping yet another inch away from herself.

CHAPTER FORTY-SEVEN

Jess

Where's Piggy?" Bryan asked as he closed the door from the garage.

He'd just gotten home from work two days after the beer incident and was used to Piggy greeting him with butt wags and snorts when he came through the door.

Jess, sitting at the kitchen table reviewing witness statements for one of her new cases, let out a long sigh and said, "At Aunt Nina's."

"Why?" he asked as he threw his keys in the bowl on the console table just inside the door.

Here we go.

Jess cleared her throat to steady her voice. "Because I think she's lonely, and he's caged up all day while I'm at work. I think it's best that he stays there, and I'll see him a few days a week. I hate it, but it's for the best."

"You don't need to leave him over there. I'll let him out. I can start coming by during the day."

"What about when you're in court or away for training?" Jess asked.

"That's not very much. Few days a month," he replied nonchalantly as he made his way to the fridge and grabbed a beer.

"No, I hate when he has to be up all day when neither of us can get to him. And I've always been a little nervous after that break-in attempt. Besides, like I said, Nina's missed him since I moved out. He'll keep her company."

"Break-in?" Bryan asked.

Jess looked at him across the kitchen before responding hesitantly, "When the screen was popped off...in the back."

"Oh, yeah. I don't think that was a big deal. Like I said, probably just those juveniles." Bryan waved it off as he popped off the cap on the beer bottle and tossed it over the island into the trash can.

Attorney Jess entered the chat. "It was a big enough deal to put cameras up." She looked up at him, awaiting his response.

"To make sure you're safe while I'm away. And a dog would help with that. Robbers tend to avoid houses with dogs. That's probably why they left that time and didn't break in. I'll bet Piggy went berserk and ran them off. Besides, he was caged up when you worked in Dallas wasn't he?"

"I had a dog walker because I was making six figures," Jess explained curtly. This clearly wasn't about the dog anymore. It was a power struggle to see whose ego would prevail.

"Nina lived by herself for years before you moved in. She's also got Ruth over there almost every day now. And he might trip her while she's trying to walk around. You don't want her breaking a hip. She's already in bad enough shape as it is," Bryan continued. Ever the master problem finder.

Jess dug in. "No, this is the best move. Nina is excited to have him, and it won't put pressure on either of us while we're at work. Piggy is an attention whore anyway, and Nina will spoil him rotten. He can always come back, but we're going to give it a try." Her voice was firm, her position unwavering.

The truth was Jess was starting to circle the wagons. She didn't know what was going to happen, but something told her to start getting things in order. Moving Piggy was also a test to see how Bryan would handle it.

"Well, I wish you would consult me about these kinds of decisions before you make them. You're going to have to start including me from now on. That's how relationships work."

"I'll bring him over on the weekends. It's going to be fine. And besides, you didn't ask me before putting a deposit down on the venue."

"You didn't hear a single word I just said," Bryan protested, his anger starting to rise.

They were interrupted by his phone ringing. Bryan pulled his work phone out of his pocket. He looked at the screen and ignored it.

"Go ahead, answer it." Jess's tone was snappy. "I've never been important enough to you before to not answer a call."

He opened his mouth to answer but was interrupted by his personal cell ringing. With a huff, he grabbed it off the counter and answered it.

Jess could barely hear the voice on the other line from her side of the kitchen, but it sounded like Topher's.

"Alright. I'll look into it first thing tomorrow," Bryan said, wrapping up the conversation.

He was about to hang up when Topher started speaking again.

"Understood," Bryan answered, tight-lipped.

Topher must've set him straight on not answering his work phone.

The distraction broke his focus from her. When he hung up, he ignored her and went upstairs. Jess breathed a sigh of relief and returned to her work.

CHAPTER FORTY-EIGHT

APRIL

Jess

Basketball game tomorrow at six, not seven," Bryan informed Jess as he took his tie off. He'd been interviewing witnesses all day and had just come through the door. "I'm going to shower before we eat," he said over his shoulder as he headed toward the stairs.

"Okay," Jess acknowledged.

Left alone again, she started folding the cheese into the béchamel sauce for the enchiladas she was making as the recipe on her phone instructed. Something caught her eye in her peripheral, and she looked over to her left to see Bryan's phone on the counter. He never left his phone lying around. It was always either in his pocket, in his hand, or sitting right next to him. His reasoning was that he didn't want to miss a call from work.

Should I look at it? This could be her only chance to get some information on exactly what Bryan was up to. Topher's words about not searching for information came back to her. She might not want to know.

As she was deciding what to do, the shower cut on upstairs, and she instinctively grabbed for the phone, knowing she only had a few minutes before he plodded back down the stairs.

The screen illuminated when she picked it up, and there was a photo of the two of them from the Biltmore the day they got engaged set as his background. She swiped up to find it password protected. Keeping an ear to the pipes to gauge how much time she had, she started inputting guesses. She tried his baseball numbers from high school. Not it. His badge number. Not it. His birthday. Not it. Her birthday. No, again.

Her palms grew sweaty. She was afraid she was going to lock the phone, and he would know she was trying to get into it. She dropped it back on the counter where he'd left it and returned her attention to finishing the enchiladas.

She set the table with two tall glasses and filled them with water. She grabbed a beer and set it at Bryan's spot as well, then made them each a plate. Locating napkins and silverware, she added them to the table, sat down with the food, and waited for Bryan to join her.

With nothing else to do, she stared out the bay window that looked out over their backyard. The steam from the food wafted up in front of her, creating a glaze over the scene.

A small subdivision of around a dozen cookie-cutter houses ran behind their property. Most of its inhabitants were young families. Jess often watched from her windows as the street threw block parties a couple of times a month. The parents would set up lawn chairs or sit on the back of tailgates and drink cocktails from their insulated tumblers, while their kids engaged in yard games and played flashlight tag when the sun went down. She wished they could join, but Bryan always had an excuse for why they shouldn't. Jess eventually stopped trying, then got so busy with work she didn't have the time.

Today, there was a young boy in a G.I. Joe getup running around the yard of the house behind theirs with a plastic lightsaber. Nothing was safe from the fierce, young warrior. A cherry tree, his tricycle, and anything else that he happened to lay eyes on all took a good whacking. He even tried a swipe at the dog, which trotted off toward the front yard away from the young Jedi. After a moment, a man Jess took to be the boy's father emerged from the garage with a jacket for the boy and another lightsaber and challenged him to a duel.

Jess watched, amused. The boy swung valiantly, and his dad let him get a few strikes in before falling to the ground in a dramatic, mock death. The boy stood triumphant over his fallen enemy, raised his lightsaber to the sky with both hands, looked up, and yelled something indistinguishable. His father laughed, rose from the ground, and scooped the boy up. They disappeared into the shadows of the garage, presumably to their own supper.

Finally, Bryan emerged from upstairs. He padded across the living room looking at his phone, smirking. His hair was still wet. When he got to the table, he clicked his phone shut and set it on the table face down on the other side of his placemat from Jess.

He said grace, and they started to eat. His phone dinged, and he ignored it to compliment her on the enchiladas. She thanked him and asked about his day. His phone dinged a couple more times, prompting him to flip it over and take a look.

"I've got to take this. Work," he said as he pushed away from the table and left through the door to the garage.

Jess could see him pacing the driveway through the living room window, one hand holding the phone to his ear, the other shoved into the opposite armpit. His facial expressions oscillated between concern and frustration.

Two things bothered Jess. First, his work phone sat by the bowl where they kept their keys on the console table just inside the door to the garage. He was talking on his personal phone. Second, having dinner together when they were both home in time was something Bryan revered with the enthusiasm of a pulpit preacher as exhibited by his outburst after they toured the wedding venue in January.

She ate by herself, put the dishes in the dishwasher, and grabbed a book to settle on the couch with.

When Bryan came back inside, he downed the rest of his cold enchiladas in a few quick bites, then suggested they pick up where they left off on one of the shows they'd been streaming. Jess agreed but she couldn't concentrate on the show. All she could think about was how it felt like they were slow dancing in a field of landmines, and the tempo was starting to pick up.

240

CHAPTER FORTY-NINE

Jess

The next evening, Jess went with Bryan to basketball. With the sun out and the temperature north of seventy degrees, the guys' families came, too. She made small talk with Courtney as they watched the guys start shooting free-throws and stretching to warm up. Topher didn't show, but Courtney mentioned something about Jason having to travel to Macon the following week once Topher got back. Jess assumed he was taking the training that Bryan was supposed to go to when he followed her to Dallas.

She ached to talk to Topher, feeling bad about losing her cool with him in Nina's basement and hoped he wasn't gone long. She wanted—no, needed—to know if he'd found anything else out but was nervous Bryan would catch her if she started texting him. As much as she hated it, she was cruising on autopilot until she had more information from Topher and she could get the Jessup case behind her.

Once the game kicked off, Courtney turned to tend to her kids, and Jess slid off the bleachers and took to the track situated just down the hill from the court.

She shared the space with CrossFit Karen in her Lululala athleisure—that probably never saw any real athletic activity outside of this track—and Starbucks Stephanie—who looked like one of those people who professed to know if their coffee was going to be good or not based on the weight of the cup when the barista handed it over the counter. The dynamic duo walked in sync as they chatted nonstop, complete with furiously animated hand gestures. From the sounds of it, there was some high school teacher that had the audacity to give one of their sons a B-. Jess said a silent prayer for the teacher and picked up her pace so she wouldn't have to be near them. She needed a good endorphin boost, so she kicked her pace up to a quick but sustainable jog. After half an hour, she felt much better and walked a couple of cool down laps.

On her way back up the hill to the court, she passed the women again, presumably planning their next attack on a retail store manager. Or maybe a restaurateur who dared to keep the ice at the wrong temperature for their skinny margaritas.

After the game, the guys hung around to shoot the shit for a few minutes before everyone meandered off to their cars. Jess climbed in the passenger side of Bryan's truck while he and Jason chatted, each leaning over a side and facing the other across the bed.

The men wrapped up their conversation after a few minutes, and Bryan climbed inside. He cranked the engine and threw the truck in reverse.

"What do you want for dinner?" he asked.

"Mmmm. I don't know. We have some leftovers at home," Jess offered.

"Let's just grab something in a drive-thru. That way we don't have to fight about who's doing the dishes," he suggested with a poke to her ribs. Jess loathed doing the dishes, so she didn't argue.

Back at home eating their dinners out of Styrofoam boxes at the kitchen island, Bryan caught her up on his cases. Jess wanted to point out the fact that he didn't like her talking too much about work after hours, but she didn't want a fight, so she refrained. Turns out, Bryan was in a fighting mood because he pivoted hard.

"Why were you wearing sunglasses today?"

Jess almost dropped her water glass as she set it down. The conversation shift came out of nowhere, and her body started to tingle in an unpleasant way. "Because it was bright."

He looked at her as he closed his box. "Sure it's not so you can look at other guys?" His tone inflection said *question,* but his face said *statement.*

"Babe, you know I have sensitive eyes. I wear them when I'm just driving down the street or outside to walk the garbage down to the curb."

"You've never worn them around my friends," he said matter-of-factly, his jaw tightening under his skin.

Jess paused. Wondering where the hell this was coming from and how far he was going to push it. "Yes, I have. I wear them on the boat, when I'm driving to work, my God, Bryan. I can't even believe we're arguing about something so exiguous."

He narrowed his eyes at her. "Exiguous? Is that one of your fancy legal words? Trying to talk over my head to get me to shut up, huh?"

The words scraped across her skin, and she reacted, saying, "Did you ever think about becoming an attorney? You really know how to turn everything into a deposition."

His tone became laced with venom and his eyes darkened. "You can't handle the heat so you turn to mocking me?"

Jess threw her head back, closed her eyes, and exhaled. "Can we just forget it? I wear sunglasses. It's not a new thing. Maybe you just noticed. That's the end of it."

Bryan grunted, pushed away from the table, and walked off toward the stairs without another word, but Jess knew he wasn't done. Even without him in the room, she could feel the charge in the air. Her defiance waned with the uneasy feeling that started in her chest and was creeping outward to her limbs. She stared out the window and wondered if Topher was right.

Maybe she should start planning her exit.

CHAPTER FIFTY

Jess

Jess was alone at the house getting ready for work when her mother called.

"Hey, Mom," Jess said as she picked up.

"Hey, honey. How's my Georgia Peach?"

"Oh, I'm hanging in there."

Marcie launched into a sales pitch. "Well, that's good. Listen, I know it's a little early, but we're trying to figure out where to go for the Fourth of July this year. Your dad had the idea of renting a house on Lake Austin, and you know they'll be booked up before Easter, so we have to get one soon. Anyway, how long do you think you'll be here for? We're trying to figure out if we can do four bedrooms, or if we need five since your Aunt Shannon has decided to come with your cousins. Won't it be so wonderful to see them again? I know your dad is thrilled to see his sister. I think it's been nearly half a decade now since we've been together. Anyway, if we're all here for just a couple of days, we can probably make four—"

Jess interjected her mother's ramblings. "Uh, I'm not sure if I'll be there this year, Mom."

"What? You're not coming home for the Fourth?" Her mother sounded taken aback and disappointed.

Jess fidgeted with the phone. "I don't know, yet. Bryan and I haven't discussed it."

"Well, I know that, but we have to book soon if we want to get that week. The houses are going fast. Anyway, I thought before you moved you said you'd be back for the holidays. You know, that's the only reason I let you go." She tried a stab at some humor. Jess knew it was her mother's way of trying to not get emotional.

"Let me talk with Bryan about it, and I'll let you know," Jess responded.

"Okay, just make it as soon as you can so I can let Dad know about booking the house. There's only a couple left," Marcie explained, the apprehension thick in her voice.

"I will," Jess promised before hurrying off the phone, feeling close to a breakdown.

She knew she was delaying the inevitable by forcing her mind away from the idea of leaving Bryan whenever it came up. For one, she didn't want to think about it. And there were people depending on her to get out of jail that drew her to the office each day, further delaying a decision on whether or not to leave the man she loved.

Bryan could brew a fight out of anything, especially the best of intentions. Jess was coming to find that was his specialty.

They were in his truck on a backroad one afternoon after work when she told him she wanted to go back to Dallas by herself for a weekend. He took issue with the plan, accusing her of being embarrassed of him again if she didn't want him to come with her. The conversation was going in circles, and Jess shut down with the all-too-familiar pang of dread brewing in her stomach. This time her armpits started to tingle with stress sweat, and she felt her hips tighten. She sat silently and watched the tall grass go by outside her window, trying to keep the tears at bay.

"Oh, so now you're going to give me the silent treatment, huh?"

Jess didn't respond. She knew it was a bad idea, but there was no winning either way. Damned if she did, damned if she didn't.

"I wouldn't do that if I were you," he warned.

"What?" she kept her face to the window.

"You know what," he spat. "Your mind games. Not talking to me. You think you're smarter than me because you went to law school. Playing your psychological bullshit games you learned at work. I'm not an idiot, Jess. I can see what you're doing. I'm not your experiment."

Jess had defended herself so many times by this point. It seemed like they had this fight once a week now. Him accusing her of playing mind games when he was the one who came home from interrogating criminals to do the same thing to her. She refused to get pulled into his trap again, so she clamped her mouth shut.

"You know what? I think I've had enough of you today," Bryan said as he hit the brakes hard, sending the truck into a violent nosedive.

He brought them to a complete stop in the middle of the road. Without missing a beat, he flung open the door and started walking down the road in front of the truck.

Jess scrambled over the console into the driver's seat. She was angry and scared but needed to get out of the middle of the road before someone came barreling over the hill and slammed into the back of the truck. Shutting the door, she shifted the truck into drive.

Bryan hadn't looked back once. He had moved over to the white line, looking straight ahead as he walked.

Jess pulled the truck alongside him and rolled down the passenger window.

She pleaded with him. "Bryan, get in. We can talk about this at home."

He ignored her and kept walking. She checked the rearview again to make sure she wasn't going to get nailed in the rear.

Her tone became more desperate. "Bryan, please get in the truck. Before you get killed."

He shrugged apathetically and said, "Maybe that's for the best."

She pleaded with him another minute or so until a car finally appeared in the rearview. Jess hit the accelerator, passing Bryan and maneuvered the car to the shoulder, pulling in front of him on the side of the road. Punching the hazard buttons, she watched him come up in the rearview. The car whizzed by on her left as Bryan passed on her right, walking past the truck.

Her throat constricted, and she let her head fall back against the headrest as the tears streamed down her face. She was equally alert and tired. Part of her trying fervently to figure out what to do, and another part not caring if they sat on the side of the road all night.

He stopped walking and sat on a nearby fire hydrant for a few minutes, looking around at anything except Jess. She wondered what his motive was. Was he trying to make it look like Jess had kicked him out of the truck? Paint the picture to the town that she was the bad guy?

A couple of cars had passed by since the incident started. One of them stopped by Bryan and appeared to ask Bryan if everything was okay. He nodded and waved them on.

Eventually, he made his way back to the truck. He started coming up on the driver's side, so Jess moved to climb back over the console into the passenger seat. She briefly hesitated, wondering what he might do once he got back behind the wheel. Slam them into a tree. Steer them into an oncoming car. But it's not like she could fight him off if that's what he wanted to do, so she climbed over and slipped her seatbelt on.

He climbed in and drove them home without a word, and Jess knew she was running out of time.

CHAPTER FIFTY-ONE

Topher

Topher watched where Bryan's brass fell on the gun range. About four yards in front of the concrete pad where the rifle benches sat. They were completing their semi-annual pistol qualifying for the bureau. Topher and Bryan each shot at least a couple times a week, and Jason shot three-gun competitions on the weekends.

Topher was the regional pistol instructor, so he had to keep an eye on his office, plus the Region Eight agents joining them today. He positioned Bryan at the end of the range to minimize the chances of his brass mingling with others.

Yet again, he was faced with deciding how much information to let Jess in on with his plan to run a ballistics test. He hadn't been able to bring himself to tell her that he'd found out Tweety Bird was Thomas Ravello's uncle and that Suarez and Silva were half brothers the night he'd gone to visit Mateo. All he'd been able to get out was he suspected that Bryan could be blackmailed into working with Tweety Bird. He hated keeping the rest from her, but ultimately decided to stick with the plan that the less she knew, the less she had to lie about to Bryan. He needed to talk with her again soon and see how she was doing. And for his own selfish reasons as well that he was still coming to terms with. Right now, he had to finish up training, if it would ever end.

The new Gen Z agents in the office were testing his patience. He had to stay late with several of them that week to bring them up to speed on protocols they learned on their first day as agents and promptly forgot. Some days, he was genuinely worried that one was going to mistake a loaded magazine for a PEZ candy dispenser.

He was starting to put a plan together in his head. One that would nail Bryan's ass and get Jess to safety. It might end up going against everything he stood for as an agent. But so did being a predatory piece of shit.

As Bryan popped off a couple rounds to complete the drill Topher had just called out, Topher's mind went to his cousin, Stephanie. He and Stephanie had been like brother and sister growing up. When she was twenty, she started seeing a guy she met at the community college in their hometown. Everything seemed fine at first, and Stephanie didn't change radically overnight, but Topher saw the slow shift over time. Her smile didn't stretch quite as far as it used to, and she lost weight. The bigger concern was Dave, her boyfriend. Within a few months of their relationship, he went with her everywhere. He always had a reason. Topher had tried to talk to Stephanie about it, but she shut him down and assured him everything was fine.

Within a few weeks of their conversation, Stephanie was arrested for felony drug charges. She was currently serving a twenty-year sentence. Dave had put her up to it, and Stephanie didn't feel like she had a choice. She took the fall, and she was now paying dearly for it with at least a quarter of her life. And Dave was free to manipulate others, though he was in and out of jail with domestic violence charges every few months—a testament to the fact that the system was in severe need of attention when it came to the light punishments it doled out to abusers.

Stephanie's situation was one of the reasons Topher decided to enter law enforcement after his time in the military. The hicktown cops that worked her case botched it horribly. All the evidence was there to charge Dave. But Dave was the mayor's nephew, so he was always going to get off. Stephanie never had a shot.

In addition to his duty to justice as an agent, Topher saw Jess's situation as a way to right a wrong as best he could. To bring some kind of justice to the Stephanies of the world. He was in the line of serving others, after all. And then there was Jess herself.

Topher couldn't swear on a Bible that his thoughts about Jess were always pure. He was attracted to her; there was no doubt about it. She was a rarity. Smart, attractive, and passionate. But he had no plans to act on his desires, especially not after what might be happening soon. And his gut told him as soon as Jess could get back to Texas, she'd be headed west, racing the setting sun.

"Motherfucker," Topher whispered to himself as he watched a young agent—kid probably wasn't much older than twenty-one—struggle with a magazine change.

If this was the future of the bureau, God help the citizens of Georgia. Instinctively, he started to mentally tally the number of years he had left before he could retire with full benefits, but it didn't matter. Tomorrow wouldn't be soon enough. Law enforcement years were like dog years. One year felt like the equivalent of seven.

He stepped up to the firing line to address all the agents where they could hear them over their ear protection. "You've got the rest of your life to get that mag changed when you're in a gunfight. Let's run through clearing a jam one more time."

He unholstered his gun, illustrated the drill, and reholstered the weapon.

"Tap, rack, bang. Let's go," Topher instructed with a helicopter swing of his arm over his head.

He caught the more seasoned agents giving him side eye looks. They were probably irritated they were having to run through such an elementary drill. But if you don't practice, you lose muscle memory, and if Topher had to suffer through the injustice of training a generation of screen zombies, everyone else did, too.

They finished qualifying, and Topher sent everyone out for lunch. He said he'd take care of cleaning up. Bryan offered to stay behind and help, but he was the last person Topher needed around at the moment.

"Y'all go ahead," he said.

Bryan zipped up his pistol bag. "What?"

He still had his ear protection on and couldn't hear Topher. He pulled up one muff, and Topher repeated himself.

"Alright, man." Bryan threw the strap of his bag on his shoulder as he turned to catch the rest of the group making their way to the parking lot.

Topher took down the paper targets first and threw them in the trash. He then grabbed the brass retriever and rolled it along the ground everywhere except where he mentally pinned the location of where Bryan's brass fell.

After collecting everyone else's brass, Topher circled back with a Ziplock bag and collected Bryan's with gloved hands. He only needed a couple but grabbed a handful just in case. Next, he threw a silica packet in with the brass to soak up any moisture before sealing the Ziplock and putting it in one of the pockets of his range bag. He grabbed the brass retriever again and collected the remaining casings, threw the cardboard ammo boxes away, and headed to the Atlanta office.

CHAPTER FIFTY-TWO

Jess

D o you love him?"

Jess and Topher were in Nina's basement with the dryer soundtrack playing in the background. It was evening, and Topher had called the house phone to see if Nina was asleep before he came by. Jess had been relieved to hear his voice when she picked up the line. Bryan was three hours away at Macon, taking the training at Gipstick he'd bailed on when he followed Jess to Dallas. Jess had dinner with Nina and stayed after, looking over motions prepared by her paralegals at the kitchen table with Nina already retired to her room.

Jess was taken aback by his question. "What?"

"Do you?" Topher pressed. "Because if you do, I need to step in now."

Jess looked past Topher's shoulder and drew a deep breath. "I did...for the first few months. When everything was new and...happy." Her eyes met Topher's, as if they held the secrets to all the answers she didn't know how to ask.

"But you don't now." He said it as more of a statement than a question.

It was a little uncharacteristic of Topher to drill into her, so dry and direct. But Jess knew what he was getting at. He was trying to get her to fight for herself, trying to get her out. But what he didn't understand was that it wasn't that simple.

Jess lowered herself into the white iron patio chair Topher had sat in the last time they were in the basement, staring at the floor in front of her. Piggy, who had been sniffing his way around the musty basement, came over and curled up at her feet.

Jess cleared her throat. "There was this woman I represented back in Dallas. Her name was Cathy Denmare, and she shot her husband to death. Well, he was wealthy, and everyone thought she did it for the money. I did, too, at first. Then I spent an afternoon with her interviewing her in prison and found the truth was much more convoluted. I went in expecting to hear a litany of excuses and a bullshit alibi but came out wondering how someone could be so evil to break a human being down slowly over time."

Jess's defense team had to fight an incredible uphill battle to overcome the surface facts of the case. It was true Cathy's husband had never laid a hand on her. It was true she'd always been provided for. It was true her husband had no criminal record. It was true the neighbors thought they were a completely normal family. It was true her husband was philanthropic and on the boards of several wonderful charities. It was true they'd had two kids that went on to Ivy League schools. It was true that she was living the ultimate American Dream. It was true he had a large life insurance policy. This was the story the prosecution hung its hat on.

From the inside, it was also true that he had spent years slowly breaking her psychologically by planting seeds of doubt in her. It was true he monitored her relentlessly, counting each grocery bag she brought in from her car as he watched her from the home's security system cameras. It was true he'd discouraged her from keeping connections with her family, making her believe that he and only he had her best interest at heart. It was true he told her she shouldn't work because he made enough money for the both of them. It was true she'd lost touch with her friends from college when he demanded all her time to meet his needs, "like a good wife does." As time went on, he tried less and less to cover his affairs. Cathy hoped he would leave her for one of the women he cheated with, but he never did.

Jess likened Cathy's husband to the ocean. Some days the water was calm and serene like a safe oasis. Other times, it was relentlessly pounding the shore in a mad barrage of fury, as if lashing out from a deep wound that had been triggered seemingly without warning. And it could switch between the two forecasts with a ferocious quickness, which instilled enough fear in Cathy that she never made any attempts to leave, even after the children left for college.

And then one day, one small drop in the bucket was enough to bring the whole thing crashing down. He told her she couldn't go to lunch with her mother. She snapped and shot him with his own gun. After a long and emotional trial, they prevailed, and Cathy had been able to start living the life she deserved.

Jess drew a deep breath. "And I guess what I'm trying to say is, I don't know how. I don't know how to leave." She couldn't bring herself to say the word "scared." "And I can't afford that mental load with work right now. If I don't get this man out of jail, my unit will probably have to close shop."

A mental image of David from when they met at the jail hit her. The pain in his eyes and the hope in his smile haunted her.

Topher spoke calmly and confidently, "You don't have to do like that woman and shoot him, Jess. I've got a way to get you out."

"How?"

"I think I might have figured out a way to turn him in, and he'll get some time behind bars. I'm not sure which charges would stick, so I don't know for how long. But you'll have the perfect excuse to break off the engagement and time to start a new life before he gets out."

"How do we turn him in if you said they already have eyes on him?"

"Here's where you can use big government to your advantage. The federal guys don't get along, and often the right hand doesn't know what the left is doing. I think the Department of Homeland Security is the one on his ass. So we turn him into the FBI."

"And what if they say you didn't go through the right channels by addressing it within the GBI?"

"I think I can win that one on a conflict-of-interest argument."

"What if he explains his way out and Emery and Eli are the only ones who get charged?"

With an unwavering gaze, Topher declared, "I'll testify against him."

"And you think there's enough evidence to make it stick?"

Topher's face shifted into a pained expression, and his eyes searched the ceiling. As if he had something to say but was wrestling with himself on whether or not he should do it.

All the sudden, a thought hit Jess harder than a gut punch. She had no idea what time it was, but she knew it was late. They'd been in the basement long enough.

The cameras.

CHAPTER FIFTY-THREE

Jess

Oh fuck! Fuckfuckfuck…" Jess felt like she was about to jump out of her skin in fear.

Topher approached her. "What is it?"

She paced back and forth and wrung her hands without realizing it. "He's probably checked the cameras and called me. How long have we been down here?"

"He knows you're not home?"

"Yeah, sometimes he checks the cameras, and I didn't tell him I'd be staying here late," Jess quickly explained as a wave of nausea rolled through her. She forced air in her lungs in an effort to keep the roiling of her stomach at bay.

Topher was talking again, but she couldn't hear him. She was still pacing, pinching the bridge of her nose. Scared shitless.

"JESS." Topher finally broke through her panic.

"What?"

He turned around, grabbed the patio chair, and guided her onto it. "I said I need you to breathe for me. Try this: four seconds in, hold it, four seconds out, hold it. Repeat."

Topher did the exercise with her. It helped keep her from going into a full-blown panic attack, but she couldn't get her mind off her phone wrapped in foil on the floor above them, and the consequences she was going to face when she got back to it.

"I have no idea what I'm going to tell him." Every muscle in her body was rigid with tension.

"It's going to be fine. I've got an idea. Come on." He started making his way up the stairs. Jess followed with Piggy hot on her heels.

He removed her phone from the microwave and unwrapped the foil. It took a moment for the notifications to start coming through. Twelve missed calls and twenty-three texts.

Bad. Badbadbad. Shitfuck.

A new wave of nausea ripped through her stomach.

"Okay, here's what happened," Topher started, keeping his voice low. "Nina fell, and you thought she might've broken her hip. EMS just left. Actually, no. He can fact-check that with Emery. So Nina insisted you not call 911. You couldn't get her up, so you called me to help since he's hours away. That covers if anyone saw me come here tonight, too. If he checks your phone log, you saw my truck still at the office across the tracks and called me there from the house phone because yours started an automatic update and wouldn't let you make any calls." Topher pointed to Nina's house phone mounted on the faded magnolia wallpaper and the telephone book sitting on the counter below it. "That explains why his went straight to voicemail in the foil. I doubt he'll dig in your phone for update records, and I'll wipe the memory on the phones in the office tomorrow morning. I just left."

It was a lot to take in but Jess nodded. "Okay."

Topher's confidence and presence were keeping her from a full-blown panic attack. Bracing herself, she tapped on Bryan's last missed call and steeled herself for what was coming.

He answered on the first ring. "Why haven't you been answering me?!"

Jess frantically pressed the button on the side of her phone to drop the volume.

"Nina fell, and—"

"And you turned your phone off?" He spat the words out.

"No, I haven't been able to get to it. I thought she might've broken something, so I've been trying to convince her to go to the hospital to get checked out for the last hour, but she won't."

"And you couldn't answer your phone at all? I'm on my way home Jess, Jesus. You had me so fucking worried. What the hell were you thinking?"

"It wasn't intentional, Bryan. I'm so sorry. I left my phone upstairs and couldn't get to it until Nina was taken care of."

"You can't do that to me. I thought you were hurt or worse. God, Jess. Use your brain." His voice had dropped a few octaves since he first answered but was still teeming with anger.

Jess didn't know whether she expected him to show concern for Nina and her "fall," but it was clear he didn't have any. The resentment this stirred in her made her brave.

"Nina's okay, by the way."

"Good," he replied curtly. "Now, I've got to drive all the way back to Macon, so I can get up at the ass crack of dawn for training. Text me when you get home."

No need when you'll have the cameras pulled up as soon as we hang up.

"Okay," Jess said.

"Love you, bye."

"Love you—" he hung up on her.

Looking up at Topher, Jess felt ashamed. Even though he knew the darker secrets of her relationship, him witnessing it felt like she was naked in front of him.

"I've got to go. I'm sure he's already got the cameras pulled up, counting the seconds," she said, her stomach tying into another knot.

"Are you sure you're okay?"

"Yeah, I'm fine. Thanks," Jess said in a tone that convinced neither of them and grabbed her purse off the kitchen table. There wasn't time for a therapy session.

"You've got that number…" Topher said, referring to his throw down phone.

Jess nodded. "Thanks for your help tonight."

Neither one of them moved. Jess wondered if Topher was fighting the same feelings she was.

"You're welcome." Their eyes locked, but neither spoke.

They were standing a few feet apart. The space between them felt heavy with all the things they wanted to say to each other but couldn't.

"Okay, then," Topher finally said, slowly making his way to the back door.

"I'll lock the door behind you," Jess said.

Topher flipped the switch on the wall by the door, turning off the porch light. He moved the curtain that covered the window in the door slightly to make sure the coast was clear.

"Are you sure you won't be seen?" Jess followed him to the door.

He stopped with his hand on the knob, turning to face her. Their faces were close enough she could've counted the striations in his irises. "The military spent a lot of your tax dollars training me how to move in the dark," he replied in a low tone. For a moment, she thought he might dip his head and kiss her. But he turned the knob, opened the door, and said, "I'll let you know if I find out anything else."

He slipped into the night, disappearing into the shadows of the tall grass, headed for the tree line.

Jess locked the door behind him, left through the front door, and hurried home.

She couldn't sleep. She laid there silently while a few tears escaped. Jess willed her mind to stop thinking about Bryan. She found herself thinking of Topher, which was somehow more painful than her thoughts of Bryan. Two different kinds of betrayal: the man she thought she loved turning into someone she didn't recognize, and the one she found her mind wandering to when she needed to escape the reality of her situation.

Yet another area of her brain she needed to shut off. She couldn't think of how his concern for her made her feel. It would be dangerous to pine on about how she longed to have a beer with him on a Friday by the lake, with the breeze caressing his dark blonde hair while the sun illuminated the golden strands scattered throughout as they bantered. How could she imagine the feel of his hands on her when she knew Bryan could call any minute? What good would comparing the color of his eyes with spring clover do?

She finally fell asleep with two daggers lodged in her heart, each with a man's name on it.

CHAPTER FIFTY-FOUR

Jess

Hey, Mom," Jess chirped as soon as her mother picked up.

"Hey, dear. You sure sound chipper this morning."

Jess cleared her throat. "Well, I have good news. I'll be home for the Fourth."

Marcie's tone rose several notches. "Oh, that's fantastic, hon! I'll go tell your father now. He's going to be thrilled. Is Bryan coming, too?"

No.

"I'm not sure yet," she answered.

"Okay, well I'm so glad my baby girl is coming. I'll make that dessert with the strawberries you like so much. I'll make my shopping list now." Jess could hear her mom open a drawer and rifle through its contents, probably looking for a pad and pen in her kitchen junk drawer.

They said their goodbyes, and Jess smiled, hanging up the phone. She texted Stacey the news, then dropped her phone on the kitchen counter to go get ready for her appointment. By the time she was ready, Bryan was awake and coming down the stairs.

"Who were you talking to?"

"My mom," Jess said over her shoulder as she walked to the door to the garage.

"Where are you going?"

"I have an appointment," was all she offered on her way out.

As soon as the door shut behind her, she hustled to her car and jumped in before he could interrogate her. She was already in reverse by the time he opened the door. He stared at her as she pulled out of the driveway. She couldn't gauge his expression exactly, but she was sure it wasn't good.

Her hands were shaking so hard, she had to keep a white-knuckle grip on the steering wheel to drive.

It's going to take a while to shake you off me, she thought.

It was a small step, but it was high time she started taking her liberty back.

When she returned from her waxing appointment—thanks for the inspiration, Stephanie and Karen—Bryan didn't say a word about it. He was reviewing what looked like interview notes at the kitchen table when she walked in.

He suggested they go out for dinner, and Jess agreed, thinking it might be better to be in public with him than home alone with a brewing temper. His tone and face weren't showing anything out of the ordinary, but the air around him carried the same palpable charge that accompanied his blow-ups.

"Okay. Sounds good," Jess agreed as she watched his every movement to gauge his mood.

He wasn't letting anything show, which was worse for Jess because she knew there was no way he was going to let her off the hook for brushing him off earlier. He was masking, so she didn't know how bad it was.

She started second-guessing herself, regret starting to creep in.

But what was done was done, and she knew she would've been disappointed in herself had she backed out.

Bryan pulled them into the gun range instead of a restaurant.

Jess looked over at him. "I thought we were going to eat."

"This won't take long," he responded.

Jess hated the indoor gun range. Bryan had taken her to a couple times before. The gunpowder stung her nostrils, and many of the patrons didn't seem to know what they were doing with their firearms. The place was a lawsuit waiting to happen.

They signed in at the desk and made their way through the set of glass doors that separated the store from the range. Their only company was a couple of older gentlemen occupying the second and third stalls.

Bryan walked to the far side of the range and set up in the last stall. He'd selected a paper target with a menacing-looking robber, which he clipped to the horizontal bar hanging from the cable before flipping the switch for the small motor that sent the target zipping downrange.

Jess took a seat on the bench that lined the wall behind the stalls. Thinking they would be there for a while, she removed her phone from her purse and unlocked it. She checked her emails and deleted the junk ones, many of them from stores in Texas that made her a little homesick. Before she'd made it halfway through her inbox, Bryan was standing in front of her.

"You're done?" She had to raise her voice so he could hear her over their ear protection and the pops from the rounds the older men were firing.

"Yup. Let's go eat," he yelled back.

She dropped her phone back in her bag.

Bryan shifted his pistol bag from one hand to the other and turned to head to the door. As he moved, Jess noticed he didn't take his paper target down and throw it away like normal. It was still hanging in the stall, and it stopped her in her tracks. The target had one hole in it...directly in the middle of the robber's forehead. One shot. He'd only shot once. It didn't make any sense, but Jess quickly realized it wasn't really supposed to.

The objective of their pre-dinner detour was clear, and it made her blood run cold. Bryan needed to make sure Jess hadn't forgotten who was in charge. One shot was all that was needed to let her know exactly what he could do if he wanted to. This was her payback for not submitting her waxing plans to him for approval. She'd expected a good tongue-lashing and saber-rattling of the usual sort. But this was bold, even for Bryan. And it was crystal clear.

Jess knew she was going to fully awaken the beast that was Bryan with her defiance, but she hadn't realized exactly how dangerous the beast was. She just found out, and he was more vicious than she'd anticipated.

Not wanting Bryan to know she'd registered his threat, she recovered her composure, swung her purse over her shoulder, and followed him out the door as nonchalantly as she could manage with her knees feeling as stable as a pile of Jell-O in an earthquake.

CHAPTER FIFTY-FIVE

Jess

The next day after work, Jess got a call from Nina on her way home, saying Ruth had to go early, and that she needed a prescription picked up. Jess swung by the pharmacy and was waiting for the pharmacist to fill the order in the drive-thru when a text popped up from Ruth.

"Can you switch the laundry to the dryer for me?"

It was an odd request for Ruth, but she didn't think much of it. Her mind was bouncing around between the Jessup case and Bryan's actions last night.

She got to Nina's, gave her the medication she'd just picked up, and let Piggy out. He trotted off toward Nina's room when they came back inside, and Jess went to take care of the laundry in the basement.

The light was already on and the scraping noise of the patio chair moving on the concrete nearly made her jump out of her skin. She fell back on the stairs behind her with a squeal, one heel flying off toward the concrete floor at the bottom. Topher came into view as she regained her footing.

"What the fuck?!" She whisper-screamed at him.

Nina's voice came from above. "Jess? Jess, dear, are you okay?"

She scrambled to get up and yell into the hall, "I'm fine! Just missed a step!"

Closing the door, she whirled around to face Topher. "I could've broken my neck. How about a heads-up next time?"

He turned to start the dryer. "I texted you."

Jess paused, so he went on, "Under Ruth's number."

She wiped a hand down her face. "I completely forgot about that." After removing her other heel, she descended the stairs.

He came toward her with her shoe that had bailed during her fall. "How're you holding up?"

"Uhm…I'm holding," she said, taking her shoe from him.

What could she say? *Doing great. My favorite part of the day is when the mister gets home, and I get interrogated for forty-seven things I didn't do, and if he thinks I'll leave him, who knows what he'll do. Thanks for asking. How're you?*

Topher leaned back against the washer, propping his hands behind him on the machine. He was looking at her, but his head hung low. "It's about to come to a head. I know I've been saying this for a couple weeks now, but I'm getting the feeling the feds are about to step in and bust this thing up. Probably within the next few days."

Jess didn't ask how. She didn't ask why. She just let his words sink in as she lowered herself onto the stairs behind her, studying her bare feet.

He went on, "And I think there's a good chance Bryan will end up dead or in jail by the end of it."

Jess looked up at him, still not sure what to say. Her hands felt clammy, and she balled them into fists as if that could help her get a grip on this situation that was very much outside of her control. Opening her mouth to speak, she couldn't make any words come out, so she closed it again. Her gaze floated to the floor joists above them as though they held an answer for her.

"Do you want me to step in?"

The world stopped spinning for Jess. She pondered his words, turning them over in her mind, as though they were shiny objects that she couldn't make sense of.

When she didn't respond, Topher broke through her thoughts. "Can I give you some unsolicited advice, Jess?"

She looked up at him, returning to her body. A humorless laugh escaped her lips. "Yeah, I'll take all the advice I can get right now."

He took a deep breath, scratched his chin, and said, "My mom and I didn't always see eye to eye, but she told me something when I was about ten that's stuck with me ever since. It was this: don't lie to yourself. If you're going to do something bad, call it as such. You can still do it, but don't try to justify it."

Not the kind of advice she was expecting. But it signaled he wasn't going to stand in her way, whatever option she chose. She closed her eyes, threw her head back, took a deep breath, exhaled, and asked, "You ever heard of the quote, 'You either die the hero, or live long enough to see yourself become the villain?' "

He cocked his head to the side. "Yeah, who's that from? Nietzsche?"

"Batman, actually," she quipped.

He cocked his head to the side. "No shit?"

"Yeah, someone said it in one of the movies. Anyway, my point is, the reality of the situation doesn't escape me. I just don't understand how the hell we got here. How, I got here, I mean." She sucked in her bottom lip and wrapped her arms around her waist.

Neither of them said anything for a moment. Topher shifted in his chair, and Jess could feel his eyes on her. She'd wrapped her arms around her legs and rested her cheek on her knees as her mind warred over trying to save Bryan or letting fate have its way. In her mind's eye, she saw the target from the gun range last night. One shot in the forehead. Finally, she drew a deep breath and peered up at Topher.

With finality, she looked him dead in the eyes and said, "I think you should focus on your own cases."

He opened his mouth to speak but was interrupted by what sounded like a knock at the front door.

They both looked at the door above them and froze.

The knocking returned until the sound of Nina's walker coming down the hallway drowned it out. Squeaking indicated the door's opening.

Bryan's voice pierced the airwaves, like a metal pole dragged across a chalkboard.

Jess opened her mouth but couldn't say anything. Her eyes grew wide, her heart raced, and she reached out toward Topher, terrified.

He grabbed her up off the stairs by cupping his hands around her shoulders and began looking around in the dim light. Deciding to go to his left, he pulled her behind him as he quickly moved around the backside of the stairs. There was a small nook behind the wooden staircase that butted up to a cement wall. They sidled up to the wall, but the space was so small they had to stand face to face, inches apart.

Jess could see Topher's face by the slanted light seeping through the cracks in the boards of the toe-kicks in the stairs. His eyes were narrowed, and a muscle was working in his jaw. Neither one of them breathed for what felt like minutes. She was close enough to smell his aftershave, and it calmed her in an odd way.

Neither of them moved for several seconds. Topher finally whispered for her to stay put and then crept his way around the stairs and carefully moved up the staircase.

"No!" Jess whispered and jumped out from behind the stairs.

Topher paused mid-staircase and turned to look at her.

"Let me go," she instructed and waved him back down the stairs.

He paused as if deciding whether to concede. Ultimately, he turned sideways to let her pass. Jess turned her body to slide past him, and his words caught her on the same step he was standing on.

"You sure?" he asked, his tone low and husky.

They were even closer than they were under the stairs. His nearness made her brain quit working, and she couldn't remember what he'd just said.

"No," she replied, her mouth responded in the absence of her brain function.

"I won't go out there. I'm going to listen and make sure he's gone before you go out," Topher offered, swinging his head toward the door a few steps above them.

The warm glow of the bulb above them illuminated his features and showed the lilac semi-circles framing his lower eyelids and the start of a beard she hadn't been able to see in the shadows. He looked as though he hadn't slept in days, and Jess realized he was struggling with what to do with Bryan as much as she was.

"No…no." her brain came back online. "I can't take the chance." She couldn't even explain to herself what they were doing. And she damn sure couldn't explain what her heart was feeling right now.

Jess climbed the remaining steps, the door opened with a creak, and she slipped out. Looking left toward the front door, she closed the door to the basement behind her. The house was quiet, but she caught sight of the tail end of Bryan's bureau car leaving the driveway through the window in the front door.

"Nina?" she called.

"Yes, dear. I'm back here," Nina called from the hallway off the foyer that led to her bedroom.

Jess followed the sound of her voice and found her trying to negotiate her walker through her bedroom door.

"Bryan was just here looking for you," Nina explained as she crossed her bedroom to an armchair by the window she liked to read in.

"I was downstairs doing laundry. Did he say anything else?" Jess asked.

She picked up her book off the table beside her. "No, I just told him you must've gone with Ruth to the store since I hadn't heard anyone in the house for a while."

They both knew the other was lying, and Jess felt bad for not being honest with her aunt.

She started to explain, "It's—"

"None of my business," Nina finished for her, flipping through the pages of her book as if looking for the place she'd left off. There wasn't even a hint of judgment in her tone. "You're an intelligent woman. I'm sure you know what you're doing."

Jess felt a wave of relief wash over her. One less thing she had to worry about.

She turned on her heel and headed back down the hallway to return to the basement. The house phone started ringing as she grabbed for the knob on the basement door. Ignoring it, she opened the door to find the stairs empty.

She descended them halfway to look around, but Topher was gone. Her eyes landed on the rectangle window close to the ceiling on the far wall that led to the backyard. The patio chair was under it. She'd never noticed the window before, probably since the glass had been painted black—presumably for privacy. From her vantage point, it appeared the latch that secured it wasn't in the locked position.

As she climbed out of the basement, the phone started ringing again. Jess hadn't looked at her cell phone yet, but she was sure Bryan was blowing it up, and the muscles of her hips and lower back unconsciously tightened. She expected it to be his voice when she answered the house phone, but it was Topher's. He must be calling from a burner phone since his cell was still wrapped up in foil on Nina's counter.

"You okay?" he asked.

"I'm fine. Did you leave out the window?"

"Yeah, you might want to lock that back up," he answered.

"Bryan left. He's probably riding around looking for me." The more Jess thought how close they were to getting caught, her palms started to sweat and a pit the size of the Tallulah Gorge up the highway opened in her stomach.

"I just got off the phone with him. I'm pulling him into an interrogation with me that will keep us busy into the evening," Topher explained, sounding frustrated at having to be around Bryan.

Jess's body relaxed knowing he'd be occupied for a while. "Thank you."

"Listen, part of the reason I came by was to tell you that I need you to get into Bryan's phone, his personal one, go to WhatsApp, and take photos of the text streams you find with your phone. Don't screenshot them. I'm going to get you his passcode and tell you when to look."

"Okay," Jess said. "Wait, if you have his passcode, why do I need to look?"

"Because what I'm looking for is going to come through at night, and Bryan will wipe it in the morning before I can get to it."

"Alright, but you left your other phone."

"Leave it on the back porch. I'll get it later tonight," he said.

"Done," Jess answered.

"I'll find you soon," he said, and then hung up.

CHAPTER FIFTY-SIX

Jess

Law enforcement frowned upon habits, Jess knew this . They're a good way for one to get killed. That's why Topher had instructed Jess not to form any. But sometimes they're a blessing. Apparently, Topher knew—probably via his law enforcement ways—that Nina always took her lunch from Reid's Café on the downtown strip on Tuesdays when fried okra was their side of the day, and that Jess always walked across the tracks to get it for her when she worked remotely, or Ruth got it when Jess went into work. Jess felt this was one habit she could keep as she was in public in the middle of town, and it seemed unlikely Bryan's enemies would whack her with so many eyes around.

She was working remotely that day, and at exactly eleven-fifty, she stepped out Nina's front door onto the porch en route to Reid's. The folks that worked there always had Nina's lunch prepared for her on Tuesdays and automatically charged her credit card at the end of the month. They always made sure Nina got the first scoops of the day's special. And often, the Styrofoam to-go box was overflowing with food sticking out from the sides. They would usually add an extra box for Jess at no charge. Nina had babysat several of the employees when they were kids and others had worked at the lumberyard during their high school summers as Bryan had, so they made sure the matriarch of the community was taken care of.

Jess jogged across the street, walked up the bank to the railroad tracks, navigated her way over them, and gained the sidewalk that led to the shops and restaurants. Maneuvering around the antique shoppers and kids licking their ice cream cones, she reached Reid's and opened the door to the sound of a bell dinging overhead.

The plump, retired lady at the register that sat on the glass counter to the right just inside the door welcomed her with a, "Hello, sweetie," and smile to match. Jess wasn't sure what her real name was, but her name tag said "Flo." She had a habit of using an entire palette of blush on her cheeks and always had a different shade of eyeshadow on—today was teal.

"Let me get you Nina's box," Flo said as she shifted off her stool and waddled her way over to the other end of the counter that had a line of white paper bags stretching across it.

She grabbed one of the bags, looked in it, and then turned around to the window where the cooks passed the food through and started chatting with one of the young male employees on the other side. The boy was wearing a black apron over his t-shirt and a black hat that he'd turned around backward to keep his hair out of his eyes while he worked. He listened to Flo, nodded, and turned to head back toward the fridge at the back of the kitchen.

Jess leaned against the counter by the register with her arms clasped in front of her and turned to survey the room over her left shoulder. The crowd was mostly older. Jess figured this had something to do with the fact the café was modeled after the soda fountain shops that were popular in the 1950s. Pastel colors covered every surface and Coca-Cola memorabilia dotted the walls.

There was a break in the counter just to Jess's left where the servers came in and out. Just beyond it was a line of stools where single lunch-goers usually sat.

Today, Topher was one of them. Jess spotted him and took a step to approach him, but he caught her eyes before she did and shook his head ever so slightly, slid off the stool, and walked away from Jess toward the restrooms. Jess was a little confused at first, but then she saw him discreetly slip something into the bag that Flo had pulled for Nina as he passed. He disappeared into the men's room and didn't come back out before Flo retrieved a small, round Styrofoam container from the boy that had reappeared in the window, turned around, dropped it in Nina's bag, and delivered it to Jess back at the other end of the counter.

"Tell Nina to give me a shout sometime soon. We've got some catching up to do," Flo said with a smile as she handed over the bag.

Jess promised she would, smiled back, and stepped back outside into the dreary late spring drizzle.

The bag in her hands felt like it weighed ten pounds. She wondered why he was dropping her a note instead of calling Nina's house phone or under Ruth's contact. She understood not wanting to put anything on record in a text. Maybe Bryan had said something to him about planning to check her phone. Whatever his reason, Jess trusted him. He'd given her no reason not to so far.

She wanted so badly to dig through it and find out what Topher put in it, but she could see Bryan's truck at the police station just down the street from Reid's, so she waited until she was back inside Nina's front door.

In the foyer, she retrieved a napkin that had fallen down the side of the bag away from the others piled neatly together on top of the Styrofoam containers. She heard footsteps approaching and, not sure whose they were, stuffed the napkin in her back pocket and headed for the kitchen. The footsteps belonged to Ruth, and she made her way into the kitchen as Jess unloaded the containers from the bag at Nina's normal lunch spot at the table.

"Actually, I'll take those," Ruth said, indicating the containers. "Her knee is pretty swollen today, so I'm telling her to rest it."

"Oh, okay. Here, let me get some silverware for her. Does she need something to drink, too?"

"No, I just got her some water. Thanks, though," Ruth said.

Jess dropped a fork and spoon into the bag and handed it off to Ruth.

Once Ruth's footsteps dissipated, Jess grabbed the napkin out of her back pocket and ran upstairs.

Safely alone, she pulled the napkin out and found nothing. It was a standard white diner napkin. She flipped it over. Standard white diner napkin, side two.

She slid her thumb in between the sheets and pulled it open. It looked like there was some writing that was on the innermost layer, so she pulled apart the sheets again. The square was transparent now, but there was a note written in black ink in one of the smaller squares. The paper was so thin Jess was impressed he could even write on it without ripping it to shreds.

It read: "315218. Thursday night."

She read the numbers several times to commit them to memory. This would be kind of fun, like a game of clue, if the "who done it" wasn't her fiancé, and the outcome wasn't one of them in a body bag.

She went to put it back in her pocket, but she didn't want to forget about it and Bryan somehow find it. Not that it was likely that he would get a wild hair and do a load of laundry but still. Any risk was too much, so she ran it under the faucet until it disintegrated in her hand, then dumped the remnants in the trash.

Jess waited Thursday night until Bryan's snores became a steady cadence. Grabbing her phone off the nightstand first, she then crept over to his side of the bed and grabbed his phone off the wireless charging pad on his nightstand. She slipped into the bathroom, closed the door, and made sure she flipped the switch that was for the light only, not the fan.

Her fingers were shaking as she typed in the passcode Topher had written on the napkin. It worked and his home screen popped up.

Swiping up, she saw he had no apps open. She navigated through the folders until she found WhatsApp. The increase in her blood pressure was creating a thumping in her ears. She fought back her nerves and started taking pictures of the text streams from the three conversations that came up with her phone. None of them were very long, so it was only a few photos. Jess didn't recognize any names and most of what was said didn't make sense to her, either. It was like the conversations were in code.

She swiped up to close out the app and leave his phone as she found it. Part of her wanted to pry more but she knew she was pushing her luck, so she locked the phone, flushed the toilet as though she'd used it, cut the lights, and crept back out into the bedroom.

Bryan hadn't moved, but he was mumbling something. Jess stopped, frozen in fear.

Is he waking up?

She waited to see if he said anything else. The snores started back up, and she exhaled. Quickly, she returned his phone to the wireless charging pad and crawled back in bed, careful not to wake him.

Jess was already awake when Bryan woke up the next morning. He rolled over to her and nuzzled his face in her hair while squeezing her ass. Jess was worried he would initiate sex she didn't want to have, but he didn't. Instead, he rolled over and grabbed his phone. She got up and told him she was going to make coffee and breakfast since she was planning to go to the office and wanted to get an early start.

He told her he'd be down in a few. When he met her in the kitchen already dressed for work, his mood had soured. Jess grew nervous, wondering if he somehow knew she'd gotten into his phone. He didn't offer a reason for his demeanor, and Jess didn't ask. He ate quickly standing at the kitchen island, then poured coffee in a thermos, planted a kiss on Jess's lips, wished her luck for work—knowing it was a big day for her—and left.

It was the day the judge was set to rule on David Jessup's case. Unlike the movies where there's a hearing in the courtroom with dramatic fanfare, the judge had decided to take the case under advisement after their final arguments had been made, meaning Jess and her team were simply going to wait by their computers and compulsively check their emails until they received the ruling from the judge's office.

The news that the judge signed and filed the order granting their motion to vacate Jessup's judgment and sentence hit their inboxes mid-afternoon, and they celebrated harder than college kids whose football team had just won the national championship. Shauna broke out party hats along with a cookie cake she'd been hiding in the fridge. The paralegal dialed David at the jail to give him the good news and promised they would ensure all the processing paperwork was taken care of that day to get him released from custody as soon as possible.

He cried with relief, and Jess felt a swell of pride in her team for giving up so many frustrating hours of their lives back in order to give David the rest of his.

Jack made an appearance to congratulate Jess and thank her for pushing for the unit. "Well done, Jess. You've done a fine job setting up this office. We'll meet next week to discuss new funding and raises."

Jess beamed. "Thank you for believing in me, Jack." She meant it.

He was the man she wished the partners at her Dallas firm had been when the attorney general scandal hit her. A salt of the Earth kind of person.

The party lasted another few minutes before everyone got busy on the phones arranging David's family's travel to come get him upon his release. Once everything was set in motion, Jess sent everyone home early.

As she was driving home, the same heaviness she'd felt that morning returned, not sure what she would face when Bryan came down that night.

CHAPTER FIFTY-SEVEN

Jess

That's too many, Jess thought to herself.

She knew it wasn't uncommon for all available units to respond to a call in a small, north Georgia county like Hall. Everyone wanted in on the excitement when anything happened because it rarely did. But this was more than usual. And she knew enough to know tonight wasn't a case of the nosey Deputy Barney Fifes.

Looking back down at her phone, she tapped her fiancé's name on her recent call list. Then, she put the phone to her ear, knowing he wouldn't answer.

But then he did.

"Hey, babe. I'm okay. Can't talk right now. I'll call you later." He hung up the phone before Jess could respond, and she's glad he did. She had no idea what she would've said.

A cold panic started at the top of her neck and flushed through her body.

What happened?

She wondered if she should try to reach Topher. That seemed like a bad idea, though. Without any information as to what went down, she couldn't take the risk of reaching out to him. A second wave of panic washed over her.

What if Topher's hurt? Should I drive in the direction of the sirens?

Jess paced the floor thinking through her options.

The scanner.

She quickly opened her phone and navigated to the police scanner app Bryan had downloaded for her soon after they'd started dating. She'd never used it before, and her hands were shaking from nerves. By the time she got it working, it seemed she missed the action as the dispatchers were answering routine calls like medical emergencies. She shut it off and threw her phone across the room on the couch. There wasn't much else she could do other than pace.

After a few minutes, the activity made her more anxious, so she made a cup of coffee and started a load of laundry as bizarre as it felt. She knew she'd go crazy if she didn't keep herself busy so next, she cleaned the kitchen until every surface shined like she'd coated it in shellac. Shellac...that reminded her that her hutch needed to be sealed. She grabbed a quart of polyurethane and headed for the garage.

Bryan got home around two in the morning. Unable to sleep, Jess had stayed in the garage bouncing from one DIY project to the next while she waited for him. She hit the button to lift the garage door as soon as she heard his truck in the driveway.

"What happened?" she asked as soon as he stepped out.

"There's a cartel link we've been keeping an eye on. Things started moving fast this week, and feds came in and busted it today. They needed our help getting set up. One of the undercover fed guys blew his cover, and there was a shootout." His eyes looked tired, but his demeanor was more relaxed than she'd seen him in a while. Not exactly what she expected from him after being caught up in a federal-level drug bust.

Jess's mind immediately went to Topher, and her stomach dropped. She wanted to ask if he was okay, but she knew there was no way she could without raising a host of red flags. If there was ever a time for Jess to put on an Oscar worthy performance, it was now.

"Oh my God, Bryan. Is everyone okay?"

"Everyone on our side is."

Jess internally breathed a sigh of relief. "Thank goodness." She stepped in and hugged him, every fiber of her being resisting as she did.

"Yeah, and it's going to be a long day of meetings with the feds tomorrow...well, today I guess," he said, checking the time on his watch. "So I've got to grab a shower."

They both climbed the stairs, and Jess slid in between the sheets with her head pounding as Bryan stepped into the bathroom. A dozen emotions hit her like a lightning strike to the chest. She had to force air into her lungs to keep from hyperventilating.

What now? I can't live like this.

CHAPTER FIFTY-EIGHT

Jess

Why don't they just leave?

Jess pondered the question with contempt through tears the next morning in the shower. The steam filled her lungs with each sharp inhale between sobs.

She'd awoken to find Bryan gone. He'd texted her that the FBI wanted to meet early while the crime scene was still fresh. She didn't care why he was gone; she was just thankful he was. It was a mystery how he wasn't dead or in jail as Topher had predicted. Maybe he figured out the feds were on him and threw Emery and Eli under the bus.

Her body ached to talk to Topher. To ask him what to do. She prayed, asking for guidance. And she cried some more.

Dragging herself out of the shower, she toweled off before wrapping herself in a robe. She made her way downstairs, fixed a cup of coffee, and sat at the kitchen table, staring into the mug and watching the lighter cream swirl into the dark liquid until it was a warm chestnut color. The sunrise was bathing the room in a warm glow, and she could see light clouds tinged with traces of pink out the window. It was a beautiful morning that looked entirely opposite of the way Jess felt inside. A storm was brewing deep inside, and it carried an ominous message: now that David Jessup was out of jail, it was time to figure out how to break off the engagement and get away from Bryan.

Holding this truth in one hand, there was still another one weighing heavily in her other. Part of her still loved Bryan.

Or do I love my perception of what he could be? A perception based on the man he presented himself to be those first few months. Is the man I love real? Was he real, and now he's gone? Was he ever real? Is this all in my head?

The questions intensified the pain that had been building in her chest. It felt as if there was a knife inside her trying to cut its way out. A searing pain that burned more with every memory that fought its way to the forefront of her consciousness. The blade moved slowly, popping one heartstring at a time.

Amid these questions, Jess's mind kept pulling back to Cathy Denmare. The woman she'd told Topher about in Nina's basement.

The denial she'd been subconsciously clinging to slowly illuminated from the inside out. What started as a small flame grew steadily into a roaring bonfire to reveal itself as something far more sinister than denial. It was dread. It could very well be Jess herself sitting on the stand just as Cathy Denmare had, defending herself against a world that thought she deserved to rot in jail for what she'd done.

The thought caused such a physical reaction in her, she rushed to the half-bath and dry heaved over the toilet.

Jess had known guys like Bryan back in Dallas. Cops that paraded around as "do-gooders" and "speak-for-the-deaders." At least that's what they projected in their chin-down false humility kind of way they favored. But the truth was, they wanted to play the game and one side got to them before the other did. Whether that be a life of crime from growing up in a poor neighborhood, or on the law enforcement side as a legacy. Bryan was dealt a hand that favored the more socially acceptable side of the game. He'd said it himself that night on the couch when he'd quoted Stalin's chief of police.

It was so easy to "other" the opposite side. "It's us against them" mentality. It starts in childhood. Cops versus robbers. Nerds versus jocks. Good versus bad. Jess understood it. She saw it in the courtroom. It's an extremely simplified, binary way of thinking that's comforting because of its nature of being certain. But Jess had come to realize that this zero-sum viewpoint lacked the nuance needed for much of life. Life is much grayer than most like to admit, and the legal system has neither the tolerance nor the resources to deal with this idea. Which leads to the kinds of cases that end up as TV documentaries. The ones where the cops plant the evidence and coerce the witnesses. A corrupt DA decides the case that will get through the court system and manipulate the evidence, build a story around only the evidence they want admitted, and that's the one that ends up in front of the judge and jury.

Bearing in mind her "gray" philosophy—in contrast to what Bryan claimed on the boat when they'd first started dating—Jess knew that not all cops were bad. Not all DAs were willing to put innocent people in jail for the sake of their record. But there were the bad apples—the Bryans—and Jess was coming to realize that the only way to escape a Bryan-type was to beat him at his game of absolutes. The gray wouldn't work here. In her case, Bryan was the DA, Jess was at the defense table by herself, and the jury was still out.

Jess considered her options. She could tell everyone—and by everyone, she meant *everyone*. Bryans can only exist and operate in the shadows. Once there's an awareness, once he's been outed and the darkness that hides the hideous has been illuminated, he loses his power. But she'd be going up against the hometown hero with his Sheriff Daddy *and* run the risk of her past in Dallas coming to light. Inevitably, Jess would look like the crazy one as soon as she stuck her thumb in the eye of the collective citizenry by accusing the golden child of the dearest Whitley family.

Who would I tell anyway? Law enforcement?

The Whitleys were the law enforcement. On multiple levels. And the circumstantial evidence was not in her favor, just like David Jessup.

Jess knew that convictions were very hard to overturn once they were handed down. And the court of public opinion was no exception. Once an impression was made, once accusations flew, they could be hard to shake. Exonerees like Jessup and Denmare knew this well. They may get their freedom back in the sense that they're no longer confined to a sterile six-by-eight cinder block box, but they're never truly free. The stain of suspicion follows them often all the way to the grave.

She also knew from her work as a defense attorney that it wasn't always the truth that prevailed. It was whoever could paint the best picture on the canvas that was the minds of the jury. The courtroom was semantic theater complete with costumes—the judge in the robe and the bailiffs in their uniform. You have to be more compelling than the other side. People are emotional creatures. Attorneys on both sides of a case know this and use this to their advantage.

Next option, she could try to quietly slip away in the night and get back to the safety of her family in Texas as fast as her Mercedes could take her. But even if she rented a car and threw her cell phone in the trash, Bryan would be on her like a duck on a June bug. And if she did make it back to Texas before he found a way to stop her, he wouldn't leave her alone. Just like when she went out a few weeks ago and he followed her. Bryans don't quit. And, more importantly, you don't quit on them. That would be the ultimate betrayal. And even a perceived loss of power for Bryan could spell dire consequences for Jess.

Final option: she could finish the game. Much easier said than done considering the game was like playing chess with a chess master who'd designed the board, engineered the pieces, and changed the rules whenever he felt like he needed an edge. She would also have to betray herself in order to protect herself. Something she'd been doing all along, but now she would have to step her game up without the distraction of the Jessup case—and she'd have to do it well.

This was a delicate, deadly dance she was about to do. Bryan needed control, and what Jess was about to do was going to shake that up in a major way. She would have to make sure she made the right moves at the right time. Bryan was like a hound on a scent when it came to her emotions and intuitions. He could usually sniff them out in seconds. In fact, she was surprised he didn't notice how revulsed she was when she hugged him last night. He must've still been coming down from the raid.

But Jess knew she had to be careful not to overdo it. Too much compliance would alert him even faster. She might as well color her hair purple and wear a neon sign on her forehead that read "poser."

But she would comply a little longer if it meant saving her future.

What other choice do I have?

CHAPTER FIFTY-NINE

Topher

Merriam-Webster didn't have a word for how angry Topher was. He knew he should've told headquarters to give him someone else when he was tasked with starting the Flowery Branch office. But the big wig had given him Bryan—probably a favor owed to Sheriff Daddy—and Topher had decided to give him a shot against his better judgment. And that had gotten him here, in a meeting with the head of the FBI Atlanta field office, who was sucking out all the air out of the small conference room they shared with Flowery Branch Police Department with his oversized ego. They were taking over the investigation Bryan had been working on. Or, more accurately, the scheme he'd been running.

The fourth motivation for Bryan's undercover operation—the one Topher hadn't shared with Jess because he didn't think Bryan could pull it off—was the correct one: Bryan had been working with the feds. It wasn't about the money—although Topher had a hard time believing he hadn't benefitted by having Emery and Eli cozy up to the plug and run some drugs for a cut, unbeknownst to Tweety Bird—or impressing sheriff daddy. Or only because he was being blackmailed by Thomas Ravello's uncle, Tweety Bird, in retaliation for Ravello's death. It was all three of those motivators, plus a dash of hubris and a pinch of "fuck you" to all his colleagues, and you had a cop named Agent Whitley who (probably) took dirty money to protect the cartel—under the guise of being blackmailed—from the federal agencies he was working under cover for to bolster his career and impress his dad. He was either the stupidest man alive or the slickest bastard on the planet.

That explained the undercover athleisure couple. They weren't there to catch Bryan. They were there to step in and help if anything went down. And probably keep an eye on Bryan to make sure that he was a credible source.

Topher had Jason stay late with him at the office last night working on an audit, waiting for the emergency lines to light up like a pack of firecrackers on the Fourth of July. Once they heard the commotion from the calls coming through on the city officer's scanners down the hall, they rushed over to the scene—a recently shut down concrete plant just north of downtown Flowery Branch—in Topher's bureau car. They arrived to find several local units already on-site and EMTs administering first aid, but it wasn't to Bryan. The earthy smell of gunpowder and the metallic scent of blood tinged Topher's nostrils.

He had to fight to push the images of Afghanistan out of his mental space that the smells evoked. At least there weren't any screaming children this time. Just two grown men laying in their own blood. One was clearly deceased, and the other was groaning, barely conscious. Topher had seen enough wounds to know his weren't survivable. A few yards away, a man Topher recognized as Tweety Bird from the case file photos was sitting on the ground, his head hung low with his hands cuffed behind his back. A federal agent was emptying his pockets with gloved hands.

Scanning the rest of the scene, Topher expected to find Bryan somewhere in handcuffs. Maybe already in the back of a federal vehicle. Instead, he was in plain clothes talking to a small gathering of feds who were counting kilos of cocaine and clear bags of black tar heroin in the back of a white utility van, and Topher instantly knew he'd underestimated Agent Whitley. Bryan had played both the cartel and the feds. He'd made deals with both sides and somehow hadn't gotten caught or killed. It was a miracle, really.

Topher had to give it to Bryan. He was a sly motherfucker. Keep your friends close, your enemies closer. He must've realized he was running on borrowed time. A drug ring with connections far-reaching was bound to get picked up by multiple federal offices. Bryan rode the wave as far as he could solo, knowing it was a short-lived game. Then, once the feds started picking up on the scent, he switched sides and acted as though he'd been working undercover instead of actively working with the cartel to save his skin and secret kickbacks.

Damn, he made a good cop. If he was slippery enough to best Topher, he had skill. But what he had in expertise, he lacked in morals. What a waste.

Back in the conference room, Topher was mentally shooting Fed Boss in the forehead when the star of the show made his appearance. Bryan sauntered in with a cup of coffee looking rested and freshly shaved. What kind of sick fuck sells out the cartel, watches two people get murdered, and then gets a good night's sleep?

Topher hadn't slept a wink. The few minutes he wasn't overseeing the processing of the crime scene or answering asinine questions from all the federal agencies showing up, he was chain smoking, slamming cups of black coffee, and thinking about Jess. He wasn't worried for her safety, since the rest of the members of the drug ring that weren't arrested at the site of the bust had been apprehended at various places through the night via no-knock warrants carried out by the FBI and some county-level gang units. There wasn't any immediate threat to anyone's safety after such a devastating bust. It would take any lingering members a while to regroup before attempting any retribution.

Within a couple minutes of Topher and Jason arriving on scene last night, Topher overheard Bryan's brief call with Jess to let her know he was okay. He wondered what she must be feeling. But he never got much time to think about it before someone else came up to him needing information.

As he sat now in the small conference room, absolutely seething, he wished he could talk with her. But it wasn't the time or place. And he needed all his remaining energy reserves to pull some professional decorum together and get through the next round of meetings, which ended just before lunchtime.

Everything that needed immediate attention had already been situated, so Topher finally headed to his truck to go home and clean up before he had to come back and answer more questions for the new round of federal fuckheads that were en route. It was going to be a long next couple of weeks, if not months.

"Topher!" Bryan called, stepping out of the police precinct in pursuit.

Topher ignored him and kept walking to his truck. He hadn't even been able to look directly at him last night, and he had even less patience to deal with him now.

"Hey, man. I know you're pissed. I want to apologize," Bryan pleaded as Topher opened the driver door.

He continued to ignore him, threw the cold contents of his coffee cup out on the ground behind him, and tossed the cup to the passenger floorboard. By now, Bryan had closed the gap.

"Listen, I get it. I fucked up. And I know you probably hate me." Topher mentally filed that one under "understatement of the century."

Topher briefly considered jumping in the truck and backing over Bryan's sorry ass, but he knew there might be eyes watching from the precinct, so he turned and faced him.

"Look," Bryan went on. "I didn't know what else to do. I got in a little over my head with this one and didn't want to bring it to you and admit I fucked up. I asked a fed buddy of mine for some advice, and well, I guess he couldn't keep his mouth shut. So, they came to me and told me they were taking over, and that I had to stay undercover for them."

"Bullshit."

"I'm telling you, man. I didn't have a choice," Bryan insisted.

"I've heard toddlers tell better lies. Save it for your buddies in there." Topher swung his head toward the precinct over Bryan's shoulder.

"It's the truth. Swear on my life."

Topher took a step toward his subordinate. "Want me to go back in there and have the boss man corroborate that story?"

Bryan opened his mouth to speak, then shut it.

"Because of you, some are going to get away," Topher said, taking a step toward Bryan. "What you didn't know is that Region Eight had some leads that could tie in to all this shit, but those are probably going to go cold now and—" Topher stopped himself. Bryan wasn't worth the explanation, nor could he keep his mouth shut to save his life. "So now you've put all of us in danger, including your own fiancée. You pinched the turd off halfway and now you're going to have more shit up your ass than you want to deal with. And we're going to have to deal with it, too. You swatted a motherfucking hornet's nest, undermined the integrity of this office, and blew an entire case that would've saved countless lives all because of your little *fucking* ego. I've met murderers who have more consideration for others than you."

He'd taken a step toward Bryan with each point he'd made until the bills of their ball caps were close enough that Topher could smell the coffee on Bryan's breath.

"You may not realize it for a while," Topher went on, "But you're going to come to regret what you've done. And you better hope to God that no one else gets hurt in the process, or I *will* make you regret every last *miserable second* you've spent on this Earth. And that's not a threat or a promise. That's a fucking fact."

If Topher had to stare at Bryan one more second, he didn't think he would be able to quell the primal desire brewing in his chest to grab his rogue subordinate, drag him to the train tracks fifteen yards in front of his truck, and hold him there until a train came. As if reading his mind, a train whistle ominously blew in the distance, and the ground began to tremble.

Turning on his heel, Topher climbed into the truck, cranked it with more force than necessary, and took off to his house to get some rest. But not before he checked in with Jess, who beat him to the punch.

CHAPTER SIXTY

Jess

Jess was at work, fighting back tears in the bathroom as she pulled out her phone and texted Topher under Ruth's contact. Another person she had to lie to. And another lie she had to tell herself: that this was the best thing, and the only way. He wouldn't be protected otherwise, and Bryan already had him in danger, like her. Her heart protested as her head moved her thumbs across the screen to text him: "Everything is good. Thanks for your help." A new wave of dread washed over her as she pushed send.

A green message popped up almost immediately: "call me."

She couldn't do it. It was more than she could handle emotionally. And Jess knew she needed to find a place deep inside her to store those feelings for now. If she allowed them too much of her mental space, they might keep her from doing what needed to be done.

Jess wasn't so naive to think she could run away from them forever. There was no doubt in her mind they would find their way to the surface with a vengeance one day. She learned in her twenties that you could push them away for a while, but they would always find their way out. She just needed to keep them at bay a little longer.

Dropping her phone in her bag, she tried to ignore the sound of it ringing over the clacking of her heels on the tile of the justice building's floor as she went back to her office to put out other people's fires, while the one consuming her life grew brighter, beyond the point of containment. But she could only play firefighter until lunch. Her office would have to fend for itself this afternoon as she had a meeting with Scar at the jail she couldn't miss.

CHAPTER SIXTY-ONE

Topher

On top of his loathing for flip-phone T9 texting—kids these days really don't know how easy they have it—Topher needed to hear Jess's voice. He needed something to gauge her statements on. That and, well, other reasons.

He waited briefly for a response before deciding to call her. The phone rang through to the voicemail with no answer.

Fuck.

She's going rogue. Topher had seen enough fight in her eyes in Nina's basement to know it would win out over the fear. Jess was smart, intelligence combined with grit was a combination that Bryan had misjudged in Topher's estimation.

Topher almost felt bad for Bryan for a brief second. Just briefly. Then images of the dead men from last night slid into his mind's eye, instantly evaporating any amount of pity that Topher might have felt.

The next twenty-four hours were another whirlwind. Meetings, phone calls, paperwork, federal agents trying to claw their way into every orifice they could find for more information. Topher knew it was a big case, but he didn't realize exactly how far out it reached until he saw the levels of brass coming in to get the scoop firsthand. Of course, they didn't tell him much. He was just a peon that could provide what they needed. The relationship was in no way reciprocal. But the sheer number of agents that descended on Flowery Branch from a smorgasbord of three-letter, overfunded federal agencies told him Whitely had handed them something much larger than a run of the mill cartel connection.

But it didn't matter much to Topher now for two reasons. One, because the feds were taking over so the case was officially out of his hands. And two, because Jess kept invading his mental space like she had every day since he'd taken her and Bryan out on his boat last fall. He was coming to terms with the fact that he hadn't been heeding his own advice and had been lying to himself about her. Without a single word or intimate touch, she'd completely changed what he wanted in life. He no longer believed his destiny was celibacy. Whenever he saw a couple or a family, he unwillingly thought of Jess. The life that had seemed like something out of reach suddenly seemed possible. The thought made him hate Bryan more than he already did.

He drove home after his long day of briefing feds and made a beeline through the house to his fridge to grab a beer, and then to his back deck that overlooked the lake. There was no point in trying to find rest he knew wouldn't come. He swiped a beer from the fridge before stepping through the sliding glass door onto the deck.

His work phone rang, and he pulled it out of his pocket.

"Yeah, boss?" Topher answered.

The ballistics expert from the Atlanta office on the other end of the line got straight to the point. "The casings you gave me are a match. Do you have a case number you want me to note it under?"

"No, I do not. Thanks for your help." Topher punched the screen to end the call and threw the phone on the table beside him.

Dropping into one of the patio chairs, he pulled off his ball cap and then used the edge of the table beside him to pop the cap on his beer bottle. After a swig, he set it down and reached for the cigarette pack resting in the middle of the table.

With his first cigarette, he considered having Bryan arrested for murdering Thomas Ravello now that he had the ballistics evidence to back it up. He'd pulled a shell casing from the evidence tub that held items from the Ravello shooting stored at headquarters. It was stuffed at the bottom of a paper evidence bag and wasn't listed on the bag log, almost like it had been thrown in as an afterthought. He found it the day he'd met Jess for lunch when he told her to be careful. Of course, he couldn't be sure the casing was Bryan's until a test was run, but Topher knew the gang Jesus Silva ran with was notorious for using suppressors on their guns so they could shoot from their vehicles in drive-bys. This meant the shell casings stayed in the car, minimizing the evidence that could connect them to a murder. Based on this information, the fact that a shell casing was found at the scene—which was also left out of the investigation report—had been a problem for Topher. And now the ballistics expert just confirmed it was the missing link Topher had been looking for to confirm Bryan murdered Ravello.

If he had Bryan arrested, he doubted the charges would stick. It was more likely the Feebs would step in and sweep it under the rug now that Bryan was the teacher's pet. But it might buy Jess some time to get the hell out of town and off the radar.

With his second Marlboro, he considered going public with the information. Stir up enough outrage so that action had to be taken if for nothing else than damage control. Who was he kidding? Topher wasn't the kind to sit around and wait for the court of public opinion to take Bryan down, and there probably wasn't even the time for that. Not to mention the fun he would start with the already pissed off cartel.

By the first drag on his third cigarette, he was reaching for his keys. He wasn't sure exactly where he was headed, yet. He cranked the

Tacoma and steered back toward Flowery Branch, willing himself to come up with an option. Any option that didn't involve the immediate end of his career.

CHAPTER SIXTY-TWO

Jess

So much blood, Jess thought to herself as she examined her left hand in the faint glow of the hallway light streaming through the cracked bedroom door.

Just beyond her glistening, red fingers lay Bryan. Crumpled on the floor, he was lying on his side in his boxers with his hands and feet bound together with a small rope and his face turned down. He was still—not the sleeping kind. He had shallow cuts all over his body, none of which appeared to be deep enough to penetrate anything vital. But enough of them to allow major blood loss. Death by a thousand cuts. Literally. Her gaze shifted back to her hands, her right one this time. The knife from the kitchen she always cut fruit with shone in the light, crimson and sticky.

A sound interrupted her thoughts. He whimpered.

Not dead, yet.

Jess stepped closer to his body so she could get a better look at his face. His eyes were closed. He didn't acknowledge her presence, so she took the tip of the knife and pressed it into his forehead, pushing his head back so he was facing her. A small trickle of cherry-red oxygenated blood seeped out at the point of contact.

She held the pressure until he finally opened his eyes.

"Did you know the best way to kill someone is with salt?" She asked rhetorically.

His eyes widened as he registered one of the boxes of salt he'd purchased in Jess's other hand. The white around his irises a stark contrast to the dark blood that covered nearly his entire body.

Another sound stopped her in her tracks.

She looked to her right. The sound was coming from the floor near Bryan's side of the bed. She squinted in the dark until she made out the rectangular shape of his phone. The screen was black, but she heard a voice coming from the device. She shifted toward it in her crouched position to pick it up, her joints felt stiff. The phone lit up as she lifted it off the floor.

The screen read "911." He'd called the police. The time elapsed on the call was two minutes.

They'll be here soon.

As if on cue, the faint wail of a siren started slicing through the silence of the night.

Should I run?

She awoke with a start. Before she even realized it, she was sitting up in bed, looking to her left, where Bryan lay sleeping. No blood or blade in sight. She could hear him snore faintly and see his face with his jaw slack in the blue glow of the light that came from the Wi-Fi extender plugged in the outlet on his side of the bed.

Jess rested her elbows on her bent knees and combed her fingers through her hair, sucking air in until her breathing normalized.

And at that moment, the true weight of the situation came crashing down. Like someone had released a thousand pounds of bricks directly on top of her. She didn't know if the dream was a premonition or simply a nightmare. But she did know two things: Bryan was a monster, and the reality that one of them might not make it out of the relationship alive was as clear as ever.

Any lingering denial had been wiped from Jess's consciousness by this point. Moments of mental friction of an existential magnitude would occasionally pierce through the fabric of everyday life for Jess. It seemed new revelations came daily for her, like sheets of rain pummeling her. Every time she came close to regaining her sanity, a new round slapped her. She felt constantly barraged by new bombshells.

One came through the next day as she poured over the witness statements at work. A thought floated in from some unknown origin that shocked her because it would have been an abhorrent rumination in any other relationship. She found herself truly wishing Bryan would find someone new. And if that thought wasn't disturbing enough, the realization continued to unfurl itself like a black rose: there very well could be another person. But the Bryans of the world, like Cathy Denmare's husband, don't simply cheat and move onto the next person. Once someone is in his clutches, under his thumb, he may color outside the lines for fun, but he wasn't going anywhere. His possible infidelity wasn't a symptom of the state of the relationship. It was his MO.

She didn't have time to be angry at herself. There would be plenty of time for that later...hopefully. Right now, she had to get started on leaving. She knew from working with victims of coercive controllers as an attorney that leaving was a process, not an event.

Jess felt like she didn't know what she didn't know. Everything she thought she knew about coercive controllers, and herself, was in question now.

What else? She wracked her brain for other useful information from the training. *Where to not be assaulted.* He hadn't been physically violent with her, yet, but Jess knew it could very well be coming.

Stay out of the bathrooms and kitchen. Or any room with hard surfaces and sharp objects. Get to the living room or bedroom when he escalates.

Jess was still thinking about all this when she pulled into the driveway that afternoon. She'd taken off work early, thinking she could get more work done at home than in the office since the interns, paralegals, and her investigators were all trying to share the office, getting in each other's way. She probably could've found a jury room to duck into, but she needed lunch and decided to continue home once she was in the car.

CHAPTER SIXTY-THREE

Jess

Let's go to the tavern tonight," Bryan suggested as he stared into the empty fridge across the kitchen from Jess at the table. He was referring to a joint up the road that had live music, cheap wings, and cold beer.

Jess shifted a stack of folders on the kitchen table in front of her. "I'm really tired. Can't we just pull something out of the freezer?" All Jess wanted to do was soak in the tub and try to forget what her life was.

"I think they brought that dish you like back. The one with the peppers," Bryan teased with an enticing tone.

"Why don't you go and bring me back a to-go box. Call Topher or Jason. I'm really overwhelmed and just need to chill."

"Overwhelmed with work?"

"Yeah."

"Then go with me to dinner, and let's talk about it. You can get it off your chest while I get some beer in my belly. Come on, let's go." He swaggered across the kitchen, kissed her on the cheek as he passed by, and grabbed his keys he'd deposited in the bowl on the entryway table when he came in a few minutes earlier.

She didn't have the energy to fight him, so she followed him out the door, still dressed in her work clothes.

The tavern was already buzzing with a mostly blue-collar crew of patrons when they arrived. Jess had left her blazer in the car but still felt out of place in her attire. Bryan didn't seem to notice and ordered three beers when the waitress came by. Two for him and one for her.

Bryan ended up doing most of the talking. He told her about a BOLO put out by the bureau's Perry office in middle Georgia.

"Some psycho killed his whole family down near Valdosta. There's reason to believe he might be in the area. So keep your head on a swivel for danger and don't go anywhere by yourself that you don't have to," he instructed.

"Why do they think he might be in the area?"

"Some tips that've been called in," Bryan explained.

"Then, why aren't you out looking for him?" Jess pressed incredulously. It felt like an attempt to isolate her.

"Region Eight is on it." His tone was clipped.

"So is he in *this* area, or is he up in Region Eight?"

"How about you let *me* be the investigator and quit playing your stupid twenty questions game?" As he finished, the waitress dropped their beers off and took their orders.

Neither of them revived the topic when she left, each taking sips of beer. Bryan did most of the drinking. He rarely drank more than a couple of beers, but a couple of city officers Jess recognized from basketball showed up as they finished their dinner and convinced Bryan to play a couple games of pool. Jess declined to join their game and sat in the booth by herself swiping through apps and checking her email on her phone until Bryan was ready to go home.

Jess was concerned about the number of drinks he had in the relatively short window they were there. Her suspicions were confirmed when he swung the truck wide as he pulled them out of the parking lot, driving them into the opposite lane.

"Bryan, I think I should drive," Jess blurted out, grabbing the handle on her door.

"Why?"

"I had less to drink. Just pull over here at the gas station, and we can switch," she said, pointing at the Chevron just across the intersection.

"Jess, I'm a police officer. You think I'd drive us drunk? You think I'd be that stupid, given what I do? You act like I don't care about you. Like I would put you in harm's way when I'm always the one who's tried to protect you! ALWAYS!" His tone escalated to a yell, making Jess's left ear ring. The gregarious fiancé from earlier was gone.

Jess sat silent, wishing for them to be home. She needed to get out of the car before he did something even more reckless than driving them intoxicated.

"You know what," he said, his tone having dropped back down to a conversational level but with suspicion injected into it like venom. "You're trying to control me. That's what it is. That's what's going on here. Yeah, you want to be in charge and tell me what to do. Order me around like some little bitch. Well, I've got fucking news for you. That shit doesn't fly with me. I won't be a part of the wussification of men going on in the world today. You can fucking forget about that." He slammed his hand down on the top of the steering wheel and looked over at her.

In his inebriated state, he didn't realize he pulled the wheel as he slammed his hand down, and the movement took them into oncoming traffic.

"Bryan!" Jess screamed as they were staring down the headlights of another car, playing chicken.

Bryan swerved to the right shoulder as the other car blared its horn and swerved toward the opposite shoulder.

"If you'd stop distracting me with your whiny-ass nagging, that wouldn't happen. So stop before you get us killed."

Jess sat wide-eyed and tight-lipped the remaining miles home. Once he pulled them in the driveway, narrowly missing the mailbox, Jess finally exhaled.

She quickly exited the truck and went inside. Bryan was right behind her and had wound up again. Now that he wasn't having to concentrate on driving anymore, he turned his attention back to her.

"Why do you act like I'm such a bad guy? I really want to know where all this is coming from."

"I never said you were bad. That wasn't what that was about at all," Jess answered as she pointed toward the door to the garage. "It's fine. We're home now, so let's drop it."

Bryan stepped over to the kitchen counter and grabbed one of his work files off it.

"You act like I treat you like shit. Like I'd do something like this." He threw the file toward her.

Several 8x12 images of a dead woman slid out of the file and scattered across the floor. The glossy finish of the photos made the blood look fresh. Like she was in the room with them. It appeared she'd been badly beaten, a horrific death.

"Do you know how lucky you are? I don't hit you. I've never laid a hand on you!"

You don't have to.

Jess peeled her eyes away from the carnage in the photos and steeled herself for the rest of the attack. Experience told her the worst was yet to come. She busied herself by slipping off her heels.

Jess's lack of response fueled his tirade. He switched tactics since his first approach failed to get the rise out of her. "It's Stacey, isn't it? She's acting like I don't treat you well or something. Comparing me to that soft, corporate husband of hers. Is that the kind of guy you like?"

Jess was exasperated and on the verge of tears. "Please stop."

"Why won't you just answer the fucking question, Jess? Talk to me!"

"We both need to cool down before we finish this conversation. I'm going to go take a bath," Jess said, heading through the living room.

Bryan moved to position himself between Jess and the stairs.

"Don't do this," she warned. "Let me go upstairs and relax, and then we'll talk." Her warning turned into more of a plea.

"No, you're a grown adult, Jess. You can't run away from your problems," Bryan argued, folding his arms across his chest.

"I'm not running away from anything! I'm trying to cool off so we can have a more productive conversation. Just let me take a bath for half an hour."

He wasn't budging. "After we talk."

Jess couldn't keep her tone down any longer. "What's left to talk about, Bryan? There's nothing to discuss. We're arguing about stupid shit." She motioned between them. "This is doing *nothing*. We need to *not* talk for a few minutes and calm down."

Bryan remained cool. "I am calm. Clearly, you're the one who can't keep calm."

He spread his feet apart, making himself look even more imposing.

"Fine." Jess backed away. "I'll go to Nina's for the night." She moved back toward the kitchen to grab her keys.

Bryan jumped into action and ran around the other side of the coffee table, beating her to the kitchen.

Stay out of the kitchen. Get to the bedroom, she reminded herself.

Jess whipped around and ran up the stairs. She heard Bryan's heavy footfalls gaining on her as she reached the top. Making it into the bedroom just in time to close the door, she swung it closed and accidentally hit Bryan in the face with it as it latched. She quickly locked it and backed up.

What now, Jess? You know this won't end well.

"Are you fucking serious, Jess?! Open the door. NOW!" Bryan was simultaneously banging on the door and working the knob so violently Jess feared the door was about to fly off the hinges.

"Give me a minute!" Her voice carried a level of panic she wasn't expecting.

She was answered by the door rattling in its frame so violently she feared the whole wall might come down.

He rammed it a second time, the hinges barely hanging on from the first hit. Jess quickly stepped over and flipped the lock and opened the door before he broke through it.

It swung open, barely missing her this time. "What the fuck is wrong with you? I try to have a conversation with you and you hit me in the face?"

"It wasn't intentional, Bryan. I just needed a minute to myself like I've been asking for since we got home."

He moved past her into the bathroom, flipped on the light, and looked in the mirror. A small red mark was materializing on his cheekbone.

He whipped around, pointed to the mark. "You understand I could press charges against you for this? That's assault, Jess."

Jess had no idea what to say. It was like the salt and getting out of the truck in the middle of the road. He was trying to drive her crazy so that she looked like the bad partner in the relationship. Not him.

Without another word, he went downstairs, grabbed his keys, and left in his truck.

Jess sat on the bed for a long time, trying to process what had transpired. She considered calling 911 anonymously to report Bryan driving drunk. But she knew he would know it was her that called, and she was worried he might bring up the incident with the door and land her in jail, too. Should she go to Nina's?

No, I don't want him showing up at Nina's like this.

She briefly considered calling Topher. But she knew the chances of that option ending well were also slim.

Eventually, she washed her face and got in bed, staring at the ceiling and counting the trains that rumbled by as her mind battled itself. One side of her brain fought to keep her thinking of a plan to get out. The other fought to push everything down, resulting in a paralyzed feeling that had her mind drifting off, as though she was no longer in her own body.

Bryan finally came home in the early hours of the morning. She flipped onto her side, facing away from Bryan's side of the bed, acting like she was asleep. He climbed into bed without a word and started sliding his hand down Jess's back.

She prayed he would stop touching her and go to sleep. He didn't. His hands continued to roam, and he pulled her across the bed to him.

"I'm very tired. Please let me sleep," she said.

He ignored her words and climbed on top of her, kissing down her chest. Jess could still smell alcohol on him. He must've found another drink while he was out.

"Bryan, stop," Jess said firmly.

He acknowledged her this time and pulled back. "Why? Who're you fucking?"

"What?" Jess's heart hit sixth gear, and her armpits tingled with stress sweat.

"If you don't want to fuck me, then you're getting it somewhere else." Anger and accusation dripped from his words like blood from a wound.

"You're crazy. Get off me." She fought to get out from underneath him by bucking her hips.

He held strong and kept her pinned beneath him, his beer breath tickling her face making her want to vomit even more than she already did from stress.

"Then prove you're not," he demanded, shifting his legs to force hers open.

The more Jess resisted, the harder his grip on her became.

"That's fine. I know how you like it rough."

It seemed her resistance fueled his desire to dominate her. Nothing she said stopped him. Jess gave up trying to fight him since the tension in her muscles made his movements hurt worse. He got progressively rougher until he finished.

He rolled off her, panting, and then started snoring within a couple of minutes.

Jess rubbed her wrists where he'd been gripping, which were already sore. She wasn't sure if he'd torn something between her legs.

Maybe she needed to scrap a planned exit and get it over with tonight.

CHAPTER SIXTY-FOUR

The polymer stippling dug into Jess's left palm like 100-grit sandpaper as she wrapped her fingers around the grip of Bryan's service pistol and quietly removed it from the holster. Her right hand wrapped comfortably around the other side of the grip. Her thumbs lined up on the right side of the gun like a skewed equal sign. Being a leftie, she pushed forward with her left hand and pulled equal tension back with the right, creating an iron grip on the weapon. Even though the bedroom was almost pitch black, Jess could find her grip on a pistol upside down and blindfolded. Perk of growing up in the South. Being proficient with firearms was a rite of passage for a Texan.

Since it was his service pistol, which had to be ready to perform at a moment's notice, she was almost positive a round was already chambered, but she pushed the slide back slightly to double check. A glint of silver poking through the black affirmed her suspicions. She released the slide, her hands shaking. She wondered if this was the same gun used to kill Thomas—if Bryan was the one who pulled the trigger. More importantly, was it the gun that was about to kill Bryan now?

Jess kept both of her hands on the gun at low ready and slowly turned to her left where Bryan was out cold on their bed, exhausted from his exertions on her.

She had to think quickly. Was she going to do it or not? He could wake up at any second. She would probably need to wake him, so he would lunge at her, and then she would have to act fast and shoot straight.

Will anyone believe me? Am I ready to face the consequences if they don't? I'll have to fabricate some more defensive wounds. The marks on my wrists might not be enough. People don't believe you unless they can see the black eyes and the bloody noses or broken ribs. Just like Cathy Denmare.

Her heart was trying to pound its way out of her chest, and her feet grew clammy, sticking to the wood floor.

Her upper arm muscles engaged to lift the weapon, but she stopped herself. The lines of his face were just visible in the darkness. Memories of their first dates came to her, flooding her with emotion. The laughter, jumping in the lake together, the cuddling, the intimate moments all vied for her attention, begging her to remember the good times.

But as she shifted her weight, she felt the burning between her legs from what he'd just done. It was enough for her to raise the weapon. Most of Bryan's head disappeared behind the orange fiber optic sights as she trained the gun on him.

Can I do this?

She was ripped from her thoughts by the bellowing of a train whistle. She hadn't even noticed the vibration of the floor as the massive locomotive made its way through the center of town just a few hundred yards away.

The disruption was enough to back her down. She replaced the gun in the holster and laid on the chair in the corner by the bathroom door where Bryan always dropped it for the night. Quietly, she tiptoed back to her side of the bed and sank into the embrace of the comforter, exhausted but unable to release herself to sleep. Something had changed.

It wasn't Bryan she feared anymore. It was herself.

The next morning, Bryan apologized to her for being "intense" as they lay in bed. Jess was on her side facing away from him, hating the feeling of his body on hers as he nuzzled his face into her hair.

She had to know. She had to know if he was a murderer. Even after what he did last night, there was still some small part of her clinging onto the idea that the Bryan she had met was still somewhere in there.

"I heard something the other day," she began, staring unfocused toward the window.

"Heard what?" The vibrations of his voice into her hair made the hair on her neck tickle, but the feeling didn't invoke sensuality.

"I heard a rumor about that shooting from last year," she threw out, testing the waters. She knew he would know which one she was referring to.

The comment pulled him out of sleep's grasp, and his words were crisper when he answered, "What about it?"

"Something about it might've been a cop that shot him," she answered, and then held her breath, unsure how he would respond.

He didn't miss a beat, and his tone was even as he asked, "Where'd you hear that?"

"At the café in the justice building. I was waiting on Shauna, and some Gwinnett officers were sitting nearby. I overheard their conversation," Jess lied.

Bryan exhaled, and she could feel his body go rigid with tension. In the fiery light of the sunrise stretching through the blinds, she watched him roll over and sit on the edge of the bed with his back to her.

He spoke apprehensively. "The way things went down in the report isn't how it actually happened."

It felt like every cell in Jess's body stopped in its tracks. Her heartbeat felt louder than the cars passing outside on Atlanta Highway.

He went on, "I got accused of murder. And I didn't murder anyone. I defended myself."

Neither of them said anything for a moment as Jess digested his words.

Topher was right.

Jess nervously pressed, looking over her shoulder at him. "Then why didn't you just say that? If it was a true self-defense situation and you'd never had any issues on your professional record in the past, why would telling the truth be a problem?"

Bryan turned so he could face her over his shoulder. His expression pleaded for her understanding with pain in his eyes. "It was in Dekalb County. The DA down there ran for office on a platform of cracking down on police brutality. He'd nail me to a cross to prove to his constituents that he was holding true to his word. Taking me down as a state agent instead of a local beat cop—something that would make regional if not national headlines—would be his dream come true." He paused for a moment before continuing, "I didn't have a choice, Jess. I had to say that it was Jesus Silva in the Hellcat that did it—and I know for a fact it was Silva in the Hellcat, because I had been casing him less than an hour before I met with Ravello. As I was getting information from Ravello, he saw the Hellcat coming down the road toward the parking lot I met him in and started yelling that I was working with Silva. He went for his gun in his waistband, and my instinct took over." He dropped his head, but she could still see his profile. His jaw worked, and he squeezed his eyes shut.

Jess sat with his words for a moment, studying his face to gauge his sincerity. It was hard to tell.

When he spoke again, his voice was filled with angst. "You don't have to believe me. I'm sorry I didn't tell you before. I didn't know how." His words tapered off at the end, and she thought she might've heard a sniffle.

He got up abruptly and put on his running clothes, adding that he might be gone for a while before going down the stairs. Jess didn't ask questions because she didn't care where he went. She just needed him the fuck away from her. Once she'd heard the door close downstairs, she jumped out of bed to shower and leave for work before he got back. Then she remembered it was Saturday.

Shit.

She went downstairs, made coffee, and sat at the kitchen table, staring out the window. Of all the thoughts her brain could pick to focus on, she couldn't quit thinking about how much she hated the monkey grass that grew around the perimeter of the pine straw island in the backyard.

Thinking a physical activity might help pull her out of her spiraling thoughts, she went upstairs to change into some old clothes.

As she pulled a grungy t-shirt over her head, her mind continued searching for options. She wondered about the Witness Protection Program. Vanish, change her identity completely, and relocate in the middle of the night. But she hadn't witnessed a crime. They wouldn't help her. As far as they knew, she was just an ungrateful woman that should've thought twice about who she went on a date with and should "just leave." Very few understood her dilemma.

She went back downstairs and looked through the tools in the garage for a shovel. Hedge shears. Cleaning chemicals. A fire poker. Jess had never thought of how the average American household had a lot of things that could be weaponized should the need arise until now. She paused every time she saw a new object that could be used to inflict pain and suffering until she located a shovel.

She then opened the garage door, walked around the side of the house to the backyard, and began digging up the ratty monkey grass.

"Be gone," she said as she tossed a clump into the wheelbarrow she'd found lying upside-down in the side yard, presumably abandoned by one of the craftsman's former owners.

It took her a while to root out all the plants. After she dumped the final clump, she wiped her brow with the back of her gardening gloves and leaned the shovel against the side of the wheelbarrow. Then, staring at the shovel, she had a thought.

She took hold of the handle again and looked it up and down. Another item that could be used to inflict pain or cover one's tracks after doing so. It was old, and the wood was dry as a bone and splitting. The blade was dying a slow death as rust ate away at it. It didn't have much life left in it, especially not after uprooting the monkey grass. She was surprised it made it to the end. But that was the last project it would complete. Firmly gripping the handle, she leaned the shovel a little to the side and stepped on the blade, testing it with her weight. It immediately protested with cracking sounds. She increased the pressure until the wood finally split above the collar where the blade and handle met. Officially decommissioned.

She threw the pieces of the shovel on top of the plants in the wheelbarrow. Removing her gloves, she headed inside to cool off and grab a pen and paper to make a list.

After jotting a few things down, she checked over the list, sliding her thumb down the side of the paper as she went. She noted the place to get each item beside it and dug some cash out of her purse.

That should do it.

She'd have Bryan pick up the items before the weekend ended.

CHAPTER SIXTY-FIVE

Jess

Kind of like Thomas," Jess snapped, losing control of her wits for a moment.

Bryan had been hounding her about the "psychopath from Valdosta" again out of nowhere after work on Monday. Jess had gone into the office and spent most of it looking at autopsy photos from a case they were about to file post-conviction motions on. Looking at murder victims was something she hoped she never got too used to. Bryan had beat her home, already having showered and changed, which meant his gun was hopefully upstairs in the bedroom on the chair by the bathroom door. He'd started in on her right after she'd walked in the door, reminding her once again that she could end up dead if she didn't listen to him.

"Thomas Ravello," she repeated. "I guess he didn't listen well enough and ended up dead."

Jess couldn't hold it together anymore. Emotionally exhausted was an understatement. The stress of trying to act like everything was fine while she feared her life—and not because of some guy from Valdosta that may or may not even exist—had become too much.

"I told you. That was self-defense. And I was cleared from any wrongdoing." He slowly started in her direction from where he'd been across the kitchen by the fridge.

Jess fought to keep her voice steady. "Was it?"

"What're you going to go to my bosses and whine about some hearsay from a few Gwinnett courthouse Paul Blart security guards? You think they're going to believe you?" His eyes bored holes into her, and Jess was suddenly aware of his physical prowess as he moved closer. He stopped halfway across the kitchen and let out a maniacal laugh before launching his next assault. "Just like your boss in Dallas?" His words seared into her like a hot iron, burning their way through her skin to her heart. "That seemed like it went well for you. You look a little confused. Should I remind you of how everyone thought you were a liar? You lost your credibility. Kissed your fast-track career goodbye."

Jess's initial instinct was to correct him. To remind him that her claims were true. He'd always said he believed her. But now it was clear he never even cared. It was another chess move in his ruse of trust-building. Another tactic to get her walls down, expose her vulnerabilities. And, where a devoted lover would have taken his time kissing his way over her insecurities until they melted away so she felt safe, Bryan stockpiled them for moments like now. To weaponize them against her.

You knew he would do this when you confronted him. Get your head back in the game.

Jess tapped into the last calm reserves of her mind that had eluded her before. She willed them back to draw on them for this next part. It was time to break out the ace she'd hidden up her sleeve. She calmly clasped her hands in front of her. The move was more to stop them from shaking than to look authoritative; the latter was a bonus.

"I thought you might say that. But I wonder what the investigators would say about all the supplies you've been collecting over the past few months. You know the paint thinner, the bleach, the tarps, the new shovel, all the drop cloths, oh, and your murder weapon of choice, all that salt."

The color began draining from Bryan's face as he slowly took another step toward her, realizing she had him pinned on two fronts. She continued, "And because you're a cop, you knew to buy them over time at different locations, often paying with cash. Once I confronted you with the evidence of Thomas's murder, you couldn't let that kiss your fast-track career to the FBI or taking daddy's place as county sheriff goodbye. So you had to take matters into your own hands. And how convenient was it that you just happened to need all this stuff right around the same time."

His face shifted from fear to anger as his wide eyes narrowed at her, and he lit into her with vengeance.

"Who put this idea in your head?" he demanded. When she didn't respond right away, his anger escalated rapidly, taking his tone along with it. "TELL ME!"

Jess stared back at him stoically and hoped the fear gripping her chest wasn't translating to her face. She did a mental checklist of her surroundings: she was by the door to the garage with Bryan on the other side of her, away from the door. She had to keep it that way.

"So, here's what's about to happen. I'm going to leave this house, and you're going to let me go, and no one else will know," she explained as she quickly pulled her phone from her pocket, unlocked it, and played the video she'd obtained from Scar, which clearly showed Bryan acted as the aggressor in the shooting he was investigated for, not in self-defense as he'd claimed.

"But if I don't walk out of this house in the next few minutes, the rest of the world will know you killed Thomas Ravello in cold blood." She'd already drafted an email that contained the video on an account Bryan didn't know about. The recipient list consisted of two dozen reporters at various news outlets, local and national, and podcasters. Topher was copied on it as well. If nothing else, Jess knew he would get it in the right hands. And the final recipient on the list was Bryan himself. That would help her with what might be coming next.

She quickly hit send, which was followed by a "woosh" sound, confirming its departure. Keeping her tone as even and calm as she could, she explained, "There's a ten-minute delay. I can pull it back but only if I hit I-985 southbound without sight of you in my rearview mirror. Otherwise, you might want to go ahead and start consulting criminal attorneys."

He ignored her last comment and continued in his heightened tone. "Topher put you up to this? *Didn't he*? And I bet you're fucking him, aren't you?"

Jess said nothing, holding firm to her stoic expression.

"AREN'T YOU?!" New nuclear level activated.

"I'm telling you. You don't want to do this Bryan. Just let me go," Jess warned, keeping her composure.

"Get in the truck," he ordered, grabbing his keys out of the bowl in a rage, knocking the rest of its contents on the floor.

"No," Jess said, panic creeping in.

She slipped her hand in her back pocket and hit the button on her key fob that started her car.

Bryan heard the engine crank. "Yeah, we'll take your car. Even better. He'll probably be excited to see you and come outside."

CHAPTER SIXTY-SIX

Topher

Topher was staying late in the office working through the mound of paperwork Bryan had gifted him with his rogue actions when he heard the call come through on the scanner. The panic button at Jess and Bryan's had been triggered. He beat every city officer out the door and nearly caught air with his truck as he sped over the railroad tracks, running the red light on the other side.

He didn't even bother with the driveway once he reached the house, sliding directly into the front yard. Jess's car was running in the driveway, and the garage door and door to the house from the garage were both open. He didn't hear anything, but he drew his pistol and cleared the house anyway. Empty.

Fuck.

The sirens were just now reaching his ears. He jumped back in the truck and pulled out his phone. While the app loaded, he scanned the yard for a sign of where they went. Tire marks. They started at the very edge of the driveway and onto the road for just a few inches. Easy enough to miss if you weren't looking for them. The grass to the right of the concrete was disturbed as though someone had taken a hard, fast left out of the driveway.

The app had loaded, and he saw the blue dot moving south on Atlanta Highway, confirming they were moving in the direction the tire marks and grass had indicated. Dropping the truck in gear, he hurried in the same direction.

He frantically thought through the options where they could be headed. They? Topher's investigative mind kicked back in. He didn't have enough information to determine it was both of them. It could be Bryan with Jess's phone. It could be Jess in Bryan's truck. His gut told him it was both of them. None of the options made him feel any better about the situation.

He grabbed the phone again and looked at the location. The dot had taken a hard right and was headed west on Lanier Islands Parkway, which was the direction of the lake. Toward Topher's.

They were headed to his house. Handing him home field advantage.

Game on, motherfucker.

CHAPTER SIXTY-SEVEN

Jess

Bryan continued to hound Jess en route to Topher's house. They were in his truck. As soon as Bryan mentioned taking her car on his way out the door, she threw her key fob on the ground in front of her and smashed it with one quick stomp of her heel, then kicked the pieces into the grass. Obviously, his vehicle was available, too, but she wasn't going to make it easy on him. Without missing a beat, he grabbed his keys and ordered her into the truck. Her feet had felt like lead as she made her way to the truck, Bryan breathing down her neck. Getting in was the last thing on earth she wanted to do, but she knew it was her only shot at keeping him calm. Maybe she could talk him down on the way to Topher's. And if not, she trusted Topher to take control of the situation once they got there.

She wanted to cry, but the tears were frozen in place by fear. His driving became more erratic with each mile.

"You thought you'd get away with it, huh? I fucking knew it," he spat at her. "I knew it since the basketball game. That's why you always wore those sunglasses. So you could look at him and not get caught. You goddamn *whore*!" He punched the dash, sending a crack shooting through the media screen.

Jess crawled into the corner of her seat as far away from him as she could get.

They blew through the intersection of where McEver Road expanded to four lanes and crossed over the four lanes of Lanier Islands Parkway, running the red light. A car heading south on McEver had to swerve sharply and run off the road to narrowly miss nailing them in Jess's door. She screamed, but Bryan remained unfazed. He had a wild look in his eyes. It was almost animal-like.

As the truck approached one hundred miles per hour according to the speedometer, Bryan turned toward her and reignited his interrogation. "Are you wearing a fucking wire?" He demanded.

Jess clutched the door as they veered toward the shoulder. "Slow down!"

"ARE YOU?!" Bryan refocused his eyes on the road and reached over, grabbing hold of her button-down shirt by her chest.

"Stop!" She tried to swat his hand away, but his grip was too firm, and he ended up ripping off the top button, exposing her chest.

When they got to Topher's, his bureau vehicle was in the drive. Jess sat frozen in her seat and prayed he was there.

Bryan cut the engine and took the key as he jumped out, leaving his door open.

"Come out you fucking coward!" Bryan screamed, banging on the front windows.

He then proceeded down the side of the house toward the back deck and dock, yelling more insults and threats.

Jess thought briefly about running and banging on a neighbor's door. But she knew he would catch her. Without flight being an option, her mind kicked into fight mode and started planning.

She moved quickly while his attention was off her, searching the console to find nothing of use. She then turned to the glove box, hurrying as Bryan turned around and headed back up the side yard to the truck, banging on each window of the house he passed on his way back.

The glove box had both items she was looking for. She quickly retrieved them, shoved them between her back and the seat, and shut the compartment.

"Where's your fucking boyfriend, huh? Call him!" Bryan said as he made his way around the open driver door.

"Bryan, stop. Let's go home and talk about this. There's nothing going on." She pleaded with passion as if her life depended on it when in reality, both of theirs did.

Bryan climbed back in the truck, reversed them out of the driveway, and whipped them around. Jess braced herself, holding onto the door to keep herself from banging her head against the window. They raced back down Lanier Islands Parkway the way they'd came.

CHAPTER SIXTY-EIGHT

Topher

Topher was chasing the blue dot, checking its position every mile. Once Bryan and Jess had reached his house, the dot stopped for a couple of minutes. He was still on Atlanta Highway and floored it when traffic would allow. After a couple miles, he got stuck for several minutes while a semi-truck carrying some SUVs tried to back into a used car lot, blocking both lanes of traffic as he poorly maneuvered his way into the parking lot.

Topher cussed and checked his rearview to assess the situation behind him since there was no way around the truck. Not knowing how long it would take for the truck to clear the road, Topher cut the wheel and reversed into the opposite lane, cursing the truck's poor turning radius as he shimmied around to the tune of honking horns.

Slamming the accelerator, he backtracked up Atlanta Highway to the intersection near the office where he turned left and crossed the railroad tracks again. He pulled up his phone again to check Jess's location. It had started moving again back toward McEver Road once it departed his house.

"Take a left, you piece of shit."

Bryan did, at the same time Topher took a left to head south on McEver Road. They were now headed directly toward one another, just a few miles apart, on a winding, two-lane road.

He pulled all his faculties together to formulate a plan, knowing he had a couple of minutes at best to decide what was going to happen next.

Topher kept his AR underneath the backseat of his truck. The rifle would be the move if this turned into a hostage situation. Otherwise, he trusted himself more with the 1911 pistol he kept in his console.

His decision was made not a moment too soon as he spotted Bryan's Dodge coming down the hill on the opposite side of the bowl McEver Road dropped down into, where it crossed a small channel of the lake—the same channel that connected the marina where Bryan kept his boat with the open water. The Dodge was flying, and Topher was pushing past seventy miles per hour, lethal speeds on a two-lane road. Topher knew he needed to decide and execute within mere seconds. Thankfully, there were no cars left in either lane between the two trucks barreling toward each other.

He slammed on the brakes, violently dropping the front bumper of the truck toward the ground. Once he'd slowed enough that he was confident he wouldn't flip, he snatched the wheel to the left and skidded to stop. The move put his passenger door facing Bryan and Jess's direction just short of the bridge.

Drawing his 1911, he trained it on the driver's side of the windshield, waiting until they were in range to confirm it was Bryan driving and not Jess. But they never made it close enough for him to see who was behind the wheel.

CHAPTER SIXTY-NINE

Jess

Jess's mind searched for the right moment to act. She didn't know what it was going to look like, yet, but she trusted she would find an opportunity.

They came up on the intersection, where they'd run the car off the road just a few minutes ago. Jess prayed Bryan would take a left instead of continuing back toward Atlanta Highway. He did just that, and Jess instantly knew when she'd get her opportunity. Just a couple more miles.

She reached behind her with her right hand as he sped them down the curvy road, passing slower cars over the double yellow line. She wasn't sure she could pull off her plan, and it was going to leave some questions that might land her in jail. But, if that's what it came to, she would take being tried by twelve than carried by eight any day of the week. Maybe the items she'd hidden in the toolbox of the truck bed would be enough to keep her a free woman.

The hill Jess had in mind came into view a minute later. They started descending, heading for the bridge that crossed the lake at the bottom of the hill, and she reached her right hand behind her to grab the items she'd removed from the glove box.

As they neared the bridge, picking up speed on the downhill, Jess's heart jumped into her throat. It was beating so fast it felt like it was going to come out of her body. She looked at her fiancé and wondered if the man she'd fallen in love with was still there. But the images that came to her so quickly the night she stood over the bed with his gun were gone. What's more, she had given him an exit back at the house. He chose not to take it, sealing his own fate.

Three-hundred yards. Bryan punched the dash again, launching into another rant about how she was a "fucking lying cunt." Two-hundred fifty yards. They passed a family in a van going the other way, bouncing along to the radio with the windows down, towing a pair of jet skis. Two-hundred yards. His phone rang, and he reached down to the pocket in the driver door to retrieve it. One-hundred yards. She had to time her move just right. The bridge was only around eight car lengths long, and a late move could send them into the far bank of the channel; she had to time it just right. Fifty yards.

Bryan dropped the phone back in the door pocket and started laughing the same humorless, maniacal laugh he used in the kitchen earlier. "There he is. Your knight in shining armor. You're texting him, aren't you? Where's your phone?"

Jess whipped her head back up to the road ahead. She saw Topher's Tacoma barreling down the hill opposite the one they were headed down. Something in her subconscious mind made a decision faster than she could think through in her current state of panic, and the final gap in her plan was filled with Topher's presence. She wasn't worried about being tried by twelve or carried by eight anymore.

Suddenly, the Tacoma's nose quickly dropped toward the ground as they drew closer, indicating he slammed on the brakes, and his truck started to turn.

"What the—" Bryan started to speak.

The distraction gave Jess the edge she needed. She grabbed the first object behind her back and secured half of it to her left wrist, cupping the other side in her left hand. She took a deep breath, said a quick prayer of thanks that she was a leftie, and lunged with the object. The handcuffs caught Bryan's right wrist, the hand he had on the steering wheel, and she squeezed to lock them. Before Bryan could react, she yanked the wheel hard to the right.

The truck slammed through the concrete girder of the bridge—deploying the airbags—and hurtled outward over the lake for a split second before gravity took over and began dragging them toward the water. Thankfully, there were no boats directly below them in the channel, a miracle on a warm spring day.

Bryan let out a string of panicked expletives. Jess took a deep breath, pushed her head back against the headrest, and braced for the weight of the vehicle to punch her in the back.

The time from when the truck tires hit the bridge to hitting the water was only around three seconds or less, but it felt like a lifetime to Jess. The truck hit the water leaning toward the driver's side. The impact was a feeling Jess would have a hard time describing. She'd been in a serious car wreck before, hit from behind. It was a violent affair that had totaled several cars. But it didn't compare to this. Hitting the water was much more disorienting than the wreck. The seatbelt caught her, and she felt a snap in her collarbone. The weight of the engine block immediately started pulling the front end below the lake's surface. Water poured in at an alarming rate since chunks of concrete flying from the bridge had busted the windshield, and the impact with the water had further damaged it.

Jess looked to her left to see Bryan laid out over the steering wheel, unconscious and bleeding from his forehead just like he was in Jess's dream a few weeks ago. He hadn't been wearing his seatbelt.

Squeezing her eyes shut, she fought to keep her senses straight. It was time to move. She hadn't even thought to look for a handcuff key in the glovebox as her initial plan didn't involve her being handcuffed. She went to unbuckle her seatbelt and had to push her feet against the floorboard—now completely underwater—to lessen the tension on the belt. It came free without issue, so she didn't need the seatbelt cutter she'd gotten Bryan for Christmas, the second item she'd pulled from the glovebox.

What now? How do I get the fuck out of here?

Why hadn't Topher pulled her out, yet? That was his truck, wasn't it? She had to figure something out in the event he didn't reach her in time.

She took in gulps of air as she pressed against the broken windshield with her hands, but the water pressure was too great for her to move it, and the more she pushed, the more water poured in through the cracks. Turning to the passenger window, she pressed the rubber node on the bottom of the seatbelt cutter against the glass with all her strength until the metal tool inside made contact and broke it. She was able to push it out just as she took her last gulp of air. The cab was now completely submerged.

Grabbing the window frame with her right hand, she tried to pull herself out, but she could only get her upper half out of the window before her cuffed hand stopped her. She pulled harder, determined she would pull Bryan's dead weight out with her if that's what it took to get to oxygen. But no matter how hard she pulled, he wouldn't budge. She turned around to look at him and realized his left arm was mangled in the steering wheel, preventing him from moving.

Panic clawing at every fiber of her being, she quickly turned to the glove box to try and find a key before it was too dark to see anything.

She pried the latch open with her free hand and started sorting through the contents that poured out of the box, floating upward. Her lungs burned. She didn't have much oxygen to begin with, and she was rapidly expending it with her escape efforts. Her ears throbbed, probably a combination of deprivation of air and the building pressure of the water. Every cell in her body screamed for air.

Black started closing in from her peripheral vision. And then a strange thing happened. The panic slowly slid into calm. Her lungs still burned, but she closed her eyes and let the peace come over her. In her mind's eye, she saw her grandmother's face. It was from a memory when she was a kid. One of her favorite summers that she'd spent at her grandparents' house. They were making a pie together. It felt like she was there. On her tiptoes on the pink wooden stool her grandfather had made her, trying to help her grandmother pour the sugar into the mixing bowl as she giggled. Happiness.

Somewhere far away she felt a slight bump. The truck had come to rest at the bottom of the lake. But she was still in her grandmother's kitchen. After a couple more seconds, her nostalgic vision began slipping away, fading into the black that had almost finished claiming her. She felt very tired but calm. Everything was going to be okay. The last thing she registered before her senses gave out was the sensation of being pulled.

CHAPTER SEVENTY

Topher

G oddamn it!" Topher yelled as he watched the truck burst through the barrier of the bridge and hit the water.

He scrambled out of the truck and over to the side of the bridge as fast as he could manage. He waited briefly for a sign that either one of them was conscious. As the front tires of the overturned truck sank below the water, he knew neither was coming out without help. The water around the truck was littered with floating objects that had spilled out of the toolbox: a can of paint thinner, a tarp, a bleach-sized bottle of muriatic acid, and a coil of rope. He instantly knew what Jess had been up to in her silence since the drug bust. If he wasn't worried about the seconds ticking down to her death, he would've felt a surge of pride for her.

A small crowd of people from other cars who'd seen the truck go over was starting to descend on the bridge. Topher kicked into military mode and started barking out orders. He instructed the people on the bridge to call 911, and then quickly turned his attention to a nearby boater. He ordered him to motor closer to the sinking truck before he jumped in.

The entire cab was submerged by the time he hit the water, leaving only the taillights and trailer hitch still above the surface. He opened his eyes but couldn't see much other than shapes in the murky water. He swam closer to the truck and tried to grab the window well, but the truck started sinking faster.

Running out of air—the impact of the water had nearly knocked the wind out of him, and his lungs were running on whatever oxygen reserves they could pull from—he had no choice but to resurface. Treading water, he took several deep breaths and then dove back down. He couldn't see much through the bubbles streaming toward him as the truck sank lower. After a couple broad strokes, he could make out the white of the license plate and shifted his strokes to bring him to the right side of the truck. The front of the cab had come to rest on the bottom of the lake with the bed still sticking straight up toward the surface. The pressure was building in his ears, but he pushed that and the burning of his lungs aside and kept swimming downward until he reached the passenger window. Once there, through blurry vision, he saw Jess's dark brown hair suspended around her, as if she were floating in space. A second shape, Bryan, was suspended just beyond her, neither were moving.

Topher leaned in the window just enough to wrap his left arm around Jess's waist and pull her out, which was a task, as the truck continued to slowly rotate upside down. He was able to pull her out, but she abruptly stopped once her waist was out the window. Topher pulled back, thinking maybe she'd regained consciousness. He knew from his military training that drowning victims could fight their rescuers in their panic. When it was clear she was still unconscious, he tugged again, but she wouldn't budge.

Pushing her hair out of his way, Topher leaned in the window to assess the problem. The light was dimmer inside the truck, so he had to feel around. He followed Jess's left arm that was stretched out behind her with his hand until he ran into another one and realized Jess and Bryan were cuffed together.

He prayed he hadn't lost his handcuff key in the jump and dug in his pocket until he found it. It took a couple of tries since he couldn't see what he was doing, but he was finally able to unlock them and pull Jess through the window, his lungs feeling as though they were engulfed in a fireball. He wrapped both arms around her waist, planted his feet on the bottom of the truck bed that had now come to rest completely upside down, and pushed them toward the surface.

CHAPTER SEVENTY-ONE

Jess

Jess awoke slowly, her senses struggling to regain function. She heard a familiar male voice. However, her attention was quickly pulled away as her ears protested and her lungs burned violently. Her diaphragm heaved, and she began coughing.

More of her senses returned, and she was lying on her side.

Where?

Her right cheek was pressed against something hard and kind of gritty. The male voice started talking again in a hurried fashion with authority.

Topher.

The coughing subsided, and she was finally able to open her eyes. She was lying on the deck of a boat. Topher was huddled over her, yelling directions to the driver, a fisherman. The man was on the phone—it sounded like he was talking to a 911 dispatcher—and Topher was directing him to tie them to the nearest dock.

Jess coughed, and Topher turned his attention back to her. His expression was a mixture of fear and disbelief. She tried to sit up to explain.

"Whoa. I don't know if that's a good idea." He helped support her as she tried to lift herself. "Here. Let's get you set up on this," he said as he guided her over to the center console so she could rest her back against it.

"Are you okay? Tell me what hurts the most." He started looking her over.

"Everything. Nothing. I don't know. I think I'm okay. Maybe," she choked out as best she could while she rested her head back on the console.

She took shallow breaths. It was easier for Jess to list what didn't hurt than what did. There was no doubt in her mind her collar bone was broken. It felt like someone had seared it with a hot iron.

"No cuts or anything?" he asked, continuing to check each of her limbs.

She shifted so she could look back and see what the owner of the boat was doing on the other side of the console. The man was occupied with maneuvering them slowly toward the dock and still answering the dispatcher's questions.

"Topher—" she began to explain, but he cut her off.

"He tried to kill you," he said matter-of-factly.

He gave her a look that let her know he had her back. He had it like Bryan never had. She didn't have to lie or pretend anymore. She could leave that with Bryan thirty feet below her under the blue water on the bed of Murder Lake.

The realization reduced Jess to sobs—of fear, but mostly relief. Topher quickly slipped off his overshirt and pulled it around her shoulders. She melted into it and wept as he pulled her in and held her.

She doesn't remember how long they stayed like that. Until the shrills of the first sirens reached them. Before the first responders arrived, she needed to do one last thing. She pulled away from Topher and crawled toward the side of the boat. The boat owner had left them alone at some point to run up the dock and flag down the emergency personnel.

Her right hand made its way over to her left hand that bore the gold handcuff Bryan had put on her when he got down on one knee at the Biltmore Estate nearly four months ago. She hadn't taken it off since.

It was snug, but she was able to work it over her knuckle with some effort. She didn't even look at it before she unceremoniously let it fall from her fingers over the side of the boat into the blue water below. It was a small weight to shed, but with it, Jess felt the burden of the control that she'd been secretly living under for the past year begin to dissipate.

She was finally free.

CHAPTER SEVENTY-TWO

Jess

Jess realized in the months following Bryan's death that her life made much more sense. If they had children, this would be a much different scenario. She was thankful the only thing she had to worry about was Piggy, and that her job allowed her an excuse to get him to the safety of Nina's house.

She smiled down at her pup now as she walked him before work and decided she would take him to her parents' home that weekend for a short getaway. The thought stopped Jess in her tracks. She realized how she could finally think further than the end of the day again.

After the wreck, her parents had flown to Georgia to help her decide what to do next. Thankfully, they respected her space and didn't try to pry. Jess promised she would tell them everything in time.

She had to stay in Georgia while the GBI investigated the accident. She recognized that she probably should've been scared, but she wasn't. Nothing they could do to her could be worse than what she'd been through the last year. Anything the law could throw at her was no rival for the mental agony of having the person she loved, the man she was prepared to give her future to, break her down slowly and methodically under the guise of protection, making her question everything she knew.

Jess also knew Topher would streamline the investigation process, and he did just that. She was brought into the Atlanta office for two interviews, which seemed more of a formality than anything, and the case was closed in less than two weeks. The investigators concluded that the evidence suggested Bryan had plans for Jess's murder in retaliation for her exposing his guilt in the shooting of Thomas Ravello, leading him to attempt a murder-suicide once she released the video. A few of the media outlets she'd emailed the video to ran a story for a news cycle or two. Jess didn't respond to any requests for comment, and the story died quickly, replaced by the next national political scandal.

Jess's parents hired Ruth full time, and Jess moved back to Dallas where she began practicing law again as a sole practitioner while drafting plans to open a domestic violence shelter.

To get started, she took out a business loan to get her practice up and running, then used the remainder of her savings to get the shelter off the ground. Then, a check came in the mail one day. It was the full amount of Bryan's life insurance policy from the bureau. Without hesitation, she used the money to hire more employees and expand their resources. She had no idea he'd added her as the beneficiary and had a sneaking suspicion Topher had a hand in it.

Topher...

Jess's heart ached when she thought of him. She never said goodbye. The last time she'd seen him was the day of the wreck. She couldn't bring herself to face him for a goodbye. As much as it eviscerated her, she knew there wasn't room for him in this phase of her life. She had a lot of emotions to unpack and a lot of thinking to unwire. But just thinking of Topher brought on a round of tears that made her cut her walk with Piggy short that morning. Piggy didn't seem to mind, panting heavily in the August heat. Jess unlocked the door to her townhome, the one she'd painted haint blue the day after she moved in, and Piggy ran into the living room to find a toy. Jess beelined to her room and curled up on her bed. Emotion and confusion bubbled up, tightening her chest as it intensified, and overtook her. She tucked herself into the fetal position and shook with sobs. She felt raw, exposed.

While Jess was free from Bryan physically, but his residue was a stubborn thing.

There had been a vast resource network to help her and people like her, men and women, on the other side of a relationship with a Bryan. They were quick to identify her as a victim so she didn't have to do it herself, which relieved an unmeasurably heavy burden. And they were quick to help her find a therapist. But no one, not even the therapist, could tell her what to do with the part of herself that still loved Bryan. Or the part of him Jess wanted to believe had been real. She couldn't figure out if it was really him she loved, or the perception of what she believed he could be that she was still in love with. Maybe it was the defense attorney in her that always tried to find and protect innocence wherever she could find it. But perhaps it was time to let that part of herself go. Or was it?

The questions kept coming: was she any better than Bryan for what she did? Did she let him turn her into an ugly person that ended up being worse than him in the end? She didn't have the answers to those kinds of questions that plagued her, and she knew she may never get the answers.

Maybe it was simply her conscience's way of dealing with it, but she felt like the starving child that stole the bread. The end justified the means.

Right?

It was the same argument she'd chided Bryan for espousing at times, so she felt like it was a bullshit way to see the situation. Topher's words from Nina's basement came floating back to her like mist encroaching on a lake on a fall, cool morning, slowly enveloping her until she couldn't ignore it any longer: *Just don't lie to yourself.*

So...she'd done something bad. But then she would chat with a man and instantly feel a pang of guilt. It didn't matter where or what the circumstances were. It could be at the grocery store. The bank.

The post office. A completely innocent encounter would make her feel like she was doing something wrong. And the regret plaguing her would vanish. Everyday acts of life shouldn't feel illicit. That was going to take some time to unwire. She was surprised at how quickly those neural circuits solidified, and she already knew they were going to take longer to disassemble than they took to create.

Why was it so hard for me to see it?

Jess was able to pin the answer to that question down to two main ideas. First, Bryan was a master manipulator who operated via subtle undercurrents that made Jess feel like she was in control. He never said, "don't do this." Instead, he planted seeds in regular conversations and followed those up with accusations, not too different from an effective prosecutor. And if that didn't work, he would manipulate her with his mood and indirect threats. All methods aimed at getting her to do what he wanted without directly ordering her around.

The second reason, she realized, was because admitting she was a victim carried the pejorative idea that she was weak. She was a trial attorney. According to Jess, there wasn't a weak bone in her body. She'd sat beside and counseled monsters of all kinds in her career, fighting zealously for them against seasoned prosecutors that were intimidating to most. But she was aware of exactly who she was dealing with in those cases. Their character had already been exposed via their criminal behavior. She didn't have to flesh it out. She'd overestimated her ability to deal with abusers because they'd already been labeled for her as such.

Jess had to come to terms with the fact that she was still human. And that meant she had vulnerabilities, whether she wanted to admit it or not. And Bryans know exactly how to exploit those vulnerabilities. They do it with a white glove, which allows them to wormhole their way into the lives and beds of the unsuspecting. Whether it be business relationships, family relationships, friendships, or lovers. The good people give life, and the bad suck it out of them and weaponize it against the good ones in a parasitic cycle.

Now that she was free, it was time for her to start helping others who'd fallen into the same trap.

CHAPTER SEVENTY-THREE

ONE YEAR LATER

Jess

Jess spent the morning checking on the construction progress of the new shelter. They were less than two months from opening their doors with most of the work already completed. The playground was getting delivered later that week, and she was already planning to spend the weekend picking out furniture and decor. The budget was tight, but she refused for her shelter to feel like a clinical space. She was going to ensure it felt like the home for the survivors, even if it meant painting every last wall herself.

As she drove to the office, she reflected on her own progress. She likened herself to spring in the South. There were still some brown, muddy places that needed work, but there was also new growth that brought forth green and blossoms.

She arrived just before the lunch hour and decided to relieve the team. Once they left, she took a seat at her desk to tackle emails.

Before she could get her computer unlocked, her office phone started ringing and lighting up. A call was coming through on the crisis line.

"How can I help you?" Jess answered.

"Uh, hello, is this the crisis helpline?" A woman's voice whispered on the other side.

"Yes, it is. Are you safe?"

"Right now, yes. I don't know how long I have. I need help," the voice replied, thick with distress.

"That's why I'm here. What can I do for you?"

She walked the woman through a safety plan and where to find resources to help her formulate a way out of her situation.

Shortly after, her cell phone rang. She didn't recognize the number, but she knew it was a Georgia area code. Thinking it might be Nina or Ruth with a new phone, she answered it.

"This is Jess."

A familiar voice on the other end of the line chimed, "Hey, Jess. It's Topher."

A warmth spread through the same place in her chest that was used to freezing up in fear, and she smiled.

A WORD FROM THE AUTHOR

Abuse doesn't discriminate. It doesn't give a damn about the size of your bank account, your age, ethnicity, profession, IQ, or who your daddy is. Abusers may have personal preferences. But no one is immune. It's something all of us will encounter at some point in our lives, whether it be directly or someone you know. And, most importantly, the worst abuse can be without any physical violence.

It goes without saying, physical assaults are unacceptable. But you also need to know these signs: isolation, financial restriction, denied privacy, keeping tabs on their partner at all times, throwing objects near or around their partner, and more. These behaviors often manifest themselves in subtle ways. For example, isolation may look like: *you're a married woman. Girls' night out is for single women who want to pick up guys.* Or financial abuse could be a strict budget that wasn't mutually agreed upon.

We're blind to the things we don't want to see in people we want to believe in. Everyone has layers like an onion. Maybe some of the layers of bad people are good. But they're buried in enough of the bad layers that they're spoiled. It's the moments these good layers slip through that lead us to believe if we can help them, or change the circumstances, the good layers will shed the bad and blossom into the healthier, better person we believe they can be. Perhaps this happens to some when the wind blows the right way and they're surrounded by the right people. It's impossible to have all the answers.

Regardless of the reasons behind the behavior, you do not have to live in fear or isolation. Reach out to the National Domestic Violence Hotline at 1-800-799-SAFE(7233) to find out about the resources available to help you make a plan to leave and keep yourself safe after you do. You can also find additional resources on my Instagram: @authorhmpalmer.

ACKNOWLEDGEMENTS

First and foremost, I thank God for His many blessings.

Thank you to the abuse survivors who were so gracious in sharing your stories with me.

To my beta readers, all of you greatly shaped this novel. Y'all helped push me to the finish line. I am so grateful for each and every one of you.

Thank you to everyone who helped me escape my own Bryan.

And finally, to anyone who has stared in the face of evil and still mustered the courage to escape an abuser, you are my hero.

ABOUT THE AUTHOR

H. M. Palmer writes thrillers because it's cheaper than therapy. She's a graduate of the University of Georgia and escapes to the mountains whenever possible. When she's not writing—or procrastinating on writing—she enjoys listening to podcasts, hiking, traveling, and is constantly searching for the best fries in Atlanta.